EUREKA

William Diehl's bestsellers include *Sharky's Machine* and the three
Martin Vail Novels: *Primal Fear, Show of Evil* and *Reign in Hell*.
Several of his books have been made into motion pictures, and all
have been received to great acclaim. He lives in Woodstock, Georgia
with his wife, Emmy Award-winner Virginia Gunn.

Praise for Eureka:

'Infidelity, murder, murky secrets, a deeply affecting love story and an
old-fashioned showdown . . . this novel serves notice that Diehl is one
of the best thriller writers working today.' *Publishers Weekly*

'Another rousing Diehl actioner . . . page-turning fun.' *Kirkus Reviews*

Primal Fear

'Shocking . . . as much psychological thriller as legal drama . . . Diehl
delivers,' *People*

'Suspenseful . . . a horrifying crime story.' *United Press International*

Show of Evil

'Spine-tingling' *New York Times*

'A crackling good yarn.' Larry King, *USA Today*

EUREKA

WILLIAM DIEHL

WILLIAM HEINEMANN : LONDON

Published in the United Kingdom in 2002 by William Heinemann

1 3 5 7 9 10 8 6 4 2

William Heinemann
The Random House Group Limited
20 Vauxhall Bridge Road, London SW1V 2SA

Random House Australia (Pty) Limited
20 Alfred Street, Milsons Point, Sydney,
New South Wales 2061, Australia

Random House New Zealand Limited
18 Poland Road, Glenfield
Auckland 10, New Zealand

Random House (Pty) Limited
Endulini, 5a Jubilee Road, Parktown 2193, South Africa

Random House Group Limited Reg. No. 954009

www.randomhouse.co.uk

A CIP catalogue record for this book
is available from the British Library

Papers used by Random House
are natural, recyclable products made from wood grown in
sustainable forests. The manufacturing processes conform to
the environmental regulations of the country of origin

Printed and bound in the United Kingdom by
Mackays of Chatham plc, Chatham, Kent

ISBN 0 434 01045 6

This book is for my wife,
Virginia, who defines
everything good in my life
for the past twenty-five years.
I love you in my heart.

So we beat on, boats against the current,
borne back ceaselessly into the past.
                    —*The Great Gatsby*
                    F. Scott Fitzgerald

PROLOGUE

1945

If you're a cop, the best thing you can hope for is to have a partner like Ski Agassi. That, and a beautiful lady who loves you. I was thinking about both, lying on my hospital bed watching morphine drip into my arm. It started as a small bubble, very slowly turned into a teardrop, then silently fell into the tube. I was concentrating on that process, wondering how long it would take for that drop to weave its way through my veins and into my brain when the doctor came in.

His name was Meisel, a short man with alert eyes and graying hair and a jovial attitude that helped, considering the situation. I had a hazy recollection of having met him briefly when I had arrived at the L.A. hospital the night before. He had a large envelope under his arm.

"Morning, Sergeant Bannon," he said. "How's the pain?"

"I'm kinda numb all over."

"Good. If it becomes a problem, call the nurse and she'll give that little knob a twist and make it go away."

"Thanks."

"What do they call you, by the way?"

"Zee."

"Like the letter zee?"

"Yes, sir."

He nodded.

"Okay, Zee, here's where we stand. They did a pretty good job back at Walter Reed. Basically your left leg is fine. And they've got the bones in that right leg lined up. The ankle is still a mess but we'll take care of that in due time. The good news is that I'm the best there is at this kind of thing. I'll get you back on your feet without so much as a limp. The downside is it's going to take time."

". . . okay."

"How does six months sound?"

I didn't know how to answer that. It had already been three, six more sounded like forever.

He didn't wait for an answer. Instead he took an X ray from the envelope and slapped it against the windowpane. He pointed to the bones in my right leg. The leg looked a lot better than the first time I had seen a picture of it. Then, the bones looked like a bunch of scrambled, broken toothpicks. The shinbone was shattered in a half-dozen places and the ankle was twisted almost backward.

The bones still looked like toothpicks but now they were straight, and held in line with metal pins. The foot still looked like it had been tacked on as an afterthought.

"We're looking at three more operations. One to get the shinbones back together and two more on that ankle. Then two to three months teaching you how to walk again. At first you'll be staggering around like a drunk stork."

I laughed. "Better than crawling," I said.

Meisel nodded and smiled broadly. "Good attitude. At least you're back in California. How about family? You're not married?"

I hesitated a minute and said, "No, sir."

"You list your next of kin as Ski Agassi?"

"My partner when I was a cop before the war. I . . . haven't really been in touch for a while."

"Hmm."

He pulled a chair up and sat beside me.

"I've reviewed your records, Zee. It helps me to know how you got your wounds."

"I was a traffic cop, Doc. Drove my jeep over a land mine."

"You were trapped in your jeep with your legs almost broken off and you took out a German Tiger tank with a bazooka."

"Wrong place at the wrong time."

"They don't hand out Silver Stars and Purple Hearts for driving over land mines. Look, I've treated a lot of wounded soldiers. I know there's a certain amount of guilt involved in survival. But you have to help me help you to get well. Your frame of mind will have a lot to do with how fast we accomplish that. I'm an expert at the mechanics. But you need friends for support."

"I'm just not ready to . . ." I paused, trying to frame the rest of the sentence.

"Hell, son, heroism is not a choice you make, it's made for you. It certainly isn't something to be ashamed of. I don't care what you tell people, tell 'em you broke your leg skiing in the Alps for all I care. But you need support in this effort. You're facing a long and dreary process. The last thing I need is for you to go getting depressed on me."

He slapped his hands on his knees and stood up.

"Besides," he added, "if you think you're going to be a burden on people who care for you, you're wrong. You'll be a bigger burden if you cut them out."

"Hey Doc," I said, as he started toward the door.

"Yes?"

"What day is it?"

"It's August tenth."

"Christ, I've really been out of it. The last thing I remember was getting on the train. That must've been . . . two weeks ago? I keep losing time with all this morphine."

Meisel stopped and stared at me with curiosity.

"They kept you very sedated on the train because of your foot."

"I guess so. I don't remember the train ride. I barely remember meeting you last night. Anyway, thanks."

He came around the bed and leaned over.

"You don't know about the bomb?"

"What bomb?"

"My God," he said. "We dropped something called an atomic bomb on Japan five days ago. It wiped out a whole town called Hiroshima. We dropped another one on Nagasaki yesterday. They expect the Japanese to surrender within the week."

"Aw c'mon." *It's all that morphine,* I thought.

"Zee, the war is over."

I just stared at him.

"And I slept through it," I said finally.

He started laughing, a big belly laugh. And then I joined him. The first time I had really laughed in a long time. He was shaking his head as he walked toward the door.

"It's you and me against that leg from here on out, Zee. We start at eight in the morning. No food or drink after midnight. I don't want you puking on me in the middle of the operation."

Ski showed up four days later.

*   *   *

The big bear of a man appeared in the doorway. He was wearing a red silk tie and a white shirt under a dark blue suit, expensive, the kind that comes with only one pair of pants. And he was carrying a black briefcase. I remembered him being heavier, perhaps a little taller, a bit younger, a lot sloppier. That's the way the memory works. Nothing changes in your mind. Nothing ages. Everything is just as you last saw it and I hadn't seen Ski in four years.

"That must've been some big dog that bit you," he said, nodding at the cast on my leg.

"You look like a damn stockbroker," I said. "That what happens when you make lieutenant?"

"It's my Sunday suit. I decided to come formal now that I outrank you."

That tickled me. Some things never change. He pulled a chair over beside the bed, sat down, and my hand disappeared into his giant paw.

"I missed you, pal," he said gently. "You're lousy when it comes to writing home."

"Ah, I didn't have anything to say you couldn't read in the papers. How'd you find me?"

"I'm a cop, remember? I'm also your next of kin. They kept me informed."

"Meisel called you," I said.

He smiled. "That, too."

"He's part shrink," I growled.

"It's nice to have a sawbones who gives a shit," he said. "Called anybody since you got here?"

I stared at him for a second or two and shook my head and that ended the Q and A. For the next thirty minutes he brought me up to date on the squad. Lieutenant Moriarity had retired and moved to Florida to fish out his life. A guy named Mancusa, who needed a road map to put his socks on, had made captain. Jerry Fowler, one of our pals in homicide, was killed in a car wreck one night on the way home from a bar. Ski had replaced me as sergeant and then moved up to lieutenant when Mancusa was promoted.

"All I do is make assignments, chew ass, or pat people on the back, whichever's appropriate. It's dog work. I miss the old days."

"Waste of a good cop," I said, my speech beginning to slur. "Th'
Ponder Man."

Agassi was one of the best homicide cops I ever met. We made a
good team. I'd pick clues out of the carpet and he'd ponder. That's
what he was best at, pondering. He would sit and stare into space and
all the clues and evidence would swirl around in his head and come together like the pieces in a jigsaw puzzle. Then I'd step back in and tie
up the loose ends. He once solved a murder case pondering and making phone calls while sitting in a hospital bed with a bullet in his side.
There were still some loose ends to that one.

"Oh, I have a lot of time to ponder," he said.

He reached down, picked up the attaché case, put it carefully on
the bed beside me so it wouldn't rattle my leg, and snapped it open. It
was full of file folders.

"Four years of pondering here," he said. "I call it the Eureka File.
The doc says you're gonna have a lot of free time on your hands for the
next couple of months. Maybe this'll keep you from getting too bored.
Call it a welcome home present."

The morphine was taking me down and my eyes were drooping.

"You're obsessive," I mumbled.

"Completely," he said with a smile. "Meantime, I'll drop in every
week or so. Least I can do since I'm next of kin." He patted my hand
but I was in never-never land before he got out the door.

A few days later when I was lucid enough to open the briefcase and
start looking through all the information, I was astounded. There were
copies of public records, news clippings, interviews, bits of historical
facts to put all the information in perspective, as well as his own evalua-
tions and observations. The material was arranged chronologically,
starting at the turn of the century; an amazingly articulate archive of a
case that had haunted me since I had left the force in the fall of 1941 to
join the Army. I recalled some of the facts, but not in the contemplative
and explicit detail with which Ski had arranged them.

During the next few months, as I explored and scrutinized the
documents, sometimes with gossamer, narcotically induced hallucina-
tions, sometimes with clearheaded and discernible perception, the Eureka affair took on a narrative life that I knew would draw me back to

people who were engraved in my mind, and to a place I thought I had left behind forever.

It had all started at the turn of the century, at a time when eighteen million people still rode horses, there were only eight thousand automobiles on the horse paths called roads, and most lamps still used kerosene. . . .

Book One

CULHANE

1900

The two young men who rode over the crest of the hill were a study in contrast. One was tall and lean, his black hair curling around his ears, his dark brown eyes bright and naive. The other was an inch or two shorter, with a tight, muscular body, light brown hair clipped short, and pale blue eyes that were wary and cautious.

Ben Gorman, the taller of the two, was Jewish. The other, Thomas Brodie Culhane, was Irish. Gorman, seventeen, was the son of Eli Gorman, the richest man in the San Miguel valley. Culhane, six months younger, was the orphaned son of a deep-sea fisherman and a washerwoman.

The two young men had been playing baseball on the other side of the rise, on a ball diamond laid out on the flat, comparatively dry side of the hill. It had been a ragtag pickup game with nine boys from Milltown, ten miles away. Brodie and Ben and three of the Milltowners made one team. Five against six. But with Ben, the mastermind with the magic arm, who could throw the ball like it was a lightning bolt, and Brodie, the slugger who hit the ball with the same energetic fury with which Gorman pitched, on the same team, it was so one-sided that the losing team quit after five innings and they all headed home.

As usual, water was running down from the hills, splashing in from the ocean, falling from the sky, gravitating to the haphazard collection of buildings that called itself a town. A valley town that lay at the bottom of a high, forested ridge that surrounded a broad bay in the Pacific Ocean and that attracted water the way honey attracts a bear.

The two horses, Ben's a sleek, brown, thoroughbred stallion, Brodie's a pure white stallion, shied away from the muddy road but even the hillside was soggy and the two boys had to keep them in tight rein so the horses wouldn't slip and fall in the slime. Brodie hated mud. Had hated it for all his seventeen years—at least as far back as his memory went. And now daily spring rainstorms had turned the mud into syrup. Even in the dry season, when the mush turned to dust and stung your eyes and got in your mouth and in the wrinkles of your clothes, it was still mud to Brodie. It conjured memories of his mother struggling over a boiling cauldron of murky water, dropping railroad workers' clothes into it and watching it turn the color of chocolate as she stirred the muddy duds.

It was a tough town they were riding into, a mile down the hill. The main street, deeply rutted and sloppy from the rains, led past a rough-and-tumble collection of bars and eateries; basic essentials like a grocery store, a hardware store, a pharmacy, and a bank; an icehouse that served the town's only industry, a fishery; and several docks to house the fishing boats. Several homes, wooden shacks really, huddled behind the main drag, shelter for the people who worked in the town and the tough rail-layers. And behind them, hidden among the trees, was a long barracks that housed the Chinese workers, who kept to themselves, had their own stores, bars, and, it was rumored, an opium parlor, although nobody knew for sure since only Asians entered its grim confines.

It was one tough town, where table-stakes poker games were played behind storefront plate-glass windows in view of God and all his children; where fancy ladies advertised their cheap allure from windows above the hardware store; where, in the middle of Prohibition, bars advertised bar-brand drinks for twenty cents and imported brands for two bits. It was a town founded by hard-boiled railroad gandy dancers at the end of the track, where the sheriff, who had once ridden with Pat Garrett, kept the peace riding down the middle of the unpaved main street with a .44-caliber Peacemaker on his hip and a strawberry roan under him.

The railroad gandy dancers, who finally had a wide-open town where they could raise hell when the grueling job of laying track was over for the day, had named it Eureka.

Eli Gorman, Ben's father, often warned the two boys to stay out of the town, to ride the ridge of the mountain on their way to and from the ball diamond, but they were thirsty and decided to get a soda pop at the pharmacy, one of the few legitimate businesses in town. To Ben, who lived in the biggest mansion on the Hill, it was an exciting adventure, a quick trip to Sodom. But to Brodie, who had been brought up in a frame house on the edge of the harsh and violent village, it merely bolstered his hatred of the entire environment.

As they approached the main street, the horses became nervous and jumpy.

The moment reminded Brodie of the day he and Ben had first met. It was at this same intersection, four years ago. Brodie was walking back from the baseball field, had his glove tucked in his back pocket. As he crossed Main Street, he saw Ben Gorman riding up the road from the beach.

Two blocks up Main, in a saloon called Cooley's Ale House, two drunks were arguing at the bar. Nobody paid much attention; drunken words and brawls were common among the hardworking railroad men. Then suddenly, one of them pulled a pistol from his back pocket and took a shot at the other. The bullet clipped an ear. The injured man backed through the swinging doors of the saloon, drew his own gun from an inside pocket, and fired a shot at his assailant, who was hit in the side. The man with the bleeding ear backed all the way out the swinging doors, shooting away as the other one charged toward him. Bolting through the door, the one who had started the gunfight was hit again and, as his knees gave out, he emptied his gun at the man with the pierced ear. They were only a few feet apart. The one with the bleeding ear was riddled with bullets. He threw his hands into the air and fell backward off the wooden sidewalk into the muddy street. The other crumpled like a paper sack on the wooden sidewalk. Both men were dead in seconds.

Down the street, Ben's horse bolted and reared up at the flat smack of gunshots. Ben leaned forward in the saddle, hauling in the reins, but the horse was totally spooked. It began to back down the hill. Brodie dashed into the muddy road, grabbed the bit on both sides of the horse's mouth, and held tight.

"Easy, boy, easy," he whispered in the stallion's ear. "It's okay, it's all over." Without taking his eyes off the spooked horse, he asked Ben, "What's his name?"

"Jericho."

Jericho started to bolt again, lifting Brodie's feet out of the mud, but he pulled him back, still whispering, staring into the fiery, fear-filled eyes.

"Easy, Jericho, easy. It's all over. Calm down, son. Calm down."

The horse grumbled and started to back away but Brodie had him under control. He gently stroked the horse's nose.

"Got him?" Brodie asked.

"Yeah, thanks. I don't think he's ever heard a gunshot before."

"Must not spend a lot of time in Eureka."

Ben held his hand out. "M'name's Ben Gorman."

The younger boy shook the hand. "Brodie. Brodie Culhane."

They decided they deserved a soda. Ben rode his horse slowly up the street to the pharmacy while Brodie clomped beside him on the wooden decking that passed for a sidewalk, shaking the mud off his boots.

"Sorry about your shoes," said Ben.

"They was brought up in mud," Brodie answered.

They got to the pharmacy, and Ben jumped off Jericho and tied him to the hitch rail. They both looked up the next block on the other side of the street, where a crowd had gathered around the two bodies.

"I never saw a shooting before," Ben said with awe.

"Happens once or twice a month. Sometimes I pick up a dime for helping Old Stalk stuff them in the box."

"You touch them!" Ben's eyes were as round as silver dollars.

Brodie laughed. "They're dead; they don't bite."

"Two sarsaparilla sodas," Ben said and reaching in his pocket took out a handful of change and smacked four pennies on the small round table as they sat down. "My treat," he said.

As they sat down to drink their sarsaparillas, Brodie's mitt fell from his pocket, and Ben snatched it up, admiring it for a moment before handing it back.

"You a baseballer?"

"I play a coupla times a week."

"Where?"

"They got a diamond down toward Milltown. Kids from the school play sides-up there. One side or the other always picks me. I ain't much at catching but I can knock the ball clean out of the field if I get a bite at it. How about you?"

"No," Ben said, shaking his head and looking down at the floor for a moment. "I'm from up there," he said, jerking his thumb toward the Hill as if embarrassed to admit it. "Aren't enough kids in our little school to get one team together, let alone two. But I practice pitching. I throw at an archery target."

"You any good?"

"I can pitch a curve. I'm not much at batting but I can sure pitch."
He paused a minute, and said, "Think they'd let me play?"

"Sure, 'specially if you can pitch. Pitchers are hard to come by. I usually go on Thursday and Sunday. I get off those days. I gotta work Saturdays."

"How old are you?" Ben asked.

"Fourteen comin' up. How about you?"

"I turned fourteen in September." They sipped their drinks for a minute or so and then Ben asked, "Where do you work?"

"I wrangle horses for the railroad. Up at end-o'-track. Get outta school at one, go to work from two 'til six. But it pays good—twenty-five cents a day."

Ben almost swallowed his straw. His weekly allowance was more than Brodie made working five days a week.

"How do you get to the ball field? Must be three, four miles over there?"

"I walk."

Ben thought for a moment, then said, "Tell you what, I'll meet you up at the ridge road at two on Sunday. I'll bring an extra horse."

Brodie smiled a cautious smile.

"Yer on," he answered.

Almost four years and they had been as close as brothers ever since.

"We're gonna catch it if Mr. Eli finds out we come down here," Brodie said, as the horses slogged through the mud.

"Then we won't tell him," Ben answered with a brazen smile.

"Yer old man knows everything." He paused and rephrased the thought. "Mr. Eli'll know we were in town before we get home. No way we can lie to him, Ben."

"Yeah, yeah, yeah." Ben reached over and slugged Brodie's arm. "Gotta live dangerously once in a while."

They reached the edge of town.

Eureka was the unfortunate legacy of a robber baron named Jesse Milstrum Crane. In 1875, Crane, a con man and gambler, escaped west to San Francisco with a trunk containing close to a million dollars, leaving in his wake a dozen irate investors in a defunct railroad line pillaged by him, one of many cons that had earned him his fortune. The heavyset, hard-drinking, womanizing swindler saw new opportunities in the wide-open western city. He bought an impressive house on Nob Hill, joined the best club, opened accounts in several of the city's biggest banks, and planned his grandest scheme yet—a railroad down the coast to Los Angeles, which he called the JMC and Pacific Line—and he offered his rich new friends an opportunity to buy into the company. His two biggest investors were Shamus O'Dell and Eli Gorman. As the tracks were laid south down the rugged coast, Crane was busy behind the scenes, scheming to steal every dollar he could from the company.

He might have succeeded, except one night his past caught up with him. As he was walking up the steps of his opulent home, a figure stepped out of the fog, and Crane found himself face-to-face with an eastern businessman he had cleaned out five years earlier.

"You miserable bastard," the man's trembling voice said. "You ruined my life. You stole everything I had . . ."

Crane cut him off by laughing in his face. "You whining little . . ." he started—and never finished the sentence.

The man held his arm at full length a foot from Crane's face and shot him in the forehead. The derringer made a flat sound, like hands clapping together. Crane's head jerked backward. His derby flew off and bounced away in the fog. A dribble of blood ran down his face as he staggered backward against an iron fence and fell to his knees. He looked up at the face in the fog, tried to remember his assailant's name, but there had been so many . . .

The second shot shattered his left eye. Crane's shoulders slumped and he toppled sideways to the sidewalk. He was dead by the time his killer fired a third shot into his own brain.

Accountants quickly discovered Crane's embezzlement, and Gorman and O'Dell took over the company, which included the sprawling San Pietro valley, ten miles west of the track and a hundred miles north of the growing town of Los Angeles. It was their decision to build a spur to the ocean and build estates on the surrounding heights. But the spur also brought with it "end-o'-track" and a raunchy honky-tonk, ten miles west on a Pacific bay, that serviced the roughnecks who did the harsh job of laying track and who settled arguments with fists, guns, or knives.

With them came the gamblers and pimps.

And with the gamblers and pimps came a hard-boiled young gangster who had learned his trade on the Barbary Coast of San Francisco. His name was Arnie Riker and he soon ruled the small town with a bunch of young toughs he had brought in from the big city.

As Ben and Brodie came down the road, their horses reined in, Arnie Riker was sitting on the porch of his Double Eagle Hotel, which commanded the southeast corner of the town. It was the largest building in town. Three stories, nearly a city block square, and badly in need of a paint job. It also housed a whorehouse, boasted the town's largest bar and gambling emporium, and had a pool table in the lobby. Riker's chair was leaning back against the wall of the hotel, his feet dangling a foot off the porch floor. Riker was a dandy. He was dressed in a light tan vest and pants, with a flowered shirt open at the collar, his feet encased in shiny black shoes and spats.

Four of Riker's hooligans were in the lobby of the hotel shooting pool. Rodney Guilfoyle was leaning across the table, lining up a bank shot. The sleeves of the eighteen-year-old's striped shirt were pulled back from the wrist by garters at his biceps. A cigarette dangled from the corner of his mouth. He slid the pool cue across the table and stood up. He was close to six feet tall, lean except for his thick neck and the beginning of a beer belly, which sagged over his pants. His red hair was an unruly mop. He looked through the big window in the front, and saw Ben and Brodie turn into the main street.

"Looka there," he said, "the sheeny rich kid and his pal."

He walked out on the porch, down the steps to the wood-slat sidewalk and, as the two boys rode past, he flicked his cigarette at them. It arced past Brodie's face and bounced off Ben's shoulder.

"Hey, kid," Guilfoyle said to Brodie, "who's your kike friend?"

Brodie did not hesitate. He handed his reins to Ben.

"Hold my horse," he snapped as he swung out of the saddle and landed flat-footed on the wooden walk in front of the red-haired lout.

"What d'you want?" Guilfoyle sneered, his thumbs hooked though his suspenders.

Brodie didn't say anything. He was sizing up Guilfoyle, remembering what his father had told him early on about street fighting: *Size up your foe. Look for his soft spots. Distract him. Hit first. Go for his nose.*

It hurts like hell, knocks him off balance, draws blood. Draw first blood, you win.

Guilfoyle had three inches on him and probably twenty pounds. But he was a dimwit, which meant he was slow. And he had bad teeth, rotten teeth.

"Your breath is uglier than you are," Brodie said. "I can smell you from here."

On the porch, Arnie Riker frowned and leaned forward. His front chair legs smacked hard on the porch floor.

Guilfoyle's smile evaporated. He looked puzzled.

Brodie took the instant. He kicked Guilfoyle in the shin. The big kid yowled like an injured dog, lost his balance, reached down and as he did, Brodie threw the hardest punch he could muster, a hard right straight into Guilfoyle's nose. Brodie felt Guilfoyle's bones crush, felt the cartilage flatten, felt the warm flood of blood on his fist.

Guilfoyle staggered back several steps, blood streaming from his nose, pain gurgling in his throat. Brodie quickly followed him, hit him with a left and a right in the stomach. Guilfoyle roared with rage, threw a wild left that clipped Brodie on the corner of his left eye. It was a glancing blow, but it snapped Brodie's head and he saw sparks for a moment. But it didn't slow him down. He stepped in and kneed Guilfoyle in the groin, and as the young thug dropped to his knees, Brodie put all he had into a roundhouse right. It smashed into Guilfoyle's mouth and Brodie felt the big redhead's teeth crumble, felt pain in his own knuckles.

Guilfoyle fell sideways off the walk into the mud. He lay on his back, one hand clutching his broken nose and busted teeth, the other grabbing his groin. Tears were flowing down his cheeks.

Riker stood up, his fists clenched in anger.

"Stand up," he yelled. "Stand up, you damn crybaby."

Guilfoyle groaned, rolled on his side, and tried to get up, but he was whipped. His hand slid in the mud and he fell again. He spit out a broken tooth and smeared blood over his face with the back of his hand.

Disgusted, Riker spat at Guilfoyle, and turned to the other three toughs who had joined him to watch the fight.

"Knock that little shit into the middle of next week," he snarled.

One of them reached inside the door and grabbed a baseball bat. The three of them started down the steps.

Ben had eased the horses up to the hitch rail. He got off his horse, tied them both up, and hurried to join Brodie.

The three toughs walked toward Brodie, who didn't move an inch. He was sizing them up as they sauntered toward him. He'd feint a left toward the one in the middle, smack the one holding the bat with a right to the mouth, and hopefully grab the bat and even things up.

It never happened.

A shadow as big as a cloud fell across them. Riker's hooligans looked up and Brodie looked over his shoulder.

Buck Tallman was sitting on a strawberry roan, his back as straight as a wall, his blond hair curling down around his shoulders from under a flat western hat. His face was leathery tan with a bushy handlebar mustache, its ends pointing toward flinty gray eyes. He was wearing a light-colored leather jacket with fringe down the sleeves. His sheriff's badge was pinned to the holster where his .44 Peacemaker nestled on his hip. It looked as big as a cannon.

He smiled down at Riker's young roughnecks and at the stricken Guilfoyle.

"One on one's a fair fight," he said, looking straight into Riker's eyes. "Three on one don't work with me. Understood?"

Riker didn't say anything. The three ruffians nodded and went meekly back into the hotel. Riker stared down at the beaten Guilfoyle, who was still sprawled in the mud, and shook his head.

"You're pitiful," he growled. Then he turned and went into the brothel.

Buck Tallman was a product of the previous century, of lawless western towns where violence was a way of life. Tallman had brought to Eureka the harsh morality of that frontier, had ridden with Pat Garrett and Bat Masterson, and had dime novels written about him.

Nobody messed with Buck Tallman. Everybody knew he was hired by the men on the Hill, the Olympus of the gods who owned the railroad and the land, and had friends in high places in Sacramento. They called the shots. In Eureka, Buck Tallman's job was to keep the peace within the limits they set.

*   *   *

Tallman leaned forward in the saddle and held his hand out to Brodie, who grabbed it and was swung up behind the saddle of the colorful rider.

"Thanks," Brodie said.

"What are you two doin' down here? Y'know how Mr. Eli feels about that."

"Going to get a soda," Ben answered. "We've been playing baseball up on the field."

Tallman looked back at Brodie. "You got a little shiner there. Needs some ice."

As they rode the block toward the pharmacy, Brodie put both hands under himself and swung over onto his own horse. They pulled up in front of a small shop with a large window announcing "Gullman's Pharmaceutical Parlor," with a rendering of a mortar and pestle under the lettering.

"Hey, Doc," Tallman called out.

"Yes, sir," came the answer from inside the store, and Gullman stepped out.

"How about bringin' us three strawberry soda pops? Put 'em on my tab."

"Good enough," the owner answered. "They're good and cold; Jesse just come back from the icehouse."

"Good, throw some ice in a small bag while you're about it," Tallman said.

Gullman returned quickly with the three sodas and a paper bag of ice.

Tallman wheeled the roan around and headed toward the ocean, with Ben and Brodie following. They tethered their horses to a tree at the edge of the beach and hunched down Indian-style on the sand. For a change, the sun was out. The sky was cloudless. It was so clear you could see the waves breaking at the entrance to the bay, almost two miles away.

Brodie dug some ice out of the soggy bag and winced as he pressed it against the welt on the corner of his eye. Water dribbled down the side of his face.

"You'll be goin' back East soon, won't you, Ben?" Tallman said.

Ben nodded. "Papa and I are going to Boston in a month to get me set up. Soon as school's out."

"You gonna marry Isabel?"

"Well, she's going East to school, too," Ben said, his face reddening. "But it's too early to be thinking about getting married."

"How about you, Brodie? What are you gonna do?"

Brodie picked up a handful of sand and watched it stream from his fist. "Haven't thought much about it," was all he said.

Tallman was mentor to the two boys, had taught them how to stand in the stirrups at a full gallop to take the load off the horse's back; how to draw a gun in a single, fluid move, skimming the hammer back with the flat of the hand, pointing the piece—like you would point a finger—before making a fist and squeezing the trigger, all the while without changing expression. No hint of a move in the eyes or jaw muscles. No giveaways. And stay loose, don't tighten up, concentrate on the eyes and face of your foe.

"Their eyes'll tell you when to squeeze off," he had told them. "It's a look you never forget."

"Like what?" Brodie asked.

"Plenty a things. Fear, hesitation, a little twitch of the eye, anxiousness. It's a giveaway look for damn sure. You'll know it, if ever you see it."

The talk didn't mean much to Ben, who loved a shotgun and the hunt, while Brodie loved pistol shooting.

"So who's the best shot you ever knew?" asked Brodie.

"Phoebe Moses is the best shot alive," he said without hesitation.

"A *girl*!" Ben said incredulously.

"C'mon," Brodie said.

"Phoebe Anne Oakley Moses. You boys know her better as Annie Oakley. I met her a few years ago when Bill Cody's Wild West Show was in Chicago. She shoots over her shoulder with a rifle better than me, Wyatt, Pat Garrett, or her husband, Frank Butler—who was damn good himself—can shoot with a pistol. You could toss a playin' card in the air and she'd put a dozen shots in it 'fore it hit the ground. Her and Frank are still with the show, far as I know."

"How about that abalone shell down there," Brodie said suddenly.

"What shell?" Tallman asked, casually looking down the beach.

Brodie looked down the beach. A red abalone shell was lying at the edge of the surf about fifty feet away. He had to squint to see it clearly. "The red one. Down the beach there."

Tallman didn't need to ask what Brodie wanted him to do. He simply stood up, stood straight with his hands hanging loosely at his sides. His eyes were narrowed slightly. Nothing in his face changed before his right arm moved fluidly up, his hand drawing the .44 as it passed his hip, his left hand fanning back the hammer as his hand stretched out, and

BOOM!

Both boys jumped as the gun roared.

The red shell exploded. Pieces flying left and right, the main piece jumping straight up. As it fell, Tallman fanned off a second shot and it disintegrated.

And just as quickly, the gun was back in its holster and Tallman reached up and tenderly stroked the curves in his mustache.

"You mean that one?" he said.

He took out the pistol, flipped the retainer on the cylinder open and emptied the spent casings into his hand and dropped them in his pocket, then inserted fresh bullets into the slots and flipped the retainer shut. He handed the gun butt-first to Brodie.

"Give it a try," he said.

The Irish kid took the pistol, stuck the gun between his pants and shirt so the hammer would not catch on his belt. It was on his left side, the butt facing to the right so he could cross-draw. He looked for a target. Twenty feet away a bottle rolled on the beach at the edge of the surf.

He shook his hands and shoulders loose.

His right arm moved swiftly across his body, hauled the big Frontiersman from its resting place. His left hand snapped the hammer back as he raised the gun at arm's length and squeezed his hand. The gun roared, kicked his arm almost straight up. Sand kicked up an inch from the bottle.

"Well, damn," he muttered.

"That was a good shot," Tallman said, nodding assurance. "Just a hair to the right."

Brodie smiled, dropped the empty casing into his hand and gave the casing and the gun back to the sheriff.

"How about you, Ben?" Tallman asked.

"Nah," Ben answered. "You know I never got the hang of it."

Tallman looked over his shoulder. The sun was turning red, sinking toward the horizon. He slapped them both on the shoulder.

"You boys better get on up the Hill. Be dinnertime soon."

They rode the length of the beach to the cliff trail, a wide walkway huddled against the face of the cliff, which rose six hundred feet up the sea side of the Hill and ended at the edge of Grand View, the O'Dell estate. The grand, white-columned mansion sat back from the main road at the end of a drive lined on both sides by small bushes. Behind it and six hundred feet down, the Pacific Ocean stretched to the horizon.

It and the Gorman estate were the two grandest houses on the Hill.

A one-horse surrey was coming up the road from the strip of stores that serviced the families on the Hill. The driver was a powerfully built black man in his twenties, who spoke with an almost musical lilt. His name was Noah. Rumor had it that Shamus O'Dell had bought Noah's mother at a slave market on one of the Caribbean islands. He had bought her as a housekeeper, not knowing she was pregnant. Her son had been raised by O'Dell and educated by his wife, Kate. Noah was fiercely loyal to the family, sometimes acting as a bodyguard for Shamus; sometimes watching over Delilah, who was O'Dell's daughter and one of the three girls in the carriage; sometimes driving the family automobile, a German Daimler, which looked like a formal horse carriage powered by a gas engine and was the only automobile in the valley.

O'Dell never took the car down the hill, fearing the brakes might not hold or it would get mired in mud. So he showed off in it sticking to the broad, forested, five-mile-wide northern mesa, the Hill, where the families of fourteen tycoons lived, five appearing only on weekends. Noah proudly squired O'Dell along the horse trails that served as roads, taking him to the club where the rich men and their male out-of-town guests drank at the bar or played cards. On occasion, Noah drove Delilah to the two-story schoolhouse, where tutors taught the dozen or so children of the barons who lived there year-round.

Two of the girls in the surrey were facing Ben and Brodie as they reached the top of the cliff. The third girl was sitting opposite the other two, with her back to the boys.

When Noah saw the boys, he reined in his horse.

Delilah O'Dell, seventeen and the oldest of the three, already flaunted a sensuous and independent nature that would define her through the years. She was well developed for her age. Blazing red hair cascaded down over her shoulders and curled over her breasts. She ignored Ben, fixing her green eyes on Brodie.

"Looks like you've been rolling those horses in the mud," she said haughtily.

Ann Harte, the girl sitting next to her, had just turned fifteen and was extremely shy. She giggled nervously, looked down, toyed with her purse, and murmured, "Hello."

Brodie was staring at the girl with her back to the two riders. "Oh, Del," she chastised, "that's rude." Then she turned and stared back at Brodie.

Isabel Hoffman was as fragile as Delilah was lusty. She would turn seventeen in two weeks. Jet-black braided hair hung down her back. Deep brown eyes stared softly from a face that had the quality of fine china. Sharp features accented high cheekbones. She was dressed in a white pinafore. She was always dressed in white or pastel, unlike Delilah, who favored bright, sometimes garish colors. Sometimes black, when she was feeling moody.

Today, Delilah was dressed in black.

The valley was owned by the JMC and Pacific, which O'Dell and Gorman had inherited when Jesse Crane had been gunned down. Shrewdly, Gorman had opted for a smaller share of the property—but his share completely encircled O'Dell's. The Irishman could not develop his property without entry and exit rights through Gorman's property and Gorman, knowing O'Dell's plans for the future, refused to give them up.

But O'Dell owned the six square blocks that included the town of Eureka.

"Something the matter, Del?" Ben asked.

"You know what's the matter," she chided, still looking at Brodie.

Ben thought for a moment and said, "Is this about the game?"

She finally glared at him but did not answer.

"That's between my father and yours," Ben said quietly. "We've all been friends since I can remember. What's it got to do with us?"

"Yes." Isabel nodded. "I agree."

"My father says we'll have to leave if he loses. But he *won't* lose." Delilah looked at Brodie and her full lips curled into a slight smile. "When he was young he played poker for a living. Over in Denver."

"I don't know whether my father can even *play* poker," Ben said.

"So when *he* loses," Del said with a snicker, "will *you* leave?"

"Mr. Eli hasn't talked about it," Brodie interrupted.

"He's the only one in town who hasn't," said Isabel. She looked at Ben and said, "Aren't you worried?"

"It's not for our houses, just the land in the valley."

Del looked down and picked at her skirt. Her tone became more plaintive. "Daddy has such a terrible temper. He said if that old . . . if Mr. Eli wins . . . he'll leave on the spot and go back to San Francisco and never set foot here again, and Mother and I will follow as soon as school ends."

"I'm sorry it's come to that, Del," said Ben.

"Me, too," Brodie said. "But we can't do anything about it. Just wait and see what happens."

Ben reached down and squeezed Isabel's hand.

"We gotta go. It's dinnertime."

She nodded and looked at Brodie, who wheeled his horse around as he touched the bill of his cap.

"See you at school tomorrow," he said over his shoulder.

Noah snapped his whip and the surrey moved up the road toward Grand View. Delilah looked back as they pulled away, her eyes fixed on Brodie's back as the two boys headed toward home.

The only time Brodie ever saw Eli Gorman in less than business attire was on Sunday at lunch when he sometimes wore a silk smoking jacket. Even then, he wore a tie. Short and somewhat stubby, his heavy-lidded but steady brown eyes never wavered, alert and always interested. He spoke in a deep, level voice, which he rarely raised, even in anger. His face was thick-featured, topped by thinning black hair, and concealed behind a graying mustache and goatee. Most people found his appearance intimidating.

In business he was tough but fair, a shrewd, well-informed, quiet fox who had attended some of the finest schools in Europe and emigrated to the United States with his father, a banker. He mastered the English language, had not a whit of an accent. At twenty-one, he attached himself as an intern to Andrew Carnegie, the powerful steel magnate, who later moved him into the railroad business, where Gorman proved a wily match for the robber barons who controlled the network of trunk lines that criss-crossed the country. In his mid-thirties, Gorman found himself in San Francisco, comfortably rich thanks to a generous inheritance and artful investments in his burgeoning business.

It was there he finally began to enjoy life. He met and, after a year of ardent courtship, married Madeline Lowenstein, the tall, handsome, cultured daughter of a wealthy shipping magnate. Maddy gently sanded off his rough edges and they idolized their son, Ben, who had come late in both their lives. Then fate had led Eli to robber baron Jesse Milstrum Crane, to the Frisco–Los Angeles railroad fiasco, and, ultimately, to his unfortunate partnership with Shamus O'Dell.

Now, at fifty, the old fox was a man whose persona was dictated by tradition. In his religion, ethics, family, and friendships, his life was stable and comfortable, if somewhat ritualized. He tried to keep his business run the same way. But now, uncharacteristically, he was about to risk his ownership of half the valley in a poker game that would pit O'Dell's greed against his vision.

Madeline knew about the game and supported his decision. And the boys knew about the game because it was a topic of gossip all over the valley. But it was not a subject Eli discussed openly with his family.

Eli stared across the elegant dining table at Ben and Brodie as the evening prayers began. Eli was inspired by their friendship, which transcended social standing, by Ben's ability to see the value of this young boy, toughened by the streets of Eureka but with an innate sense of honesty and loyalty. And Brodie was smart, no longer brandishing the hard-boiled attitude he first had shown that day four years ago when Ben had brought him home—a tattered ragamuffin whose mother was a washerwoman. Eli was proud that Brodie saw and admired the same values of trust and friendship in Ben. When Brodie's mother died of lung fever four months later, Eli had unofficially adopted the boy, given him a room over the stable, and paid him five dollars a week to groom the horses.

Brodie was grateful for his new life and showed it in many ways. Every Friday, starting at sundown, he voluntarily performed or directed the chores of the servants during the twenty-four hours de-

voted to prayer and atonement during which all other activities were
forbidden to Jews. When Brodie had been invited to share meals with
the family, it was his choice to wear a yarmulke—a voluntary act that
deeply touched Eli.

When the prayers were over, Eli piled food upon Maddy's fine
china plates and passed them around. He sat at the head of the table
wearing a prayer shawl, his pince-nez perched on the bridge of his nose.

"So what were you two up to after school?" Mr. Eli asked as he
chewed a mouthful of meat loaf.

A little too casual, Brodie thought. *The old fox knows.*

"We had a little problem in Eureka," he blurted, before Ben could
avoid the truth.

Ben winced but was speechless. Eli looked up and stared at his
son. His tone was quiet but firm. "What were you doing in Eureka?"

"We went to the pharmacy to get a soda."

"There's a soda shop up here on the Hill."

"We were real thirsty, Papa," Ben said. "We played baseball for two
hours."

"You don't know enough to take a canteen? A bottle of water?"

"We shared it with the kids from Milltown, sir," Brodie pitched in.
"They didn't have none."

"*Any.* Not *none.* The word is *any.*"

"Yes, sir, any," Brodie said.

"Then what?"

"There was a . . . uh . . . mix-up," Ben said.

"What kind of mix-up? Did you have words with somebody?"

"Yes, sir," said Ben.

"Harsh words?"

Ben nodded.

"So harsh they gave Thomas a bruise over his eye? Words that fly
through the air and make an eye black and-blue?" Eli was the only one
who called Brodie by his given first name.

"It was a fight, sir," Brodie said. "With a guy named Guilfoyle."

"He called me a kike," Ben said.

Maddy looked down at her plate, embarrassed by the bigoted
remark.

Eli took another bite of food.

"And you stood up for Benjamin?" Eli said to Brodie.

Brodie looked down at his lap. "He said it to me, not Ben. Besides, Ben, he does the thinkin' and I . . . uh . . . I do the . . ."

"Fightin'?" Eli said, mimicking Brodie's tough talk. "Brains and brawn, that it?"

"That's about it, sir."

"Look at me, Thomas. Don't look away, that's a sign of weakness. Always look a person straight in the eye."

"Yes sir," Brodie answered and fixed his gaze on Mr. Eli's dark brown eyes.

"You're a very bright young man, Thomas. A bit impetuous, but that's the Irish in you. Don't undersell yourself. Just because you're handy with your fists doesn't mean you're stupid."

"Yes, sir."

Eli looked at Brodie. "This Guilfoyle, is he the young hoodlum who works for Riker?"

Brodie nodded.

"And he was looking for a fight, was he?"

Brodie nodded again.

Eli nodded toward the black-and-blue streak over Brodie's eye.

"He's quite a bit larger than you."

"He whipped him good, Papa," Ben chimed in. "The miserable skunk . . ."

"Benny, *please!*" Maddy said.

"Sorry, Mother. Anyway, he only got one punch in and Brodie—"

"Yes," the father interrupted. "He whipped him good." He thought for a moment and added, "Well, I'm glad you won, Thomas. Winning is always preferable to losing. But I have forbidden you both from going into Eureka for just this reason. Are we understood on that?"

They both nodded.

"Mother, have you anything to add?"

Madeline Gorman, who had been listening quietly to the conversation, looked up from her dinner.

"I don't approve of brawling," she said softly. "But sometimes it *is* a matter of honor, Eli."

"Yes, my dear, I understand that. The point is, they weren't supposed to be there in the first place." He cleared his throat and added, "Well, enough said of that. Let's enjoy our dinner."

*   *   *

The full moon was brighter than the lanterns flittering at the corners of the wide paddock. Brodie had showered off both horses and stabled the brown. Now he stood brushing the white horse in slow, easy strokes, smoothing out his coat and sweeping the tangles from his mane, and talking to him in a voice barely above a whisper.

"Frisky tonight, huh, Cyclone?"

The horse snorted and casually stomped a hoof.

Brodie stroked his forelock, patted his neck, rubbed his soft muzzle.

"Liked that run on the beach, din'tcha? You like runnin' on the sand."

The horse growled and bobbed his head.

Behind Brodie, the end of a cigar glowed in the darkness.

"You really love that animal, don't you, Thomas?"

It startled Brodie, although it was not uncommon for Mr. Eli to stroll down to the pasture for his evening cigar. He never smoked in the house; Mrs. Gorman hated the smell of cigars.

"He's the first thing I ever owned, sir. Three dollars, imagine that. He's one handsome fellow, he is."

"Thanks to you."

"And you, sir," Brodie answered.

The white stallion, a horse bred to be ridden, had been hitched side by side with a muscular dray horse, hauling railroad ties in a wagon. The white strained but did not have the powerful legs of the dray. The driver, a big-chested, angry man, was lashing out at the white.

"You lazy son of a bitch," he roared. "You worthless, good-for-nothing nag. I'll show you who's boss."

He jumped down from the wagon and pulled a pistol from his back pocket. Brodie, who was working on the railroad that summer, jumped down from a railroad car and ran to the man.

"Don't shoot him," he begged.

The big man glared down at him. "Who the hell are you?" he growled. "Get outta my way."

He cocked the pistol, held it toward the horse's head.

"I'll buy him," Brodie cried out.

"With what?"

Brodie had five silver eagles in his pocket, his pay for the week.

"Two eagles," he said. "I'll give you two dollars." He took out two coins and held them in the palm of his hand toward the man.

"I'd rather shoot the lazy bastard," he sneered.

"I'll make it three. Is it worth three dollars to shoot him?"

The driver stared at the three silver dollars.

"Christ, yer crazy," he said. But he took the three bucks and un-hitched the horse. "How you gonna get him home?"

"I'll ride him," Brodie said.

"You ain't even got a saddle."

"I'll ride him bareback."

"Shit," the driver said, and spat a stream of tobacco onto the horse's neck. "You get on him, he'll throw you all the way to Albuquerque."

Brodie rode the horse six miles bareback, using a rope for a bri-dle. He was thrown four times and he was skinned up, his one shirt-sleeve almost torn off and a bruise on his cheek. When he got to end-o'-track he bummed a ride into Eureka on a wagon, with the horse he named Cyclone tied to the back. Then he led the horse the last four miles up the cliff walk and across the top of the hill to the Gorman estate.

Eli remembered the day Brodie came home with the animal. Skinny, its ribs standing out like a museum skeleton, its flanks festered with whip scars, its eyes crazy and fear filled.

"I'll pay for his food and take care of him," Brodie pleaded. "You can take it out of my salary."

Old Gorman had smiled.

"I think we can handle the food bill," he said. And as he turned away, he looked back and said, "I admire you, Thomas. You have a big heart, which is a gift. But it isn't much of a horse for three dollars."

Brodie had nursed Cyclone back to health and, in so doing, they had formed a bond. No one else could ride him, no one else could even climb into the saddle without being thrown head over heels. Horse and boy were devoted to each other.

"You have a natural love for animals," Gorman said, tapping the ash from his cigar. "I've watched you with the other horses and the dogs. I admire that."

He pointed to the end of the pasture, which was separated from the edge of the cliff by a high, white fence that surrounded the twenty-acre grazing land.

"Let's take a walk," Eli said, nodding down the pasture. They strode side by side, with Cyclone clopping slowly behind Brodie.

"Have you thought what you're going to do when school ends?" Eli asked. "Ben will be going back East to Harvard in a couple of weeks. How about you? The state has a very good college down in Los Angeles. Then maybe take on law school."

"I ain't   I'm not smart enough."

"You do yourself an injustice, Thomas."

"I make C's, sometimes a B or an A but mostly C's."

"There's smart and there's smart. Ben is smart about business. Someday he'll run mine, he'll be responsible for this valley. For what happens to it. But he needs somebody who is smart in other ways. Ben is naive about things. He trusts everybody. He needs someone—one person—he can trust without question, a partner who will take care of things Ben doesn't see."

"You mean like somebody who can take care of a guy like Guilfoyle when he smarts off?"

"I mean somebody who understands why people like Guilfoyle are the way they are. Someone who understands that and will handle that part of the business. The kind of smart Ben will never be."

Brodie twisted his apple into two pieces, and held one half behind him. The horse gently took it from his hand and ate it.

"I . . ." Brodie started to say and then stopped.

"You what?"

"I don't wanna be a roughneck all my life."

"I don't imply you should. What I am saying is that it takes a man of unique talents to handle the roughnecks. My son doesn't have that kind of talent."

"And I do because that's where I came from. That it, sir?"

"You grew up in that life. Now you've seen the other side of the coin. I'll be glad to stand for your schooling."

"I don't wanna go back to it, Mr. Eli. You spoilt me that way."

"*Spoiled.* I spoiled you that way."

"Spoiled."

"You've already risen above that, Thomas. But railroading is a harsh business. It not only requires shrewd business sense, it requires a man who can think ahead of trouble and handle it."

"And that's me?"

"I see that kind of strength in you, yes."

They reached the end of the meadow and walked to the corner of the high fence that marked the edge of the cliff. To the south, past two neighboring houses and O'Dell's mansion, they could see the glow of Eureka.

"I had a vision the first time I saw this valley," Eli said softly, almost to himself. "And I still see it. I see a pretty village at the bottom of the valley. I see decent homes for workers. I see this valley, the way it is now, lasting forever. A place for good people to live and flourish. I see Ben and Isabel Hoffman marrying, they've been sweet on each other since they were children and she's a nice Jewish girl. I see them raising a family here, surrounded by its beauty. And I see you watching his back, keeping the law. But it won't happen as long as O'Dell owns half the valley, and Riker and his ilk run Eureka."

"Buck Tallman keeps the law, sir."

"Buck is an honorable man, but he's in his fifties. He tolerates gambling and womanizing and hard drink and brawling. He keeps it controlled, but he was a town-tamer, Thomas. He is from another time. My vision of the valley will never become a reality as long as men like Buck let men like Riker have their way. And my vision won't happen if O'Dell has *his* way. He will chop down the trees, turn all of this into power plants and paper mills and shanties for the workers. It will become a slum like Milltown."

Brodie was uncomfortable talking about the subject. It was not something Eli had ever shared with either of the boys. But his curiosity was rampant.

"Couldn't you just, uh, buy him out?"

"Been tried, Thomas. This has been going on for two years. O'Dell owns the part of the valley that includes Eureka. He's a rowdy himself and a spoiler. Our problems could never be worked out. The game was O'Dell's idea—although I must admit it is the only solution."

Brodie hesitated for a moment and then said cautiously, "What if it doesn't turn out the way, uh . . ."

"It?" When Brodie hesitated again, unsure if he had overstepped his bounds, Eli said, "Ah. You're referring to the game."

Brodie nodded. "Everybody knows about it, sir. The whole town's talking."

"And what are they saying?"

Brodie turned to Cyclone, held the other half of the apple in the flat of his hand, and the horse took it. "That O'Dell's a gambler and you ain . . . aren't."

"So they think O'Dell will win?"

"Well, that's what they're saying. Riker's giving five-to-one odds favoring Mr. O'Dell."

"You familiar with poker?"

"When I lived down there, I used to play a little penny ante with the other kids."

Eli looked at the youth for a moment, then reached in his pocket, took out some bills, and handed Brodie ten dollars.

"Bet this on me to win. You'll win fifty dollars after you pay me back the ten."

Brodie took the bill and stared at it for a moment or two. Ten dollars was a lot of money to Brodie.

"I never knew you to play poker," he said, folding it carefully and putting it in his pocket.

Eli puffed on his cigar and said, "You know who Andrew Carnegie is?"

"I know he's real rich."

"He's a steel man, Thomas. Made his fortune manufacturing steel. When I was a young man back in Pittsburgh, he took a liking to me and he moved me up in the business. He and some of his rich friends had a poker club. Played once a week. A tough game. Fairly large stakes. One day he invited me to play and I told him I couldn't afford it."

Brodie laughed. "What'd he say to that?" he asked.

"He said, 'You can afford it if you win.' He sat me down and in one afternoon taught me some of the secrets of poker. Then he gave me two hundred dollars and told me to come to the game that night. I won seven hundred dollars. And became a member of the poker club."

"What were the secrets?" Brodie asked eagerly.

Eli looked out at the shimmering reflection of the moon on the ocean.

"The most important one," he answered, "is the art of the bluff."

Brodie watched Eli walk back to the house, saw the back door open and close. He leaned on the paddock fence for a long time, thinking about everything Eli had said.

Now, suddenly, he had to make some hard decisions.

And then there was the other problem.

He went in the barn and came back with another apple. He broke it in half, gave one to the horse and took a bite out of the other one to chase the dryness from his mouth. He got a bridle and a blanket, slid the blanket over Cyclone's back, and put the bit in the horse's mouth. Slinging the reins over the horse's back, he jumped on and quietly rode out of the paddock and down through the woods to a pathway near the cliff's edge. Brodie rode south, toward the lights of Eureka. The O'Dell mansion was lit up like a church, its lamps flickering through the trees.

He turned the horse back into the woods and stopped, slid quietly off his back, tethered him to a tree, and gave him the rest of the apple.

"Be quiet, now," he whispered, then ran his hand down along Cyclone's mane and slid the blanket off his back before sneaking into the woods. He walked a hundred or so feet to a greenhouse and slipped inside. It was dark. He walked down the aisle of flowers and plants to the rear of the glass shed and stopped, looking back at the big house a hundred yards or so away. A light glowed in the corner room. A signal.

"You're late," a soft voice said from the darkness.

It startled him.

"I . . . we, Mr. Eli and me . . . we had a talk," he stammered, and before he could say anything else, she moved quietly from the darkness, gliding to him and putting her arms around his waist.

"I was afraid you weren't coming," Isabel Hoffman whispered.

She was so close he could feel her heart beating, a rapid tapping against his chest. He could smell her hair, feel her breath against his throat. In his young life he had never known such longing, never felt a connection with anyone that went so far beyond friendship.

"We have to talk about something," he said, but she lifted her face to his and kissed him. Her lips were wet and trembling with desire,

and he was overwhelmed by her ardor, as he always was and had been
for the two months they had been meeting secretly, two or three times
a week, in her mother's greenhouse. It was a tryst that had begun with
a note he found in his geography book one morning. It had started innocently enough. They had met at the bakery on the Hill to study for a
test. Ben was at his father's bank, where he worked after school for
two hours every day. She had been a little flirtatious at first, then their
mutual attraction escalated quickly. She was like a lure, shimmering on
the end of a line, and he was hooked.

Now his emotions were in turmoil. He knew how Ben felt about Isabel, but his own longing for her had masked any sense of betrayal.

He was so dizzy with longing he took her in his arms with passion-
ate desperation.

She took the blanket, pungent with the odor of the stallion, spread
it on the soft earth in the darkness of the greenhouse, lay down and
drew him gently to her, and, in a voice quivering with desire, she said,
"I never knew it would be like this, Brodie. I never imagined it would
be so wonderful . . ."

The Social House, as the men on the Hill called it, commanded the
northern crest of the valley and had once been a large, sturdy barn
and stable, owned by a horse breeder from San Luis Obispo, thirty or
so miles away. When the horse breeder died, Eli Gorman bought the
property from his estate.

The barn was refinished with teak and mahogany walls, Tiffany
windows and lamps, and a slate bar imported from Paris. Fourteen bar
chairs lined the bar, and fourteen tables and chairs occupied the
sprawling, cathedral-ceilinged main room, each chair with a brass
plaque identifying a member, nine of whom lived in sequestered mansions on the Hill. The other five had elaborate cottages and came from
Los Angeles or San Francisco on weekends and holidays.

There were two other rooms, one the office of the manager of the
club, a fluttery little perfectionist named Weldon Pettigrew who had
been the concierge of a Chicago hotel, the other occupied by the telephone switchboard, run by a widow named Emma Shields, who had
been trained in New York. The barkeeper, Gary Hennessey, had been
imported from a hotel in New Orleans and spoke with an accent that
was part Irish, part New York, and part Cajun.

Through the years, three apartments—for Pettigrew, Hennessey, and Mrs. Shields—had been built beside the clubhouse, and five small offices had been added to the clubhouse so its members could conduct business in private. Shields was the only woman allowed in the club except on rare occasions, when entertainers were brought in from San Francisco for the evening, and on New Year's Eve, when all the family cooks prepared a feast and the new year was ushered in properly.

At all other times, it was a place where the tycoons gathered to smoke cigars, sip brandy, talk business, play cards, and keep in touch with their businesses by special long-distance phone lines. There was no restaurant. If a member wanted to eat, food was cooked at home and delivered by servants.

Tonight was a particularly special occasion at the Social House.

Tonight was the poker game between Eli Gorman and Shamus O'Dell.

The boys went to Brodie's room on the pretense of studying, but quickly sneaked off through the woods to the Social House, Ben clutching his father's opera glasses so they could see better. They cautiously entered through the back door and went up the stairs to the storage loft, crawling over cases of whiskey and sweeping away spiderwebs until they found a secluded place where they could watch the main floor without being seen.

They stared down at the arena.

All the tables but one had been moved to the side of the big room. A single table, with a felt cover and three chairs, held down the center of the room, spotlighted under the chandelier. Six bar chairs formed an arc five feet away from the empty spot at the table and six more were behind the chair opposite it. They were separated by an occasional brass spittoon. There were large Waterford ashtrays in front of each place at the table, with matching water glasses beside them and a Waterford pitcher to service them. The chandelier cast a sphere of light on the table. The twelve chairs were outside the orbit, in the dark. From the setup, Brodie figured there would be twelve spectators, six facing the empty seat at the table and six behind the dealer. Nobody would be seated behind the two players.

The game was set for 8:00 P.M.

Fifteen minutes before game time. The ritual began.

Buck Tallman arrived first, carrying a saddlebag. He draped his jacket over the middle chair. He was wearing a bright red vest, a white shirt with a blue string tie, and tan leather pants. The boys had never seen him that elegant. He carefully rolled up both his shirtsleeves halfway to the elbow. He sat down and growled across the room to Hennessey.

"A cup of black coffee if you please, Mr. Hennessey."

He planted the saddlebag close to his right, opened it, took out ten virgin decks of cards, and placed them side by side in front of him. Hennessey, who was wearing a tuxedo for the occasion, brought the cup of coffee and placed it on the felt next to Tallman's elbow. He nodded his thanks.

Spectators began to filter into the room and fill the gallery.

Eli Gorman arrived two minutes before the hour. He was dressed in a dark blue suit. A gold watch chain draped between the vest pockets on either side of his chest. He was carrying a black leather doctor's satchel. He shook hands with Tallman and placed the satchel on the table.

His chair was below the boys. He sat with his back to them, but Brodie checked his position with the opera glasses. They would be able to see his hand over his right shoulder.

Gorman took out a thick packet of land deeds tied with twine and laid them next to the decks of cards. Then he took out a packet of ten-, twenty-, and hundred-dollar bills, stacked them in individual stacks, and counted out ten thousand dollars.

O'Dell was five minutes late, dressed in a garish light blue suit, an open-collared checked shirt, and a gray derby, which he hooked over the arm of his chair. His goods were in a small leather suitcase. He put his deeds on the opposite end of the line of cards from Gorman's. He counted out ten thousand dollars in tens and hundreds.

Hennessey poured each of them a glass of water. O'Dell ordered a glass of Irish whiskey. Gorman shook his head when Hennessey looked at him. The bartender vanished into the darkened room.

Twenty thousand dollars lay on the table.

Tallman said, "Gentlemen, the game is poker. I will deal for each of you. Five- and seven-card stud and three-card draw, no wild cards. In straights and flushes, high card wins. If it's a push, the pot will carry over to the next game. The ante is ten dollars. The limit is table stakes, the minimum bet will be ten dollars. The first player who can't call a bet is out. Winner takes all, the deeds and twenty thousand dollars. Either player may ask for a new deck at any time. If so, the deal goes to the other player. I will flip a coin and the caller will select the first deck. Then you will draw a card for the first deal. We will take a fifteen-minute break whenever any of us requests it. Any questions?"

There were none.

Ben leaned close to Brodie's ear. "What's table stakes?" he whispered.

"Means you can bet whatever's in the pot."

Tallman said, "Then we'll begin. Shake hands, gentlemen."

"Forget it," said O'Dell.

Gorman looked at Tallman and shrugged. He took his pince-nez from a vest pocket and set it near the end of his nose. Tallman took out a silver dollar and flipped it.

"Heads," O'Dell snapped. The coin landed on the table, spun around, and came up tails. Gorman selected a deck and Tallman broke open the seal, took out the jokers, dropped them in the saddlebag. He swept the cards around the table, mixing them up, and splayed the deck out between the two players. Gorman pulled an eight, O'Dell turned a jack.

"Your game, Mr. O'Dell."

"Five stud," O'Dell said, in a high-pitched tenor voice that was a sharp contrast to the voices of Tallman and Gorman.

"Ante up," said the dealer. O'Dell threw a ten-dollar bill in the center of the table and Gorman covered it.

"The game is five-card stud," Tallman said. He shuffled and arched the cards together several times. He lay the deck in front of O'Dell, who cut them.

Tallman dealt the first card to Gorman. Both got one card down and one up. Eli lifted the corner of his hole card, let it snap back. A six of hearts.

Gorman drew a four of clubs. O'Dell, a seven of diamonds.

"Seven bets. The limit is twenty."

O'Dell bet twenty dollars. Gorman called.

Sixty dollars in the pot.

Second up card: O'Dell, a queen of diamonds, Gorman, a nine of hearts.

Tallman: "Queen bets. The limit is sixty."

O'Dell bet the limit again. Once again Gorman called.

A hundred and eighty dollars in the pot.

Third card: O'Dell, a seven of clubs. Gorman, a two of spades.

O'Dell had the lead with a pair of sevens. Gorman had a nine high. One card to go.

Gorman's expression never changed as he stared over his glasses with his heavy-lidded eyes, glanced back at his card and stared back at O'Dell.

At this point, O'Dell's open hand was a winner. The only way Gorman could win was if he paired his nine on the last card and O'Dell didn't help his sevens. O'Dell sneaked a peek at his hole card. Gorman just stared at him, studying his expression, his eyes, any tics he might discern. O'Dell's hole card could triple his sevens or pair either of his other three cards for two pair. The odds were strongly in O'Dell's favor.

Tallman: "The limit is one-eighty."

O'Dell shot the wad. Gorman folded and O'Dell pulled the bills and piled them loosely beside his left elbow. Gorman had lost ninety dollars on the first hand.

The game went on. Hennessey moved quietly, like a ghost, filling drinks.

The winning hands went back and forth. Brodie kept the opera glasses on Eli's hand and watched with surprise when Eli folded a winning hand of five-card stud, folded again when his down card gave him a straight to O'Dell's three of a kind. In one seven-card game, Eli had a well-hidden flush, O'Dell obviously had three of a kind. Eli called O'Dell with a large bet, then folded the winning hand.

Cigars and cigarettes glowed in the dark. Smoke curled upward, lured by the heat of the chandelier. The game went on. In a five-card draw hand, Eli drew one card to a four-card heart flush and caught the fifth heart. O'Dell drew two cards. He bet two hundred dollars and Eli called him. O'Dell had three kings.

"Beats," Eli said, and threw away the winning flush.

Brodie was astounded. *What kind of bluff was he playing?*

When the pot was high, Eli was purposely losing every bluff he tried. Brodie was confused. *What was the art of the bluff Mr. Eli had talked about—throwing away winning hands?*

At 10:15, Eli called for a break.

"The old man must be gettin' tired," O'Dell whined in his high voice as he headed toward the bar with most of the gallery. Eli stood up and stretched and worked the kinks out of his shoulders and neck. Buck Tallman intertwined his fingers and snapped them, then shook them out.

"How do you feel?" Tallman asked.

"Just fine."

"Maybe the cards'll start falling a little better."

"The cards are falling just fine," Eli answered.

"The way I figure, you're down about two thousand."

"The night's young."

At 10:30, Tallman announced, "Let's play cards."

O'Dell strolled back to his seat. Eli was already seated.

"You got any objections to raising the ante to twenty bucks?" O'Dell said, looking at Tallman.

"Mr. Gorman?" he asked.

Eli shrugged and said, "Why not make it a hundred?"

There was an audible reaction from the gallery. Tallman tried to control his surprise. O'Dell snickered. "What's the matter, Gorman, you so tired you wanna go home early?"

"Do I take that as a 'yes'?" Tallman said.

"Hell, yeah," O'Dell said and threw a hundred-dollar bill in the pot, which Gorman covered. Since Gorman had called for a new deck, it was O'Dell's game.

"Mr. O'Dell, your call."

"Draw poker."

"The game is draw poker," said Tallman, and dealt each man five cards down.

O'Dell picked up his hand, squeezed the five cards out. He had three eights, and a ten and six of mixed suits.

Eli watched his reaction while slowly shuffling his hand by slipping the top card under the bottom one. Then he looked. He had three kings, a five, and an ace of hearts.

"The limit is two hundred dollars," said Tallman. "Cards?"

O'Dell bet the two hundred and Gorman called.

"The limit is six hundred. Cards, gentlemen?"

O'Dell took two cards.

So, thought Gorman, *he, too, had triples or a pair and was holding an ace kicker.* Gorman only took one. He held the kings and the ace, hoping O'Dell would figure him for two pair or four cards to a straight or flush.

"Goin' for that inside straight again?" O'Dell bit. He chided, "Don'tcha ever learn?"

He looked at his two new cards. He had not helped. His best hand was triple eights.

Gorman watched him closely, looking for anything, a tic, a flinch, a hint of a smile. O'Dell licked his lips, took a sip of whiskey.

"Mr. O'Dell, the limit is six hundred," said Tallman.

O'Dell thought: *Got him. Didn't help his two pair or fill his straight or flush.*

"Bet a hundred," said O'Dell.

"The limit is seven hundred."

"Two hundred back at you," said Eli.

It caught O'Dell flat-footed. He sat for a moment. *Gorman figures me for the opening pair. He probably had two pair going in so he figures even if I paired my openers he's got me beat.*

"The pot is nine hundred dollars."

Gorman had tried bluffing too many times before.

"Call," O'Dell said.

Gorman laid his hand down and spread out three kings.

O'Dell's eyes narrowed and his face reddened, but he said nothing. His three eights were beat. He threw in his hand.

"Three kings wins a thousand dollars," said Tallman.

Now Eli had O'Dell's holdings down to sixty-nine hundred; Gorman had sixty-seven hundred. A mere two hundred dollars separated them.

"I'd like a new deck," Eli said again.

Tallman held the old deck between two hands and tore it in half, dropping the pieces in the saddlebags. He opened a new deck, mixed and shuffled them.

"The game returns to Mr. O'Dell," he said.

With the right hand and the right timing, Eli could take O'Dell. O'Dell, playing arrogantly, had not counted his money. It lay in a loose pile by his elbow. But Eli knew. He had been counting both his money *and* O'Dell's. Now Eli had to play cautiously. The stakes were getting so high, if either of them made a mistake it could cost them the game, the stakes, and the valley.

O'Dell called seven-card stud.

Tallman: "The game is seven-card stud."

The players anted up a hundred apiece.

"The limit is two hundred. Cards to the players."

He dealt two cards facedown to the players. O'Dell lifted the corners of his two cards. An ace of spades and a jack of hearts. Gorman peeked at his two cards, but Brodie could not see them well enough to read them.

Tallman dealt each a face card.

O'Dell: jack of spades.

Gorman: four of diamonds.

"Jack bets," said Tallman.

O'Dell bet two hundred. Gorman called the bet.

Tallman: "The pot limit is now six hundred."

He dealt the second cards up.

O'Dell: three of hearts. "Jack, three," said Tallman.

Gorman: jack of clubs. Tallman: "Jack, four. Jack, four bets."

Gorman studied the cards.

"Check," he said.

O'Dell bet a hundred dollars. Gorman called the bet.

Tallman: "The limit is eight hundred."

O'Dell: jack of hearts. "A pair of jacks and a club three," Tallman said.

Gorman: three of hearts. "Heart jack, diamond four, a heart three. The pair bets."

O'Dell's tongue lashed at his lower lip. He started pulling hundreds from his pile.

"Eight hundred," O'Dell snapped.

In the darkness, there was a sudden spate of whispered chatter.

"Quiet please, gentlemen," Tallman admonished softly. "The bet is eight hundred. Pot limit is sixteen hundred dollars."

Gorman studied his three face cards: jack, four of diamonds, three of hearts. He stared across the table at O'Dell, who was wearing what could pass for a smile.

"Call the sixteen hundred," Gorman said.

Tallman sighed. "The limit is thirty-two hundred. Cards to the players."

He dealt the last face card to O'Dell: an ace of spades. "A pair of jacks, three, and the ace of spades," said Tallman.

Gorman caught a four of diamonds. "Two of diamonds, jack of hearts, three of hearts, four of diamonds. Three cards to a straight." He looked at Gorman, who was expressionless.

"The pair still bets. The limit stands at twenty-four hundred," Tallman said.

O'Dell said, "I'll make it easy on you, old man." He counted out twenty hundred-dollar bills and dropped them in the pot.

"The bet is two thousand," Tallman said. He looked at Gorman, who was staring at O'Dell. "Two thousand buys you the last card. The pot stands at forty-four hundred."

Gorman hesitated. Was this a sucker bet to keep him in? Why would O'Dell make a soft bet? He studied O'Dell's hand. A pair of jacks, an ace, and an eight. Possibilities? Three jacks or three aces. He had the cased jack of clubs and a cased ace. Either a pair of eights or a hidden pair in the hole. Unless all three of his hole cards were eights, he could not have four of a kind. Odds for a straight or flush were zero. A full house was the best hand he could have. With a pair of jacks showing, Gorman figured O'Dell had either two pair, jacks and possibly aces, or a jack high full house.

Eli would know after the last down card was dealt. If he had a full house he would check, gambling that O'Dell would bet, and O'Dell could raise him out of the game.

At this point, a full house, four of a kind, or a straight flush could beat Gorman.

Gorman called the two-thousand-dollar bet.

"The pot limit is sixty-four hundred dollars."

An audible gasp from the darkened gallery. Hennessey brought Tallman a fresh cup of coffee, his sixth of the night, and he took a breath and a sip.

The last card.

Gorman watched O'Dell take a quick, cursory look at his down card, which told Gorman that O'Dell had his full house, probably jacks and a pair of aces or eights.

Gorman bent his hole card up, looked at it, and let it snap back on the felt.

Brodie got a quick look at it. A three of diamonds.

A pair of threes! Brodie thought. *What are his other two hole cards? Even if Eli had another three and a pair of jacks, O'Dell's full house would beat Gorman's. This was a hand Eli couldn't bluff.*

O'Dell did exactly as Gorman anticipated. He checked.

Either he had two pair and was hedging, or it was a sucker bet. He'd figure Gorman, with a straight, would bet. O'Dell would raise him and drive him out of the game.

O'Dell swept up his stash and counted the hundreds. Gorman's expressionless eyes watched him. He had sixty-nine hundred dollars left.

He looked across the table at Gorman's neatly stacked cash. Easy to count. Sixty-seven hundred dollars.

Gorman looked at him for a minute or more. O'Dell finally looked away, lit a cigarette.

Gorman bet a hundred dollars.

The bet reduced O'Dell's stash to sixty-eight hundred, Gorman's to sixty-six hundred.

The pot was sixty-six hundred, the maximum bet.

"Looks like you're gonna get your beauty sleep early tonight, old man," O'Dell sneered. "You think you can bluff me out with a little straight?" He counted out a fistful of hundreds and dropped them in the pot. "The limit: six thousand six hundred dollars."

He leaned back in his chair and smiled.

Eli sat quietly for a moment. Then he counted out his last dollar and dropped sixty-six hundred dollars on top of O'Dell's bet.

"I'll just call," Eli said. "If you've got that filly, let's see it."

O'Dell's left eye twitched. He looked at Gorman but saw only the dead stare he had seen all night.

He turned his first two hole cards over. An ace and a jack.

"Jacks full," he snarled. "Let's see that little straight of yours."

"Oh, I have the little straight," Gorman said, and smiled for the first time during the evening.

Gorman turned his first two hole cards over.

An ace of diamonds, a five of diamonds.

O'Dell started to reach for the pot.

Gorman turned over his last card. A three of diamonds.

"But they're all diamonds," Gorman said. And he laughed. "A straight flush."

O'Dell stopped and looked at the trey of diamonds with disbelief. He wiped his mouth with his hand. Beads of sweat gleamed from his forehead. He looked at Gorman with hate.

The gallery began to babble. Hennessey poured himself a double bourbon.

"You kike bastard," he bellowed, grabbing his full house and throwing the cards at Eli. A couple hit Eli's chest, the others fluttered to the floor.

Tallman slammed his hand on the table.

"This was a gentleman's game. Act like one!" he ordered. "Ace-five straight flush is the winner." He took O'Dell's stack of deeds and placed them on top of Eli Gorman's land titles. "Winner takes all."

Eli stood up and raked nineteen thousand eight hundred dollars into his satchel.

O'Dell was left with two hundred dollars, only enough for an ante. He would be beat on the first up card. He was trembling with rage. The gallery was crowding around Gorman, slapping him on the back, congratulating him, thanking him for saving the valley.

O'Dell threw his suit jacket over his shoulder and propped his derby on the back of his head. He started toward the door and over his shoulder he yelled, "Hey, Gorman."

Eli stared at him through the friends gathered around him.

"I just want you to know that I sold the six square blocks of Eureka to Arnie Riker this afternoon for a dollar. You got rid of me, I'm leaving tonight. But you're gonna have Riker up your ass until the day you die."

The celebrating was over, and Ben and Brodie had gone off to bed. Eli decided to have a final cigar and told Maddy he would be upstairs in a few minutes. He went out the back door, snipped the end off his stogie, and lit it. He heard Brodie's voice down near the stable and followed it out to the paddock.

Brodie was feeding Cyclone an apple, telling the horse about the game.

"It was really somethin' to see," he said softly to the white horse.

The remark surprised Eli.

"Do you have something to tell me, Thomas?" he asked.

When Brodie didn't answer, the old man went in. "I can read you like I can read a hand of cards. I can see it in your face."

"See what?"

"A kind of admiration toward me I've never seen before."

"Well, sure. You won the game."

"Not just that."

Brodie could not lie to Eli Gorman. He stuck his hands in his pockets and thought for a moment and said, "We was . . . were . . . there, Mr. Eli. Ben and me were hiding up in the loft."

"What!" he snapped, his face clouding up.

"Ah, c'mon, sir, you think we could pass it up? We were behind you and we had the opera glasses. I saw every hand you played." Brodie flashed his crooked smile. "You were really something, Mr. Eli."

Eli glowered for a moment more, then the glower slowly turned to a smile. He nodded.

"I should have guessed," he said. "Too good a show to miss, eh?"

"But I got one question," Brodie said.

"What question is that?"

"On that last hand? Why did you only bet a hundred dollars?"

"Did you watch him? He's a sloppy player. He never counted his money, he just piled it up. I'm a numbers man, Thomas. I knew after every hand where we both stood.

"The pot was sixty-four hundred dollars. I knew O'Dell had his full house already, he barely looked at his last card. And I had my straight flush. O'Dell had sixty-nine hundred, I had sixty-seven hundred. By betting a hundred dollars, it limited the pot to sixty-six hundred, which is what I had, so there was no way he could bet me out of the game. When I beat him, he had two hundred dollars left, just enough for an ante and one bet, so he was beat. Had I bet the limit, he could have raised me four hundred, and with only two hundred left, I couldn't call the bet and he would have won."

"I saw you throw in four winning hands during the night."

"Actually five. So he pegged me for a poor bluffer. On that last hand, he figured me for a small straight and thought I was trying to bluff him out with a small bet when he checked. There's no way he wasn't going to bump my hundred-dollar bet and run me out of the game."

Brodie shook his head. "You didn't have your winning hand until the last card."

"That's right. If I hadn't drawn that three of diamonds when he checked I would have checked, too. He would have won the hand, but I still would have had sixty-seven hundred dollars.

Eli ground out his cigar, started for the house, then stopped and turned back around. "Did you learn anything tonight, Thomas?"

"Oh yes, sir. I learned two things."

"And what were they?"

"The art of the bluff," Brodie answered. "And the luck of the draw."

Writing the letters was the hardest part. He had already packed all his belongings in two saddlebags, which were under his bed. His entire fortune—four hundred dollars, most of it paper money—was in a cigar box tied with twine in the bottom of one of them. He had twenty gold eagles in the pocket of his only suit, blue serge, a bit shiny at the elbows. He put the pocket watch Eli had given him once, as a Hanukkah present, in his jacket pocket.

He sat down on the edge of his bed and reread the letters he had written to Mr. and Mrs. Gorman and to Ben. He had struggled over the words for two days, writing and rewriting. He was no poet and he knew it. In the end, the letter to the Gormans was simple and to the point. A thank-you note for all they had done for him. It was time for him to leave the sanctuary they had provided, leave their care and affection. Time to find his own way in the world. They would understand.

"You have been the family I lost," he finished. "I thank you for the offer of college, but I think we all know I am no student. It is time for me to find my true place in this world. I will miss you two and Ben and this house. I love you in my heart. Thomas Brodie Culhane."

The letter to Ben was harder.

"You are the brother I never had and the best friend I will always have," he wrote. "You and Isabel have your future planned out. Right now, I have no future. There is nothing here for me in Eureka. I will leave Cyclone at the sheriff's office. I'm sure Buck will bring him home. Take care of him for me. He's the first thing I ever bought with my own money that was worth a damn. I leave this place to take on the world, Ben. I know you will understand. If you ever need anything—

anything—I'm sure you will find me and I'll come running. Have a good life, and thanks for taking care of me all these years. Brodie."

The letter to Isabel was impossible. He wrote and rewrote it a dozen times, crumpling each one and throwing it on the floor.

"Dear Isabel," he finally wrote. "You and Ben will be going back East to start a new life in a few weeks. He is the man for you. He loves you dearly and will bring magic to your life. It is time for me to leave here and look for my future. I will remember you forever. Brodie."

He rode down the pathway and tied Cyclone to a tree, gave him an apple to munch on, and looked up at the Hoffman house.

The light was on in the corner room.

She had sneaked out and was waiting for him.

He decided to wait until she went back to her house and leave the note for her in the greenhouse.

Then he thought better of it. Her mother or father might find the letter.

Even worse, it was a cowardly way to bow out.

But he approached the secret hideaway fearfully. Thirteen years of poverty and the loss of two parents he adored had left him emotionally barren. He had learned affection and self-respect from the Gormans, had found in Ben a brother figure in whom he had confided his fears and his joy.

But Isabel.

Isabel was different. Isabel had been his first love. She had awakened emotions he had never felt before. Each eagerly had surrendered their virginity to the other. She had revealed in Brodie a gentleness of spirit that both awed and terrified him.

How can I say good-bye, he wondered, *when my heart aches at the thought?*

He knew what he had to do, knew he had to dig deep down inside himself, to reach back four years, to search for and rekindle the cynicism, the toughness, the solitude of the kid who had grown up in Eureka and who, when his mother died, had cowered alone in his bed in the corner of the laundry until Ben had come and found him and taken him to the Gorman mansion and a new life that was far beyond his wildest dreams.

Payback time.

He entered the greenhouse resolutely.

She rushed from the darkness before he was halfway to the back. She was wearing a nightgown and a silk robe covered with tiny embroidered roses.

His throat closed. He couldn't swallow.

"Daddy told me about Mr. Eli. Isn't it wonderful! It turned out so perfectly," she said joyously.

She threw her arms around him, hugging him, and her hair swept his face. He kept his hands at his sides.

She stepped back and looked up at him, and saw something she had never seen before. There were tears in his eyes.

"Brodie . . ." The first hint of apprehension.

His lips moved but no words came.

"Brodie," she said, lowering her head a trifle, staring at him, her head cocked slightly to one side.

He touched her cheek and realized his hand was shaking.

"Something's bad," she said, and tears flooded her eyes. She put two fingers against his lips. "I don't want to hear anything bad. Please."

"Isabel . . . I've got to . . . I have to go away."

"What do you mean, 'go away'? Where? Where are you going?"

He looked at the ground. He could not stand to look at her face, at the tears edging down to her chin.

He shook his head. "I don't know. But it's not fair for me to stay here."

"Fair! *Fair!*"

"Look at me, Isabel. Please. I got nothing. All the clothes I own wouldn't fill the corner of a closet. I got four hundred dollars in a cigar box and that's all I got in the world . . ."

"Stop it!" she said.

"Ben loves you. He can give you everything you want."

"I don't care!" she cried, tears streaming down her cheeks. "I love you, and I know you love me."

"I left a note for Mr. Eli and Miss Madeline, and one for Ben. I'm leaving, Isabel. I'm leaving San Pietro valley for good. It's best for everybody. Especially you."

"It is *not* best for me," she said, anguish accenting every syllable. "You care about Ben, you care about the Gormans. Don't you care about me?"

"We're just kids," he said harshly. "It's puppy love."

"That's what you think? *Puppy love?*" She was crying hard now. "Is that all I mean to you?"

He couldn't stand the hurt. He reached out to her but she backed away, into the shadows at the back of the greenhouse. She sat down on the hard earth.

"You're just throwing me away." Her voice was like a whispered wail, a cry in the night, her grief so deep that Brodie did not know how to respond.

"I gotta go," he said in a voice he didn't even recognize. "It's best for everybody."

"How do you know what's best for me?" she moaned. "I thought you loved me. I thought you would protect me and . . ." Her voice dissolved into more tears.

Jesus, he thought, *why won't she understand?*

"My heart hurts," she sobbed. "It will never stop hurting. You've turned my dreams into nightmares."

"Isabel . . ."

"If you're going, then go. Get away from me."

He stood his ground for a few moments and then backed down the aisle to the door. He couldn't tell her there was a crushing hurt in his heart, too.

As he turned the doorknob, her voice came to him from the darkness.

"I read a poem once," she said in a voice tortured with misery. "It said 'First love is forever.' And I believed it."

He ran from the greenhouse, ran to Cyclone, jumped on his back, and rode down the path, away from the Hoffman house and around Grand View and down the precipitous cliff road from the Hill to Eureka.

The town had gone crazy. It was like New Year's Eve. The bars were full, men were staggering in the street, shooting their guns into the air. Some of the girls were dancing on the wooden sidewalk. The news was out about Riker.

Light from town spilled out on the beach, and Brodie leaned back and smacked Cyclone on the rump. He dashed off down the beach.

"Go, boy, go!" Brodie yelled, as the stallion galloped in and out of the surf as he loved to do. They raced past the town, and then Brodie wheeled him around, and they trotted back to the swimming beach. Brodie slid off his back and for the next two hours he talked to the horse, emptying his heart out, explaining to him why he was leaving.

He understands. I can see it in his eyes. He knows I gotta do this.

The wagon to end-o'-track left at 5:00 A.M. And the weekly supply train to San Francisco left at seven. The sun was a scarlet promise on the horizon when he led Cyclone up to the sheriff's office and tied him to the hitching post. He threw a saddlebag over each shoulder and went into the office. The deputy was half-asleep at his desk.

"What you doin' down here this time a day?"

"I gotta go out of town," Brodie answered.

He laid an envelope on the desk.

"My horse is tied up outside and I got a note here for Buck. I'm asking him to take the horse back up to the Gormans for me."

"Hope the hell nobody steals him," the deputy said, looking out the window at Cyclone. "I'll keep an eye on him."

"Thanks."

The wagon was loaded with hungover iron workers when Brodie climbed aboard. A few minutes later, the driver cracked his whip and they started up the hill. As the wagon reached the crest, Brodie looked back at the town where he was born and where his life had changed forever in the years since the death of his mother. A great sadness flowed over him. Then he turned his back on Eureka and dismissed it.

Good-bye forever and good riddance, he said to himself, and he knew he would never return.

Fate had other plans for Brodie Culhane.

1918

In the spring of 1917, a dispirited President Woodrow Wilson, the liberal idealist who had ardently resisted America's intervention in the war in Europe, was finally forced to admit the inevitable: America was about to be drawn into the most savage conflict in the history of warfare. In 1914, nine European nations were embroiled in what would become known as the Great War, a conflict unparalleled in its brutality. On one side, France, Italy, Great Britain, and Russia, among others. Opposing them, Germany, Turkey, and the Ottoman Empire.

It quickly became apparent that World War I was to become a campaign of mud, trenches, barbed wire—and machine guns, the first time the deadly weapon was used in a major war.

By the time the United States entered the conflict, the trench war was approaching its grotesque and barbaric finale . . .

A thick fog laced with the smell of death lay like a shroud over the battlefield. Then there was a howl in the sky as a star shell arced and burst, briefly revealing a ghastly sight. Silhouetted in the heavy mist was a wasteland of staggering destruction. Trees, fragmented by constant artillery shelling, were reduced to leafless, shattered stalks. Fence posts wrapped in rusting barbed wire stood like pathetic sentinels over trenches that snaked and crisscrossed the terrain. Shell holes, surrounded by mounds of displaced earth, were filled with rancid rainwater. There was no grass, nothing green or verdant, just brown stretches of mud, body parts dangling from endless stretches of wire, abandoned weapons, and corpses frozen in a tragic frieze of death.

And there were the rats, legions of rats, scurrying back and forth in the no-man's-land, feasting on the dead.

A few hundred yards beyond the haze-veiled scene, the Germans were gathering for another attack—there had been dozens through the years. The star shell burned out and darkness enveloped the shell-spotted battlefield.

Brodie Culhane was chilled even though it was early September. His boots and socks were soaked and he had removed his puttees, which were in rags. Damp fog wormed through his clothing and clung to his skin. The machine-gun nest he had set up had an inch of water in it from a rainstorm the night before. There wasn't a spot of dry ground for miles in any direction. It made him think of Eureka. All around him was mud. Mud as demanding as quicksand, sucking a man's legs down to the knees with every step. As he stared into the darkness, another star shell burst overhead, illuminating the grim no-man's-land that lay between his machine-gun line and the Germans.

From Switzerland to the English Channel, the French had lined their border with trenches and barbed wire, four rows of each separating

them from Germany. Now, almost four years later, the grim sight before him defined what had become known as the Western Front.

He was dying for a cigarette. And in the deadly silence, a song suddenly echoed in his head.

> K-K-K-Katy, K-K-K-Katy,
> You're the only g-g-g-girl that I adore . . .

*It was their first day on the line. They were marching down a road
past a park on the outskirts of a French town called Château Thierry,
heading north toward a game preserve called Belleau Wood. One of the
squads started singing, as if it were a parade. One platoon singing one
song, a second company answering with another.*

> K-K-K-Katy, K-K-K-Katy,
> You're the only g-g-g-girl that I adore,
> When the m-m-m-moon shine's, over the c-c-c-cowshed,
> I'll be w-w-w-waiting at the g-g-g-garden door.

Answered by:

> You may forget the gas and shells, parlay-voo,
> You may forget the gas and shells, parlay-voo,
> You may forget the gas and shells,
> But you'll never forget the mademoiselles,
> Hinky-dinky parlay-voo.

*They were still singing when the Germans fired the first volley. Ma-
chine guns. His men went down like string-cut puppets.*
Barely six months ago.
Baptism day.

Behind him, the radiophone buzzed, its ring muzzled to prevent the
enemy, a few hundred yards away, from hearing it.

The radioman, a clean-cheeked youngster, answered it, cupping
the mouthpiece with his hand. He gave the receiver to Culhane, who

could feel the youngster's hand shaking as he took it. The nineteen-year-old had developed the shakes after only two weeks on the front.

"Culhane," he whispered.

"Brodie, this is Jack Grover. The major wants to have a chat. I'm on the radiophone by the five-mile post."

"Stay where you are," Brodie answered, "I'll come to you. You'll never get that tricycle of yours through this damn muck."

"Appreciate that," Grover answered with a chuckle, and the radio went dead.

"Relax, kid," Culhane's voice was calm and deep as an animal's growl as he handed the phone back to the radioman. "Nothing's gonna happen for three or four hours. Think about something else. Think about your girl back home or Christmas or something. Fear's worse than the real thing."

He checked his watch in the masked glow of his flashlight. It was three-fifteen.

"I gotta run back to HQ," he told the kid. "Cover the stutter gun." He grabbed his rifle, crawled out of the nest, and headed east in a crouch toward the dirt road four hundred feet away, mud snatching at his boots with every step.

Grover was waiting on the motorcycle when Culhane emerged from the dark. His clothing and face were caked with mud, he was un-shaven, and his eyes were dulled by lack of sleep.

"Jesus, you look like hell," Grover said as Culhane clambered into the sidecar.

"Haven't you heard, this *is* hell," Culhane answered. Grover wheeled around and headed back down the muddy road.

Temporary HQ was a two-room bunker a mile from no-man's-land. It had wood-plank floors, sandbags for walls, and the ceiling was made of fence posts and logs. The first room was occupied by the top sergeant, a beefy old-timer named Paul March. Wooden planks stretched be-tween upended ammo boxes substituted for a desk. A radioman named Caldone was huddled over his equipment and a runner was catching a nap on a cot in the corner. A tattered piece of burlap served as a door to the other room, the major's office.

"How's it going up there?" March said to Culhane.

"Wanna take a guess?"

"No thanks," March said. "Let me be surprised in a couple of hours when we join you for tea and crumpets." He walked to the burlap curtain and knocked on the wooden frame that supported it.

"Yes?" The voice from inside the room was deep, with the soft roll of the South in it.

"Sergeant Culhane's here, Major."

"Good, show him in."

They entered, saluted, and Major Merrill walked around his desk to grab Culhane by the arm.

"Good to see you, Brodie," he said.

"Glad I'm still around."

The major was a big man, broad-shouldered and muscular, his hair trimmed almost to the scalp, his dark blue eyes dulled by too many attacks and counterattacks and too many "regret" letters written to mothers or wives or sisters. He was a year younger than Culhane, but the war had put ten years on his face. Culhane had served under him for two years, starting when the battalion was formed in South Carolina. Merrill was a compassionate man in a business where compassion was a liability.

"Jesus, you're a wreck," he said to Culhane.

"So I've been told," Culhane answered. Haunted eyes peered out from his mud-caked face.

Major Merrill looked Culhane over.

"Sergeant March," the major called.

"Yes, sir," March answered, peering through the burlap curtain.

"Do you think you can find me a pair of dry boots, ten-and-a-half C, and some dry socks and puttees?"

"Yes, sir. Right away, sir."

To Culhane, the major said, "I could hear your boots squishing when you came down the steps. A soldier has a right to go into battle with dry feet, damn it. Sorry I can't get you a fresh uniform."

"I'll be up to my ass in mud two minutes after I leave here, anyway," Culhane said. "But it'll be nice to have dry feet for a little while. Thanks. Okay if I smoke?"

"Of course."

Merrill watched Culhane's mud-caked hands as he took out a

pouch of tobacco, papers, and matches wrapped in tinfoil to keep them dry. Not a tremor, he thought, as he watched Culhane roll the cigarette and light it.

Culhane took out a roughly sketched map and spread it out on Merrill's table, but Merrill pointed to the other curtain in the room.

"There's a makeshift sink and some clean water in there. Why don't you wash up before we talk. My razor and strop's in there if you want to grab a quick shave. I'll get us some coffee."

March came back with fresh footwear, and Culhane put on the socks and boots. When he returned to Merrill's office, there were two tin cups of coffee sitting on the table. Merrill took a silver flask from his back pocket and laced both with brandy while Culhane rolled another cigarette.

"According to our intelligence, whoever the hell they are, the Germans are lining up to take another crack at us," Merrill said.

"What a surprise," said Culhane. "When?"

"Dawn."

Culhane looked at him for a moment, then asked, "What's the weather look like?"

"We're supposed to pick up some wind about sunrise. That'll clear the fog, then it's going to be a bright, sunny day."

"A break for us, for a change."

"If we can stop them this time, I think they're beat. They need to make this breakthrough and get behind our troops. Brodie, you're going to have to . . ."

". . . stall their front line at my forward post until you can move the company up," Brodie finished the sentence.

Merrill laughed. He had not laughed for some time. Culhane could sense a lot more relief in his laughter than joy.

"Where will you be?" Brodie asked.

"Fifty yards behind you. The company will move up to within fifty yards of your position before the Krauts start shelling us. I'm gambling that they'll think we're in the trenches, and pepper the trench line between them and us. If they find out we've moved back from the line, they'll raise their big guns and blow us to hell and gone. Your gunners are our front line. As soon as you make contact, we'll attack."

"How long do I have?"

"With the mud? Ten minutes. Can you hold them for ten minutes?"

In a place where a minute equals an hour anywhere else in the world? He shrugged. "If that's what I gotta do, that's what I gotta do."

Culhane turned his hastily sketched map toward Merrill and pointed out his positions as he spoke. "I got ten machine-gun nests set up along our perimeter with overlapping fire. Max Brady's in charge of the line. I got sappers out there planting mines in the trenches only. The mines are marked with circles on the map. I've got my two best shooters on the road and Rusty, the human ear, in a trench about fifty yards out. They should hear something before the shelling starts. The Krauts have four trenches to cross, a lot of wire, the mud, and the mines. The trenches are laced with 'em, Major. Warn our boys to jump across them. If they fall in one, there's a four-in-one chance they'll land on a mine."

"Classic setup for an ambush." Merrill smiled. "You outguessed me."

"I need the fog to lift, because if we can see them, we can hold them in place. But if the fog holds and they get right on top of us before we can engage them . . ."

He let the sentence die.

"So you have fourteen men holding that line?"

"Actually eighteen, counting me. We have two radiomen and two corpsmen up there, too."

"You travel pretty light."

"I got the seventeen best men in the company. You got the rest."

Merrill leaned forward and stared at the map. "So we need the fog to hold, to cover us," Merrill said, "and then lift just as they attack so you can zero in on them."

"That's about it. My two point men and Rusty the Ear are out there listening for movement. They'll fire flares when they're sure the Krauts are on the move. Then you can lob some star shells over them and, with luck, we'll get a nice look at 'em."

"They'll charge at that point."

Culhane nodded. "And move their artillery down the road. If they lead off with a tank, we can take it out with grenades. If they bring on the caissons first, we'll kill the horses and stop their artillery dead in its tracks."

"It's a daring plan," Merrill said. Then he nodded. "But if it works, we can drive them right into the river. They'll have to surrender."

"A lot's gonna depend on the fog."

Major Merrill reached in his pocket and took out a lieutenant's gold collar bar, put it on the desk, and slid it toward Culhane.

"I knew you'd be ready, Brodie," he said. "You're the best I've got. I'm giving you a battlefield commission. Colonel Bowers approved it last night. I don't have a commissioned officer left in this company."

Culhane stared at the bar for a full minute. He reached out with a forefinger and spun it around.

"How'd you like to tell some kid's mother that her son was blown to bits for five miles of mud, Major?"

"I do," Merrill said quietly. "I write the letters every day. I tell them their sons died heroes."

"There aren't any heroes in a slaughterhouse."

"Brodie, in four years, the battle lines along the western front have moved less than ten miles in either direction. It isn't about taking ground, it's about artillery and machine guns and bodies. We're expendable because we can be replaced. The guy back on the production line cranking out those howitzer shells and firing pins and cannon barrels, he's the one who's important."

"So whoever runs out of ammo, guns, and bodies first loses?"

"That's about it," Merrill said. Then added: "I'm giving you a battlefield commission. You're the best Marine I ever met."

They finished their coffee in silence. Somewhere to the west, they heard a shell scream to earth and explode. The tin cups jittered for a moment and some dirt dribbled down from the ceiling of the bunker.

"I'd like to pass on that. The reason you don't have any comms left is they're the first ones the Krauts knock off. I'll do whatever you call on me to do, but I'll keep my stripes if it's all the same to you."

"You're a lifer, Brodie. Do you realize what life will be like for a Marine officer when this is over?"

"I may not stay in. If I'm not rat meat by the time this is over, I'm thinkin' of taking a crack at civilian life again."

"You're throwing away what, fifteen years?"

"Closer to sixteen. I lied about my age. But I think it's time I went back to the hole I left."

"Where's that?"

"California. Called Eureka. Sits right on the Pacific. That's where I first learned to hate mud."

"Why go back to it, then?" Merrill asked.

"My best friend lives there." Brodie smiled and added, "I've got a godson I've never seen."

"What'll you do there?" Merrill asked.

"There's a sheriff there, an old-timer. He was kind of a mentor to me. Taught me to ride and shoot, do things with a sense of style."

"You thinking of taking his place?"

"Nobody'll ever take Buck Tallman's place," Brodie said. "Better get back. Dawn's just around the corner. Thanks for the dry boots and the coffee."

Merrill stood up, offered Brodie his hand, and they shook. Saying good-bye, just in case.

"Just remember," Brodie said as he brushed through the burlap doorway, "once it starts you'll have ten minutes. And not one minute more."

Rusty Danzig huddled against a battered sandbag in a shallow trench forty or fifty yards in front of the machine-gun line. His eyes were closed and his legs were curled up beside him. His rifle was resting against his legs. He could have been mistaken for dead or asleep, but he was neither; he was listening.

He had his ear pressed against a piece of burlap to keep it dry, and he had been listening for two hours in the darkness. Not for sounds he knew. Not for the sound rats make skittering across a board or chewing on a corpse, or the *thunk* of a shell as it splattered deep into the mud before exploding, or the sound barbed wire makes when the wind rattles it. Danzig was listening for the unusual. The sound of boots slogging through the mud, or a metal canteen accidentally scraping against an ammunition belt, or someone trying to muffle a cough. The sounds of life in a field of death.

Danzig was a South Boston tough guy who did not take well to orders. He would nod, say "Yes, sir," and then do it his own way. He was a short, burly, black-haired man who had great ears. He claimed he could hear a fly clear its throat from a hundred yards away. He was fifty yards in front of Culhane's foxhole, in a trench that was mined on both sides of him. The second most dangerous position in the planned ambush.

The most dangerous spot was reserved for Big Redd, whose father

was a Chiricahua Apache, his mother a white schoolteacher from Min-
nesota. The big Indian was the forward sniper. Redd had once told Culhane that he had joined the Marines just to get off the reservation,
where his father was a drunk and his mother the schoolmarm. *The
Marines got the best of that deal*, Culhane had thought. *We got a great
tracker and hunter, with the instincts of a mountain lion.* Eyes, ears, and
nose were part of the combination. The tall, muscular man could smell
a horse half a mile away with the wind at his back. His job: listen for
the sounds of an advance and, as soon as possible, shoot the lead horse
pulling the caissons with a clean front-on shot, two inches to the left of
its foreleg and a little higher. A heart shot that would drop the horse in
its tracks. Then pick off drivers, officers, whoever he felt was worthy
of an old frontier Sharps .30-caliber shot to the head. Delay the line,
cause chaos, and when it got too hot, run like hell. Culhane once asked
why it was Redd's favorite assignment even though it was the most
dangerous. Redd's answer: *Because* it was the most dangerous.

The number-three suicide spot was reserved for Lenny Holtz,
from Bend, Oregon. Son of a crippled lumberjack and his bitter wife. A
born sharpshooter who, like Culhane, had lied himself into the
Marines at fifteen. He was a sapper along with Danzig—first planting
mines in the three trenches between the Marines and the Germans
and, if he didn't blow himself up, then acting as Redd's backup. Anybody that got past the Indian's Sharps rifle was meat for Holtz. His
shooting eye was as flawless as Danzig's ears.

The three best men Culhane had were in the most vulnerable positions. The ten machine gunners were spread across a fifty-yard-wide
perimeter. Max Brady was his lead gunner. Their job, once the charging Germans reached the farthest trench, was to lay down a deadly .30-
caliber barrage, force the survivors of the gunfire to jump into the
mined trenches, and create panic in the German front lines until Merrill charged with the rifle company. Newsmen had nicknamed the
Marines "Hell Hounds" because they screamed like wounded dogs
when they engaged the enemy in hand-to-hand combat. Throw in mud,
fog, and barbed-wire fences, and in the red glow of sunrise it became a
howling, bloody ballet of death. The American Marines aimed not only
to kill the Germans but to break what fighting spirit was left in the war-
weary German infantrymen. Culhane thought it would work, but, he
knew, not without taking its toll . . .

*   *   *

Max Brady orders the machine-gun barrage. The Germans fire back. In the first exchange, a sniper bullet rips through the bridge of Brady's nose and takes out his eye. He stuffs a handkerchief in it and keeps firing.

Red dawn. The fog turns pink in the sun's early rays. Danzig hears it first. A hundred and fifty yards away, a horse snorts. At almost the same instant, Redd smells horse flesh. But before either can fire a flare, the German .88-millimeter howitzer barrage begins. Merrill was right. The Germans are shelling the no-man's-land between the two enemies, gambling that the major has moved his forces into the trenches to await an attack. Danzig is caught in the middle of the deadly onslaught from the sky.

"Rusty, get outta there now. Run for it. Come in, come in!" Culhane yells. The beefy Bostonian jumps from the trench and zig-zags toward them, a chunky silhouette in the pink mist. He is yelling, "A hunnert-fifty yards, a hunnert-fifty yards," as the howitzer barrage rains down around him. Ten yards from Culhane's position, a bomb explodes. It is a few feet away from Rusty. He is knocked to his knees, clutching his throat. Blood spurts between his fingers.

Culhane fires a red flare, signaling Merrill to attack, and then jumps out of the foxhole, runs to Danzig, and pulls him to his feet. He shoves Danzig into the foxhole a moment before another .88 goes off.

At their posts, Redd and Lenny peer into the mist. They can hear the horses snorting and the wheels on the caissons squealing. They are getting too close for comfort. To their left, the whole trench area is being bombarded.

And then a miracle. The wind comes.

The mist swirls and blows away.

The road is bound on both sides by four-foot-deep ditches. In the morning's glare, Redd sees the first horses. Four of them, pulling a heavy gun. He aims, finds his mark, and fires. The Sharps kicks into his shoulder, then the lead horse's head flips up, and the animal falls straightaway to the ground. A moment later, Lenny Holtz drops the other horse in the lead team. The remaining pair panic; eyes scared, nostrils flared, they bolt. Redd's next shot takes the driver. He topples forward into the crazed horses. Lenny drops the third horse and the fourth breaks loose and gallops past them. The second horse team goes crazy. A commander, obviously an officer, is screaming at the second driver to get his horses under control. Redd waits a moment until he gets the officer's profile in his sights, aims just in front of his ear, but before he can fire, the side of the German's head erupts. Lenny has beaten him to it.

"Redd, come on, the shelling's stopped!" Lenny yells. "We gotta get out of here!"

But Redd sees something else. Behind the second caisson is a tank. A stubby little box topped by a tin can of a turret, with a cannon swinging back and forth. Below it is a window with a machine gunner, both looking for targets.

Behind him, he can hear Merrill's troopers yowling.

"Go on," Redd yells back. "I'm going to get me a tank."

"You're nuts."

"Sure am." And Redd runs up the gully toward the Germans.

"Well, shit," Lenny snarls, and follows him up the opposite side of the road. Behind him, he can hear Merrill's yowling "hounds" as they wallow through the mud toward the advancing lines. Ahead of him, Lenny sees another German officer ordering several men to shoot the four horses in the second team and push the caissons into the ditch so the tank can get by. Lenny kills him and begins picking off the men who had been ordered to shoot the horses.

Redd doesn't shoot anything. He just keeps running up the gully toward the tank.

With the firing of Culhane's flare, Merrill blows his whistle, a shrill signal that the attack is on. The company, in staggered lines, races toward the enemy as the morning wind sweeps across the battlefield and the fog swirls away. A hundred yards in front of him, the front element of the German line is mowed down as the machine-gun trap opens up on them. The Hell Hounds charge forward through the mud and the battle becomes even more surreal.

A white horse, like a manic ghost, its eyes crazed, its nostrils flared, suddenly materializes from what's left of the fog, gallops into the attacking force, knocking men down and stomping them as it snorts and whinnies with fear.

"What the hell!" Culhane says. He screams "Kill the horse!" as the crazy animal flails among the advancing Marines. A soldier shoots it in the leg and the hobbled animal goes even crazier, whinnying wildly and kicking out its back legs even as it begins to fall. Culhane jumps from his nest, runs toward it. For a moment, his mind sees an image of Cyclone, the beautiful white horse from his youth on the Hill, then quickly flashes back to the frantic horse, and he fires a shot from his .45 into its brain. The horse's head snaps and it collapses. The wave of Marines sweeps on.

Culhane races back toward his machine gun, hears the banshee scream of the howitzer shell, feels the hot concussion smack his back, the shower of mud, a searing pain in his right leg as he is blown into his shallow foxhole. Culhane looks down at his leg. It is shredded by shrapnel.

He thinks he hears somebody, somewhere, screaming, "Corpsman! Corpsman!"

Big Redd sticks close to the wall of the gully. The German artillery line is in havoc. They are too busy shooting horses, shoving them into the gully to clear a path for the tank, and getting shot, to pay attention to him as he creeps up beside the tank. On the other side of the road he can hear Merrill's men charging the trench line.

In the tank, the machine gunner sees Redd as he steps back to grenade the tank. He fires a burst.

In the ditch, Redd ducks as bullets spout along the rim of the gully. He falls against the wall, spins about ten feet down it, jumps up, the Sharps already against his shoulder, and fires one shot. It zings down the machine gunner's barrel and hits him in the forehead.

Redd lobs two grenades under the front of the tank's screeching gears. Both grenades do the job. The tread splits in two and rolls off its runners. Crippled, the tank turns to the right. The turret man swings the cannon toward Redd, but before he can get off his shot the tank goes over the opposite side of the gully and crashes on its side.

*   *   *

Lenny crawls out of the ditch and runs toward the advancing Marine line. The German infantrymen are still bottlenecked at the trenches; hundreds are being slaughtered by both the American gunners and the mines when they jump into the trenches for cover. As Lenny jumps over the last trench, his foot slips in the mud. He scrambles to keep from falling into the deadly pit. He tries frantically to get a handhold but the mud defeats him. He slowly slides over the rim of the trench, flips over, and falls headfirst into it. When he hits the murky floor, he hears the deadly click of a mine as it is triggered. He dives away and rolls over as the bomb explodes. The blast slams him against the trench wall, showers him with shrapnel, and blows off the lower part of his left arm.

Above him, the attacking Marines jump across the trench.

"Hey," he yells, "somebody gimme a hand!" He holds up his good arm and one of the charging Marines falls to the ground, reaches down and pulls him out of the death trap. It is then that Holtz realizes his other arm is gone at the elbow.

"Maybe I shoulda said 'gimme an arm,'" he moans, before passing out.

As Merrill leads his men toward the embattled Germans, he runs past Culhane's foxhole and drops down beside him.

"The trap's working like a charm," he says and then he sees Culhane's leg. "Sweet Jesus!" he cries out.

"Don't let 'em take my leg, Major," Culhane says, his voice so weak Merrill can hardly understand him.

Merrill looks through the charging company of Marines and sees a red cross. "You, Corpsman, get over here!" he orders.

Culhane grabs a handful of Merrill's shirt.

"I got you your ten minutes, Major." His voice gets stronger. "Don't . . . let . . . them . . . take . . . my . . . leg." He begins to shake. Shock is setting in. The corpsman drops beside them and puts a tourniquet on Culhane's upper thigh.

"Promise me, damn it!" Culhane yells above the din of battle.

Merrill grabs a leatherneck by the arm. "Listen to me," Merrill bellows, shouting above the sounds of the Hell Hounds screaming, the peal of bayonets clashing, the thunder of guns. "You stay with your sergeant, get it? You stay with him when you get to the field hospital. You stay with him when they operate, and you tell whoever takes care of Culhane that I said if he takes off that leg, I'll personally take off one of his."

"Yes, sir, Major Merrill."

"Th'nks," Culhane stammers, and Merrill races into battle. He doesn't hear Culhane's last whisper before he passes out: "Good luck."

1920

The winter rainstorm passed quickly and bright hard sunlight urged buds into blossoms in the winter garden Madeline had loved so much. Eli shifted in his wheelchair and stared at the flowers through the large library window. His mind, as sharp as it ever was, raced back through time and he remembered the first time he saw her. San Francisco. She was wearing a pink dress with an enormously wide-brimmed hat and she was framed by ferns in the corner of the Garden Terrace restaurant. Thirty-two years old and she hadn't looked a day over twenty, and when she smiled as they were introduced, he was immediately her captive.

His memory dissolved into another image. A young boy in tatters, with such an arrogant, cocky smile, standing beside Ben the first time Eli ever saw him. He saw that image reflected in the window but he seemed older and taller, no longer a teenager but a man in a uniform. Then he snapped out of his reverie and realized he *was* staring at a reflection.

"Hi, Mr. Eli," the voice behind him said.

He wheeled his chair around and looked up at Brodie Culhane in Marine dress blues, medals—a Purple Heart, Silver Star, French Croix de Guerre—gleaming on his chest, eyes as bright as new coins, the smile as challenging as ever. He had grown into a handsome man, his face a bit lined by age and harsh experience. And he was leaning on an oak cane.

"Well, look at you, Thomas," Eli said affectionately and held out his hand. Brodie clutched it eagerly. Eli's hair, what little he had left, was white and his body looked ravaged, his legs mere twigs, but his face seemed as smooth and ageless as ever.

Brodie leaned over and put his arm around the old man.

"I knew you'd come home," Eli said, embracing him, patting his back. "Sooner or later, I knew you'd come back to us."

Brodie hooked a chair with the crook of his cane, pulled it to him, and sat down as Eli wiped his eyes with a handkerchief, then blew his nose.

"So, how's the leg?"

"Another month and I can throw away the cane."

"Look at you! I wish Maddy were here to see you. Not a day went by she didn't mention you."

"I'm sorry," Brodie said. "I know how much you must miss her. I tried to write you from the hospital but, you know me, I never was much for writing."

"How long were you laid up?"

"Eighteen months. They put my leg back together with glue and tape. I had to learn to walk again, but it's almost good as new."

"Did you stop at the bank and see Ben?"

"Not yet. Mr. Graham was on the train with me. He remembered me. Dropped me off here on his way home."

"They have a taxi now, you know. Very sophisticated. My God, Ben will faint with excitement when he sees you."

"How's his pitching arm?"

"Not what it used to be. He coaches the high school team now."

"Got a high school, huh?"

"It was time for a good school. We have twenty-two families living on the Hill now. There are a few families in Eureka who attend. And the kids from Milltown come over on the bus."

"And Eureka has a sidewalk and paved streets. Never thought I'd live to see that day."

"Well, Riker had to do something. You hardly see a horse and carriage anymore. All automobiles."

"Is Cyclone still alive?" Brodie asked. "Last time I talked to Ben, he said the old boy was still kicking."

"And still as handsome as ever, like his owner."

"I wonder if he'll remember me."

"Animals have an amazing memory. It may take him a while but I'm sure he hasn't forgotten."

"He's twenty-three now. And my godson is almost twenty. I can't believe it."

"Quite a young man. Fair college student but more interested in football and girls."

"Ben says he's not interested in banking."

"He'll be twenty this year," Eli said, waving his hand. "He's got plenty of time to make up his mind. He's down in Los Angeles with Isabel. They'll be back tomorrow. Why didn't you tell us you were coming in today?"

"I like surprises. Isabel as beautiful as ever?"

Eli nodded. "Like Maddy, she gets prettier every day. She has a birthday coming up in a few months. Thirty-seven. I think she'd rather forget it."

"And Buck?"

"Slowed down some but he's fine. Tells everybody he's sixty. Hell, he's got to be at least seventy but nobody knows for sure."

"Is that why I'm back here?"

"You're back here because we miss you. And Ben needs you. We talked about that once, a long time ago."

"I remember the conversation."

"I've worried over that a lot. Was it I who drove you away?"

"Don't think that. It was time for me to leave here, see what the rest of the world looked like."

"Well, you certainly accomplished that."

"Seen London, Paris, New York, Chicago. Been down South."

"Everybody needs a home to come back to, Thomas."

"My room over the stable still available?"

"I'll build you a house."

Brodie laughed. "What would I do with a house?"

"Get married. Have a family."

"We'll talk about that later. I hear Delilah came back to Grand View after the O'Dells were killed."

Eli nodded. "She turned the place into a private club. Well, that's what she calls it. It's a high-dollar bordello. She has a small casino; excellent restaurant; beautiful, educated young women. Movie stars come up from Los Angeles. Businessmen from San Francisco and points east. They come in private train cars, Stutz Bearcats, yachts. She's made her own fortune in addition to the one her father left her."

"I found out about the O'Dells in the *New York Times*. They ran a list of all the victims when the *Lusitania* went down. I was reading down the column and all of a sudden there it was. Shamus and Katherine O'Dell, San Francisco."

"I suppose Shamus had his good side, he just never showed it to me. And Kate was a fine lady. Loved him dearly, although I'll never know why."

"Water under the bridge, Mr. Eli."

"It's hard to forget the past when you live with it every day."

"It's that bad?"

"Prohibition starts in two weeks. Things are going to be tough around here. Social House is a private club so we'll be alright. And they'll never shut down Grand View. I know a couple of senators and at least one governor who've visited the place. The good news is, it may put Riker out of business. I've tried to buy him out since the night O'Dell left. The town is still as rotten as ever. It attracts rowdy crowds from fifty miles around."

"Prohibition won't hurt Riker. If anything, he'll make more money. He'll board over the windows and put up a front door with a peephole, just like they're gonna do in New York and Chicago. Hell, the Feds'll be too busy worrying about the big cities, they won't be snooping around a little place like this."

"That's bad news," Eli said. There was still anger in his tone after all the years.

They talked for several hours, about Eureka, about what Brodie's job would be, about Ben, whose dream for the valley was more elaborate than Eli's. About plans to form a county board, get a new prosecutor, clean up Eureka. No decent middle-class families would live there the way it was.

"You'll be special deputy under Buck," Eli said. "When he retires, you will become sheriff of the whole damn shebang."

Twenty years and nothing had changed. Eli Gorman had a plan and Brodie Culhane was the last piece to fall into place.

The conversation finally wore Eli down, and Brodie and the nurse helped him to bed for his afternoon nap. Brodie strolled across the big backyard, past Maddy's winter garden, and through the trees to the barn. The white horse lounged near the far end of the paddock, chewing on grass. His winter coat was matted and there were snarls in his mane, but he looked as strong as ever.

Brodie whistled to the horse. The white's ears went up and he responded immediately, peering across the length of the paddock with curiosity. Brodie whistled again.

"C'mon, pretty boy," he said softly. "I got something for you."

He had brought two apples from the house.

Cyclone loped down the length of the paddock, approaching Brodie cautiously at first, sniffing the air, grumbling and snorting, his ears standing straight up. He'd come close and back up, come closer and back up.

"Look what I got," Brodie said, and held up one of the apples.

Cyclone moved closer. Brodie held the apple between his hands and twisted it in two. The horse watched, his nose checking the air. Brodie rested half the apple in the palm of his hand and held it toward the horse. Cyclone snorted, bobbing his head up and down. He walked sideways, away from the apple, and leaned his long neck out, checking it. Brodie leaned through the fence and held it.

"C'mon, boy," he said softly. "Pretty boy, come and get it."

Finally he came close enough to roll back his lips and snatch the apple-half with his teeth. He munched it noisily and stepped closer, sniffing for more.

"Do you remember, pretty boy? Is it coming back?" He took the makings from his pocket and awkwardly began to roll a cigarette. A piece of shrapnel had injured his left hand and it was difficult. He finally prepared the paper and then the wind blew the tobacco off. "Damn," he said, and started over. When he finished, the butt looked like a small pretzel but he got it lit and took a deep drag, all the while talking softly to Cyclone. He gave the other apple-half to him, and this time Cyclone came closer, let him pet his muzzle.

Brodie went into the barn, found a brush, and entered the paddock. The horse backed up, his eyes cautious and uncertain. Brodie broke the other apple in half, and this time Cyclone came over and got it. Brodie very slowly began to brush his side. The horse was still skittish, but he stood still as Brodie brushed his sides and then his mane and then finally stood close to him and petted his long nose.

"Wanna go for a ride?" Brodie asked gently. "You'll have to wear a saddle. I got a bum leg, I don't think I can handle you bareback."

Cyclone grumbled but held fast. Brodie returned to the stable and came back with a blanket, bridle, and saddle. Every move was slow and easy. He put the blanket on Cyclone's back first. The horse jumped a bit but Brodie soft-talked him, then eased the saddle over the horse's back, reached under his belly and buckled the straps. So far so good. He put the bit in his mouth and laid the reins over Cyclone's back, and the horse bolted. He trotted a dozen yards away and stopped, his ears twisting, his nose testing. Brodie held the last half of the apple in his palm. The horse slowly returned, this time bumping against him before taking it.

"Let's give it a try, pal," Brodie whispered. He leaned on the cane and got his right foot in the stirrup. The horse grumbled but stood fast. Brodie swung his injured leg carefully over the saddle and sat down.

Cyclone backed up, started to bolt again, and Brodie leaned over his neck. "Easy, pretty boy. It's just you and me." He kept talking, and walked Cyclone around the paddock a few times, then eased him into a trot. They circled the paddock a few times and Brodie steered him to the gate, reached down, and unlatched it. Cyclone walked slowly out of the paddock.

"Okay, son, let's go for a ride."

He rode around the barn, then down the path toward the ocean walk. The sun was slowly sinking toward the horizon, its reflection shimmering on the waves far out toward the entrance of the bay. The path was overgrown and unused, and Brodie walked the horse down it. Through the trees he saw the Hoffman house, and a moment later the greenhouse. He stopped and stared at it through the trees.

Even with memories of the war fresh in his mind, it had been the worst night of his life.

He went on, riding down to the wall around Grand View and then heading along it toward the road. From inside the house he heard music, strident military music, yet with a different kind of beat. He stopped and listened to the faint tune. There was something familiar about it. He rode down to the road and turned in front of the house.

Tall iron gates protected the house from intruders. A small guardhouse was situated on the far side of the gate but it appeared to be unmanned. Rows of tall hedges bracketed the road that led to the white-columned mansion a hundred yards away. Behind it, beyond and below the sheer cliffs, the ocean was serene. A Japanese gardener was meticulously snipping the grass around the gate. He saw Brodie and, smiling, he stood up and saluted.

"Speak English?" Brodie asked.

"Yes, suh, very good."

"Miss Delilah is an old friend. I'm going to ride down to the house and say hello."

"Need to call first," the gardener said, pointing to the guardhouse.

Brodie eased Cyclone through the gate. "It's a surprise," he said. The gardener stood motionless as Brodie trotted down the paved road to the house. The music got louder as he reached the house and tied the horse to a fence post. He got his cane from the saddle pocket and went to the door. He could hear the music more distinctly now and realized it was a recording of "Memphis Blues" he had heard in Paris years ago. He rang the doorbell.

A minute passed, then the door opened and Noah stood there. He was wearing a blue jacket, tan cord pants, and immaculate knee-high leather boots. He stared curiously at Brodie for a long moment.

"What's the matter, Noah, don't you recognize an old friend?"

Curiosity melted into a smile.

"Mistah Brodie?" Hints of the Caribbean still haunted his accent. "Mon, look at you. Ain't you the fancy one."

"You're not looking too bad yourself. May I come in?"

"Yes, suh. I'll tell Miss Delilah you're here. Mon, she is goin' t'be some surprised."

Brodie entered a wide, two-story foyer. A winding staircase faced him on the other side of the large room and led to a balcony on the second floor, with four hallways leading away from it. It was a pleasant room, with handsome stuffed chairs, antique tables, Tiffany lamps, vases of flowers, and two large davenports. In a stained-glass window over the doorway, a knight was challenging a dragon with his lance while a lovely damsel cowered nearby. High above the vaulted room, a crystal chandelier shed a comforting blanket of light down on the room. There were several closed doors leading away from the foyer. Brodie heard the laughter of young women behind one.

"Now aren't you the dashing one," a dusky voice said from above. Delilah stared down from the balcony, decked out in a dark green, floor-length dress and a wide-brimmed hat trimmed with white roses. Her red hair was braided in a ponytail draped over her shoulder.

Brodie smiled up at her.

"Going to the opera?" he asked.

She looked at the cane.

"Can you make it up the stairs?"

"I'm a little lame, I'm not crippled," he answered, and managed the broad stairway with little problem. She led him into her apartment and turned around.

"Does a girl get a kiss after twenty years?"

He started to kiss her on the cheek, but she turned her face to his, leaned hard against him, and kissed him fully on the lips, holding the kiss for half a minute before stepping back.

"I think you're blushing," she said. "Marines aren't supposed to blush."

"I haven't been kissed like that for a long, long time."

"How're you doing, Brodie?"

"The leg's almost healed. The rest of me's whole."

"Thank God for that." She laughed.

"I wasn't sure you were here," he said, and pointed to a Victrola in the corner. The needle was scratching endlessly at the end of the record. "Actually, I was attracted by the music. Is that record by James Reese Europe and the Hell Fighters Band?"

"You've heard them?" she said, lifting the needle off the record.

"I saw them. In Paris. The French loved the band. Called it 'Le Jazz Hot.' Almost made me want to dance and I don't know a step."

"Well, you'll have to come by. I've got all twenty-four of his records. We'll play music and I'll teach you the Charleston."

"I'll take you up on that."

"Have you seen Ben?"

"Not yet. I spent a couple of hours with Eli."

"The stroke almost did him in but he's handling it well."

"How about you? I hear you're the richest lady in California."

She arched her eyebrows. "Just California?"

Brodie laughed and sat down on a settee. "You live here?"

"I run a tight ship here. Have to make sure my high-class clientele is happy. Three rooms are all I need. What are you drinking?"

"A little bourbon and some ice."

"So you haven't seen Ben or your young Eli or Isabel yet?"

He shook his head.

"Or Buck?"

"Nope."

"Stick around. He comes every night at six to have a cup of coffee and look at the young girls."

"How is he?"

"Not as quick as he used to be but tough as ever."

"You know what they say, myths never die," Brodie said.

She chuckled. "Nice to think so. Back to stay?" she asked.

"Why not?" Brodie answered ruefully.

"That's the best news I've heard since Prohibition," she said as she filled a pebbled glass half full with hundred-proof Kentucky bourbon, dropped two ice cubes in it, and poured herself a little Scotch. She raised her glass to him.

"Here's to sin," she said. "Without it, we'd both be up the creek."

They touched glasses.

"So Prohibition doesn't worry you?"

"Honey, it's going to make my business much sweeter and your job a lot livelier."

"I haven't taken a job yet."

"You will, Brodie. That's why you came back. It's what friendship and love are all about. And I haven't used the word 'love' seriously in a very long time."

"Eli says everybody has to have a home to come back to and he's right. Eureka ain't much but it's all I got. I couldn't stay in the Marines. I got a battlefield commission the night I was wounded. A year later they upped me to first lieutenant while I was in the hospital, and they made me a captain just before I was discharged. No future, nice pension."

She sat down on a crimson davenport and leaned back on one elbow.

"Why did you leave, Brodie?"

He shrugged. "To see the world."

"Uh-huh."

"You want to know the truth? I was running away from what I just came back to."

Brodie rode Cyclone back to the stable and gently took off the saddle and bridle. "I'll be back tomorrow," Brodie said softly. "Be like old times."

In the darkness, a cigar tip glowed. "Let's hope so," a voice said, and Ben Gorman stepped into the light.

"Give you a start, brother?" he asked. The two men rushed together, hugging and laughing like children. They walked briskly back
to the house, both chattering away, cutting each other off with one
story after another. Ben didn't talk about the future. He didn't have to.

A cool September afternoon nine months later.

Brodie Culhane parked his Ford under the trees behind the bank
and turned off the ignition. He took out the makings and struggled to
roll a cigarette. He focused on the job, folded the thin paper around his
forefinger and sprinkled tobacco into the groove. Then he started to
twist the paper with the thumb and forefinger of both hands. It was almost perfect and he smiled to himself, licked the glued edge of the paper, and twisted it shut. It wasn't a work of art but it was better than
smoking harsh store-bought cigarettes. As he lit it, he heard the back
door of the Ford open and close.

"I hope that's you, Slim," Brodie said, blowing a smoke ring and
not turning around.

"I get real nervous meetin' before dark," came a jittery voice from
the floor of the backseat.

"Hell, you called me. What's so urgent?"

Slim was a skinny little man who worked the desk at Riker's Double Eagle Hotel. He picked up an extra five a week by keeping his ears
open and passing information to Culhane.

"Sompin's in the wind."

"Like what?"

"Riker brought in four toughs from outta town today. They came in
the hotel about four. All of 'em are heeled, I could tell when they came
to get their keys."

"How do you know they're Riker's people?"

"He made the reservations. Told me not to put 'em in the book and
be quiet about it."

"How'd they arrive?"

"Black Ford coupe."

"What do they look like?"

"You know the type. They never blink. Leader seems to be a guy
named McGurk. Has one of those purple splotches on his face."

"How long they here for?"

"Riker didn't say, but they ordered up a bottle and when I got to the door, I heard Riker mention Buck and Miss O'Dell."

"What'd they say?"

"Ain't sure, Cap'n. I just heard the names and somethin' about a piece of the action."

"Were they talking about Grand View?"

"That's all I know. I can tell you this, Riker's been jumpy as a cat all day. Like I been tellin' you for a while, he wants some of that outta-town high-roller action up there. Then there's all this talk about them on the Hill forming some kinda council and shuttin' him down. And there's those two times his boats got sunk out in the drink."

"I don't know anything about that. You think these guys are shooters?"

"All I know is I seen rods bulgin' under their coats. I know when a bozo's loaded. I'm supposed to tell Schuster when I see it, but I figure since it was Riker set 'em up, he knows if they're carrying or not."

"You off duty?"

"Just got off. I really got bad jitters meetin' like this in broad daylight."

Brodie took a five out of his pocket and draped his arm over the back of the front seat.

"Here's an extra fin. Why don't you go over, play a little poker, and keep an eye out for those four. I'm off tonight. Gonna eat dinner at Wendy's, then maybe go up to Delilah's. Call me if anything looks screwy to you."

"Okay. Thanks." The door opened and shut quietly.

Brodie drove the four blocks to the diner and went in. Wendy was barely in her twenties and had inherited the eatery from her father, who drank too much, ate too much, and a year earlier had dropped dead behind the counter one morning while fixing an order of ham and eggs.

She was a plain girl with ashen hair and a ready smile for her customers. She leaned across the counter as Brodie entered.

"Come to whisk me away to the Garden of Eden?" she said.

"I came for the meat loaf special," Brodie said with a crooked grin. "If it's real good, maybe I'll whisk you away after I eat."

"I'll settle for that."

"Where is everybody? The joint's empty."

"It's early." She reached under the counter and handed him the newspaper.

"Okay if I use the phone a minute?" Brodie asked.

"Anything for you," she said, and put the telephone on the counter. Brodie got the operator and called the sheriff's office. Andy Sloan, the assistant deputy, answered.

"Andy, it's Brodie. Anything going on?"

"It's quiet. I got a guy back in the lockup for beating up his old lady and that's about it."

"Is Bix there?"

Bix was the jailer. He had lost a leg at the Marne and hobbled around on a homemade crutch, a quiet man who made terrible coffee.

"Yeah."

"Take a drive up on the Hill and nose around, then stop off at Delilah's and hang out. I'll stop by after I eat."

"Something up?"

"Maybe. We got four heeled out-of-towners in a black Ford at the Double Eagle. I don't think they're lost."

"I'll keep my eyes open."

"See you at Grand View in an hour or so."

He hung up and took his usual booth in the corner of the place and read the paper. A few customers came in and sat at the counter. Brodie was finishing a piece of pie and washing it down with coffee when Wendy said, "Here comes trouble."

Arnie Riker was a man who strutted when he walked, swinging his arms like a soldier on parade and swaying back and forth. He was crossing the street, followed by his blond bodyguard, Lars Schuster, a muscular ex-prizefighter with the mashed nose and cauliflower ears to prove it.

"Hell, they're comin' in," Wendy groaned. "They never eat here."

"I don't think they're coming in to eat." Culhane picked up the paper and held it in front of him, staring over the top. "Just treat 'em like customers. If there's a problem, let me handle it."

Riker and Schuster entered the diner, sat at the counter across from Culhane. Brodie ignored them, stared at the sports page of the newspaper.

"What can I do you for?" Wendy asked as cheerily as she could.

"I hear you make a great cup a coffee. You make a great cup a coffee, Wendy?"

She went to the urn and drew two cups of coffee and put them in front of Riker and Schuster.

"You tell me," she said, still smiling.

Schuster ignored the cup. Riker took a sip, rolled it around in his mouth, and swallowed it.

"Not bad," he said. "Maybe I'll stop in now and then—when I'm feelin' blue. Coffee perks me up."

"You feeling blue?"

"Yeah. Maybe you heard, I lost a fishing boat the other night. Lucky there was a Coast Guard boat nearby and they pulled my boys out."

"That was lucky," Wendy said. She was getting nervous.

"Or maybe it wasn't luck." He swung the counter seat around and stared at Culhane. "Maybe a boat full of Feds came aboard first and threw all my fish overboard and pulled the plug on the boat, and then the Coast Guard pulled up to make sure nobody got hurt."

Culhane ignored him.

"It's happened to me twice now. Always way out there," he waved toward the ocean. "Never anywhere near shore, and they never make a case against me or any of my people. Don't that seem odd to you?"

Wendy walked away to wait on a customer. Riker continued to stare at Culhane.

"I said, 'Don't that seem odd to you?' " he repeated.

Culhane laid the paper aside.

"Was that crack aimed at me?"

"It was a 'what if' kinda question. Like what if the big shots on the Hill wanted to dry me up without causing a big investigation here."

"I wouldn't know anything about that."

"You're the law around here. You're just waiting for Tallman to drop dead of old age."

Culhane smiled. "Haven't you heard, Riker, Buck's gonna live forever. Maybe you ought to stop *fishing* at night."

"Ain't you the funny one."

"What're you crying to me for? I don't have anything to do with the Feds. And I don't know anybody in the Coast Guard."

"Maybe your pal Bucky has friends in high places. Or Gorman. Or some of those other big shots on the Hill."

"I wouldn't know, Riker."

"I'm not sure I believe you."

"I don't give a rat's ass whether you believe me or not. But if I was you, I wouldn't call me a liar."

The blond muscleman started to get up.

"Where are you going?" Brodie said to him.

"Relax, Lars, we're just talkin' about 'what if' here. Ain't that right, Culhane? For instance, what if I owned a piece of Grand View? Me and Delilah would be partners and maybe all this harassment would go away."

"Maybe it would go away if you had a heart attack. Or 'what if' somebody stuck a .45 up your ass and blew your brains out."

"Hey there," Schuster said and stood up.

From the corner of his eye, Brodie saw a black Ford wheel from behind the Double Eagle Hotel onto the main drag a block away and screech toward the Hill. Four men were in the car.

"What the hell . . ." Brodie said.

The phone rang and Wendy answered it.

"It's for you, Brodie."

He grabbed the phone. "Yeah?"

"It's me. Don't use my name." Slim whispered on the other end of the line. "They just left here."

"Thanks, Andy." He hung up and headed for the door. The blond henchman jabbed a thick finger into Brodie's chest.

"Mr. Riker's still talking to you," he growled. Brodie grabbed the finger, bent it back almost to the wrist, heard it crack. The gunsel bellowed. Brodie twisted the bodyguard's arm up and backward, grabbed the back of his hair, and slammed his face into one of the stools. Blood squirted from both sides of his face. He made a gurgling noise, and Brodie lifted his head and slammed his face onto the stool again.

Riker, eyes bulging, was riveted to the spot. Brodie threw the limp hoodlum on the floor, reached under the gangster's arm, and pulled a .32 from his shoulder holster. He turned and aimed the pistol at Riker.

"I ain't heeled," Riker screamed, holding his hands high.

Brodie jammed the hoodlum's .32 under Riker's chin and frisked him anyway, then grabbed a handful of his shirt.

"Where's that bunch of yours going?" he demanded.

"I don't know what you're . . ." Riker stammered.

Lars groancd, raised himself up. Culhane kicked him in the jaw and he fell on his back.

"If that bastard ever touches me again, I'll kill him on the spot," he whispered in Riker's face, and shoved him into a chair, which flipped backward. Sprawled on the floor, the gang leader trembled with fear as Brodie aimed the .32 at him.

"What if I just put you out of everybody's misery," Culhane said. Then he pointed the gun toward the ceiling and emptied the bullets on the floor. He turned and dashed out the door.

Wisps of fog drifted past the sprawling Grand View mansion, leaving damp streaks on its ghostly white facade and dampening the hedges that led to the front door. The full moon was a hazy aura in the mist.

The black Chevrolet cabriolet pulled up to the tall iron gates, and a hard-looking man got out and walked to the postern, where a security guard stepped out on the other side of the gate.

"Do you have a card, sir," he said in a flat, no-nonsense voice. The hard-looking man took a .38-caliber pistol from under his arm and pointed it straight at the guard's forehead.

"Will this do?" he hissed with a nasty smile.

The guard studied the gun and the face behind it, then walked over to the gate, unlocked it, and pulled one side open. The armed man stepped inside, stuck the gun in the guard's back, led him back to the postern, and shoved him inside the small guardhouse.

"Sorry, pal," he growled, and slashed the guard viciously across the jaw with his gun. The guard grunted and collapsed on the floor. The gunman pulled the telephone lines from the wall, walked back outside, and jumped on the running board of the Chevrolet.

"Okay," he said, and the car inched down the long drive through the fog to the house. The gunman jumped off the running board and three other men piled out of the car behind him. The leader was Charly McGurk, a slick-looking little weasel wearing a gray fedora. There was a purple wine-stain birthmark on his right cheek. He put the gun back under his arm and they went to the giant double doors and he rang the bell. Inside, he could hear chimes gently stirring. A minute later, a burly chocolate-colored man with temples beginning to show a little gray opened the door. Noah's eyes widened as the gunman put a hand on his chest and eased him backward. His cohorts followed him into the mansion.

They entered the wide, two-story foyer. McGurk looked up the winding staircase that faced them, then turned his attention to Andy Sloan, who sat at a table sipping coffee. Sloan jumped to his feet as the four men entered, and his hand fell on the butt of a holstered .38.

"Don't do nothin' stupid," said McGurk. "Sit down."

Culhane decided to take the old horse trail up the cliff to Grand View. It had been widened and there was a wall separating it from the drop to the rocks below. He started up the road, downshifted into low, and hugged the steep rise on his left.

Halfway up he ran into fog and slowed to a crawl, the transmission groaning as the Ford climbed toward the top.

At Grand View, three hooligans stood behind McGurk, their hands resting inside their suit jackets.

"We're here to have a chat with the lady of the house." He turned to Noah. "You—dinge—go get her."

Noah's jaws tightened. He looked at the deputy, who thought a moment before nodding. Noah went up the stairs, knocked on a door at the head of the steps. A moment later it opened and Delilah, handsome in a pale yellow evening gown, stepped out and glared down at the four men. She said something to Noah, who disappeared down one of the halls leading from the balcony.

"Who the hell are you?" she said sternly.

"You must be the O'Dell lady, all that red hair and all," McGurk said with a sneer.

"So what."

"So Mr. Riker wants to have a chat at the hotel. He sent us up to bring you down there."

"What's the matter, does he have a broken leg?"

McGurk rolled his tongue across yellow teeth.

"He said he wants to see you . . ."

She cut him off. "He wants to see me? Tell him he knows where I am and to come alone. Or maybe try a phone call, unless he's forgotten how to talk, too."

"Mr. Riker wants you to come along with us," said McGurk in a harsh voice just above a whisper. "He wants to have a little friendlylike chat *now*."

Buck Tallman stepped out behind her. His pure white hair flowed down over his shoulders. He was wearing a buckskin vest over a plain white shirt, and dark brown flared pants. A .44 Peacemaker was hanging low on his hip and his badge glittered where it was pinned to the holster. His right hand hung loosely next to the six-gun.

"Well, well, if it ain't Buffalo Bill hisself," McGurk said, and chuckled. "You ain't invited, old man."

The tall lawman moved Delilah behind him and came down the stairs, his eyes glittering behind hooded lids. One of the gunmen walked to the middle of the room. The sheriff reached the foot of the staircase, strode resolutely forward, and stopped a foot from him. The other three goons divided up. McGurk near the door, another one next to Andy Sloan. The fourth thug sidled to the lawman's right and lounged near a side door to the foyer. They had the room covered.

"He said . . ." the lead gunman started.

"Shut up," the lawman said in a deep, gravelly voice. Then: "You oughta brush your teeth sometimes, your breath smells like a dead cat's."

As Culhane neared the top of Cliffside Road there was a shot, then another, and then Grand View exploded with gunfire.

For an instant, Brodie's mind flashed back to a foxhole near the Somme, to a white horse racing through the fog, to lying in the hospital, where he had made the decision to come back to San Pietro. He flashed back to the fear he felt getting off the train, knowing he was really back in Eureka.

Now he knew that something terrible was waiting at the top of the Hill.

What he didn't know was that the events of the next few minutes would change his life again, would be beyond his most terrifying nightmare, beyond fear of death or the fear of battle that lay behind him.

Another gunshot cleared his mind. He slammed on the gas and skidded around the curve, into the drive to Grand View. More gunfire. Brodie wheeled up the drive and skidded to a stop. An armed and wounded gunman staggered out the front door, reeled sideways along the row of hedges. Brodie saw the wine-stain birthmark on his cheek, jumped out of the Ford, using the open door as a shield.

"You there, McGurk, drop the gun," Brodie yelled.

McGurk, still lurching along the hedge, turned and fired a shot that hit the windshield of Brodie's car. It exploded, showering the inside of the car with shards of glass.

"I only ask once," Brodie muttered as he laid his arm on the sill of the door window, aimed an Army .45, and fired a single shot. It hit McGurk just above the left eye. His body arched into the air, the gun spun out of his hand, and he fell into the hedge with his arms spread out like he was singing an aria at the opera. He stayed there.

Brodie ran toward the door of the mansion. He didn't bother to check McGurk, he knew he was dead. When he reached the door, he flattened himself against the wall, then whirled around the corner and dove into the house.

A moment later, a shot rang out. Then another. And another. Quick shots. Bang, bang . . . bang.

A second or two later, a woman's scream split the dense night air like an axe splitting a log. And she kept screaming.

Although he didn't know it then, Thomas Brodie Culhane would hear those screams for the rest of his life.

Book Two

BANNON

1941

CHAPTER 1

It was just another day in Los Angeles.

A black Rolls-Royce hearse, glass sides draped with silk and lace, carrying a fifty-two-year old movie star, has a flat and holds up traffic on Sunset Boulevard for forty-five minutes. As a crowd gathers, his wife rolls down the window of her limo and yells, "He got a heart attack screwing some seventeen-year-old slut," over and over again.

Out in Los Feliz, a four-year-old girl has gone missing for most of the day before she is discovered next door, floating facedown in the backyard pool.

A twenty-two-year-old unemployed Mexican named Suarez Bailuz kills and robs the forty-two-year-old clerk of a greengrocery on Racine and then, for no apparent reason at all, shoots her dog, a toothless little pup, fourteen years old and blind in one eye. Then he steals her '36 Ford, runs out of gas in Coldwater Canyon, and shoots himself. His nineteen-year-old wife, who does not have a radio, reports him missing when he doesn't come home for dinner.

On the west side, a forty-one-year-old ex-Marine, who had lost a leg in the trenches in 1918, spends most of the day drinking in a bar, staggers out the door, loses his balance, and falls in front of the right front wheel of the Ventura bus. A woman standing nearby faints and somebody steals her purse.

Out in Westwood, the manager of a movie theater smacks his wife for spilling his dinner and she returns the favor by stabbing him in the back of the neck with an eight-inch boning knife. He runs out of the house and drops dead on the front lawn, in front of some kids playing stickball in the street. While they stand around laughing and pointing at the knife that is still sticking in his neck, the investigating officers

99

go in the house and find the new widow sitting at the kitchen table, smoking an Old Gold and reading *Look* magazine. She offers them a beer.

On La Cienega, a forty-six-year-old bartender shaking a martini drops dead of a heart attack.

And in the press room at homicide central, the police reporter of an L.A. gossip sheet is griping because he has nothing to write about.

"Just another day at homicide central," the desk sergeant, named Conlin, says as he closes out the log at the end of his shift and scribbles the time and date—7:00 P.M., May 26, 1941—at the bottom of the page.

My partner, Ski Agassi, and I were running late getting back to the station house when the call came in. A woman had drowned in the bathtub in a pleasant subdivision called Pacific Meadows.

"Ah hell, let's take it," I said, "we're only two minutes away." I U-turned and headed west on Santa Monica.

"Let the new shift catch it, Zeke," he growled. "We don't get overtime for these jaunts, y'know."

"It'll take a half hour," I said, snatching up the radio mike and calling the desk, while Agassi shook his head. Regulations ruled that any unobserved or accidental death should be considered a homicide until the coroner said otherwise. It was a courtesy for two homicide detectives to take the call.

"I'm starving, Zeke," groaned Agassi, who at forty-two weighed in the neighborhood of two hundred sixty pounds. The boys at Division called us Laurel and Hardy—but not when we were in earshot.

"You're always starving," I said. I was three inches shorter and a hundred pounds lighter.

Pacific Meadows was a deceiving name. A low slope shielded the tiny community from the ocean so there was no view of the Pacific. And the neighborhood was built on the shoulder of the slope as it rose to form one of the many canyons that separate L.A. from the Valley, so it could hardly be called a meadow. But it lived up to the serene promise of its name. It was a pleasant oasis neighbored by a sprawling rundown section of L.A. that had not yet recovered from the Depression.

The houses of Pacific Meadows, mostly one-story stucco or brick bungalows, were built close together and, although inexpensive, always seemed freshly painted. The lawns were well kept, the streets clean of debris. The neighborhood was a mix of once-affluent families—who had lost everything in the Crash, survived hard times, and had begun to rebuild their lives on the low end of the scale—with civil servants, who had weathered the catastrophe with low-paying but regular jobs. Bus drivers, court clerks, secretaries, office workers, schoolteachers. Salt-of-the-earth types. Pride and perseverance was reflected in the pleasant, well-kept environs, the sounds of kids at play, an occasional dog barking, the clatter of lawn mowers. It was the kind of community where people kept their door keys under the welcome mat.

We passed a house I recognized. I had been here once, about five years earlier, just after I was promoted to the homicide division. A man, whose name I couldn't put my finger on, had taken a leisurely bath, donned his best Sunday blue serge suit, stuffed towels under the cracks of his garage door, and then cranked up his used Studebaker and waited for carbon monoxide to end his misery.

He had been the vice president of a textile company in New Jersey, with two kids in private school and a small estate on the affluent side of the tracks, when the Crash wiped him out in '29. For six years, he and his family moved from place to place, riding the rails, flopping in Hoovervilles, living off soup kitchens and handouts, struggling to keep the family together. His two children had grown into teenagers with little hope of overcoming the social stigma sudden poverty often carries with it. When they reached the coast and California became the Pacific Ocean, he lucked out and found a job as a stock clerk in a hardware store just off Melrose. Over the next two years, he worked his way up to assistant manager, making enough money to rent a house in the Meadows and buy a used car. Then he was passed over for the manager's position.

It was his final humiliation; hope had betrayed him once too often.

I remembered his wife and kids staring mute and dry-eyed as a couple of cops carried the sheeted stretcher out of the garage, their dreams of a new life wiped out by the turn of an ignition key.

Agassi also was familiar with the place. He had once considered a house in Pacific Meadows before finding one more to his liking on Ogden Avenue in Hollywood. Agassi had the kind of pleasant face that big men often affect to offset their intimidating size, but now he wore a frown, a reaction to what he called my "eager-beaver attitude."

"He doesn't have a wife waiting dinner on him," Agassi grumbled at the windshield, mostly under his breath.

"What did you say?" I asked.

"Grab a left here," Agassi replied.

The house was three blocks from the corner, a pleasant redbrick, one-story with a front porch and a white picket fence surrounding the front yard, split by the walkway to the front door. The left half of the yard was neatly mown and smelled of fresh grass. The other side hadn't been touched. A spotless green '39 DeSoto sat in the driveway.

People were standing in front yards, staring with morbid curiosity at the house and chatting in whispered tones. A cop was interrogating a man and woman in the yard of the house next door and taking notes. His partner was standing by the front gate with his hands clasped behind him, like a sentinel on the bank of the River Styx. He came out to meet us as we parked behind the patrol car. He was Officer Ward King, he told us, and his partner was Howell Garrett.

"What've we got?" I asked after the introductions. King ran the essentials as we headed toward the front door:

"Verna Wilensky. Mid to late forties. Lived alone—her husband was killed in a 126 four years ago. Lived here about sixteen years, owns the house. The woman next door found her. Garrett's talking to her and her husband now."

"Good enough," I said. "Keep them on tap, we'll want to talk to them, too. Any idea how long she's been dead?"

"No, sir, but judging from conditions in there, my guess is since last night." Agassi checked his watch. It was 7:18. He sighed with resignation.

The sickening, sweet smell of death tickled my nose as we entered the house. King took a small jar of Mentholatum from his pocket and handed it to me.

"You may need this," he said. I dipped a dab from the jar with my index finger and spread it under my nose.

Ski did the same, saying, "Jesus, I hate this."

"I know you do," I said gently. After three years together, there wasn't a lot we didn't know about each other.

The house was neat as a Marine barracks, nicely appointed with expensive furniture. There were framed prints by the Masters on the walls. A leather sofa, with two easy chairs facing it, dominated the center of the room. A large étagère that looked like an antique commanded one wall and the floor was covered with a Turkish rug. In one corner was a large, cathedral-style, ebony Magnavox with a Stendhal turntable attached to it. I didn't know much about furniture but I knew record players. The Stendhal was the best turntable made, with a price tag that would scare John Rockefeller.

Two windows were open, their chintz curtains fluttering in the breeze.

"I opened the windows to air the place out," King explained. "It's back this way." He clicked on his flashlight and led the two of us through a bedroom with a large canopied bed to the bathroom.

I suddenly said, "Chester Weatherspoon."

"Huh?" Agassi said.

"I just remembered the name of a guy who killed himself out here a few years ago," I said.

"Terrific," Agassi said, and rolled his eyes at King.

"You'll need this, Sergeant," King said, and handed me the torch. "The fuse is blown but I didn't want to touch anything until you got here."

"Good procedure," I said. "How about Bones?"

"On his way."

It was a large bathroom, about eight by eight. King's torch picked out the details of the room. Facing us: a large old-fashioned tub with legs that looked like the paws of a gryphon, a window behind it with a dark shade pulled down. To our right: the sink, imbedded in a large counter covered with jars of creams, expensive brands, not the kind you find in Woolworth's, a sterling silver comb and brush, a bottle of Chanel No. 5, a pair of clip-on earrings, a tube of toothpaste, a small hand-painted jar filled with bobby pins. Above the sink: the medicine cabinet, with a shelf between sink and chest. The side of the shelf near the tub was wrenched away from the wall and slanted toward the floor. To the left: the toilet, with a bathrobe carefully folded on it and a pair of slippers beside it, a door that I assumed led to a closet, and a full-length mirror. A small stool squatted beside the tub. On the stool: a candlestick holder almost obscured under the melted remains of a taper, a drinking glass with a half inch of clear fluid in the bottom, a pack of Chesterfields, a leather-and-chrome Ronson cigarette lighter, an ashtray. A couple of movie magazines lay on the floor beside the stool.

The stench was much stronger than in the foyer. Ski took out his handkerchief and held it over his nose.

"Why don't you go in the living room, check out the desk," I said. "Get a line on survivors. We're going to have to notify somebody about this."

"Thanks," Agassi said, and hurriedly left the room.

Then to business.

Verna Wilensky looked to be about five-three or five-four and heavy for her size, one-fifty, maybe one-sixty pounds. Her dark hair was cut in a pageboy. Her eyes were open and her face was beginning to bloat. She was lying on her left side, her right arm bent at the elbow and trapped under her body, her left arm floating half submerged like a water-soaked tree branch. Both hands were tight-fisted. Her knees were doubled up as if she were sitting sideways in the tub. Her face was underwater. The radio lay against her left shoulder. There appeared to be scorch marks on her shoulder and a dark bruise on her right temple just above her ear.

"I hate it when they die alone," King said.

"Everybody dies alone," I answered. "Get used to it."

We heard the siren of the meat wagon as we walked back outside, and a moment later it pulled into the driveway behind the DeSoto. The coroner, Jerry Wietz, fondly known as Bones, got out and stepped over the small fence as he walked across the lawn to the porch. He was about six feet tall and skinny as a scarecrow, with short-cropped white hair and jet-black eyebrows over brown eyes.

"Hi, Zeke," he said, offering me a stick of Juicy Fruit gum. "What've we got?"

"Widow named Verna Wilensky. Mid forties. Dead in the bathtub. Her radio's in the tub with her. Next-door neighbor tagged her about half an hour ago."

I didn't offer any more information or make any suppositions. I knew Bones liked to work from scratch.

"Well, let's take a peek," the coroner said. I led him and his photographer to the scene, offering him King's torch.

"The radio's still plugged in," he said.

Bones turned to King and said, "The fuse box is probably in the kitchen, son. If you don't find a spare thereabouts, use a penny. Got a penny?"

"Yes, sir."

King left. Bones unplugged the radio and draped the cord over a corner of the sink counter. He turned his chin up an inch or two and sniffed the air, then aimed the light into the tub, slowly swept the length of the body with the light, reached in, and touched her throat.

"Happened last night," he said.

A minute later, the lights came on. He gave me the flashlight, walked slowly around the entire inner periphery of the room, his eyes checking everything, and said to his cameraman: "Wide-shot from the door, close-up of the shelf where it's pulled out from the wall there, full on the tub, two snaps of the body from feet and head, a full of her, and a tight on her head and shoulder. Also a close-up of the stool."

He picked up the glass with his index and middle fingers, took a whiff.

"Gin drinker," he said, and put it back.

"I'm gonna have a chat with the neighbor while you're doing your work," I said.

I gave King his flashlight and went next door.

Garrett, a beefy cop who talked in a half-whisper, filled me in on the details. According to the neighbors, Loretta and Jimmy Clark, Verna Wilensky was their best friend. She had come home, as usual, at 5:30 P.M. the night before. They had chatted for a minute or two, then Wilensky had decided to mow the lawn. When darkness crept up on her, she went inside. The DeSoto was in the driveway when Clark and her husband left for work that morning, which was normal. When they got home and the car was still in the same place and the yard still half-mown, Mrs. Clark had gone over to check on her. The front door was unlocked, as were most front doors in the neighborhood, and her nose led her the rest of the way.

"Good enough," I said. "I'll take it from here."

Loretta Clark was a wisp of a woman, her hair cut in a bob. Her blue eyes were red from crying and she clutched a lace handkerchief in her hand like she was afraid it would fly away. Jimmy Clark was a slab of a man, with stooped shoulders, very little hair, a bulge for a stomach, and eyes fading with age. She did most of the talking.

"How long has Mrs. Wilensky lived here?" I asked, after expressing my condolences.

"We moved here in '27," she said.

"It was the day Lindy flew the Atlantic," Jimmy interrupted. "She invited us over to listen on her radio. That's how we met."

"She had been here about three years at the time," Loretta continued. "I guess 1924, maybe."

"How about family? Kids, parents?"

She shook her head. "They were both only children, parents were dead. They never had kids."

"They?"

"Verna and Frank, her husband. He was killed by a hit-and-run four years ago. A truck went through a red light and ran him over."

"He was on his motorcycle," Jimmy added.

"I don't know what we'll do without her. Losing Frank was bad enough but . . ."

She let the rest of the sentence dwindle out and started sobbing.

"Would you like a drink of water or something?" I asked.

She turned to Jimmy and said, "Get me a highball, would you, Jimmy?" And then turned quickly to me. "Will that be alright?" she asked, as if taking a drink of liquor violated some unwritten rule of the dead.

"I'm sure Verna won't be offended," I answered, and Jimmy left on his chore.

"She was the most generous person I ever knew," Loretta Clark went on. "We went to the movies once or twice a week and she always bought the tickets. And she had wonderful taste, nothing but the best for Verna. She called me 'Sis,' that's how close we were."

"Where was she before she moved here?"

"Texas. But she never talked about it. She was shy in so many ways. Hated to have her picture taken. It even embarrassed her for us to say thanks, that's just how she was."

"How'd they meet?" I asked.

"He owned an auto repair shop. Something broke in her car and she took it there to get fixed. He brought her home on his motorcycle. We were astounded. She wasn't the adventurous type at all. After he left, she was absolutely giddy. They clicked right from the start. Six months later they were married and they were perfect together. She was gaga over him and he absolutely adored her. It took her three years to get over the accident."

Jimmy returned with a highball the color of battery acid and she knocked down half of it without taking a breath.

"What was her maiden name?" I asked.

"Hicks," Jimmy offered. "Verna Hicks."

They talked a little longer but I learned nothing new, excused myself, and headed back to the Wilensky bathroom.

Bones had finished his work and he began a ritual I had watched dozens of times over the years. He lit a Lucky Strike and paced slowly back and forth in front of the tub while he verbalized his initial reaction:

"Last night the widow Wilensky starts to mow the lawn, runs out of light, decides to finish in the morning. Comes in, mixes herself a gin and tonic, fills the tub, lights a candle, turns on the radio, and settles in for a smoke and a drink with her favorite movie magazines. At this point, her life is suddenly being measured in seconds. When the water gets tepid, she starts out of the tub. Her foot slips. She reaches out to keep from falling, grabs the shelf with the radio on it. The shelf pulls loose, she falls back in the tub. The radio is right behind her. In an instant, it turns from an instrument of pleasure to a deadly weapon. It hits the side of her head and falls into the water. There's a loud pop, about as loud as a .22 going off, maybe a spark or two, but the widow Wilensky doesn't hear it. If she had put a toe in the tub, it would have given her a nasty shock, like sticking your finger in a lamp socket. If she'd put her foot in, it would have knocked her across the room, maybe killed her if she had a bad heart. But fully immersed? A hundred and twenty volts hits every pore in her body, every orifice. Everything stops at once—heart, lungs, liver, brain, the works. She's dead instantly." He snapped his fingers. "Just like that, she's the late widow Wilensky."

"Very poetic," I said with a smile.

Bones stopped pacing and took one last look at the cadaver. "Of course, that's off the cuff, but I think an autopsy and the pictures will bear me out."

"Usually do," I said.

"Thanks, m'boy," the coroner said with a fleeting grin. "Okay, let's get the cleanup squad in here and take what's left of the lady downtown. I'm pretty backed up. Maybe day after tomorrow before I finish the post."

"Fine. I'll sit on my report until then." I shrugged. "What's the hurry, right?"

Bones nodded. "Wherever she was going," he said, "she's there now."

Bones left and the cleanup boys moved in. King and I walked out on the porch, and I rolled a cigarette and lit it with my Zippo.

"How about the dog?" King asked.

"Dog?" I said. "What dog?"

"There's a dog in the backyard. Should I call the pound?"

"The pound?"

"That's the routine when there's an animal involved and nobody to take care of it."

"That's okay, I'll take a look. You and Garrett can go along, we'll finish up here."

"It was a real honor working with you, Sergeant Bannon," King said. "I read all about you dropping those four bozos on that western set over at Columbia last year."

I smiled. "Don't believe everything you read in the papers," I said.

"I read the reports."

I laughed and said, "Don't you have anything better to do with your time?"

"I got two more years before I can take the exam for third-grade detective," King said. "I'm studying."

"Well, I got lucky that time," I said. "Thanks, King. You did a nice job here."

"Maybe I could put you down as a reference when I make the application?" He said it as a question, as if he were talking to some-one else.

"Sure. Ward King. I can remember that," I said.

"Thank you, sir," the cop said, and flipped his forefinger off the bill of his cap. He had a ramrod kind of walk. A stiff ass, I thought, but he did good work.

Agassi was avidly reading through the papers from a hefty strong-box he had found in the large bottom drawer of the desk. There were stacks of bound checks and several papers lying on the desk. Ski Agassi loved research, loved going through papers and files and piec-ing together the everyday lives of victims. I loved visual details.

"Boy, this lady was really organized," Agassi said. "Got bank records dating back to 1924. No will so far. No letters, nothing to connect her to anyone."

"Keep digging," I told him. I went into the kitchen and dropped the cigarette butt down the drain, then flipped the light switch by the door. The backyard lit up like Christmas.

I opened the door and stared down at a hulking mix of German shepherd, Irish setter, and God knew what else. Red with streaks of black in thick fur. Gold-flecked, inquisitive eyes. Paws the size of salad plates. His tail whisked the back porch.

Sitting down, he came up to my chest.

He growled at me, and I stared back at him but stood very still.

"It's alright, he's friendly," Loretta's voice said from next door.

"He's growling at me."

"He wants a bone," she said. "When he wags his tail and growls that way, he wants a bone."

I looked down at him, then cautiously reached out and scratched the top of the dog's head. "Sorry, pal," I said, "I'm fresh out of bones."

"Try the icebox. Verna gets them from the butcher. Dog food's in the pantry."

I left the door open and checked the refrigerator, found three shank bones wrapped in red butcher paper, and took one back to the dog, who clamped teeth the size of railroad spikes on it, turned and started out to the yard, then stopped. He looked back over his shoulder at me, then he went down the steps, loped out into the yard, found a suitable dinner spot, circled it a couple of times, lay down, and chomped on his treasure.

"What's his name?" I asked.

"Rosebud."

"*Rosebud!*" I gasped. "He's a male, for God's sake! That's an awful name for a big mutt like that."

"I know. She named him after a character in a movie she saw. She just loved the movies."

"It wasn't a character, it was a sled."

"You mean like a kid's snow sled?"

"Yeah, a snow sled."

"She never told me that. Just like Verna. She had a screwy sense of humor." She paused for a moment and said, "What's going to happen to him now?"

"Couldn't you take him?" I suggested.

"We have two cats. He hates them and they hate him."

"Then I guess he'll go to the pound."

"They'll put him to sleep!" she said with alarm.

"Maybe somebody will adopt him."

"That's where she got him," Mrs. Clark said. I could hear a new sob coming. "They were about to put him to sleep and she just couldn't bear the thought. Actually, she went to get a smaller dog."

"He must weigh seventy, eighty pounds," I said, watching the big dog tearing up the bone.

"He's such a sweetheart. She lets him in at night. He's trained."

"Swell," I said.

"How terribly sad," she said. "First he loses Verna, now they're going to give him the gas. He deserves better."

I closed the door and went back to the living room.

"I hate a day like this," I said. "It's depressing. The great American love story." I sat on the arm of one of the sofas and started rolling another cigarette. "Two lonely people meet, fall in love, work hard, weather the Depression, buy a little love nest in a nice neighborhood. What happens? He gets ironed out by a hit-and-run and she fries herself in the tub. Simple but sad."

"Maybe not quite," Ski said, still rifling through the papers in the strongbox.

"Maybe not quite what?" I asked.

"Maybe not quite so simple," the big man answered.

CHAPTER 2

He had taken off his jacket, his tie was pulled down, and he had pulled his suspenders off his shoulders. He had been sweating and his handkerchief was stuffed in the back of his shirt collar. The lid of one of those large fireproof steel boxes was open, and there were stacks of documents, wrapped with rubber bands, spread out in piles on the desktop.

"What do you mean?" I asked.

"I thought I might find something to lead us back to where she came from," he said without looking up. "Maybe find some relatives or something."

"And?"

"This, which I think you'll find most interesting."

He dropped a large bundle of what looked like letters in a separate pile. They were bankbooks. Lots of bankbooks.

"Check this out," he said. He opened one of them and leafed through the pages, stopping now and then to make a comment.

"I figure her salary was forty bucks a week, that figure appears every Friday so I assume she got paid weekly. Nothing else stands out . . . except the papers on the house—paid in full at the time, in March of 1924, four thou. There are four car registrations, all paid in full at the time of purchase, the last was the DeSoto, bought in September 1939—looks like she got a new car every three years or so. Always cash. There are the usual bills for water, electricity, taxes. But lookee here. On the third of every month, like clockwork, five hundred smackers automatically go into her savings account. She paid the house loan, the cars, the furniture out of it, and very little else. Five C's a month, Zeke, the deposit slips are here but no mention of where the money came from. I went back ten years so far. Every month, like clockwork, on the third. And here's the kicker—her savings book."

He laid it down in front of me. Verna Hicks had $98,400 in her savings account.

"Jesus," I said.

"Yeah. All these financial records were in this box. It wasn't even locked. Her house and car papers, everything; even her husband's birth and death certificates and life insurance policy. Paid her five grand. And a bill of sale for Wilensky's business. She sold it two years ago. Seven thou and nickels. But not a mention of the five hundred. It isn't some kind of investment, the backup papers would be here. What do you think of that?"

"Maybe she had a married friend."

He was digging through other bankbooks and flipping through them. He whistled through his teeth.

"These books go back, let's see, here's one from twenty-six, twenty-five . . . and that five hundred keeps popping up. Damn, Zee, her savings book shows she had these deposits going back to 1924. She opened it with four grand cash. She's been banking that five a month for, what, seventeen years! Right through the Depression and all."

He took out the car papers and checked them out.

"She paid twelve hundred cash for the DeSoto."

He looked at me. "Hell, she could've been living uptown with that kind of dough."

"Well, she must've been saving it for something."

Agassi shrugged. "What?" He dug around in the box and came up with a small green envelope and dumped a small key into his palm.

"Safe deposit key," I said. "Maybe there's something there. What's the bank?"

"West Los Angeles National. There's two things missing," he said.

"What?"

"No birth certificate. And no will."

"Ninety-eight G's and no will?"

"Yeah, and she was totally organized. I mean, every scrap of paper she ever got's in here. But no will or B.C."

"How about her purse?"

"I emptied it. The usual woman things, her wallet, and car keys.

The wallet has eighteen bucks in it. According to her license, she was born April 14, 1894. She just turned forty-seven. That's it."

I took out the makings, rolled one, fired it up, and took a long pull, then said, "You know who gets all this and the savings account if there's no beneficiary?"

"The state."

"Yeah."

"That don't seem right somehow."

"Yeah, whoever said life's fair?"

He handed me a newspaper clipping from the *Times*. A two-column shot buried on the business page, it showed a group of women and one guy standing in a cluster around a small, plump brunette who was smiling sheepishly. The short story that accompanied it told us that Mrs. Verna Wilensky had celebrated her sixteenth anniversary with the Los Angeles tax assessor's office. It was dated seven weeks ago.

"This everything?"

Agassi nodded. "Not another personal thing in the whole damn house. I went through the closets and drawers while you were next door. Nada."

"A paid-for house and car, ninety-plus grand in the bank, and no will."

I smoked for a few moments in silence, leaning back and blowing the smoke toward the ceiling. I stared down at the collection of checks and deposit slips, picked up the clipping. Then it hit me. I walked into the bedroom and then back into the living room.

"Do you notice anything peculiar?" I asked Ski.

"Other than the small fortune in the bank?"

"Pictures," I said. "There aren't any pictures of *any*body, except that clipping from the paper. No pictures of her, her husband, no family shots. Nothing."

Ski stared at me blankly.

"Even the picture of her in the paper is kind of goofy. She isn't looking at the camera. She's staring down at the floor."

I went back to the bathroom, stared at the broken shelf near the tub, pictured the corpse in my mind.

A very shy lady. A lady without a history for almost twenty years. No family pictures, not even a picture of her late husband. Not a wedding pic-ture, or vacation shot with the Grand Canyon in the background.

So who was she saving the money for?

I got a queasy feeling in the pit of my stomach.

"How about the Clarks?" I said.

"The who?"

"People next door."

"What about them?"

"You'd think if she didn't have any family she would've left some-thing to her best friends."

He thought about that for a minute and nodded.

"Or at least left it to her dog," I said.

"There's a dog?"

"Out back, gnawing on a bone."

"What happens to it?"

"The pound."

"Well, that's pretty shitty."

"Want a dog?"

"I got three kids, a goldfish, two canaries, and a dachshund who hates strangers. How about you?"

"I live alone, no pets allowed."

"Too bad, so the dog goes to the pound. What do we do now?"

"Look, we don't know a damn thing about this woman before she moved here in 1924," I said. "The Clarks say she came from Texas somewhere. Her license says she's forty-seven. She didn't just hatch seventeen years ago. Where the hell was she for the first thirty years of her life?"

"Well there ain't anything in this house that'll tell us the answer to that question."

"I want the house sealed. Nobody else in or out."

"Aw, c'mon, Zeke."

"Tomorrow I take the bank, find out where the checks came from, and get into her safe deposit box; maybe there's a will in there. You take the job, see if somebody down there knows anything about her that might fill in her background. Maybe we can find a survivor. Then check Motor Vehicles, see if they have any further background on her."

Ski shook his head and rolled his eyes.

"What're you building, Zee?"

"Precaution."

"Precaution," he said dejectedly. "Precaution of what?"

"Just precaution. That's our job, Ski. Got to be cautious."

He growled under his breath and got up.

"I'll post a man at the door."

"Until after the autopsy."

"Right."

"This lady didn't want anyone to know her before she was thirty—or apparently since. Let's find out why. I'll take everything we've got, go over the records when I get home, put together everything we know about her."

"How about the people next door? Maybe we should take another crack at them."

"They're not going anywhere. Let's see what we come up with. Maybe it'll jog their memories. I'll lock the place down. Take the box out to the car. I know how the smell gets to you."

"You're a jewel, Zee."

"Fourteen carat."

"Then can we stop and get something to eat? I'm starving."

"You're always starving, Ski."

"I eat for three."

I closed and locked the windows, then went to the back door and looked outside. When I opened it, Rosebud stared at me. A nub of the bone lay at his feet.

"He's probably hungry," Mrs. Clark said. She was on her back porch with another drink. Jimmy sat beside her on the porch swing, sucking on a beer. "His bowl's under the stairs. She leaves it there during the day in case he wants a snack."

"What are you, his guardian angel?"

"Somebody has to care."

"You're doing more than your share," I said. "This dog eats better than I do. By the way, do you have any photos of Verna?"

"She was funny about that. Hated to have her picture taken."

I got the bowl, went into the kitchen, opened a can of Ken-L-Ration, and gave it to him. It vanished. He sat down and licked his chops. Then he looked over at the door. On a hook beside it was his leash.

"Ah hell." I sighed.

I leashed him up, got the rest of the bones from the refrigerator, stuck a couple of cans of dog food in my pockets, got the front door key from under the mat, locked the front door, and we went out to the car. I opened the door and the dog jumped in the backseat without being invited.

I got behind the wheel and laid the bones on the seat beside me. Agassi didn't say anything until we were a block or two away.

"What's that?" he asked, nodding toward the butcher-paper bundle.

"Dog bones."

"I'm not that hungry."

"I thought you'd eat anything, Agassi."

" 'I save the bones for Henry Jones 'cause Henry don't eat no meat,' " he sang the line. It was an old blues song.

"I know, he's an egg man," I said, finishing the line.

We drove another block. Agassi looked at the dog.

"I thought he was headed for the pound."

"I'll take him tomorrow."

"Uh-huh."

Another block.

"What's the hound's name?"

". . . Slugger," I said.

CHAPTER 3

I lived on Barker Avenue, a quiet road off Sunset near La Mirado. They hadn't paved the road in front of the house since the CCC came through in 1936, but I had learned to maneuver the potholes and ease over the six-inch ridge between the road and my driveway without breaking an axle. The driveway ended at the house. No garage. There was a weather-worn tin mailbox on an erect four-by-four beside a cement walk up to the front door, a couple of dusty oleanders under the windows, and a cyprus tree near the street. The front lawn was fairly respectable and was freshly mown. The kid three doors down made thirty cents every ten days cutting it for me.

All in all, a respectable family neighborhood without the desperate sense of community pride of Pacific Meadows. Nobody was trying to impress anybody. People minded their own business, and if you were a little on the eccentric side, and wanted to fill your yard with plastic purple doofus birds or cement over the grass and paint it chartreuse, nobody would give a damn.

I decided Rosebud needed a name change, so I was going to reprogram him simply by calling him Slugger from now on. When I was a kid, my first dog was a little white mutt with a black circle over one eye, kind of like the dog in the *Our Gang* comedies. I called him Skippy. My mother was always finding fault with him. "It's sinful the way that dog goes around wetting on the trees," or "It's sinful the noise he makes when he drinks." Everything Skippy did was sinful and ultimately he started answering to "Sinful" and ignoring "Skippy." He lived until he was about thirteen and he was "Sinful" for most of his life.

I pulled up in the driveway, parked, got out, and went around to the other door and opened it.

"Okay, Slugger," I said, "welcome home."

He stared at me with his big tongue hanging out.

I stepped back, clapped my hands, and said, "Come on, Slugger, let's go."

Nothing.

"You Slugger, me Zeke," I said. "Let's go."

He just looked at me.

"Damn it, Rosebud, I . . ."

He was out in a flash, walked straight to the mailbox and peed, then to the cyprus tree, then to a couple of the shrubs. Then he lay down in the middle of the lawn, rolled over, and began twisting to scratch his back. Then he got up, shook off with a great flapping of his big ears, walked to the front door, and sat down.

Reprogramming was going to take a while.

The house was a white bungalow with green trim that was built the year Calvin Coolidge was elected president. A nice living room, a kitchen with an alcove that protruded from the house and looked like it was an afterthought. It had a nice space under it where Slugger could get out of the sun or rain. The dining room could accommodate a table and about four people comfortably. Since I never had company anyway, I had turned it into an office, with a child's blackboard and several different-colored chalk sticks, and two erasers so I could slap them together to clean them. The bedroom was large enough to fit a double bed, a dresser, two bedside lamps, and an easy chair and lamp for reading. The bathroom had a good-size tub and a stall shower.

My record player was the most expensive thing in the house. It was in the corner of the living room and had record shelves made of orange crates on both sides of it.

Beside it was a battered bookshelf my father had left to me, filled with his eclectic collection of books: *Leaves of Grass*; James Joyce's *Ulysses* and *The Dubliners*; *Winesburg, Ohio*; *Moby Dick*; *The Collected Poems of Edna St. Vincent Millay*; Byron's *Don Juan*; *Poetry and Prose of William Blake*; *A Tale of Two Cities* and *David Copperfield*; *A Farewell to Arms* and *The Sun Also Rises*; *War and Peace*; *The Red Badge of Courage*; Conrad's *Lord Jim* and *Heart of Darkness*; two Dashiell Hammett novels, *The Glass Key* and *Red Harvest*; a collection of Shakespeare's works, Roget's Thesaurus and a Webster's dictionary, and his favorite, *The Great Gatsby*.

When I was a kid, he read aloud to me from all these books, although I didn't understand most of the words at the time. In his fading years, when the gas he had inhaled on the Western Front had taken its toll and breathing came hard to him, I took up the chore and read to him. It was an evening ritual. He sat in his rocking chair and I would read for an hour or two until he finally fell asleep. He slept sitting up; breathing was particularly difficult when he lay down. Sometimes I would simply open a book and start reading passages to him or he would ask me to read something in particular. He loved poetry, and would often stop me and correct my cadence.

Some quotes had stayed with me through the years, and sometimes after a particularly difficult day I would turn to the bookcase and read aloud to myself. Among his favorite verses were the opening lines of "The Dream," which he often recited to my mom:

> *Love, if I weep it will not matter,*
> *And if you laugh I shall not care;*
> *Foolish am I to think about it,*
> *But it is good to feel you there.*

But I think his favorite was Shakespeare's sonnet:

> *When, in disgrace*
> *With fortune and men's eyes*
> *I all alone beweep my outcast state*
> *And trouble deaf heaven with my bootless cries . . .*

As he neared death, his choices became more melancholy and he often asked me to recite the last lines of Millay's "To a Poet Who Died Young":

> *Many a bard's untimely death*
> *Lends unto his verses breath;*
> *Here's a song was never sung:*
> *Growing old is dying young.*

My mother was never the same after his death. She kept the flag from his coffin, still so carefully folded by the honor guard at his funeral, on a night table beside her bed, sweeping her hand gently across it each evening as she said good night to him. Within a year of his passing, she had fallen into a deep depression. She died in the state hospital for the insane.

That experience—going to visit her, holding her hand as she stared bleakly and unspeaking at the ceiling, ignoring the occasional screams and hyena-like laughter of the other patients—still invaded my nightmares at times.

I opened up some windows to air the place out and let Rosebud into the backyard. The tenant before me had dogs, which accounted for the fenced-in backyard. The dogs also had dug up the yard until it looked like a bunch of archeologists had been digging for dinosaur skeletons back there, which accounted for the "no pets" edict. The landlord had made a halfhearted attempt to iron out the yard and had thrown some rye grass around, but now there were more weeds than grass. Near the back there were a yucca plant and a couple of shrubs, which would give Rosebud something to pee on.

I wasn't good about lawns. I didn't like cutting them, I didn't like watering them. And I didn't like sitting on them in a canvas beach chair reading dime novels. So basically, the backyard looked like a deserted battlefield from the Great War.

I let Slugger out and he immediately laid claim to the yucca plant, the shrubs, and everything else over six inches tall in the yard.

I went into the office and put my case on the table and emptied it, making neat stacks of things so I could find them easily, then went into the living room and piled a stack of ten records, randomly selected, on the player. The first to come up was Basie's "Sent for You Yesterday and Here You Come Today." It got my blood running and I went in the kitchen, poured myself a slug of Canadian Club, dropped one cube of ice in it. I went back to my office and sorted through the check receipts, putting them in order, and then listed them by bank and date on the blackboard, looking for patterns. But there wasn't anything to really go on. It was like trying to play a tune on a piano with no black keys.

So I packed it in for the night, took a hot shower, sprinkled on a little talcum powder, got into my silk pajama bottoms, and went into the living room. Rosebud was sitting in front of the record player with his head cocked to one side, listening to Benny Goodman's "China Boy."

He looked like that cute little white RCA dog who had grown up and turned out to be a big ugly mutt.

I turned off the player, locked the doors, turned off the lights, and got in bed. Rosebud came up beside the bed, looked at me for a moment or two, then made that little circle like he was chasing his tail in slow motion, lay down, and snorted.

A minute after I turned off the light and arranged myself for sleeping, I felt him crawl onto the bed. He did it with sly caution. A leg, then another leg, then his back legs, then his body sliding across the covers. It took him about five minutes to make the journey. Then he crept around again in that little circle he made before lying down. He settled in, gave a big slobbery sigh, and he was out.

He snored.

CHAPTER 4

I awoke from a deep sleep to hear Rosebud scratching on the back door. A moment later he came into the bedroom, sat next to the bed, and growled at me. I opened one eye and stared at him.

"Don't you ever bark, Slugger?" I said.

I hip-hopped barefoot back to the kitchen, let him out and left the door cracked for him, fed him and filled his water dish. I went to my bathroom, shaved and showered, and put on my dark suit, the one I wear when I'm going to be talking to nice, decent, everyday people who are anxious to cooperate with the law and usually tell you more than you want to know. Muscle and blackjack not required.

I put another can of dog food in Rosebud's bowl, refilled the water dish, and put them outside in the little cave under the alcove.

He watched every move, and when I started back into the house, those dark eyes followed me to the door.

"Try not to bark or make a ruckus," I told him. "Spend the day looking for Slugger."

Fifteen minutes later I was tooting the horn in Ski's driveway. I picked him up every day. He had a brand-new Plymouth but his wife, Claire, used it to take kids to school, go shopping, and do whatever women do all day long to make life pleasant for the rest of the family.

My five-year-old used Olds needed new shocks, the fan belt squealed like a pig on the way to the slaughterhouse, and I had to stand on the brakes to slow down, not an easy thing to do since I had to move the seat all the way back to accommodate Agassi's frame and drive with the tips of my toes. There was a hole in the upholstery on the passenger side, which was covered by a blue embroidered pillow with a couple of palm trees framing yellow letters that said "Welcome to San Diego." And it had that old-car smell, a mixture of oil, gasoline, cheap carry-out food, and an ashtray that hadn't been emptied since Hitler was selling hand-painted postcards on the streets of Vienna. It got me there, which was all that mattered.

We stopped at Wally's coffeehouse, which is on the way, and got coffee in paper cups and a bag of sinkers, and Ski read the newspaper as he always did, running an occasional headline by me if it was something he thought I needed to know or a comical item like: ESCAPED KANGAROO KICKS PREACHER TO DEATH AT BUS STOP.

As we pulled away from the curb, a flatbed truck went by, going the other way. There were two large billboards on the bed. Red letters on a field of white:

BUY BONDS
KEEP AMERICA FREE
JOIN THE ARMED FORCES TODAY

Two starlet types in red-and-white bathing suits were standing on a little perch to keep from falling out, waving blue high hats, while a loudspeaker over the cab was blasting Kate Smith's "God Bless America" loud enough to raise the dead.

Ski started grousing. "I hate Kate Smith," he snapped. "I really hate hearing her bellow when I'm not fully awake yet."

Smith wrapped her song and Irving Berlin's forlorn voice began moaning, "Oh, How I Hate to Get Up in the Morning."

"I hate that, too," he growled.

"Why should you care," I said. "You're forty-two, you got a wife and three kids, and you're sixty pounds overweight. They'll be drafting blind men before they get to you."

"Christ, you're thirty-four. They'll never get to you either. Besides, you're a cop. Immediate deferment."

"That sounds unpatriotic," I said.

"I think you *want* to go if we get into it with the Krauts," he said. "Mr. Gung Ho."

I started laughing and he finally broke up, too, and turned back to the paper.

"So what's the plan for the day?" he asked.

"I go to the bank, you check where she worked. We'll meet at the Kettle for lunch."

"How about Moriarity?"

"What about him?"

"It's an accident. He's gonna want to know what the hell we're up to."

"Let's see what we come up with. Then we'll worry about the lieutenant."

"Great, just great," Agassi moaned.

CHAPTER 5

The drive to the West Los Angeles National Bank took me past the entrance to Pacific Meadows. There was a small sign beside the road into the neighborhood that read:

PACIFIC MEADOWS

NO SOLICITATIONS   SPEED LIMIT 10

WE HAVE CHILDREN

It was a nice touch, the kind of understated warning you usually find in snottier neighborhoods with a lot of flowers around the entrance gate, and private police who patrol in unmarked cars and make more in tips at Christmas than I make in a year. Across the main drag from the entrance was a strip of necessity stores: a candy store and newsstand, dry cleaners, drugstore, greengrocer, butcher shop—which I assumed was where Verna Wilensky got Rosebud's bones—a shoe cobbler, and a burned-out shop on the end, with an empty lot beside it.

A few blocks farther on was a small nameless village that was showing the signs of restoration. Freshly painted shops mingled with shuttered stores that were still waiting for tenants getting back on their feet from the Depression.

The West L.A. National was on the ground floor of a freestanding, three-story building that had professional offices on the upper floors. The entrance was in the middle of the block and had brass-trimmed, etched-glass doors and a small plaque next to it that told me the bank was founded in 1920 by Ezra Sutherland. It was cheerier than most old banks I was familiar with. The teller cages were mahogany. The high glass partitions, which had become popular when

John Dillinger and his pals were fond of making sudden withdrawals from banks, had been removed. There was a long table down the middle of the room where depositors could fill in their slips. A vase of fresh flowers held down its center. On the right side, behind a hand-carved railing, were several desks where clerks made loans and did whatever else clerks do in a bank. All boasted freshly cut flowers in vases. Four towering cathedral windows lined the walls, providing warm sunlight to the big room. A large glass chandelier hovered majestically overhead.

In the far corner on the left was a stainless steel Standish-Wellington vault, its door standing open. In the center of the far wall was a door, which I assumed led to the president's office, and another, probably to a secretary's office. A pleasant-looking woman in her mid to late thirties occupied a large desk in front of the big shot's office. A single red rose, flared out in all its glory in a fluted bud vase, sat on a corner of her desk. It was a pleasant room, less threatening than most banks.

I took off my fedora and walked the length of the bank to the woman with the red rose. Her nameplate said she was Amy Shein, executive secretary, and a plaque on the door behind her told me the office was occupied by Rufus Sutherland, President.

"Good morning, Miss Shein," I said and showed her my buzzer. "Sergeant Bannon, Los Angeles Police Department. Is Mr. Sutherland busy?"

She looked a bit alarmed when she saw the badge but got over it quickly and smiled.

"May I tell him what this is about?" she asked pleasantly.

"It's a routine matter," I said. "Nothing serious. No crime has been committed."

"Well, thank goodness for that," she said, and went into the office. She was gone for less than a minute, then came out and stood at the door and motioned me in.

"Mr. Sutherland, this is Lieutenant Bannon from the police department," she told the boss.

"Sergeant," I said. "But thanks for the promotion."

Sutherland smiled from behind a teak desk that wasn't quite as big as a basketball court and just as barren: a leather blotter holder, a pen and pencil set, and a telephone. There were two large, framed

Audubon originals on the wall behind his desk. One was an eagle. I didn't recognize the other bird which was red and black and quite a bit smaller. Behind him, on top of a cabinet that matched the desk, were a dozen framed photographs of all sizes, family pictures. Otherwise the room was as impersonal as a form letter.

Sutherland was a tall, erect man in a blue summer suit with a white breast-pocket handkerchief. His salt-and-pepper hair was a little too long for a banker's and he had a tennis player's tan, manicured fingers, and brown eyes behind wire-rimmed glasses.

"Rufus Sutherland," he said, extending his hand. We shook and I took the chair he motioned to. I could feel tension in his hand.

"I hope this isn't something serious," he said. "My daughter . . ."

"Nothing like that," I interrupted. "It has to do with a customer of yours. Verna Wilensky."

He seemed relieved and then: "Is something wrong with Verna?"

Obviously the news had not reached the bank yet.

"I'm sorry to tell you this," I said. "Mrs. Wilensky is dead. An accident at her home."

"Oh my God," he said, sitting up even taller in his chair. "What happened?"

I gave him as much information as was necessary without getting into bloated faces floating under bathwater and other lurid details. I could tell the news upset him.

"She was one of our most dependable depositors, certainly the most loyal," he said. "Came in once a month to go over her statement. Never complained. A lovely lady with more than her share of bad luck. I assume you heard about her husband."

I nodded. "Are you familiar with her account, Mr. Sutherland?"

"Well, no more than for most of our depositors. The tellers and secretaries handled her everyday affairs. But she always stopped in to say hello. Used to come in with that big dog of hers." He leaned forward and a smile played the corners of his mouth. "Big old stud named Rosebud, can you imagine?"

"We've met," I said with a smile.

"Well, what can I do for you, sir?"

I picked up my briefcase, sat it on a corner of the massive desk, and snapped it open.

"We found these papers in her desk. Mostly banking things. She has quite a sum of money on deposit and we haven't been able to locate a will."

"Oh my goodness," he said. "Hard to believe she was intestate, she was meticulous in all her dealings."

"Apparently both she and Frank Wilensky were only children. I'd like to locate survivors if there are any, before the state gets its greedy hands on her estate: life savings, house, car, et cetera."

"That's very considerate of you."

"I understand she came here from Texas."

"Well, I'm not real sure. It's been a long time. My father was director at the time. That was back in the early twenties. He died several years ago and after that Millie . . . Miss Harrington . . . handled her affairs."

"The thing is this," I said. "She accumulated a rather large amount of money, apparently from a five-hundred-dollar-a-month stipend. But we haven't found anything to indicate where that money came from. I am hoping the bank might give us a lead. It could be a member of the family, a child, relative. Would it be possible for us to go over her accounts and see the checks that were deposited?"

The request made him nervous. He stroked his chin and cleared his throat.

"That is, of course, confidential. Do you have a court order . . . ?" He said it tentatively, as though unsure of himself.

"I can get one but considering the nature of her sudden death and the very real prospect of the state stepping in to take over, I was hoping we could do this right away. Better than having the state boys trooping in here waving subpoenas in everybody's face. They aren't known for their manners."

"I see."

"All I want to do is go back through her records and see if there are any names, addresses, anything that we can follow up on. I'll of course keep this all on the Q.T. An hour or two is all it should take."

He thought about all of that for a minute or two. He seemed a little nervous about circumventing the court. I took out my badge and ID and laid them in front of him to reassure him. He perused them, then looked up sharply.

"Homicide division?" he said.

I gave him my most reassuring smile. "Just routine, Mr. Sutherland. Anytime there's an unwitnessed death, we have to investigate. She was dead for almost twenty-four hours before her neighbor found her."

"I see," he said. He took off his glasses, folded them, and tapped them on his desk for a moment, then reached under the ridge of the desk and pressed a button.

A moment later, a handsome woman came in through a side door. She was tall, five-seven probably, late twenties, with ebony-black hair down to her shoulders, severe black eyebrows over gray eyes, and million-dollar legs sheathed in sheer silk, at least from the knee down. She was wearing a tailored, double-breasted charcoal-gray suit with a small diamond-and-ruby pin in the shape of a dolphin on her lapel, and an oyster-white, high-necked silk-and-lace blouse. She stood as straight as a Marine topkick. Pure elegance. She also had a million-dollar tennis tan like the boss.

"Millicent, this is Sergeant Bannion from the police department. Sergeant, this is our vice president, Millicent Harrington."

"It's *Bannon,* no *i,*" I said, taking her hand. She had a sturdy tennis-player's grip and a smile most women would kill for. I hadn't been as close to a woman this aristocratic since I brushed against Katharine Hepburn at a premiere at Grauman's a year or so ago. She was the star of the picture. I was picking up some after-hours change spotting dips for the manager of the theater.

Then my mind started working overtime. She had the same tan as Sutherland, her stockings cost more than my entire wardrobe, and the pin in her lapel spelled Tiffany. And a vice president. Sometimes I hate being a cop.

"I have some bad news," Sutherland said. "Verna Wilensky is dead."

Her reaction was immediate and profound. She gasped and pressed the fingers of one hand against her lips. Her eyes widened to the size of silver dollars and then began to tear up. She sat, keeping her knees locked together, and seemed to sag into her suit. Sutherland whipped the handkerchief from his breast pocket and handed it to her.

"Sorry to be so abrupt," he muttered, and sat back in his chair.

Her backbone stiffened again. "What happened?" she said after dabbing her eyes.

"She slipped in the bathtub and drowned," I explained. "I'm sure it was painless. She was kayoed . . . knocked out instantly."

"Poor Verna," she said sorrowfully. "She had so much going for her. Then she loses Frank, now this."

"She died intestate," Sutherland said. "Sergeant Bannion is hoping we can find something in her file that will lead him to a relative or some legitimate kin. Would you help him, please? Whatever he needs."

I didn't bother to bring up the *i* he insisted on putting in my name.

"Of course," she said, and laid Sutherland's handkerchief on the corner of the desk.

"Thanks a lot," I said, shaking his hand, and followed Miss Harrington into her office.

"You might want to open a window," she said. "It's a bit stuffy in here."

I slid the window up and looked down in the parking lot behind the building. There were two cars near the back door, a Rolls-Royce Silver Wraith and a yellow Pierce-Arrow convertible with leather seats the color of the sky on a clear day.

It completed the package, as did the office—right down to the pale yellow silk drapes and sky blue carpeting that tickled my ankles. Pretty cushy, I thought. A gorgeous woman, a million-dollar office, a Pierce-Arrow ragtop. Sutherland was keeping this lady in grand style.

I looked around at the paintings on the wall, the antique furniture, the Mueller radio built into the wall. On her desk there was an eight-by-ten photo mounted in a sterling silver frame with its back to me and an elegant, hand-painted pencil holder that looked like it could have been a gift from the King of England.

"This is very impressive," I said.

She was smart, too, to go along with everything else. Her eyes narrowed ever so slightly and one corner of her mouth turned up in what was almost a sneer.

You blew it, I thought. *She knows you're on to her. Get back to business.*

She picked up the handpiece of a white phone, dialed a couple of numbers, then, "Jane, bring me the Wilensky file, please . . . yes, everything." She hung up.

"So, Sergeant Bannon, what exactly are you looking for?"

I decided to play it straight up.

"As you know, the state is going to get the estate if we can't find a family member with a legitimate claim. Mrs. Wilensky had almost a hundred gra . . . a hundred thousand dollars in her savings account, most of which came from a, uh, stipend of some kind she got every month."

Jane, a mousy young woman with dirty-blond hair, came in with a large accordion folder, put it on the corner of her desk, and left without a word.

"Five hundred dollars," she said with a nod.

"I was hoping we can get a lead off the cashier's checks. You do keep a record of them, don't you?"

"No, bank checks go back to the issuing bank when they're cashed. We do make photocopies, although I doubt it will be much help to you."

"How come?"

"They were always cashier's checks. No names, just the issuing bank."

My disappointment was palpable.

"Can we look them over anyway?" I asked.

"All of them?"

"I'm sorry, I know you must be awfully busy, but sometimes the smallest thing . . ." I shrugged and let the sentence die.

"All the way back to the beginning?"

I nodded. "Nineteen twenty-four, I think." I leaned down to get my briefcase and my jacket flopped open. As I sat up, I saw her eyes fixed on the Luger under my arm.

"Will it make you more comfortable if I put this in my pocket?"

"I'm sorry. I'm well accustomed to firearms, I'm a member of the Bel Air Skeet Club. I've just never seen a hidden weapon except in gangster movies."

"It's concealed."

"Pardon?"

"It's called a concealed weapon, not a hidden weapon."

"Oh. Well, don't put it in your pocket on my account."

I opened the briefcase and showed her the contents. "These were in a lockbox at her house. Statements going back to the mid twenties.

There was some other stuff, papers on the car and house, bill of sale for Frank Wilensky's business. But no will and no birth certificate. Seems strange for someone that, uh . . ."

"Meticulous?"

"Yeah, meticulous."

"So, you want to see the copies of the original checks and deposit slips."

"Please."

For the next hour or so, we went through checks and deposit slips and I made notes. When we were through, I had a list of all the cashier's checks going back to the original $4,000 cash deposit. At one point my Parker pen ran out of ink and she loaned me a gold fountain pen with no trade name on it. I felt guilty just leaving my fingerprints on it.

"How about a break?" she said, finally. "Coffee?"

"Sounds great."

She went to the wall behind her desk and slid back a panel. There was a small stove and refrigerator behind it. A French coffeemaker was sitting over a low flame. She poured coffee into two bone china cups and put them on matching saucers.

"How do you take it?"

"Two sugars, a splash of milk."

She dropped a couple of cubes of sugar into one cup and got a bottle of real cream out of the refrigerator.

"Will cream be alright? I've never been much for milk."

"I'll just take the cream, forget the coffee."

She laughed then, a genuine laugh that came from somewhere around her ankles.

"This is quite a setup," I said. "Do all VPs have offices this cushy?"

She turned the framed photo around. It was a shot of Millicent and Sutherland in tennis togs. He had his arm around her waist.

"Only if you play tennis with the boss," she said.

"Oh," is all I could think to say.

"Of course, it helps if the boss is your father."

I almost swallowed my tongue.

"It's been fun watching your deductive brain at work," she said with a smile, and leaned back in her chair. "Are you usually this impulsive drawing conclusions?"

I could feel my face turning color.

"I hope not," I said. "If I am, there are a lot of innocent men dancing to the piper."

She cocked her head slightly.

"Dancing to the piper," I repeated, "means doing time. Prison. Look, I'm sorry I misjudged things. I've never seen a woman executive with an office this impressive. Or one dressed like you are."

"Well, there aren't too many of us around—yet. But that'll change, so you may as well get accustomed to it."

"Suits me fine," I said. I nodded toward the radio. "What kind of music do you like, classical?"

"I like classical."

"Tchaikovsky?"

She smiled, the kind of smile that made me feel I wasn't in on the joke.

"Is that the way I strike you? Tchaikovsky?"

"Well, who then?"

"Actually I prefer Tommy Dorsey although I think Miller's easier to dance to. And Duke Ellington when I'm blue."

This time I didn't even try to disguise my surprise? "Dorsey, huh? You must be a Sinatra fan."

"Buddy Rich."

"You're a drum freak, then?" I couldn't keep the surprise out of my voice.

"Always have been."

"Then you know Krupa's the man. He makes Rich sound like he's using chicken bones for drumsticks."

She scowled. "Krupa's all technique. Buddy has the speed and punch, and he's far more inventive."

"I never argue with a woman, but you're wrong."

"I never argue with a policeman, but *you're* wrong."

I was dying for a cigarette but there wasn't an ashtray in sight.

"Look, I'm about to get the heebie-jeebies for a smoke. Mind if I step outside for a couple of minutes?"

She opened a drawer and produced a china bowl that looked like it was on loan from a museum.

"You really want me to put ashes in this?" I asked, taking out the makings.

"It's an ashtray," she said. "Here, try one of mine."

They were Sherman Select, an inch longer than regular cigarettes and half as thick, with a gold filter on the end. The paper was light blue. Three bucks a carton if they cost a penny. The gold case they were in cost more than Verna Wilensky's house.

She got up, walked around the desk, produced a gold Dunhill lighter, and lit my cigarette. The tobacco was mild and sweet, not harsh like the Prince Albert pipe tobacco I used.

"Thanks."

I took a couple of good drags and let the smoke hang around in my lungs before I blew it out.

"It'll take about three of these to get one good smoke," I said.

She chuckled. "My grandfather used to roll his own."

"I like to roll 'em. Sometimes it gives you a little time to think when you're kicking wits around with some bohunk." Her face went blank again. "Interrogating some hooligan. That's before we take him to the back room and go to work on him with a rubber hose."

She laughed again, this time without taking her eyes off mine.

"Let me get back to business for a minute," I said, and took the safe deposit key from my vest pocket. "Can we make use of this?"

She stared at the key for a long time. A safe deposit box is supposed to be sacred, except, of course, if the G-men want to take a peek.

"I can get a court order to go into the box," I explained, "but all I'm looking for is a lead. The state boys will come snooping around soon enough when they get a whiff of what's involved here."

"I take it you and the state boys don't get along."

"I've got nothing against them except where this kind of thing is concerned. Somebody's got a right to that estate and for my money it isn't the state of California."

"Maybe she left it to her dog," she said, and then suddenly jerked straight up. "My God, what's happened to Rosebud?"

"He's bunking in with me temporarily, until I find some of Verna's relatives who'll take him on. It was that or the pound."

"You took Rosebud in?"

"He wouldn't have it any other way. I offered to get him a cabana at the Beverly Hills Hotel but he preferred slumming with me."

She crooked her finger. I followed her out onto the floor of the bank to the vault. A uniformed guard was sitting on a stool reading

Argosy magazine. When he saw Millicent Harrington, he jumped up as if a bug had bitten his rear end.

"George, my friend wants to visit his safe deposit box. Why don't you just sit back down and read your book, I'll take him back."

"Geez, Miss Harrington, I'm sorry. It's been a real slow day and . . ."

"I won't tell if you don't, George," she said. She led me back to the stainless-steel box room, found the matching key on a hook, and went down the row of stainless steel drawers until we got to the right number. She put both keys in, opened the door, and took out the metal strongbox. It was small, the smallest size available.

"Not much in here," she said, after leading me to a private room where we could examine the contents.

It was a bust. Just some love letters tied with red ribbon. I flipped slowly through them. All of them were from Frank, all to "Vernie my love": birthday cards, Christmas cards, some just telling her how much he had missed her during the day. Frank was a real romantic. I could understand why Verna Wilensky had wanted to die when he was killed.

The last one was different.

The envelope was yellow with age and there was no writing on it. Inside was a yellowed sheet, the ink faded and almost illegible. All it said was "Two more days. I can hardly wait." I looked at the back and checked the envelope once more. Nothing else.

"What do you make of that?" she asked.

"Who knows? Not the same handwriting as Frank's. Pretty old, judging from the fading and all. Maybe she was seeing somebody before him."

"Loretta Clark might know."

"Her neighbor?"

"She came in with Verna occasionally," she said. "Nice lady. Verna called her 'Sis.' "

"She told me."

There was nothing else of consequence in the box.

I put the note back in the envelope and returned the pile to the box and we put it back in the vault.

"By the way, what's your first name?"

"Zeke. My friends call me Zee."

"I'm Millie."

"Millie Harrington?"

My eyebrows asked the question.

"I was married once, right out of college. It was mostly rebellion, I guess. My father hated him. His mother hated me. And it turned out we weren't all that crazy about each other. So after six months we decided to go our separate ways. It was very amicable. We decided not to trade money. We used to call each other occasionally, but that eventually died of attrition. I haven't seen him in a couple of years."

"I'm sorry."

"Nothing to be sorry about. How about you?"

"Haven't even gotten close."

"Glad to meet you, Zee."

"Glad to meet you, Millie."

We returned to her office.

"I'm sorry that was such a flop," she said.

"It wasn't a flop," I said. "Almost all the cashier's checks were sent from banks in the San Pietro area. San Pietro, San Luis Obispo, Yucca Springs, one from Mendosa." I ran my finger down the list, quickly counting up banks in that general area. There were one hundred ninety-six deposits, including the money from the sale of Wilensky's shop and the original $4,000 deposit. Quickly figuring as I ran down the list, at least two-thirds of them had come from up there. I decided to make an accurate tally that night.

"Would it help if I got you a list of all those banks and who the managers are?"

"That would be a big help."

"I could even call some of them and suggest they cooperate with you."

I thought about that briefly but decided to finesse that idea for the moment. "I think maybe surprise might be more valuable to me at this point."

She picked up the phone and got Jane again and told her to get up the list from the state bank registry.

"Anything else?" She asked.

"Something that's been gnawing at me since last night. How often does someone come in off the street with four thou in cash?"

"Not very often."

"Can you imagine a woman coming all the way from Texas, which is where she told everybody she was from, carrying four large in her suitcase?"

"Four large what?"

"A *large* is a thousand dollars."

"Oh. Well, yes, it is unusual."

"So maybe she wasn't in Texas. I mean, that's a large chunk of cash even if she just carried it around the block."

"Yes, it is."

"Especially in 1924 when women were a little less, uh . . ."

"Independent?"

"Yeah, independent."

"So what does that lead you to believe?"

"That maybe she never was in Texas. That maybe before she showed up here and bought a house, she may have lived someplace else nearby."

"That's very interesting. And how would you go about finding out?"

"I have no idea."

She laughed again.

"Think about it," I said. "That was almost twenty years ago and there's been a Depression during that time. Banks went out of business, apartment houses closed down, a lot of people have died. And by the way, there were no photos in the house. Not a single picture except a clipping from the newspaper several weeks ago. So to be practical, I think I have to consider this: that Verna Hicks Wilensky was born that day in 1924. Whoever she was before that is just so much history and very possibly a waste of my time."

"You mean you may just forget the whole thing?"

"Not exactly, but if I draw a deuce then I'll have to let the state take it all."

"How about Rosebud?"

"Well, one thing's for sure. It's one part of her estate the boys will definitely not be interested in."

"Will you keep him?"

"It's against my lease."

"Somehow I don't think that worries you too much."

"Thanks," I said and smiled. "I'll take that as a compliment."

"As it was meant."

"There's one other thing," I said, taking out one of my business cards. "If the state boys should show up, give me a call, will you? I'm racing the clock on this and I'd like to know when the dogs are at my heels."

"I think what you're doing is quite noble," she said.

I let that pass by.

"One other thing. If it's just one of them that shows up, be sure to check his ID. Try to remember the name and buzzer number, it'll be in the upper-right-hand corner. They're supposed to travel in pairs, it's a rule. A house, a car, and a hundred grand adds up to a lot. In my business, people get killed for a lot less. One of them just might let greed outrun his brain."

I wrote my home number across the top of my card. I don't know why. Well, yes, I do. I was dreaming.

She looked at the card and snapped it with a fingernail. Then she abruptly changed the subject.

"Just out of curiosity, what does a cop do for fun? Besides adopt stray dogs."

"Go to the movies. Grab a good meal somewhere. Take a dip in the ocean occasionally. How about you, besides tennis?"

"I like to dance," she said.

"No kidding. Jitterbug?" It was a joke. I couldn't imagine her swinging around and kicking up a storm on a dance floor.

"Of course. Do you dance?"

I leaned across the desk toward her and said, "Promise you'll never tell anyone what I'm about to say?"

She crossed her heart with a finger.

"I once won a loving cup at the Saturday-night jitterbug contest at the Palladium. To Benny Goodman's 'Don't Be That Way.' Me and Julie Cluett. We also got twenty bucks."

"Were you in high school?"

I shook my head. "Four years ago. I was scared to death one of the boys on the force would find out. Now when I go, I tell the guys I'm doing security."

"How often do you go?"

"Whenever there's a big band. I don't dance much, I just stand up around the bandstand with everybody else and listen. He's going to be there next week, you know."

"Who?"

"Tommy Dorsey."

"At the Palladium?"

"Yep, with Buddy Rich, Sinatra, the Pied Pipers, the whole gang."

"I've never been to the Palladium," she said.

It sounded like a pick-up line but I knew better.

"It gets very hot and crowded."

"Are you going?"

I smiled. "I'm doing security that night."

She laughed again. Then she paused and asked, "Do you ever need an assistant?"

And there it was. One thing she wasn't, was shy. A lady whose cigarettes cost more than my car was pitching me. I wondered how long it would take for the novelty of that to wear thin.

"Look," I said, "let's put it on the table. I wouldn't know a dish of caviar from a bowl of Wheaties."

"So? I've never met anybody who was dancing for the piper. What's that got to do with anything?"

I couldn't think of an answer for that so I just stared into those gray eyes.

"Well, if you do decide you need an assistant, my number's Vandike 2578. I'll write it down for you, it's not in the book."

"Vandike 2578. I remember things like that."

"How about that? A cop who loves dogs and dancing and remembers phone numbers."

I took out the makings.

"Want to try one of mine before I leave?" I asked her.

"I . . . yes, why not?"

I rolled two, fanned them dry, and gave her one. She lit hers with her gold Dunhill, I lit mine with my Zippo.

Obviously a match made in heaven.

CHAPTER 6

I met Ski at a restaurant on La Cienega called the French Kettle, which was a high-sounding name for a lunchtime hangout for reporters, politicians, and cops. The prices went up for the dinner trade. The place was owned by an ex-prizefighter named Andre De-Court, who was once a very promising middleweight. He was one of those good-looking Frenchmen with dark shiny hair, a straight nose, and green eyes. The story goes that Andre worked his way up the rankings to a match with a muscle-bound hammer named Ray Rowles, who was next in line for a title shot. Andre was the favorite and the odds were up to about fifteen to one. Andre decided it was time to quit before he started looking like Slapsie Maxie Rosenbloom, who in turn looked like a bus had run into him, so he took all his savings, laid it off on Rowles, beat him to a pulp for seven rounds, and then lay down and took a nap. He used the winnings to open the restaurant, then took a rematch with Rowles, played with him for two rounds, and knocked him all the way to Madagascar in the third. Then he retired for good.

It was one of those high-ceilinged, wood-and-brass eateries that looked more like a cattle baron from Denver owned it than an Americanized Frenchman. There were booths around the perimeter and cubicles filled in the middle of the room. They all had high, etched-glass partitions, which looked fancy and expensive but were there mainly for privacy. When newsmen and politicians talk, they want privacy. Cops don't really care, they don't have anything to say. The place opened at 7:00 A.M. and closed at 11:00 P.M. In the morning they served eggs Benedict to die for, and the sandwich menu at lunch was two pages

140

long. I couldn't afford to eat there at dinner. If I wanted to spend that much money for a meal I'd go to Chasen's. I had never been there either.

Andre was always there, seated in a small booth for two in the front of the place near the cash register. He always wore a tuxedo. At seven in the morning he was in a tuxedo. He changed the shirt three times a day and he wore a very subtle cologne that made you forget he once earned his living with sweat and a right uppercut. He also carried a tab for the breakfast and lunch trade, which was a nervy thing to do—newsmen, politicians, and cops not being known for their credit ratings. The newsies and dicks because they didn't make much money, and the politicians because they were on the take from the start and who's going to sue the mayor or a city councilman for stiffing a check or two?

He got up when I came in and gave me a fifty-dollar smile.

"Zee," he said, "*Bonjour*. Ski is here already. Over by the window in the corner." He led me over there, handed me a leather-covered menu the size of the *Rand McNally World Atlas,* and retreated to his post.

Ski was devouring a large piece of Boston cream pie, which was his idea of an hors d'oeuvre.

"Why do you always eat your lunch backward?" I said.

"I don't like to start with a bowl of weeds with a tomato sitting in the middle of it."

The waiter came by and I ordered a corned beef on rye and a Coke.

"Sorry I'm late," I said. "I met a new friend."

"Oh yeah? Male or female?"

"Female."

"She a looker?"

"Your jaw would hit the floor if you laid eyes on her."

He gave me a nod of approval.

"Rich?"

"Her old man owns the bank—and she has an office that would make Marie Antoinette jealous."

He beamed lasciviously. "Do I hear wedding bells?"

"Yeah, sure, Agassi. I met her three hours ago and rolled her a cigarette. That was my big trick for the day. One of her cigarettes cost more than my car."

"Which would be what, thirty or forty cents?"

"Very funny. So, what kind of a day have you had?"

He finished the pie and pushed the dish aside like a kid finishing a vegetable plate.

"Well," he said, "I didn't find a lot about who she was. But I found a lot about who she wasn't. I talked to everybody at the tax office. Talked to them privately. She told just about everybody there she was from Texas. One of them she told she was from Waco, another one from San Antone, then there was Dallas, and Wichita Falls, which I thought was in Kansas. She arrived on the scene as Verna Hicks in early 1924. Was very discreet about her private life. Nobody knew she was dating Wilensky until she got married. Nobody's ever been to her house, in fact few of them even know where it is. She was an excellent worker, always punctual, never missed a day. An ideal employee according to her boss. She turned down promotions several times."

"Probably because the money wasn't worth the responsibility, considering she had that five C's floating in over the transom every month."

"My thoughts exactly. Anyway, I went back to the station house after I left there and called the Bureau of Records in Waco, San Antone, Dallas, and Wichita Falls, and then checked the state bureau in Texas. Guess what?"

"They never heard of her."

"You got it. The DMV here says she originally gave an address on Highland. I checked it. The street number doesn't exist and never did. She changed it to the Meadows address when she renewed the license. They don't check those things unless you get stopped for something serious."

"In other words, Verna Hicks doesn't exist prior to 1924."

"Exactly."

"Now why doesn't that surprise me?"

"But why did she suddenly surface then?"

"Because she had to be somebody, Ski. Apparently when she moved here she decided to stay awhile. The net is, she could be anybody from anywhere, even her age could be a phony."

Our meals arrived and he dug in.

"Your turn," he said. "Did you come up with anything—besides Miss Vanderbilt?"

"I want to put it all together on the board. The checks came from a lot of different banks. Once or twice from here in town. But most of them seem to have come from up around San Pietro."

He looked up sharply when I mentioned San Pietro.

"Hell, that's Culhane territory," he said.

"Culhane? He's running for governor."

"Not officially. He's about to announce. He's running against Claude Osterfelt and Dominic Bellini."

"I read something about it in the paper but I didn't take it seriously. Whoever heard of him?"

"The *Times* had a big spread on him last week. World War I hero. Racket-buster. Cleaned up his town, ran the gangsters out. It used to be called Eureka, which was like Frontier City, USA. Open gambling, prostitution. During Prohibition they served drinks over the bar. The sheriff was an old gunfighter named Buck Tallman. You have heard of him, right?"

"That was a long time ago. That's history. Wasn't he shot in a whorehouse or something?"

"Something like that. I'm thinking of running up to San Pietro. It's only about a hundred miles up there."

"The banks aren't gonna tell you anything, Zee. All that stuff's confidential."

"I did pretty well this morning."

"Ahhh, that's because you rolled Little Miss Rich Britches a cigarette and showed her your heater." He thought for a moment and added, "Are you hunching on this?"

"Can't say."

"I'm your partner. You think there's more to this than just an accident, don't you?"

"I don't think Mrs. Wilensky was knocking down five hundred bucks a month for years and then slipped in the bathtub and got fried. That much coincidence makes me nervous. I'm not sure, but I think the check trail leads to San Pietro."

"Moriarity's gonna laugh you outta the office."

"Hell, it's worth a shot."

"Moriarity's gonna have a seizure."

"I can con him into it."

"Culhane's a tough character, Zee."

I shrugged. "We're both lawmen. Maybe he'll work with me."

"Uh-huh. Maybe I'll lose fifty pounds in my sleep tonight, too."

CHAPTER 7

We split up again; Ski was going to check out the crime reporters at the downtown newsroom, some of the old-timers who might know more about San Pietro than what had been reported through the years. The newsies always had something in their back pocket. Stuff that was all rumor with maybe ten cents' worth of truth in it. Stuff they couldn't back up properly. Maybe they had a city editor who'd been sued once and was gun-shy of everything if they didn't have pictures, sworn statements, three sources, and a sworn statement from God that it was on the level. Ski was good at tapping them. He'd been around seven years longer than me. He'd go in with a pint of Seagram's Seven in his pocket, tell some jokes, give them a little piece of gossip they couldn't use, then sneak around to the subject and take out the bottle.

"What are we looking for?" he asked.

"I don't know," I answered truthfully. "Maybe just a word here and there."

"It's what, seventeen years ago?" he said. "And for all we know, she was on Mr. Somebody's sleeve long before she showed up in Pacific Meadows."

"I know it, I know it," I said. "It's worth an hour or two. Maybe something happened up there in the early twenties, some two-bit scandal not worth an inch of ink down here. Something that'll give me more to go on than a bunch of bank names."

Ski went his way and I went down to the main newsroom of the *Times* to look up Jimmy Pennington, who was one of the best reporters in town. We had started out at the same time, about two years after Verna Hicks Wilensky wandered into town with four grand in her girdle, a new name, a new house, and a new life except for somebody from the past who was underwriting her five C's a month. I could feel the nudge in my gut. Maybe it was because I've known a lot of people who disappeared. Just vanished, click, like that. I was in Missing Persons for two years. But this was the first time somebody had *appeared* out of nowhere. No previous history. No birth certificate. No high school prom pictures. Zip. But she had to appear from someplace before she appeared in West L.A.

Pennington and I were both rookies at our respective jobs in those days and I helped Pennington out when I could, giving him a tip that put him an hour ahead of everybody else. In those days there were seven newspapers, including the gossip sheets. An hour is as good as a week in the life of a breaking story. In exchange, he mentioned my name whenever he could. One hand washing the other. Now he was the top-slot reporter. The only homicide he would be interested in was if the mayor knocked off his mistress in the presidential suite of the Bel Air Hotel. But he had a memory like an encyclopedia, so he was worth a trip across town.

I stopped in the coffee shop on the corner, got two cups of black coffee, and took the elevator to the third-floor newsroom. I found Jimmy, sleeves rolled up to his elbows, talking into two phones at the same time, one cradled between his ear and his shoulder. With his free hand he was taking down notes. He was short, five-seven, but husky, had curly blond hair, and loved the ladies.

I sat on the corner of his desk, put a coffee in front of him, and rolled a cigarette. He mouthed, "Light that for me," which I did. I stuck it between his lips and he kept writing and talking at the same time, the butt bobbing between his lips like the cork on a kid's fishing line. He finally hung up one of the phones and wrapped his hand around the mouthpiece of the other.

"What's up?" he asked.

"Want to pick your brains a little."

He rolled his eyes. "I'm covering two stories at once and I got a deadline in two hours." He held up a finger and said, "Okay, Ned, I need all you can get me in one hour, got that? Sixty minutes. The beast is breathing down my neck. Thanks." He hung up the phone and flopped back in his chair like a man who had just suffered a coronary.

"I don't have a brain left to pick right now."

"What do you know about Thomas Culhane?"

"Jesus, Zee, don't you ever read the papers? There was a three-column profile on him last week, second section front."

"I mean the stuff that wasn't in the papers."

His eyes narrowed. "What're you on to?"

"Nothing. I have to go up there on a civil matter. I hear he's a tough cookie."

"You're in homicide, what're you doing chasing a civil matter?"

"It's an accidental death. I need to find a survivor to close out my report."

"Uh-huh."

"That's all there is to it," I said, which at that point was true.

"He likes cops. He's been one most of his life." He paused and took a sip of coffee. "Why would Culhane get tough with you?"

"Who says he's gonna get tough? You know me, I just like to have a leg up."

"What kind of civil affair is this, again?"

I could see his nose twitching.

"I'm looking for a family member. It's an accidental death and I don't want to file the report until I notify the survivors."

"That's why Bell invented the telephone. That's this gadget here." He pointed to one of his phones.

"Ski told me Culhane was bad news, but you know Ski. He can make a federal case out of a hard sneeze. I happened to be in the neighborhood and I thought I'd get your take on him."

He opened a desk drawer, which was his filing cabinet, and rooted around in the cloud of clippings that puffed up out of it. He finally found what he was looking for, snapped it out of the pile, and slammed the drawer with his knee.

"Here. That's thirty inches on Culhane. Three pictures. He's running for governor, you know, or did that get by you, too?" His face screwed up like he had just swallowed a tumbler full of white vinegar. "Jesus, what are you smoking these days?" he said, looking at the cigarette I had rolled him.

"You heard the one about beggars being choosers?"

"I ran out of Camels an hour ago and I haven't been off the phone since." He took another drag. "I don't think Culhane has any secrets in his closet. He's tough; hell, he had to be to clean up Eureka, which was what the town was called before they dolled it up and started calling it San Pietro. It used to be the meanest town in central California. Now it's a playground for people with real money, the kind that tip with Ben Franklins and give their kids Cadillacs when they pass the fifth grade. But he runs the county with an invisible whip. You get out of line and *crack!* you got a welt on your back and you don't have any idea where it came from. On the other hand, he can be a charmer. He can get a smile out of a dead cat. You won't have any trouble with him. Like I said, he loves cops. Hates reporters, loves cops."

"How come he hates reporters?"

"He played rough back when. One of his cops . . . what was his name? . . . it'll come to me . . . anyway, the cop knocked off a mobster named Fontonio, who was taking over the mobs up there. You know, starting a gangster's union—everybody joins up or they end up floating facedown to Hawaii. Woods, that was the cop's name, Eddie Woods. He claimed self-defense, there was a gun in Fontonio's hand; except everybody who knew the man, including his wife and bodyguards, said Fontonio was afraid of guns. Didn't carry one, didn't have one in the house. That's what bodyguards are for. Then they couldn't trace the heater. The boys up in Sacramento were about to look into it when Woods resigned, the D.A. dead-docketed the case, and that was the end of that."

"So why does Culhane hate reporters?"

"Some of the muckrakers implied Culhane had Woods do the job. It did look pretty fishy. But Culhane said he had nothing to do with it. Then Woods said Culhane had nothing to do with it. And when Woods quit, the case went bye-bye. Culhane never forgot that. He said the press tried to ruin his reputation and, as far as I know, he's still got a hard-on about it. He's Irish just like you: you don't get mad, you get even. Culhane gets mad *and* even. That isn't in the story. It's irrelevant now."

"When did this happen?"

"I vaguely remember it. We're talking mid twenties, thereabouts. I was just finishing college at the time and you were one of the Dead End kids. You know me. I remember weird stuff but I can't remember what I had for lunch."

"What happened to Woods?"

He shrugged. "Hell, I dunno. I heard he was a P.I. down here, but that was a long time ago."

"I have great respect for your memory, Jimmy."

"It's a gift. My old man was a card shark. He could count cards in his sleep. Must be in my blood."

The phone started ringing again. He snatched it up and snapped, "Pennington; hold on a minute." He cupped the mouthpiece.

"No kidding, what's your interest? Are you on to something?"

"Like I said, it's a civil thing. If it works out, it wouldn't rate more than three lines on page twenty-two."

"You wouldn't shit me after all we've been to each other?"

"When did I ever shit you?"

"This got something to do with that lady who took a bath with her radio?"

"How'd you hear about that? I haven't even filed a report yet."

"Scuttlebutt."

"I'm trying to locate a relative so I can let the family know before it hits the obit page."

"Oh."

I don't think he believed me, but the other phone started ringing again and the clock ticked closer to his deadline and he got busier than a centipede running across a hot rock. I thanked him, took the clipping, and got out of there before he got any nosier.

CHAPTER 8

I stopped at the grocery and picked up some tomatoes, a bottle of milk, and a pint of chocolate ice cream, and walked to the end of the block to Lupo's butcher shop. Lupo was about five-five and all muscle, one of those people without a neck. His head was shaped like a fat pumpkin, with skimpy black hair, and he had bull shoulders that bulged out just below his ears, and a torso that went straight down from under his arms. He could carry a side of beef between his thumb and forefinger. His apron was splattered with blood and he wore rubber boots folded over at the knee. I was afraid to bring up sensitive subjects like sanitary conditions when I was in the shop.

"How about a nice T-bone or porterhouse steak, Zee," he said with a grin.

"Thirty cents for a pound of steak?" I said. "The cows must be on strike."

"That's a good one."

"How about some bones for my dog?"

"Since when you got a dog? What kind?"

"I don't know, Lupo, he doesn't have a birth certificate."

"Another good one," he chuckled. "How many bones you want?"

"How does six sound?"

"Six! He must be some big dog. What's this hound's name?"

I thought about that for a minute and finally I said, "His name's Rosebud."

"*His* name?"

"He's a used dog, the name came with him. I tried to change it to Slugger but every time I call him that, he looks around to see who Slugger is."

150

He wiggled a finger at me and I leaned toward him.

"He'll come to Rosie," he said in a low confidential voice. "Anybody asks, tell him you named him after Slapsie Maxie."

He was sitting under the yucca plant staring up at a mockingbird that was singing like a blue jay, when I walked out on the back porch.

"Hey, Rosie," I called, "how about a bone?"

He came loping across the yard and leaned against me, and I scratched him behind the ears. We went inside and I dished out his can of food and put it on the floor, and he went at it like a hyena attacking carrion. Then I gave him a bone.

"You can eat that in here," I said, but he walked to the screen door and waited for me to open it. "You're some creature of habit," I said, and let him out.

I took out the clips Pennington had loaned me. Culhane's was a surface biography, no scandal attached. His picture showed a handsome man with a hard jaw and sun-creased skin. He was dressed in a dark suit, white shirt, and a striped tie, and wearing a black fedora— mischievous pale eyes under the brim, and a vague smile. He was leaning against a wall, with his thumbs hooked in his belt. Beside it was a second picture of a younger Culhane, dressed in a workman's shirt and dark pants, with one of those round, peaked hats the cops wore back in those days and the puttees he probably had worn in the Marines. He was stern-faced and looked ill at ease in front of the camera. He had his foot on the running board of a four-door Ford ragtop. Beside him was the sheriff, Buck Tallman, who was sitting on a big roan. Tallman was a tall, erect man in a western shirt and a buckskin vest, who obviously ran the county from the back of a horse and used a .44 Peacemaker as a convincer. He had a ten-gallon hat pulled down over gentle eyes, and a proud smile under a handlebar mustache. It was a face that demanded respect, a face that concealed a harsh life on the frontier and a lot of history he probably wanted to forget or had rewritten through the years. He could have been fifty or a hundred and fifty. Together, they kept the peace, which, according to the story, was not as easy as it might sound. Eureka had been like a border town, wide open, noisy, and mean, a town where gambling, boozing, and whoring were the main occupations. Under those circumstances Tallman was not an anachronism, although he might have become one by the time the two of them had decided things were changing and it was time for San Pietro to change, too.

From the story, I learned that Culhane was born in 1884 in that wide-open, sin-ridden town. In 1900, at the age of sixteen, he lied about his age and joined the Marines, ending up on the Western Front, a sharpshooter who won a Silver Star, a Purple Heart, and the French Croix de Guerre in the last battle of the Somme. He came home in 1920 and went back to work as a deputy sheriff.

In 1921, Tallman was shot down in what the paper described as "the massacre at Grand View House, the town's most respectable fancy house." A new county council immediately named Culhane the sheriff. A year later he was duly elected to the post on the promise that he would clean up San Pietro County and "make it a town and county we will all be proud of." During the years that followed, he kept that promise. He drove out the mobsters and gentrified San Pietro. Now it was a thriving tourist town.

There was a sidebar relating to the 1922 arrest and conviction of a gangster named Arnie Riker for the murder of a young woman named Wilma Thompson. Riker, of course, had claimed he was framed by Culhane. Not surprising. I never met a hooligan yet who didn't cry "frame" when faced with the goods. He got the gas chamber, later commuted to life without parole on an appeal.

All in all, a favorable piece without a hint of the kind of scandal and corruption that must have been rife during the early days, and one that gave no hint of the stuff I had been hearing from Ski and others about Culhane, except for one thing. When asked about his political platform, Culhane told the reporter, "You'll find out when I'm good and ready to tell you."

That sounded like the Culhane I was expecting to meet.

CHAPTER 9

Lieutenant Moriarity gave me the deadeye when I tapped on his door. Moriarity was a short, bulky, almost bald guy, with eyes like a ferret and a voice an octave lower than an opera basso. He had been a cop so long he didn't remember that early in his life he had been a bouncer in a speakeasy where drinks were served in shot glasses and you got a dirty look if you asked for water on the side. That had been twenty-five years ago, when he was twenty-one years old with no plans for the future. The war had changed that. When he came home in 1918 with a couple of medals and a machine-gun hole in his side, a captain he had served with suggested he take a shot at being a cop.

He had been on the P.D. ever since, understood the politics of working in a city where the real rules weren't written in any book and where his main job was to keep his captain happy, which meant a minimum of annoyance. The best way to keep Moriarity happy was to "keep it all minimum," which was his way of saying don't rock the boat, don't look for headlines, solve your cases as fast as you can, and stay out of what little hair he had left. With that in mind, he didn't get too upset if occasionally you beat on some bohunk's head to get a piece of important information or gentled a confession out of some obstinate lowlife with a few swift, well-aimed kicks where it hurts most. He called it the glove option, as in "always use a glove if you gotta get rough. I don't wanna see some riffraff on the front page looking like he walked into a waffle iron." He also believed that the best crime reports were those that stayed as close to the bone as possible, his theory being that the less said, the less the ambulance chasers had to go on. "The guy's dead, he has a hole in his head, he was lying in the gutter, period. Don't get poetic, save that for the D.A."

Violating the basics could earn you a serious talk with the boss, which meant a chewing-out people someplace in Idaho could hear. A couple of years ago, some of the boys sneaked into his office one night and nailed leather straps to the armrests and legs of one of the chairs in his office and affixed a pot to the backrest. It was a pretty good parody of the hot seat. Instead of having a stroke, Moriarity loved it. He put it in the corner of the office, which was pretty barren except for his desk and chair, a coatrack, a small conference table in the corner, a couple of real chairs, a framed picture of FDR on the wall behind him, and an American flag in a wooden holder on the corner of his desk. If he pointed to the hot seat when he called you forth, he was planning to rearrange your ass.

On that morning, he was drinking black coffee and scanning the morning *Times* when I tapped on the door. He waved me in. I stood in front of him and rolled a cigarette.

He looked me up and down. I was wearing my best off-the-rack Bond blue suit, a white shirt, and a reasonably decent tie.

"Where's the funeral?" he asked.

I took that as an invite and sat in the chair across from him.

"So what's on your mind, Bannon. And I'm hoping deep down inside it isn't going to make me dyspeptic."

"The Verna Wilensky thing," I said, lighting the butt.

"The one got fried in her tub?" he said, surprised.

"That's not the problem."

I ran the litany on her, finishing with, "She didn't have any birth certificate, no insurance policies, nothing like that. Five hundred a month for seventeen years. That's uh . . ."

He gave me the deadeye. "A hundred and two grand. What's the matter, drop out of school before they got to math?"

"Ho, ho, ho."

"Hell, she probably had a sugar daddy. Who cares? She drowned in the bathtub, for crissakes, what else do you need to know? And keep that crap about her lollipop money outta the report. It's distracting."

"I'm curious about something."

"You ain't got enough to do? I can fill your plate if you're bored."

"You know me, I like to bundle 'em up nice and neat. She was in her forties, all alone, her husband got waxed in a car wreck four years ago. No survivors and no will. Maybe we can find some relatives who'll give her a decent burial and a headstone."

"We're cops, Bannon, this ain't the bleeding hearts club. Tell it to the Red Cross."

"They're only interested in the living."

He dug a Tampa Nugget out of his desk drawer and lit it. It smelled like he was smoking a Hershey's bar. He stared at me for a minute or two.

"This isn't one of those nudges you get, is it, Bannon?"

"I don't like coincidence. There's a lot of it here."

"That ain't what this is about. You're lookin' for something else here, I can feel it in my bones."

He growled, and gnawed on his cigar.

"We dug up some things," I said, and gave him a report on what Ski and I had learned the day before, including Wilensky's shadowy past and the mysterious cashier's checks. I left out the background check on Culhane.

"I'd like to take one more day and run up the coast."

He squinted his eyes and looked at me suspiciously.

"Where up the coast?"

"San Pietro."

"San Pietro? That's Culhane territory."

"So I've heard."

"The same Culhane who's running for governor against Osterfelt and Bellini."

"The same."

He gave me the deadeye.

"So, what about Culhane?" I asked innocently.

He responded as only Moriarity can. He was a product of what I call the bureaucratic system of ambiguous response. Moriarity could be standing knee-deep in a pouring rainstorm and if you asked him if it was raining out, he would probably respond with something like, "It's hard to say" or, more likely, "I think Gary Cooper shoulda played Rhett Butler." In the bureaucracy, the less specific you get, the safer you are. So when I asked about Culhane, he thought a minute, and said that he had heard that Culhane was everything from a demagogue to a commie; from dangerous, tough, heartless, corrupt, merciless, and a cold-blooded murderer to heroic, compassionate, charming, and, as far as the citizens of San Pietro, California, were concerned, "Joan of Arc with a pecker."

"What do *you* think?" I asked.

He thought for a minute and said, "I think God has a great sense of humor."

I smiled and waited, but he didn't have any more to say on the subject.

"So, why get so excited about Culhane? I'm going up there to talk to a couple of banks."

"Thomas Brodie Culhane. His friends call him Brodie, everybody else calls him Captain. Nobody calls him Tommy or Thomas or anything kin to it."

"How come?"

"How would I know? Maybe he doesn't like the name."

"Well, he's stuck with it."

"Not if he doesn't say so."

"That's the way he is, then?"

"That's the way he is."

"What's he captain of?"

"He was in the Marines in the war."

"Sounds like a real bulldog."

"If God's a bulldog, that's what Culhane is. If you're going up there to snoop around, dance on your tiptoes."

"I'll avoid him."

"He'll know you're there before you do."

"Maybe I should make a courtesy call."

"If he doesn't beat you to it."

"Hell, all I want to know is who's been supporting Verna Wilensky for all those years."

"Read about it in the scandal sheets."

"It's not a hundred miles. I can be back late tomorrow night."

"I suppose you wanna take Agassi up there with you?"

I didn't want to push my luck, so I told him I thought I could handle it alone. "I'm just gonna check a couple of banks and see what they can tell me."

"I suppose you want a car and some play money?"

"That'd be nice. I don't trust my heap for more than twenty miles at a clip."

He sighed, opened his desk drawer, and took out a pad of expense forms and car chits. "Why don't you get rid of that junk pile. Get yourself something decent. Hell, you just got a raise."

"Is that what that was? I thought it was a tip."

"Funny. Hell, you can get a brand-new Pontiac coupe for eight hundred bucks at Nordstrom's showroom over on Welch Avenue. I just saw the ad. Tell 'em you're a cop, maybe they'll give you a break on the price and arrange a little loan."

"Maybe in your world; not the world I live in."

"Christ, what a hard head you got."

I didn't say anything. He glared up at me for a second and shook his head while he scribbled things on the two pads.

"Here's for the car, tell them to fill it up. And you can draw ten bucks for meals. Keep the receipts."

"Gee," I said, looking at the chits, "I may just lam it down to Mexico and retire."

"Send me your address, I'll put you on my Christmas card list."

"Thanks."

"Stay outta trouble up there."

"Don't worry."

"I've heard that line before. I'm still remembering the time you went up to Tahoe to pick up that firebug and ended up in the hoosegow for smacking an undercover cop."

Before I could say anything else, Moriarity shook his head. That meant he was tired of our banter. And tired of me.

"Get outta here," he said. "If you get hung up, there's a fishing camp right on the water about ten miles south of town. A buddy of mine, Charlie Lefton, owns it. Tell him I sent ya."

"Thanks."

"But don't."

"Don't what?"

"Get hung up."

CHAPTER 10

When I left Moriarity's office I checked my mail slot. There was a message from Frank Templeton, the manager of Grauman's Chinese Theater, inviting me to a screening of *The Ziegfeld Girl* on Thursday night. "Screening at 7:30, get there about 7:20. We have a couple of rows ribboned off for big shots, of which I consider you one. Yuk, yuk. Bring a friend. Frankie."

Templeton and I had gone to school together and I occasionally did some after-hours security work for him. My name was on the permanent guest list at the box office.

I sat down at my desk and looked around. Drab would be a compliment. The walls of the big squad room were covered with wanted posters, notices, the assignment board, and an enormous map of the greater L.A. area.

My desk was in the center of the room, surrounded by other desks, all of which looked pretty much alike. On mine were an in- and out-box, with a telephone, a notepad, and a gaudy ashtray from The Oyster Bed in Ventura. There was a typewriter on the stand next to it. The ashtray and a half-finished report in my in-box were its only distinguishing traits. I leaned back in my chair and thought about Millicent Harrington and Zeke Bannon. The picture was pretty bleak.

I could picture the scene: coming home for dinner and her asking me what I did in the office, and me telling her about the fellow who walks up the street after dinner to get a newspaper and a drunk jumps the curb and splatters him against a wall; or the woman who comes home unexpectedly and finds her husband in bed with a neighbor and she, unheard over the sounds of passion, gets his pistol from a drawer and walks back in and kills them both with one shot, through the back of his neck and into her forehead; or the starlet who dreams of being the next Betty Grable and is sleeping her way up the ladder and ends up in Topanga Canyon very naked, very dead, and very pregnant; or the way a man falls when shot dead, not gracefully as in the movies but like his bones have turned to dust and he has collapsed into his own skin.

Oh, by the way, darling, please pass the cream.

But I thought it might be fun for a little while to squire a lady of class around town. What the hell, a security man can always use a beautiful assistant, especially when Tommy Dorsey is providing the mood music.

A movie would be as good a place as any to start.

I called her office. The secretary plugged me through.

"Hi, this is the police calling," I said in my most threatening monotone.

"Hi," she said. "I was just thinking about you."

"Must be a slow day."

She laughed.

"Look," I said. "I hate to call on such short notice but I have an invite to a sneak preview Thursday. I thought you might like to join me."

I waited two seconds for her answer. "Sounds great!" she said with enthusiasm. "What time?"

"We'd have to be there by 7:20, so I thought we could grab a quick bite at a little place I know down the street. Is 5:30 too early?"

"Do you know how to find my place?"

"I'm a cop, remember?" I paused a moment and said, "How *do* I find it?"

Another laugh. The house was on Boxwood Drive, on the south side of Coldwater Canyon.

"Got it," I said. "Five-thirty, then."

"Yes," she said, and hung up.

I hung up, sat for a minute, then broke out in a happy laugh.

A detective named Travers looked back at me. "Geez, you musta got some good news," he said.

"Yeah," I said. "I had five bucks on a nag at Santa Anita and he came in first."

"Oh," Travers said. "I thought maybe you heard your mother-in-law just died."

I called the photo department at the *Times*, got hold of a guy in the darkroom I knew named Jerome, and asked if he could blow up the picture of Wilensky for me.

"I got two speeding tickets hangin' fire over there," he said.

"Not anymore."

"Gimme an hour."

Then I called the coroner's office and asked them if they'd dig up one of Bones's close-ups of Wilensky.

I was down in the garage waiting for them to tank up the company Chevy when Ski found me.

"Thanks," he growled. "Going on a little pleasure trip and you tell the boss you don't need me."

"I didn't think he'd go for two of us taking the ride."

"San Pietro's like the Riviera. The movie stars go up there to play around. Rich boys to play golf and act studly with their girlfriends."

"I got ten bucks for expenses. Maybe I'll run into Clark Gable and treat him to a night on the town."

"Hell, you're not gonna find anything on Wilensky, Zeke. If she had relatives, she woulda left a will."

"I got one of those feelings."

He rolled his eyes. "Sheesh. Every time you get one of your feelings, I end up in the hospital and you get a promotion."

"That happened two years ago. Aren't you ever going to get over it?"

"Nope."

Louie, the garage man, pulled the Chevy up and hopped out. He had washed it; water was dribbling off the running board. "Treat it like a lady, Zeke," he said, tossing me the keys. "She's a cream puff. I altered the radio in her. You can pick up local stations."

"Well," Ski said, "you and your little cream puff have a good time. I got stuck with Gruber for the day. He eats garlic for breakfast. The last time he brushed his teeth, Herbert Hoover was vice president."

"Give him a pack of Dentyne."

"He can't chew gum, his teeth are so rotten they'd fall out."

"Then keep the windows rolled down."

"It don't help. You stop at a light, people on the sidewalk stagger around gasping for breath." He clutched his throat and his mouth bobbed like a fish out of water. I broke up. Ski should have been in the movies.

"I'm going to miss you, partner," I said.

"What about Little Miss Moneybags?"

I shrugged. "Maybe I'll spring for four bits and call her long distance."

"Oh, that'll really impress her. If it ain't folding money, those people toss it out the car window. Loose change bags down their pants."

I laughed. "See ya later, pal."

"Be careful up there. They play rough."

I shrugged. "I'll tell them I'm an insurance man looking to give away some money."

"Oh yeah, they'll really believe *that* story."

CHAPTER 11

It was an easy drive. The traffic was light and after I passed Santa Barbara, the two-laner was almost deserted. Occasionally a truck would rumble past going south with a load of produce, the driver giving me a friendly wave. A yellow Lincoln limo passed me as I was leaving Santa Barbara. The chauffeur was stiff as a mannequin and was hanging on to the wheel as if he was afraid he'd blow out of the car if he let go. Four kids, all of whom looked to be under six, were playing tag in the backseat. One of them looked out the window as they cruised by and stuck her tongue out at me. I smiled at her and she looked as startled as if she had walked in on Mommy and Daddy having a nooner.

I thought a lot about Millie, then my mind went to work, back to the list Jane at the bank had prepared for me. The night before, I had sorted through the bank names on that list. Then on my blackboard I had listed in different colors the ones with the most checks to their credit and, vertically under them, the dates the checks were received. It boiled down to four banks in San Pietro, one in Mendosa, a little town south of San Pietro, and a bunch of banks in nearby towns like San Luis Obispo and Chino. And there was a smattering of other banks: a couple in L.A., a couple in San Diego, one in San Francisco, probably mailed when the sender was on a business trip. Then I rearranged them by dates and ended up with a chart.

A pattern had begun to emerge. No two checks were ever sent from the same bank back-to-back. They were spaced evenly, with the oddball dropping into the mix occasionally. But basically it was Bank A, Bank B, Bank C, Bank D, Bank E, Bank F, and so on. There were seven main feeders and the other three were spaced in here and there.

A check every eight or nine months, not often enough to raise any suspicions at the banks.

Somebody was being very cautious about the five hundred a month. A lot of work went into the plan, somebody was keeping track. Somebody had a little book with all this data neatly written out, the dates probably projected ahead for six months or six years. And it had been going on for at least sixteen years, probably longer than that considering she was four grand ahead when she checked into the West L.A. National and the modest house in the Meadows.

Using cashier's checks and moving from bank to bank was clever. If this was blackmail, the money trail would be almost impossible to follow—unless the blackmailer meticulously kept a list of every check, year after year. If Verna Wilensky had been blackmailing someone all these years and kept such a list, why wasn't it in a safe deposit box somewhere instead of in a desk at home where it would be easy to snatch? Perhaps Verna Wilensky was simply a fastidious record keeper. Clever or meticulous? I wondered which applied to Verna.

One thing was certain, whoever had been paying her five hundred bucks a month for all those years was either rich or corrupt.

Or both.

Five hundred dollars is a lot of money now. It was *really* a lot of money in the heart of the Depression. But the checks came like clockwork on the third of every month.

Why? What did she have on this person, if that's what it was?

I thought about the picture of Verna Wilensky, the one from the newspaper. A dumpy little middle-aged brunette in a cotton dress, staring off-camera with a shy grin. She didn't look like a woman who had done something nearly two decades ago that had kept her in niceties for all these years.

But then, they never do. When I was in Missing Persons I had a case involving a Beverly Hills banker who was as clean as fresh bedsheets: a deacon in the church, beautiful wife, three kids, perfect health, president of the Rotarians, never played around or even flirted with another woman. Mr. Wonderful. His name was Rupert Archman. Archman vanished one day and so did fifty thousand of the bank's dollars. Poof, just like that. Three months went by. Then a car drove in front of a fast-moving freight out in Burbank one afternoon. The driver was welded into the wreckage. We had to check his teeth to determine who he was.

It was Archman. Eventually we traced his footsteps. They started in Reno, where he picked up a naked dancer seventeen years old, took her down to Tijuana, blew the fifty on booze, gambling, and little brown cigarettes, and when he ran out of dough she ran out on him. So he came back to L.A. and drove his car in front of a train. No note, no nothing. He wasn't even wearing his wallet.

I always liked my partner's take on it: "Hey, two months living it up with a seventeen-year-old punch. What else could ever live up to that?"

Why? I had no idea. What did I know? I was twenty-four at that time, three years on the force. You have to be a lot older than that to crawl into somebody's brain and trace its scars with your fingertips. Maybe you never get that old.

Or maybe it was something simpler with Verna. Maybe she had an illegitimate child, couldn't take care of it, and sold it to some rich couple who couldn't have children. It wasn't that unheard of in the early twenties, even less unusual during the Depression. I was hoping it would be an answer like that, something with a little heartbreak attached. A story the sob sisters would give an arm and a leg to get exclusively:

MOTHER WHO SOLD BABY DROWNS IN BIZARRE BATHTUB ACCIDENT

But deep down in my gut I knew better.

A few miles on, I approached a dilapidated roadside fruit stand and pulled off the highway onto the crumbled macadam of the shoulder, its ground-up pieces showering the underbelly of the Chevy like shotgun pellets. The ramshackle stand looked like it had been built from washed-up beach lumber. It was at the bottom of a hill. Rows of orange trees lined the crest. There was a small picnic table beside the stand, with sagging seats and a mildewed beach umbrella that shielded one side of it from the sun. I was attracted by the hand-painted sign that told me I could get fresh orange juice for a nickel. My mouth was dry. I stared over a shelf the width of the shack, covered with oranges the size of melons, at a small, round Mexican woman the color of a pecan nut, who sat forlornly on a rickety stool in a corner of the small shack. She was reading the Spanish edition of a dog-eared paperback with a lurid cover: A well-endowed woman with her dress ripped in shreds was looking saucer-eyed at a large Chicano gent who had either murder or amour on his mind, it was hard to tell which. Behind her were several shelves holding straw baskets of apples, papayas, and some anemic-looking strawberries.

She gave me a smile that revealed two missing teeth in the center of her mouth. I learned quickly from the little woman that five cents was for the small size, indicated by a paper cup she held up that was roughly the dimensions of a Dixie cup. The only other size was big enough to hold a keg of beer. My Spanish was negligible so I took the bigger cup and pointed to a spot about halfway to the top.

"Quanto?" I asked.

"Fi'teen?" she answered, making it a question.

"Sure," I nodded.

She picked five of the prettiest oranges from the shelf, took them to a small table near the back of the shack, sliced them with a machete which she then buried in the side of the table, and started squeezing them; the juice, golden and sweet-smelling, poured into the base of the squeezer, which she then emptied into the cup. I put two dimes on the counter and told her to keep the change.

She had no trouble understanding that. She flashed her toothless smile and returned to her stool and her book.

I took a seat near the end of the picnic table under the umbrella. The juice was warm but sweet as sugarcane and I took it down in small sips, letting it wash the inside of my mouth before swallowing it. I stared up the hill behind the stand as I drank. Near its top, a young woman in a white silk shirt and jodhpurs was riding a black-and-white pinto stallion. Her jet-black hair was tied in a ponytail that snapped in the wind. She knew what she was doing. She traversed part of the hill and then wheeled the horse around as expertly as a cowboy dogging a steer and went at full gallop back the way she had come, leaning forward in the stirrups, her rump barely touching the saddle, like a jockey steaming down the homestretch. Then she pulled him around and trotted over the crest of the hill and vanished into the orange grove.

I was a long way from L.A.

I finished my juice, threw the cup into a battered garbage pail filled with sour-smelling refuse, got in the car, and went on my way.

A mile or two on the other side of Santa Maria, I saw a forest-green sign with bright yellow letters that read SAN PIETRO 2 MILES. I turned onto State Road 7. It was a narrow but well-paved road on the crest of a foothill. Pine trees shouldered up close to the road and hid the ocean from view. About a mile later, the road curved through a draw in the hillside and suddenly San Pietro lay before me. A small sign pointed south to Milltown and Mendosa. I stopped, got out, and leaned against the front fender while I took in the scene that spread out in front of and below me.

It looked as if a fist the size of a mountain had slammed into the foothill that petered out at the sea, forming a secluded bowl where the town sat as though resting in the palm of that giant hand. On three sides, the foothill sloped up for perhaps a mile. The ocean formed the other side of the village.

It was hard to imagine that the peaceful town that lay at the foot of the hill had once been one of the toughest towns in the county. I wondered how the corruption and violence had affected young Culhane, who grew up with such a spectacle representing his future. Why had he come back to a place like that after the war? Was it anger that had motivated him to go nose-to-nose with the lawless element that ran the town? Or was it greed? Was Culhane a product of under-the-table politics? Had he really cleaned up the town? Or had he merely exchanged one form of corruption for another? And was he a keeper of the law? Or was he above it?

Whatever had motivated Culhane, it had worked for the town once known as Eureka. San Pietro was now a town that might have popped off a Norman Rockwell *Saturday Evening Post* cover. The downtown section was twelve blocks long and as many blocks wide. The storefronts were white and trimmed in grays and light blues and reds. At the south end of the town, dominating a low, flat shoulder of the foothill that ran out at the sea, was a large U-shaped hotel. The open side of the U faced the ocean. An Olympic-size swimming pool surrounded by beach umbrellas and cabanas and emerald grass was embraced by the sides of the two-story resort. On the south side of the building were four tennis courts, with canvas panels facing the sea to cut the ocean's wind. Across the street was a large parking lot half-filled with Packards, Maxwells, Caddies, Pierce-Arrows, and a smattering of Rolls-Royces. A Ford or Chevy would have been as out of place in that lot as a three-hundred-pound girl in the Miss California contest.

Separating it from the rest of town was a large public park with a fountain at its center. On one side of the park was a large three-story building built in the Mexican style, with an orange tiled roof and pale yellow walls and a United States flag flying from the spire of the tower that dominated it. Facing it on the other side of the park was a movie house. On the ocean side of the park were the public docks.

Sailboats rocked serenely at its piers. Others were anchored nearby, captained by rugged individuals who preferred anchoring free of land. Farther out in the bay, a white Grebe yacht trimmed with teak drifted idly at anchor. It looked as big as a football field and sat low in the water. I reached in the car pocket, retrieved my binoculars, and focused on the yacht, sweeping the deck slowly from the stern. The brass fittings were buffed and spotless, the hardwood decks glittered in the bright sunlight, the portholes and windows were as immaculate as a Florentine mirror. I moved the glasses a little farther. A woman lay on the large front deck facing the sun, on a beach blanket that would have covered my living room. She was stark naked. A few feet away, a white-haired man in white ducks, canvas shoes, and a red-and-white-striped shirt was sitting with his feet on the rail, drink in hand, staring out to sea as though she didn't exist. I suppose if you can afford a setup like that, you take everything for granted. I hoped I never got that rich

Moving in from the sea and surrounding the village on the north and west were tree-lined streets, where I assumed the common folk lived in pleasant bungalows. Beyond the residential section, the hill rose up sharply. A wide, sweeping ridge swept around the bowl, forming a broad mesa. I was parked on one side. A golf course consumed most of the ridge to the east and north. Facing me, hidden among pines and water oaks, was where the rich obviously lived.

The roofs of mansions peeked above the foliage spotting the hillside as it rose to the crest of the foothill. A two-lane road curved up the side of the hill and vanished into the thick trees. A strip of stores a couple of blocks long wound through the trees and then, a few city blocks farther on, the ridge ended on a cliff overlooking the ocean. A three-story Victorian mansion sat as close to the edge of the cliff as was safe. From it, a narrow road tortured its way along the cliff a mile or so down into the village. It was like Olympus, where the gods of this

sequestered community could look down on the common folk and dic-
tate the mores, morals, and standard of living of mere mortals.

So this was it? A town of maybe two thousand people? A town so
serene and peaceful a lizard sitting in the sun would probably die of
boredom. A town which, like all small towns, probably harbored secrets darker than a pedophile's soul. A town that had nurtured and
reared the man who might become the next governor of the state.

As I was standing there, binoculars in hand, a black Pontiac came
down the road on my side and slowed almost to a stop. The car drifted
past me and a roughneck as big as a billboard gave me a hard stare out
of his one good eye. The other eye was frozen in one position and
stared straight ahead, while the serviceable one stayed on me until the
car was well past. Then it picked up speed again. The license plate
read SP 3 and the attitude told me they were cops. Small-town cops.
Cops with muscle who wrote their own rule books and, for nothing at
all, could give you more grief than a broken back.

Moriarity was right. They knew I was there before I did. It was
time to move on. I rolled down my sleeves, pulled up my tie, put on my
suit jacket and gray fedora, and headed down into Culhane Land.

CHAPTER 12

The road took me down the hill and into town in front of the city park. Up close, the town was just as charming and quaint as it was from afar. It was also eerie. The street gutters were spotless—no leaves, candy wrappers, or cigarette butts. A Mexican smoking a stogie was sitting on a park bench next to a wheeled refuse can with a push broom resting in it, waiting to sweep up anything alien that might hit the pavement.

Down at the city docks, to the delight of a bunch of small children, two bronze fishermen were hauling a large swordfish from the stern of a cabin cruiser. Several older citizens were holding down canvas beach chairs under red-and-white-striped umbrellas that lined the edge of the wharf; some were reading books or dozing, others were gazing out across the bay as if they expected the *Queen Mary* to come steaming into the harbor at any minute. A small arrow-shaped sign with PRIVATE BEACH printed on it was at the edge of the pier pointed northward.

The black block letters on the marquee of the Ritz theater, a two-story adobe building painted bright yellow, advertised *The Road to Zanzibar* with Hope, Crosby, and Lamour, and selected short subjects, "Shows at 3, 7, 9"; and the windowed one-sheets across the face of the theater told me that *The Ziegfeld Girl* and *In the Navy* with Abbott and Costello were coming soon.

It was a warm day, on the muggy side, but a cool breeze wafted across the bay, stirring the eucalyptus trees that spotted the city park and bringing the heat down a couple of degrees. There was a festive air about the place. Red, white, and blue balloons bobbed in the wind from shrubs and park benches; up near the main street men were setting up grills and ice-laden chests. A couple of sandwich boards spotted through the park invited one and all to enjoy hot dogs, soft drinks, and watermelon at a noontime picnic, courtesy of the Culhane for Governor Committee. The word FREE in bright red capital letters adorned the top and bottom of the boards. Culhane was upstaging the Fourth of July by a month.

The spired building facing the theater across the park was the municipal building. The big clock on the facade of the spire told me it was 11:10. The black Pontiac was maybe three blocks behind me. I turned right on the main street, which was called Ocean Boulevard. Quaint. It was paved with cobblestones and the streetlights were old-fashioned gas lamps. After that, the town got kind of creepy, as if George Orwell had come up with the concept and Norman Rockwell had hired the architect so he could do the *Saturday Evening Post* cover.

I was heading north on Ocean Boulevard with the big-money hotel behind me and another park several blocks ahead. The theater and Wendy's Diner filled the block on my left. A pleasant-looking, three-story hotel called the San Pietro Inn was on my right. It also filled the entire block. An old-fashioned bar called Rowdy's Watering Hole held down the north corner of the hotel.

After that and for the next eleven blocks, the street on both sides was a succession of stores, all built hard against each other, varying only slightly in height, width, and color: gray with white trim, pale blue with dark blue trim, green and white, white and green, and so on. There were two basic designs: gabled roof and flat roof. And they came in three sizes: small, medium, and large. They offered everything from a tobacconist and a record store to a jeweler and a restaurant advertising delicious home cooking. In between were a haberdashery, confectionary, shoe store, bookstore, newsstand, deli, pharmacy, soda fountain, children's shoe store; more services than 2,000 people could need or want. And just one of each kind. No competition here, except for restaurants, bars, and banks.

The exceptions to this architectural déjà vu were four banks and the library, each of which were brick and commandeered an entire block. They stood out like mausoleums stand out among tombstones.

The other park formed the northern perimeter of the town. I checked the rearview. Mutt and Jeff were a block behind me. I pulled into the tiny parking lot next to the library and stopped. They stopped. A block away, in the middle of the street. I pulled out and turned left, drove back past them and went to the municipal building, parked by the curb, and went up a half-dozen wide, deep steps into the building.

It was sturdily built, its thick walls holding the heat at bay. A long, wide hallway led straight through the interior. To the right were the D.A.'s office, the judge's sanctuary, and the courtroom. To the left were the police department and city jail. On the second floor were the municipal offices and the council's meeting room.

At the end of the hall on the right was Culhane's office. I decided to play it dumb, as if I had never heard of Culhane or anything else about San Pietro county. I wanted the chance to meet the man and size him up face-to-face.

I went through a glass-paneled door and came head-on to a hefty, pleasant-looking Hispanic woman in a blue police uniform, sitting behind a counter that ran almost the full length of the big room. She had a deputy's badge pinned over an ample breast, was smoking a thin cigarillo, and looked like she could handle herself just fine in any situation. A small nameplate told me her name was Rosalind Hernandez. Behind her in the corner was the switchboard, commandeered by a skinny little white lady in a plain cotton dress, who looked over her shoulder at me with a bored stare of mild disdain.

There was a small gate at the end of the counter and a door on the opposite wall, which I assumed led back to the squad room and jail. Also on the wall were two large, color photographs, one of FDR, the other of the governor, separated by a large American flag, which hung vertically almost to the floor. On the wall to my right a large, round Seth Thomas ticked forlornly as the second hand whiled away the time.

Hernandez looked at me and arched her eyebrows as a way of greeting me. I laid my card in front of her.

She read it, turned it over, turned it back, laid it on the counter, and tapped it with a finger.

"What can I do for you, Sergeant?" she asked with authority.

"Is the sheriff available?" I asked with a smile.

"No, sir," she said. "And he goes by captain, not sheriff. Captain Culhane." She said it in her official tone, without a trace of an accent. She looked up at the clock. "I expect he'll come back about five to twelve and make a pass at the gent's before he goes out to greet the voters."

"In that case I'll just wait over at the picnic," I said. "Would you give him my card? Tell him I need a word or two with him?"

She looked at a blue-covered log book, traced down the entries with a finger, and said, "No appointment?"

"Afraid not," I said.

She gave me another once-over and nodded. "I'll tell him."

"Thank you. I'll catch up with him at the picnic."

"Good luck on that," she said, and settled back to listen to the clock tick.

I drove back to the other end of town to the Pacific National Bank. The list Millicent's mousy assistant had prepared for me told me that Ben Gorman was president and manager. There was a large parking lot behind the bank. A black 1933 Pierce-Arrow limousine was parked near a rear entrance, and the chauffeur was leaning against the wall beside the door, having a smoke. I got out and went around to the front door. There was a plaque beside the twin eight-foot, brass-trimmed doors that told me: FOUNDED BY ELIJAH GORMAN, EUREKA, CALIFORNIA, 1895.

When I entered the bank, I looked down the length of the main room to what seemed to be the big shot's office. It was on the left, a corner office about the size of Soldier's Field. A secretary was seated at a walnut desk, talking into a cradle phone. A tall, slender-faced man in a checked jacket was framed in the half-open door behind her, talking to someone I couldn't see. He looked at me as I came in and pushed the door shut. I walked back to the secretary's desk and she cupped her hand over the mouthpiece.

"Can I help you?" she asked, trying to be pleasant and not doing very well at it.

"Mr. Gorman, please."

"He's gone for the day."

"Really? It's not even noon yet."

"It's Wednesday," she snapped at me. "And Mr. Gorman's business is none of yours. He can leave anytime he wishes to. As you can see, I'm on the phone. Excuse me."

I wanted to barge past her and kick open the door like Cagney might do, but instead I nodded and went back the way I came. I went around the back to my car, got in, slumped down behind the wheel, and rolled a cigarette.

The Pierce-Arrow driver finished his smoke and ditched his cigarette in a red pail filled with sand. Five minutes passed. Ten minutes.
Then the back door opened. The driver bounced smartly over to the
sedan and opened the door for the same tall, hawk-faced man I had
seen in the bank. He was over six feet, with jet-black hair streaked with
gray, and was smartly dressed in a black-and-yellow-checked sports
coat, dark gray pants, and what appeared to be riding boots. He
jumped in. As they pulled out of the lot I checked the tag. BG1.

I left the lot by the rear driveway onto Presidio Drive, a short
street between Ocean Boulevard and the waterfront. In the rearview
mirror, I saw the black Pontiac ease from behind a parked car and drop
in behind me. I decided to play a little game with my shadows. I drove
past the rear of the First Bank and Trust of San Pietro, turned left onto
Ocean, doubled back the way I had come, passed the bank, and turned
down an alley next to it. I parked, went in the bank, stood inside the
door, and watched the Pontiac park on the other side of the street.

According to my list, the head knocker here was Andrew McBurney. This time I showed my credentials to a small, blond woman with a
toothy smile and a pleasant attitude who looked to be in her late twenties. She was chewing gum.

"My name's Bannon," I said, matching her smile. "I'd like a word
with Mr. McBurney, please."

"Sure," she said. She went to the office door, stuck her nose in the
door and said, "Mr. McBurney, there's a Sergeant Bannon from the
Los Angeles Police Department to see you." I heard a muffled answer,
and she turned back to me and swung the door wide.

It was a large gloomy office. All dark wood. Shades pulled halfway
down. A dismal lamp on the corner of the desk in a puddle of light. The
parquet floors, which had been beautiful once, were scarred and pitted
as if someone had worked them over with a jackhammer.

McBurney was a short, almost bald, little Scotsman with a built-in
scowl and ashen skin littered with liver spots. He was wearing a knit
shirt open at the throat. His desk was a massive walnut antique that
came up to his chest. The rest of him protruded from its top like the
clown in a jack-in-the-box. I offered him my hand, which he took without standing and waved a hand toward a chair.

"Alright, what is it?" he asked in a no-nonsense tone.

I gave him the Verna Hicks Wilensky spiel, from the radio in the bathtub to the fact that she was intestate. He listened with a bored expression and about halfway through my presentation started drumming his fingers on the desk. Then I laid out the part about the cashier's checks. Then I sat back and waited for a response.

"That's it, that's what you're taking up my time about?" he said. "The woman's a fool, dying without a will. And you know better than to ask something like that," his voice now hissing like a snake. "Cashier's checks are confidential. It's the bank's sacred trust not to share them with anyone. If I *could*, I wouldn't show them to you. None of your goddamned business. But I *can't* show them to you, Mr. whatever-your-name-is from the Los Angeles Police Department. It's against the law. You should know that if you are who you say you are."

I felt my blood rising. I took out my wallet, opened it, and, leaning over the desk, put it in front of him.

"I am Sergeant Bannon of the L.A.P.D., sir," I said. "I was hoping we could finesse the state tax boys. I'm looking for a name, that's all. The last check from this bank was dated two months ago. Certainly it wouldn't be that hard to find."

"Are you deaf?" he said, his voice rising. "I said I wouldn't if I could. And I am not in the habit of finessing the state tax people. Commissioner Weatherly is a personal friend of mine. I certainly do not want to jeopardize our friendship—and violate the law."

He slid the wallet back across the desk to me.

"Out," he growled. He stood up. He was no more than five feet four and was wearing lime-green golf knickers, bright red kneesocks, and cleated golf shoes. He stormed past me, the shoes digging new wounds in the inlaid floor, and flung the door open.

"OUT!"

I got up and left the office, and the door slammed at my back.

The little blond secretary stared at me open-mouthed.

"Guess he doesn't want to go to the policeman's ball," I said.

"It's Wednesday," she said apologetically.

"That's what Gorman's secretary said. So what?"

"All the banks close on Wednesday at noon." She looked at her watch. "Which is in two minutes. The big shots play golf."

"Well, that shoots down a long trip," I said.

"I'm truly sorry," she offered.

"You're sweet," I said, and asked, "Is there a back door? I'm going down to the pier, save me some walking."

"Follow me," she said. "It's the least I can do."

She led me down a short hallway and opened the door for me.

"Sorry you wasted your day," she said. "If you stay over, come back tomorrow, maybe he'll be in a brighter mood."

"Anybody who wears golf shoes on a floor like that will never be in a bright mood," I said, and thanked her.

I stepped into the alley next to the bank, left my car on the opposite side of the building, walked rapidly down to Presidio, and headed for the park. When I got there, I mingled with the crowd and kept an eye out for my two shadows. They didn't show. I got myself a hot dog, slathered it with mustard and onions, picked up a Coke, then sat down on a bench to enjoy the free lunch and wait for the captain to make his appearance.

At 12:02, a maroon Packard Super-Eight touring car drove up on Ocean Boulevard, turned into the street in front of the municipal building, and parked. A hard-looking guy with short-cut brown hair and a built-in frown got out of the driver's seat and strolled around the car— a guy who was a stranger to a smile. Before he could get to the back door it popped open, and I got my first live look at Thomas Brodie Culhane.

He was about my height, five-ten and change, broad-shouldered, with a waist that a Gibson girl would die for. A hundred and seventy pounds, no fat, shaggy eyebrows over pale blue eyes, short-cut brown hair that a lot of sun had lightened, bronze skin over a craggy face, and a square jaw with hard muscles bunched up under his ears. He was wearing a three-piece blue gabardine suit. He peeled off his jacket, tossed it in the backseat of the car, and rolled the sleeves of his white shirt about halfway to the elbows. Then he pulled his tie knot down six inches and took it off over his head without untying it, and let it join the jacket. A gold watch fob arched from one side of his vest to the other. When he was stripped for action the driver handed him a freshly rolled cigarette, and Culhane lit it with a wooden match, which he fired with his thumb. He was wearing his shield on his belt. No gun.

He was followed by a taller man, a little beefy but not soft, with white hair and a wary, expressionless face. He wore a white linen suit with a dark blue shirt open at the collar. He fell in behind Culhane and alongside the unsmiling driver.

There was a crowd of about one hundred and fifty people already gathered, and they stood stone-still while Culhane arranged himself. Then he waved and the crowd broke into the kind of whoop-up you expect when the home team scores a winning touchdown against its archrival. Down near the pier, what I assumed was the high school band struck up "Hail, Hail, the Gang's All Here." They were awful. But nobody was complaining. Culhane walked across the street to the park and the crowd closed around him like water filling in behind a diver's splash. They were waving hand-painted signs: CULHANE FOR GOVERNOR, CAPTAIN TO THE CAPITOL, things like that. Several were waving American flags.

I remembered what Moriarity had said. *Joan of Arc with a pecker.* He was right about that. It was a festive occasion for a man whose life had been spent as the sheriff of a county that would fit in my glove compartment and who was getting ready to take on a couple of machine politicians who probably owned most of the state legislators in Sacramento.

He strode casually through the crowd, most of whom he obviously knew, calling kids by name, roughing up their hair, hugging the women, and shaking hands with the men. He walked in an easy lope with a touch of swagger to it. A man in control, self-assured, and cut in the heroic mold.

I stayed seated, watching his trek through the crowd. I finished my hot dog and started to roll a cigarette. That was when he saw me. He looked through the crowd and his eyes locked on me. The smile never left his lips but the eyes changed from a kind of mischievous delight to blue ice cubes. I stood up, leaned against a Monterey pine, and waited for him to come by.

It took him fifteen minutes to get there. He veered from one side of the park to the other, strolling easily through his fans and flicking a glance my way every so often. I didn't move. I let him come to me.

CHAPTER 13

I watched Culhane work his way toward me through the crowd. He didn't look directly at me but I could tell I was fixed in his peripheral vision. He took his time closing in on me, like a snake toying with a rabbit. When he was ten feet away and still greeting his fans, I took out a wooden match as he had done and snapped it with my thumb to light my cigarette. The match broke and the top half blew away in the wind. Culhane turned and looked at me, took a match out of his vest pocket, walked over to me, snapped it afire, and cupped it against the wind.

"Allow me," he said.

"Thanks," I said, taking the light.

"I presume you're Bannon."

"Zeke Bannon," I said, and held out my hand. He had a handshake like a gorilla's.

"Brodie Culhane," he said. "Call me Captain." He had a relaxed smile. If something was bothering him he didn't show it. He was a very cool customer and I was beginning to understand why the mere mention of his name perked up so many ears. He was in complete control of his environment and he was comfortable with that power. This was a guy who had brushed off fear in all its forms a long time ago.

"You got my card, then?" I said.

"And I'm dying of curiosity." He rested a hand on the shoulder of the big fellow in the white suit. "This is our ex-D.A., Brett Merrill," he said, and jerked a thumb toward the driver, "and my right-hand man, Rusty Danzig."

He took my elbow and led me to the edge of the park, out of the crowd.

"So, what can I do for you, Sergeant?" he said when we were near the street and sheltered under a big water oak. Merrill stood nearby being as innocuous as a big man can be. Danzig patrolled the perimeter of our spot in the shade like a watchdog.

"I guess you could say I'm up here on a mission of mercy."

"Oh?" he said lazily, while smiling at someone passing by. "That's stalwart of you."

"You wouldn't happen to know a woman named Verna Hicks, would you? Her married name's Wilensky. Probably left here in the mid twenties. I was hoping to find a parent or family of some kind."

He stared at me, almost bemused.

"That's twenty years ago, more or less."

"Right."

"I take a great deal of pride in knowing everybody in this domain," he said. "But I am at an age where fifteen years ago might as well be the turn of the century." He turned to Merrill. "Name ring a bell to you, Doc? I don't think we have anyone named Hicks in town."

Merrill pondered a minute and shook his head. "I don't recall anyone named Hicks ever living here."

"What did she do?" Culhane asked.

"She got dead."

That held his attention.

"Was she murdered?"

"What gave you that idea?"

"Your card. Bannon, central homicide . . ."

"Of course, right," I said, rolling my eyes in embarrassment. "No, she slipped getting out of the bathtub and pulled her radio in on top of her."

"My God," Merrill said.

"Christ, what a way to go," Culhane said, showing a modicum of concern. "How old a woman was she?"

"Her license says forty-seven."

"You sound like you don't believe that."

I smiled. "Well, you know how women are about their age."

He chuckled but said nothing. I could almost hear the cogs whirring behind his eyes. He knew there was more coming. He was waiting for the stinger.

"There's a wrinkle to the story," I said.

"Isn't there always?"

"She died without a will and left a sizable estate. No survivors, no letters, nothing to indicate anything about her prior to 1924."

"What happened in 1924?"

"She moved to L.A. Here's the wrinkle: She worked in the tax assessor's office making forty bucks a week. But she bought her house with cash. Her car, which is a two-year-old DeSoto, and several other cars before it, were all paid for with cash. And she had ninety-eight-plus grand in a savings account."

He whistled low through his teeth.

"So what brings you up here?" he said, and turned and knelt to give a kid his autograph.

"The ninety-eight large. Since 1924 she's been getting five bills a month in the form of cashier's checks. A good many of those checks came from the banks here."

He didn't look up immediately. He gave the kid back his pen and stood up slowly. The blue eyes narrowed.

"I figure if we can get copies of one or two of the checks and look for the sender's name, maybe we'll find someone that'll stand for a decent funeral or hire a lawyer to try and nix the state out of her inheritance."

Nothing changed in his face. The blue eyes just stared at me. No response.

"That sounds like a missing person's dodge," he said after a minute crawled by. "How come a homicide cop is doing that kind of work?"

"I caught the case as I was leaving for the day," I said. "My boss gave me a day or two to see if I could turn up anybody. He doesn't like the tax boys any more than I do."

"And your boss is who?"

"Lieutenant Moriarity. Dan Moriarity."

"I may have heard that name," he said matter-of-factly.

"Why here?" Merrill asked.

"Because most of the cashier's checks came from the four banks here. I was hoping you might grease some rails for me. One of the bankers threw me out of his office and the other one bluffed me out."

"McBurney called and screamed about you wanting some kind of confidential info, but he's a gruff old bastard. He's eighty-one and Scottish through and through. He saves minutes in a glass jar under his desk."

It was a nice play. He was letting me know that McBurney and probably Ben Gorman had already checked in, as well as the two comics in the Pontiac. Having said it, he changed the subject.

"What do you think of our little town?" he said pleasantly.

"Very interesting," I said. "Looks like a Norman Rockwell painting."

"Like Rockwell, do you?"

"He's a little too cute for my taste."

"What is your taste, Sergeant?"

"I'm a van Gogh man."

"Ah, so you like the new guys. I prefer the old-timers. I like Rembrandt."

"I'm younger than you are, I never met him."

He was enjoying the patter, like a dueler tapping épées with an opponent before the match gets serious.

"About the banks . . ." I started.

"Sorry," Culhane said. "I can't help you with that."

"It's against the law," Merrill interceded in a pleasant voice with a touch of the Southeast in it. "You'd need a judge's order."

"And why bother?" Culhane said. "Seems to me if somebody went to all that trouble not to be found, somebody doesn't want to be found. Just an observation."

"Because the way it looks now, her dog, the next-door neighbors, and I are the only ones who'll be there to drop a rose on her grave."

"Had a dog, huh? What happened to it?"

"He's probably sleeping under the yucca plant in my backyard."

He gave me a slow, knowing look. His lips parted in a grin. "You got a soft streak, Bannon. Better watch it; in our business that can get you killed."

"A guy could make a threat out of that," I said, smiling back.

"Nah, not a chance, not in this town," he said. "We watch over our visiting firemen."

"That why those two heavyweights have been on my tail since I got here?"

"You noticed them, huh?"

"Well, they could have been a little more obvious. One of them could have stuck his thumb in my eye."

"The boys don't get much practice. There's not much call for tail jobs in San Pietro," he said casually.

"I'm just trying to finish off the lady's days with a little class," I said, getting back to the subject again.

"Sure you are," he said. "You're not at all interested in who's been slipping her five C's a month and why, are you?"

I ignored the jibe.

"So you don't know who she is—or was?"

"I never heard that name before you mentioned it."

"Maybe you knew her under another name."

"That's possible, but if I did I wouldn't know it, now would I?"

"Well, Captain, somebody up here knew her real well."

He gave me a long, hard stare.

"You think she was blackmailing somebody," he drawled. It was not a question.

"It's an option."

"An option that doesn't concern me."

"A majority of those checks came from the four banks here in San Pietro."

"Coincidence," he said.

"I don't believe in coincidence."

He fell silent again. His eyes never left mine. Then an ironic smile crossed his lips.

"You really expect me to fall for that crap about poor little whoever not getting a decent send-off?" he said. "You're up here sniffing around and annoying some substantial citizens and you haven't got dip. When that radio cooked her, school was out. Who the hell cares what went on before? Even if she was grifting somebody, it's immaterial now. The point is, the lady's dead and whatever there was, if there was anything to start with, died with her. You're acting a little like a goddamn tenderfoot. Or . . ." he paused a minute and raised his eyebrows until his forehead wrinkled. "Or maybe there's something else going on in that noggin of yours."

I could feel the muscles in my face tightening up. He was goading me. I backed off and let my pulse slow down.

"I told you what was going on," I said, perhaps a little too softly.

"I know what you said," he answered. He put his hands in his back pockets, with the thumbs pointing down. He very slowly paced up and down in front of me. "But you could be from Osterfelt's camp or Bellini's, up here nosing around to see if you can stir up a little dirt on me. Or maybe you're planning your own little grift? Find out who was sending those checks and become the new beneficiary. See what I mean?"

"She deserves a little decency," I said quietly. "I don't give a damn if it's the President of the United States; whoever was sending her that money knows her and that somebody ought to be told."

"And you want to do the telling."

"It's my case. It's my responsibility."

He stopped pacing and just stared at me.

"Look," I said, "maybe you could prevail on one of your banker pals to look it up and pass it on to the proper individual. You can leave me out of it."

"It's against the law for the banks to do that," Merrill said. "It's confidential information protected by state law."

"Then I guess I'll have to locate the judge and seek a subpoena," I said. "What's his name again?"

Culhane said, "I wouldn't bother. Gus Wainwright's got bad breath, a bad heart, the gout, and his brain's missing about half its gray matter."

"Actually," Merrill said, "the banks are federal now. You need a United States judge."

"All for a dog and a coffin," Culhane said, shaking his head.

"I guess the nearest judge would be Homer Jennings over in Santa Maria," I said. "He's usually cooperative with the police."

Culhane's face changed an iota. The eyes, which had softened up a bit, went dead again. The muscles in his jaw tightened and loosened.

"There's nothing you can learn in San Pietro," he said sharply.

"I've got a job to do, Captain. I'm going to keep at it."

"You do what you have to do, Sergeant Bannon," he said. "I've got constituents to talk to. Have a nice trip back to Los Angeles."

He turned and went about his business.

I looked at my feet as if expecting to see the gauntlet he had just thrown down, but there was nothing underfoot except the emerald grass.

CHAPTER 14

I watched him stroll away, working the crowd, then I walked around the corner to Wendy's Diner and had a grilled-cheese-and-bacon sandwich and an egg cream. My two friends appeared out of nowhere and parked across the street.

While I was eating, I pondered the discussion with Culhane. He knew who I was, knew I'd been to see the little Scot, probably had talked to Gorman. Now he knew why I was there and he didn't believe the funeral story for a minute. He was a hard-boiled egg covered with sweet chocolate and he had just given me my walking papers.

I was also thinking about the events that coincided with Verna Hicks's departure from San Pietro, if indeed she had ever been here. I didn't have a thing. All I really knew was that Buck Tallman had been killed two or three years before Verna Hicks had shown up in L.A. Hard to make a connection there. Maybe Moriarity was right. Maybe I was spinning my wheels.

I decided to take one more shot. I walked down Ocean Boulevard and found the office of the *San Pietro Sentinel*, a narrow little building painted a pale yellow, with a gabled roof. There was a counter inside the front door and behind it a hot-metal typesetter, trays of fonts, and two desks littered with copy and notes, some of which had blown to the floor, prompted by a desktop Diehl fan that revolved in a half-circle aimed at the business end of the room.

A man in his late thirties, wearing gray work pants, a red-striped shirt, and a solid-blue bow tie, was working at the keyboard of the typesetter. He had a boyish face betrayed by thinning, light brown hair that grew to a widow's peak over watery eyes behind tortoiseshell glasses. He lowered his jaw and peered at me over the rims as I entered the office.

"Yes?" he said.

"You the editor?"

He nodded. "Charlie Goodshorn; what's your pleasure?" He had a friendly but high-pitched voice that sounded like it had never changed.

I showed him my badge. "I'm doing a little background work," I said. "I was wondering if I might check your morgue for a span of two years or so, back in the mid twenties."

He went back to work on his typesetting and said, "Sorry, sir, that wouldn't be possible. I'd be glad to help you but I can't." He jerked his thumb over his shoulder. "See that scorch mark down the wall?"

There was a jagged streak down the wall the color of hot chocolate, with arteries spreading out to the left and right of it.

"Lightning hit us hard four years ago. We saved this side of the office, but the building next door took a beating. What wasn't burned was so waterlogged we had to throw everything away. All our files and back issues were lost."

He finished what he was working on and spun around on his stool and leaned forward, hands on his knees.

"Was it something in particular?" he asked.

"How long have you been editor?" I asked.

"Since my dad died in 1933. I was working for the *Denver Post*. Really liked Denver but somebody had to take over the business."

"You a weekly?"

"We went to five days a week two years ago."

"Is it working for you?"

"Doing okay."

"Glad to hear it. I was interested in the Buck Tallman shooting. You weren't working here then, were you?"

He chuckled. "I was delivering papers back then. I know about the event but what I remember you could put in a thimble."

Another bust. I thanked him and started out the door.

"Tell you somebody who might give you a hand on that."

"Who would that be?"

"Barney Howland. He wrote for the paper for years and also shot pictures. He likes a taste every now and then, but when he's sober he has quite a memory. Likes to talk, too."

"How would I find him?"

"He's on Third Avenue just off February."

"February's a street?"

Goodshorn laughed. "The streets are named for the months of the year," he said. "Twelve streets, twelve months. Easy to remember."

"Thanks, Mr. Goodshorn."

"Want me to give him a call, see if he's in and willing to stand for an interview?"

"That would be a help."

He had an old-fashioned stand-up phone and he pulled it over, lifted the receiver and dialed a number, and waited for a moment or two. "Gladys? It's Charlie down at the *Sentinel* . . . Just fine, thank you, and you? . . . That's just wonderful. Is Barney about? Would you please tell him there's a gentleman here from the Los Angeles police who would like a word with him? Uh-huh. Alright, I'll send him on over. His name is . . ." He looked at me and raised his eyebrows.

"Zeke Bannon."

"Mr. Bannon. Thanks, dear." He hung up and said, "He's waiting for you."

"I appreciate that, Charlie."

"My pleasure," he said with a smile.

For a newspaperman, he had a remarkable lack of curiosity.

I left the news office, walked half a block to a drugstore, and invested six bits in a pint of Jack Daniel's Black Label. Then I crossed the street, walked down to the bank, and retrieved my car. There was no profit to be made trying to dodge my two shadows, so I started the car and waited until they drifted down past the bank. Then I pulled away and circled the block and pulled in behind them. I tailed them for ten or fifteen minutes as they tried to figure out how to get behind me again. Finally they pulled over and stopped. I pulled over and stopped. We sat for a while. I rolled a cigarette and lit up. I watched them, through their rear window, discussing the situation.

They decided to make their move. The Pontiac suddenly lurched ahead past the library and screamed around the corner to the right. I pulled up to the edge of the library and watched them through the trees. They drove up beside the park and turned right again at the next street. I gave them thirty seconds and then followed, pulled slowly

down to the street they had turned into, and looked. They were turning back to the right, circling the block. I went straight ahead and
turned left at the next street. I was on Third. I drove as hard as I could
without endangering anyone. The next cross street was February.

I slowed down and stopped at the third house, a pleasant, one-
story, wood-frame bungalow tucked into the quiet street three blocks
off Ocean Boulevard. A black Olds that had seen better days was
parked in the driveway, and a large collie lay in the front yard, sleeping
in the shade of the oak tree it was leashed to. I went to the front door,
and seeing no bell, opened the screen door and knocked on the glass.
A moment later the door was opened by a pleasant little woman. She
looked to be in her sixties with skin leathered by the sun and gray
locks bunched in a hairnet.

"Mrs. Howland?"

"Yes; are you the gentleman from Los Angeles?"

I showed her my credentials. "I'm Bannon from the L.A. Police Department. Mr. Goodshorn called about me."

"Is something wrong?" she said, stepping back and swinging the
door wide.

"No," I said, entering the foyer. "I'm working on a civil case involving a woman who may have lived here at one time."

"Oh my, I rather doubt it. We've been in this house since before
the war."

"No, not here in this house, in San Pietro."

She bunched up her shoulders and giggled. "How silly of me. It's
this way." She led me down a narrow hall to a basement door, opened
it, and called out, "Barnard, someone to see you."

"Who is it?" he yelled back.

"A gentleman from the police in Los Angeles," she answered, pro-
nouncing Angeles with a hard *g*.

"Well, show him down, Gladys," Howland answered in a gruff
voice. "I'm not gonna come up there and carry him down."

She nodded down a tight wooden staircase to the cellar, which was
dark and smelled of mildew. Barnard Howland was sitting in a far corner, in a makeshift office. A desk, two chairs, a typing stand supporting
an old, upright Royal, and half a dozen file cabinets lined up against the
wall. A single light hung from the ceiling over the desk. A small, ob-
long window provided the only other light. Howland was a small man

tucked into a wasted frame. The loose flesh of his face was creased by the years, and strands of white hair hung from under a green eyeshade pulled down over his forehead. I guessed he had been a handsome man in earlier years, but time and booze had eroded his looks and now he just looked like a crotchety old curmudgeon. He was wearing a shapeless pair of wool tweeds, a white shirt buttoned to the top, no tie, and a vest that was hanging open. He peered up at me through indolent, brown eyes over the top of a pair of wire-rimmed half-glasses that had slid halfway down his nose.

"Barney Howland," he said in a cracked and rheumy voice, and offered me a hand that trembled slightly. "Pardon me for not getting up. At my age, I'd rather not use up that much energy for formalities."

"Zeke Bannon," I said with my friendliest smile, and showed him my credentials. He pulled my wallet a little closer and stared at it through the glasses.

"Sergeant, eh? Homicide yet. Well." His eyes brightened a bit, and he straightened up slightly and waved me to the other chair. "What's goin' on? We don't have many homicides up here anymore, not since the good old days. Now it's silly stuff, y'know. Wives hitting their husbands over the head with a skillet for fartin' at the dinner table." He leaned forward and said with confidentiality, "A love-nest slaying occasionally. Wrong shoes under the bed; know what I mean?" He winked.

"It does seem like a well-mannered town," I said.

"Well-mannered," he sniffed contemptuously. "I like that. Hell, you can get a ticket for not cutting the goddamn lawn often enough. Now back in the twenties when it was Eureka, it was one hell of a place. Wide-open gambling, whores wiggling their little asses up and down Ocean Boulevard, loan sharks, bookies, bad boys running the town. Hell, we had a shooting a week, sometimes a couple. It was like Dodge City, for crissakes. Ever hear of Buck Tallman? Deputy for Wyatt Earp back when the West was the West. He was our sheriff. Wore a gun belt down on his hip with a .44 Peacemaker, a Stetson with sweat stains around the brim. Hah, now there was a real man. Nobody screwed with old Buck. Why, it took four two-bit gangsters to bring him down and all four went down with him."

As he spoke, my eyes grew accustomed to the limited light. Behind him on the wall were several framed *Sentinel* front pages, streaked and yellowed with age.

"I've heard about him," I said. "Wasn't he killed in the Grand View House massacre?"

"Heard about that, have ya?" He puffed out his chest as much as he could, and jerked a thumb over his shoulder at the framed mementos. "That was my story. I covered all the good ones. Shot my own pictures, too. Had a darkroom back there behind the furnace. There's my old four-by-five." He pointed to a battered Speed Graphic sitting on a Coca-Cola crate in the corner. "Old Snapper never failed me."

I got up, walked over to the framed pages, and strained my eyes to read them. The old man stood up and swung the light toward the wall. There were three of them.

The lamp threw a slash of light across the yellowed front page of one of the papers. A teaser line said: A TRAGEDY AT GRAND VIEW.

Under it, the headline: SHERIFF TALLMAN, DEPUTY, SLAIN IN GUNFIGHT.

And under it, the subhead: FOUR MOBSTERS ALSO DIE IN HAIL OF LEAD.

A four-column photograph accompanied the story, showing hospital attendants wheeling a sheeted body from the Victorian mansion; and beside it, a two-column vertical shot of the slain lawman.

On the other side, a three-column story headlined:

SACCO AND VANZETTI
GUILTY OF MURDER

Under it, another story about an auto wreck and some other stories.

The photo of Tallman showed him hands on hips, handlebar mustache accenting a hawk nose, tight belly cinched in by the gun belt slung from his hip, cowboy boots adding two inches to his height. He looked every bit the photos and drawings of gunfighters I had pored over in dime novels when I was a kid.

"So that's Buck Tallman," I said.

"Every inch a man," Howland said in his creaky voice. "Loved the ladies, loved children, hated the black hats. Every Fourth of July he'd have a showdown on the beach. Quick-drawing, keeping tin cans hopping in the air. The kids'd crowd around him getting autographs, and he with that smile would make flowers bloom. Hell, I still miss him after all these years."

"That was what year, the year of the shooting?"

"September of 1920."

"Culhane was involved in that, wasn't he?"

"Got in at the end of it. Him and Buck shot the last one down and then Buck fell dead."

I went back to my chair, took out the pint of Jack Daniel's, and put it on the desk in front of him. His eyes got young for a moment. He chuckled, and stared at the bottle.

"You must be psychic."

"I never knew a good newshound who didn't appreciate a taste now and then," I said.

He looked at me and his eyes narrowed a hair.

"So what is it you want?"

"I want to know what wasn't in the papers."

"You're not working for one of those crooks running against Brodie, are you, son? Looking under beds and what have you?"

"No, sir. I'm trying to get a line on a woman named Verna Hicks, who may have lived here back in the twenties."

"What for?"

"She died night before last. Slipped getting out of the bathtub and her radio fell in with her and cooked her. I'm trying to locate a relative or somebody who might have known her. She was a widow, no kids."

"So why do you want to know about Grand View?"

"You shook my curiosity. You know cops, we just naturally want to know the backside of the story."

He turned the bottle of Jack Daniel's slightly so he could read the label, and studied it with the kind of affection one usually associates with a grandfather looking at his granddaughter for the first time. His tongue swept his lower lip. He opened the bottom drawer of his desk and took out two old-fashioned glasses. They were dusty, with streaks of dried amber on the bottom.

"Hope you don't mind a dirty glass," he said. "My wife's temperance. Be chancy taking them up to the kitchen to wash them."

"I'm sure old Jack'll kill anything that might be lurking in those two glasses."

He worked the top off the bottle, splashed a generous slug in both glasses, and slid one across the desk to me.

"Here's to Bucky," he said, offering his glass. I clinked it and took a sip, trying to avoid a dead fly that floated to the top. Howland took a long whiff of the whiskey, then drained half his glass and let it linger in his mouth for a few seconds and pursed his lips before swallowing it, then leaned his head back, stared at the ceiling, closed his eyes, said, "godamighty damn," and sighed passionately. He sat back up, stared at the half-full glass, nodded slowly, and said with awe, "The hell with you, Seagram's Seven."

He put the top back on the bottle and slid it to me.

"It's yours," I said.

His smile was all the thanks I needed. He opened the bottom drawer and slid the bottle under a telephone book.

"What was that lady's name again?" he asked.

"Her married name was Verna Wilensky. You might have known her as Verna Hicks. Would have been in her mid twenties in 1920. Brown hair, little on the plump side, five-two or five-three. Probably good with numbers; she was in the tax assessor's office down in L.A."

I took out the two pictures and showed them to him. The blown-up shot from the newspaper was too grainy and unfocused to be of much use, and the shot from Bones's lab was grotesque at best. He took a look and then stared at me. "I couldn't recognize my mother from these," he said. "That's a long time ago, son."

He took the phone book out, flicked through the pages to the *h*'s, and ran his finger down the page. "No Hicks listed. And the name doesn't ring a bell."

"It narrows the field to none."

His laugh turned into a cough. He took out a handkerchief and wiped his mouth. "So you wanna know about that night at Grand View, huh? Well, Bucky was sheriff and Brodie was his chief deputy. Bucky and Culhane were good friends. Brodie was a hero in the big war. I think he was born about 1882 or '83, thereabouts, so he was in his thirties. Bucky was probably sixty although nobody but Buck knew how old he really was. Older'n God.

"Like I said before, the town was wide open back then. Through the years, all the action had attracted the bad element. Arnie Riker ran the criminal side of things. His sidekick was Tony Fontonio. Both of them nasty to the core. Culhane was for facing-off with them, running them out of town; but Bucky was more the live-and-let-live kind. He figured you keep your finger on them, slap 'em in the cooler if they got out of hand, things'd be alright. See, a lot of people were making money off the trade, and Bucky, he had worked the law in places like Tombstone and Silver City. Hell, he was used to dealing with gunslingers, rustlers, back shooters; Riker was a pansy in his book."

He rambled on, about how Bucky and Culhane controlled the bootlegging to make sure the town got decent hooch during Prohibition; how Culhane hated Riker and Fontonio with a passion; how Riker walked a thin line to keep on the good side of Buck Tallman.

"The trouble came when Riker decided to take a cut of the Grand View House action. You been up there?"

I shook my head.

"Delilah O'Dell owns it. It was in her family. Delilah went to Europe, to the best schools, had it in gold. Then Shamus and Kate O'Dell went down on the *Lusitania*. Delilah was always a heller. Favored her father in that respect. She came back and opened up a fancy house. I guess you knew that."

"I heard."

He took a sip of whiskey, savored it for a minute, and went on.

"A *very* fancy house. Movie stars came up there, still do. Tom Mix and Buck Jones were regulars. I hear Clark Gable, Gary Cooper, Errol Flynn, David Niven, all that bunch still come up for a breather between pictures. There's a little gambling parlor on the first floor in the back. Poker pots can run as high as a thousand bucks. Delilah runs it like it's the Ritz. Beautiful women, great food, the best of everything. Some of our leading citizens occasionally slipped through the side door. And still do."

He stopped and laughed. "Delilah could own this town if she ever threatened to write a book," he said around a chuckle. "But she's a classy lady. Would never happen."

"So what happened that night?"

"It was never proved, but the story went that Riker decided to make a major play. He brings in four tough gunmen headed by a real dangerous hooligan named McGurk, and they go up to Grand View to tell Delilah she has to kick a percentage back to Riker."

"Riker?" I said. "He's the one got gas for a murder?"

"Yeah, a year or so later. So anyway, Bucky is upstairs in Delilah's apartment having a coffee, which he usually does during the evening. His deputy, Andy Sloan, is downstairs, keeping an eye on things, when they come in. Delilah comes to the head of the stairs and wants to know what's going on, and McGurk tells her to come down and talk. At that point, Bucky enters the picture. He goes down the stairs and gets nose-to-nose with one of McGurk's boys. I think his name was Red something-or-other, and Buck tells him where to go and how to get there. There's some back-and-forth, then just like that, Red pulls his pistol and shoots Bucky in the stomach, and all hell breaks loose. There were forty-two bullet holes in the walls, furniture, and the men in the room. Poor old Andy gets his head blown off and he goes down. Only McGurk gets out of the place. He runs into the street with two bullets in him, and here comes Brodie Culhane in his Ford and drops him with a single shot in the eye. Brodie was a Marine marksman in the war, won a bunch of medals. He's not a flashy shot like Buck, he's a deadeye. Then Brodie goes into the house, and one of Riker's guys is still standing. He and Bucky are twenty feet apart on opposite sides of the room, both full of lead. Bam, bam, bam. Brodie and Buck both finish off the last of Riker's gunmen, but he gets one last shot off and it finishes Buck. According to both Delilah and Culhane, his last words were, 'Just my luck, killed in a whorehouse.' And he falls dead. Delilah was the only witness to the gunfight, and Culhane and Delilah are the only ones left when it's over."

He lifted his glass, drained the last drop of Black Jack, and licked what was left off his lips.

"And that's what happened that night at Grand View. Everybody knew Riker was behind it, but no way to prove it."

I slid his glass over and poured the rest of my drink in his glass.

"I'm driving back to L.A. tonight," I said. "You finish this."

"I can't hit it too hard, myself. I get a little giddy, she'll catch wise," he said, taking the bottle out of the drawer. "How about pouring it back in the bottle for me. I got a touch of the palsy." He opened a jar of Black Crows and offered me one.

"No thanks," I said, "I never had a taste for licorice."

"Kills the smell," he said. "Gladys has a nose like a foxhound."

I took one, rolled it into my cheek, and let it sit there while I poured half a glass of Jack Daniel's back in the bottle. He chewed his up and took another.

I took out the makings and offered to roll him a cigarette, but he shook his head. "Had to quit, gave me the cough. But go ahead, I still love the smell."

"So that was all in the papers," I said, rolling a butt. "What wasn't?"

"After it was all over, some rumors started. Riker probably started them but there were enough gossips around to spread the stories. The men on the Hill formed the county council, named Culhane sheriff, and he ran for the office about six months later. His promise was to clean up San Pietro. A lot of people didn't want to see the town dry up and go legal. The story goin' 'round was that Bucky was still alive when they both shot that last goon. Then Culhane turned his gun on Buck and finished him off. Anyway, that was all bull, just a story made up by the black hats who knew their days were numbered. The rich boys on the Hill wanted the town cleaned up and Culhane was lined up with them."

"How about Delilah?"

"Delilah laughs it off. Anyway, with Buck out of the way, Culhane was the man to dance with."

"Is there any truth to this?"

"I don't believe a word of it," he said. "Besides, only two people know for sure what happened that night, Culhane and Delilah. You got to accept their word. And Culhane did what he promised. He and Brett Merrill, the D.A., sent Riker up to the gas chamber for killing Wilma Thompson. Riker claimed he was framed and some people believed him."

"Do you?"

He shook his head as he leaned over and took a deep whiff of my smoke.

"The evidence was overwhelming. Riker had a thing for the girl. He had no alibi. Her blood was in his car, in his boat, and all over him. And there were two eyewitnesses. A girl named Lila Parrish and her date, a soldier. Later, Riker appealed the case and his sentence was commuted to life without parole. Last I heard, he was still up in Folsom dancing to the piper."

I tapped an ash off my cigarette and shook my head. "Any other scandals?" I asked.

"There was the thing with Eddie Woods."

"Who's Eddie Woods?"

"Ex-cop, one of Brodie's best. Flashy dresser and a kind of ladies' man. After Riker was sent up, Fontonio took over the mob. He was the last straw. Culhane was determined to get rid of him and shut down the town. Woods shot Tony Fontonio. Eddie went to his apartment to deliver a subpoena. He says Fontonio went for a gun and he plugged him. But Fontonio's bodyguards, his wife, and some legit people in town all said Fontonio never carried a gun. The attorney general called for an investigation, but Eddie resigned and Brett nol-prossed the case and that was the end of that."

I went back over to the front pages. One of them featured a 36-point banner headline, boxed in black:

PRESIDENT HARDING DEAD AT 57

The story ran down the left-hand side of the page. On the right, under it, in slightly smaller type:

RIKER MURDER TRIAL
GOES TO JURY

There was a fuzzy picture of Wilma Thompson, a slender blonde in a nondescript dress, wearing a coy smile, with the ocean forming a vista behind her. The picture of Lila Parrish didn't help much. She was rushing away from the courthouse and hidden behind the soldier. Short, dark-haired, nice figure.

The picture of Eddie Woods surprised me. I had expected a beefy, tough-looking cop; what I saw was a kid, maybe twenty-three or twenty-four, with a cocky grin and a pencil-thin mustache, which was the rage in those days. He was a flashy dresser, wearing a checked suit and a dark tie, and was standing in front of the municipal building.

And in the lower right corner, this:

EX-MOBSTER RODNEY GUILFOYLE
ELECTED MAYOR OF MENDOSA

With a picture of a burly, hard-looking galoot in a light-colored, three-piece suit, a cigar tucked in the corner of his mouth, and his thumbs tucked into the pockets of his vest.

"Who's this guy Guilfoyle?" I asked.

"That's a real irony, that page. After Fontonio was killed, the third man in line was Guilfoyle. He left and took what remained of Riker's gang down the road to Mendosa. It's about twenty-five miles south of here, in Pacifica County. Then all the joints moved down there with him. You probably heard of it, people call it 'Hole-in-the-Wall' after that outlaw gang because there's so many crooks down there."

"Can't say as I have," I said. "Is he still alive?"

"Oh yeah, and it's still a wide-open town. Guilfoyle was mayor for two or three terms and then he ran for sheriff. Still is."

"What's Culhane think of that?"

"They hate each other. Have for years. Guilfoyle's a killer—or has people who do it for him. But they each stay on their own side of the county line."

"Mr. Howland, thanks for the history lesson," I said. "You're one helluva storyteller, but I've got to be going."

"Sorry I couldn't help you about the Hinks girl."

"It's *Hicks*," I said.

"Right, Hicks. Come back again. I enjoyed the visit." He patted the drawer and smiled. "And Jack thanks you."

"Anytime," I said.

CHAPTER 15

It was five o'clock when I left Howland's house. The black Pontiac wasn't waiting for me.

The maroon Packard was.

The heavyset chauffeur was leaning on the front fender, rolling a cigarette as usual. When he saw me come out, he wiggled a finger at me and opened the rear door. I walked over to the car and looked in at Culhane.

"Hello again," he said in a gravelly but pleasant voice. "Hop in."

I looked around. The streets were empty.

"Don't worry, I won't shoot you." He laughed.

"What about my car?"

"Couldn't be safer," he said. "Nobody's gonna heist it, not in this town."

I crawled in and sank to my hips in an elegant, maroon velvet backseat. The plush floor carpeting belonged in somebody's living room. The car had push-button windows, a radiophone, an Atwater-Kent radio built into the back of the front passenger seat with four loudspeakers in back and two in the front, and a small cubbyhole, which held a bottle of Irish Mist, four highball glasses, and a small, hammered silver ice bucket.

"Very plush," I said patting the seat. "Where's the bathtub, in the trunk?"

He chuckled. *Okay, pal,* I thought, *just what is your game?* It didn't take long to find out.

"We got off on the wrong foot," he said. "I'm sorry; you're just doing your job."

"What about all that paranoia: I'm snooping for your competition, I'm trying to set up my own grift . . . ?"

"Forget I said it."

"Okay, it's forgotten."

"I got an hour to kill," he said, "I thought I'd give you the twenty-five-cent tour."

"Where are we going?"

"You've seen the village. We're going up on the Hill."

"What's the Hill?"

"It's where the money hides," he said.

He rested his right ankle on his left knee and took out an old-fashioned gold pocket watch. Culhane snapped it open and checked the time, and said to the driver, "We got some time, Rusty, take the scenic route." And to me, "You don't have an appointment right now, do you?"

"I don't know, my date book's back in the car."

Culhane laughed. "You got one for every occasion, don't you, Cowboy."

We drove around the park. Two small kids were on the swings. They were swinging in opposite directions and ducking every time they passed each other. An elderly gent was standing next to the slide, gently trying to coax his granddaughter, who was sitting on the top rung and hanging on for dear life, into sliding down. More Norman Rockwell stuff. Cheery little robots having the time of their lives.

"By the way, are my boys doing any better?" Culhane asked. "I had a talk with them."

"I got behind them and dogged the Pontiac for a while," I said. "In case you're interested, I'm not planning to litter the sidewalk or rob a bank. Why the hell am I getting the squeeze?"

"You've had a curious effect on some of our most substantial citizens."

"You've already told me that. I'm just doing my job."

"You sticking with that story about burying the widow?"

I sighed. "What would suit you better: I needed a day out of town because the weather's been awful? Incidentally, speaking of banks, I find it interesting that there are four of them in a town this size. I would think one, two at the most, would be sufficient."

"A lot of very rich people live up here," he said as we approached the Hill. "They like to own a piece of the institution they bank with."

"And if there aren't enough pieces they start their own?"

"That's the way it plays."

We slowed down as we approached a steel gate as imposing as the Great Wall of China. The uniformed gateman stooped over and saluted Culhane as we drove through to enter a natural greenhouse. Trees shouldered the road and formed a wall between the street and the residences, all of them shielded by the foliage.

"I'm sorry I can't help you with that bank thing," he said. "I called a couple of bank people and they are adamant about not showing those checks without a subpoena."

"I didn't have any trouble in L.A."

"You're more sophisticated down there. We're just country folks."

He said this as we passed mansions and estates, hidden back from the road among pines, live oaks, cypress trees, and eucalyptus. The lawns were manicured and bordered with flowers, all open in all their glory: yellow daffodils, roses, sword lilies, begonias, daisies as big as a spare tire. Occasionally, there was a car parked under a porte cochere or sitting in the driveway. Through the foliage I spotted a four-seat Mercedes convertible, a Rolls, two Lincoln touring cars, and a Stutz. The houses were even more impressive. No two were alike; every kind of architecture imaginable was represented in this discreet but elegant neighborhood.

The road wound its way to the top of the foothill, where it traveled along the ridge with the town spread out below us. A silver Duesenberg roared past. I glimpsed the driver, a dark-haired fellow wearing a navy blue golfer's tam cocked over one eye. A mile later, as the road turned back into the trees, we passed a gate that led to a Tudor-styled, three-story, brick-and-beamed manor. It dominated the ridge and was about two hundred yards back from the road, sitting on about twenty acres of property. The third floor had steepled and stained-glass windows. The gate was open and a black Pierce-Arrow was sitting beside the house, in front of the matching garage, in a turnaround as big as a baseball diamond. The hired man slowly rubbed wax deep into its already sparkling finish. Behind the house, the crest rolled down and away from the house to a paddock and pasture, and half a mile or so beyond it, at the foot of the cliffs, was the Pacific Ocean, looking as serene and placid as a fish pond.

"Nice little place," I said.

"That's the Gorman estate," he answered.

"He's the one who wasn't at the bank when I went calling, then walked out after I left, and drove off in that Pierce-Arrow."

"He plays golf every afternoon," Culhane said, and not apologetically. "That was him in the Duesenberg on his way to the club."

"He's got lousy manners."

"Nobody invited you to go in his bank," Culhane said, snuffing out his cigarette.

"He doesn't strike me as the sort who would worry too much about the confidentiality of a bunch of checks that were addressed to a woman who is now dead."

"You have to get to know this community," Culhane said. "Then maybe you'll understand."

"You mean they're all so goddamned rich they're innately rude?"

He threw me a sideways glance but made no response to that.

"What are we doing up here, Captain?"

"I just told you; I'm introducing you to San Pietro. The part the tourists never see."

"You invited me to leave town two hours ago."

"It was a dumb thing to do. I *was* a little paranoid. Osterfelt and Bellini are both bottom-feeders. They've got their hands in most of the pockets in Sacramento. I wouldn't put anything past them."

"Is that why you're running for governor?"

"I'm running for governor so I can get out of here. Except for my years in the Marines, I've been in San Pietro all my life. If I don't move on now, I never will. I'm almost sixty."

"I can understand that. It's a cute little spot but I can see how it could get very boring after an hour or two."

"I can beat those two bums," he said with a touch of bitterness. "Sometimes you need leadership that hasn't been tainted by longevity."

"You think you can change anything up there?"

"Probably not," he said, and grinned, "but I can sure drive the bastards crazy."

I laughed along with him. "Hell, that makes it worthwhile, then. What makes you think you can whip a couple of ward heelers like those two?"

"Numbers," he said. "Right now, no one's calling the game; it's close to fifty-fifty, with Bellini getting the edge. But those voting for Osterfelt are doing so because they think Bellini is a bigger crook. And vice versa for the Bellini voters. All I need to do is get forty percent of the voters who want an honest man, no matter who he is."

"That's pretty cynical."

"That's politics: cynicism and hypocrisy. It doesn't require anything but a quick tongue and a big grin. It certainly doesn't require intelligence or honesty."

As we came around a bend in the road, the trees thinned out and I saw a house two hundred feet back on the right. It was a three-story, classic Victorian, at the end of a pebbled drive lined on both sides with sandford hedges. There were a scattering of avocado trees interspersed with tall, slender Roman pines behind the hedgerow. I couldn't tell what was to the right of the drive behind the hedgerow, but there was a lot of land back there.

The gate was ornate and impressive, ten feet of black iron, with curlicues and spirals to make it seem less imposing. They didn't work. The gate said "keep out" in no uncertain terms, but just in case the message didn't come across, the fence adjoining it was an eight-footer with spikes at the top of the stanchions. A guardhouse at one corner of the fence completed the picture. The gates were open.

"Can we slow down a minute?" I asked.

Rusty stopped the car and I lowered the window on my side.

The house was white with pale blue trim and had five towering gables across the front. There was a twelve-foot, arched porte cochere, with beveled supports, over the entrance. The door was leaded glass. Even at two hundred feet, its facade shimmered with prismed light. The drive separated about seventy-five feet from the entrance and circled into it, forming a grass island, in the center of which was a small nude statue of a Greek goddess holding a tilted jar. Water poured from it into the small pond at her feet. There was an adjunct to the road that led straight from the covered entrance into what I assumed was a parking lot south of the mansion.

I had seen the place from the other side of the basin and knew it had a broad lawn in the rear that ended at the edge of cliff that dropped straight into the Pacific.

I was guessing there were at least fifteen bedrooms above the first floor. The main floor probably had a library, billiard room, dining room, living room, and whatever other cubbyholes were necessary to let rich people know the owner was richer. Behind the mansion, far out over the Pacific, the sky was black with storm clouds forming on the horizon. About halfway down the drive a gray rabbit stuck its head out of the hedge, looked around, and started to hop to the other side. It stopped suddenly, turned, its feet kicking up stones, and bolted back to safety moments ahead of a speckled hawk that swept across the road, its claws distended, and then pulled up sharply over the hedgerow.

No other name but Grand View would have fit.

It made the Gorman place look like a dollhouse.

"Now that's a sight," I said.

But in my mind I imagined gunshots in the night; Culhane charging through these gates in his 1920 Ford; a thug named McGurk staggering out of the house and blowing out the windshield before Culhane dropped him into the hedgerow with a single shot in the eye. I imagined Culhane rushing the living room. Three more shots. A woman's scream.

And I wondered who shot whom when those last three gunshots rang out in the night.

I sat back in the car seat.

"I'll bet the inside of that joint would give John Jacob Astor a start," I said.

"Cost you five bills to find out."

"Not likely."

He handed me one of Rusty's freshly rolled cigarettes and we lit up. Rusty dropped the Packard into gear and pulled away. The window slid quietly up as if someone in the house had prompted it.

About twenty yards ahead of us, a road curved off to our right and then dipped sharply down and curved around the cliff and out of sight. The ocean was in front of and below it. Another spectacular view. A bright red sawhorse with lanterns on both ends of it blocked the road.

"What's that?" I asked.

"It's Cliffside Road. We closed it several years ago; too dangerous." He tapped Rusty on the shoulder. "Let's take Cliffside down," he said. If that made the driver nervous he didn't show it. He stopped, got out, swung the sawhorse out of the way, got back in the car, drove a dozen feet beyond it, then got out and moved the sawhorse back in place. We started down a narrow, steep, curvy, precipitous road in first gear. There was no guardrail. Four feet from the road, the cliff made a dead drop two hundred feet straight down to the rocks and the ocean. Three feet on the other side, it went straight up. The Packard hugged the safe side of the road, rocks and pebbles spitting under the wheels. About a hundred feet along, we rounded a sharp curve and came on a wide shoulder in the road, big enough to handle six or seven cars. There was a waist-high stone wall around its entire perimeter and an old, crumbling stone bench on one side.

Without being told, Rusty pulled off on the shoulder and parked. He pulled on the hand brake and turned off the ignition with the car in gear.

"Better leave your hat in the car," Culhane said, tossing his black fedora on the seat. I did the same and followed him out on the shoulder, trying to conceal my terror. A hard wind rose swiftly up the side of the mountain from the ocean, whipping Culhane's hair around his ears. I don't like heights. I don't like narrow roads and steep cliffs. I also don't like drop-off shoulders on those narrow roads.

"It's perfectly safe," he said, walking to the edge and standing with one foot on the stone wall.

"You're giving me the creeps," I managed to tell him.

"It's okay," he said. "This is the safest spot on the road. Don't look down, you'll be fine."

I walked slowly to the stone wall. When I got to it, I reached down and grabbed it with both hands. I looked straight out at the Pacific. Black storm clouds broiled far out to sea and I could see the rain line sweeping across the ocean. A white pontoon plane with a blue stripe down the side banked into the mouth of the bay a mile away and circled toward us, flying parallel to the cliff. It circled all the way around the basin and swept in over the sailboats, then settled down slowly. The two pontoons smacked into the bay and churned twin wakes behind them. It turned and taxied slowly toward the pier.

"That big house on top of the hill is the O'Dell estate," Culhane said. "He and Eli Gorman started all this. They were partners in the railroad. One was a gruff old Irishman who mostly gambled for a living, the other was an orthodox Jew and all business. They were always at each other's throats. O'Dell wanted to sell the bottomland by the ocean for a paper mill. Gorman said he wasn't going to live with a stinking paper mill in his backyard. They put the deeds for all this property on the table, each of them put up ten grand, they played poker for the whole thing. Winner take all. O'Dell lost, and left and never came back. He and his wife died when the *Lusitania* was sunk. A caretaker kept the house up until Delilah, their daughter, inherited the house and his bankroll."

"Pretty fancy for a whorehouse," I said.

"That's a misnomer," he said. "It's a private club, and way too rich for your blood—or mine. Five hundred to join on a one-night basis, plus the cost of the entertainment. A lifetime membership is ten thousand."

I whistled through my teeth.

"You'd be surprised if I told you the names of some of the full-timers."

"Why did Delilah O'Dell do that?"

"People here despised her because she was an O'Dell, rich as Croesus and a smart businesswoman to boot. They snubbed her, so she got even, and turned Grand View into the classiest whorehouse on the West Coast, probably in the whole country."

"Prostitution is against the law," I reminded him.

"Not in this county. Neither is gambling. And neither was drinking during Prohibition."

"How do you justify that?"

"I don't have to. Buck Tallman said it best. 'You can't stop folks from drinkin', gamblin', and whorin' around. The best you can do is make it safe and pleasant for them. They pay the bills.' Does that offend your sensibilities?"

"Not a bit," I said. "I happen to work under a different set of laws."

"Hell, you know you can find a game or get laid in L.A. any time of the day or night. As long as the right palms are greased, everybody looks the other way."

I couldn't argue with that so I changed the subject. "You know, maybe I prefer old man O'Dell's vision for this place. He was out in the open about it. Put it right on the table. Soak 'em for the land, let them build a mill. Let 'em stink up the air, poison the ground, ruin the

water, cut down all the trees, and sit back and count their money. Gorman made a playpen for people with big bank accounts, charged them
three or four times what they'd pay anyplace else, and made loans
to all the peons who work for a living. Now he probably acts like a
humanitarian."

Culhane looked surprised. "Jesus, who stepped on your jewels?"
he said.

"If I have to make a choice, maybe I prefer greed over hypocrisy.
I'm giving it some thought."

I could see him staring at me from the corner of his eye, a somewhat bemused expression on his face. He was trying to figure out if I
was for real or just being contrary. He looked back at the bay.

"That's Rudy Shaeffer," Culhane said, pointing at the pontoon
plane. "He works three days a week and then flies up on Wednesday
and spends four days at the Grand View."

"How does he make his money?"

"I never asked."

When my stomach calmed down, I cautiously looked over the side,
and immediately got that queasy feeling again. Below us, halfway down
the precipice, was a small shelf covered with half a dozen pine trees.
Something glittered in the rubble that surrounded the trees. I looked
closer and made out what looked like a large, rusted bedframe. Near it,
a semicircle of steel seemed to grow out of a pile of dead branches.

"There's something down there," I said.

"It's a 1920 Chevrolet coupe," he said, without looking down. "It
gets so foggy up here at night you can't see your feet. Some nervy kid
was going downtown. He lost control of the car, didn't make the curve,
went straight over the side, and caught fire. We didn't find him until
the next morning. The road was twice as wide in those days and it had
a guardrail. It's eroded away through the years."

"Did you know him?"

"I knew everybody in town then, and I still do."

"You didn't know Verna Hicks."

"Then she never lived here."

I reached into my inside pocket and took out the five-by-seven shot
of Verna from the newspaper. I pointed to Verna Wilensky. The wind
rattled the photograph and he held it with two hands. He stared at it
and looked at me with one eyebrow cocked.

"And which one would she be?"

I pointed to the blowup and he laughed.

"I'm supposed to recognize this lady? All I can see is the top of her head and her nose. And the picture looks like it was shot at the bottom of a canal."

I showed him the original and he just shook his head. Then I gave him a look at the morgue shot.

"Jesus!" he snapped. "I hope to hell you don't show that to anybody. They'll puke on your shoes." He shoved the shot back at me.

"Why did you come down this way?" I asked. "Just to give me the willies?"

"I didn't know you had a problem with high places. My life changed forever one night, on that stone bench right over there."

"IIow?"

He didn't answer, just looked off at the horizon and tilted his head up at the sky. "Storm'll be here soon," he said.

The rest of the trip was uneventful. As we neared the Howlands' house, the first big drops of rain splattered against the windshield. Rusty pulled up behind my car and stopped. He leaned back with a sigh, his hands locked behind his head.

Culhane said, "You're a smart cop, Bannon. I appreciate that. But I say again, there's nothing here for you to learn. You ought to head back before the rain gets serious."

"Why did you take me on that little cruise?" I asked. "To let me know that there are a lot of rich people on the Hill with connections all the way to the governor's mansion and probably to the White House?"

"I don't want you to have the wrong impression about San Pietro."

I understood the veiled warning in his remark.

"I don't," I said, looking him straight in the eye. "I've put up with politics and money in my time."

I started to get out of the car. "I think I'll grab a bite before I head back to L.A. Where's the best steak in town—that I can afford?"

"The diner. A buck and a quarter. I'll give them a call; it's on the county."

"No thanks. I have ten bucks expense money. If I don't spend it Moriarity will cut me back to five the next time out."

"I've been a cop almost all my life," Culhane said. "I know about cops. I've known good ones, bad ones, crooked ones, stupid ones, and some so rotten it would make you sick to your stomach you ever put on a badge. You're a bloodhound. You stick your nose up in the air and get a whiff of something and then you bite it and don't let go. Just be careful, Cowboy. Don't get your nose stuck up the wrong dog's ass."

And they drove away.

CHAPTER 16

The rain that had started as a quiet mist developed into a full-fledged storm by the time I drove the length of the town to the diner. The wind had picked up, bringing with it dark clouds creased with lightning and heavy with a steady downpour.

My sessions with Howland and Culhane had yielded little. Howland's take on the massacre at Grand View House and the trial of Arnie Riker for the murder of Wilma Thompson was passable but shaky reportage at best, laced with sour mash and the kind of myths old-time newsmen like to spin over dinner or drinks at the bar. Culhane had completely avoided talking about the Grand View massacre and the Riker murder case and Eddie Woods.

The diner's red, flashing neon sign promised comfort from the storm. It was a classic—chrome-trimmed, with leather booths, and a long counter half circling the kitchen. The odor of cooked meat and onions and strong coffee stirred my appetite. I took a booth in the corner; ordered a rare T-bone, soft scrambled eggs, sliced potatoes and onions, hot rolls, lemon meringue pie, and a Muhlenbach beer; commandeered a crumpled but readable afternoon edition of the *Times* from the seat of an abandoned booth; rolled a cigarette; and smoked while I scanned the headlines and waited for dinner.

The story I was looking for was buried back in the second section in the obituaries, three paragraphs under the headline: WOMAN DROWNS IN BATHTUB ACCIDENT. It told me less than I knew already and ended with two lines: "The name of the deceased is being withheld pending notification of next of kin. No funeral arrangements were available at press time." Jimmy Pennington was smart enough to open the door in the event there was more to the accident than I had indicated. That's why he was the best reporter in town.

I put the paper aside when my dinner arrived, and dug in. Culhane was right: the steak was an inch thick and cooked to perfection, the rolls crumbled in my hand when I buttered them, and the beer was served in an iced mug. I was too busy devouring my meal to notice the black Pontiac pull into the parking lot and the two guys in the front seat who did not get out.

I finished a leisurely meal, ordered a second cup of coffee, had a smoke. I knew my quest for facts about Verna Wilensky's mother lode was wasted time, and the rain was showing signs of letting up. Then there was Rosebud, waiting for his dinner and bone. It was only 7:30, I could be home by 11:00, so I decided to head back to town. The waitress wrapped the bone in cellophane and put it in a paper bag for me. I tipped the waitress a buck, probably the largest tip she had ever received, turned up my collar, pulled my hat low over my eyes against the rain, and quick-stepped around the corner of the diner toward my car.

As I reached the door a voice behind me said, "What's yer hurry, bohunk?"

As I turned, an arm the size of a steam pipe wrapped around my chest, pinning both arms to my sides. The bag with my dog bone fell at my feet. A second man, a mere outline in rain and darkness, stepped in close and threw an arcing jackhammer punch deep into my stomach. It doubled me over. My hat flipped into the mud at my feet. Air whooshed out of my lungs. Sparks dimmed my eyesight for a moment. Pain swelled upward from my stomach and my dinner soured the back of my throat. I swallowed hard as he stepped in closer and landed another rib-bender. My knees buckled and I sagged toward the ground, but the guy holding me dragged me back up and growled, "Go home to your mama and stay there, big shot." As the muscleman swung his arm back for a third shot at my gut, I kicked him, with everything I had left, in the groin. I felt muscle, bone, and tissue smash under the kick. It lifted him an inch off the ground and sent him backward, doubled over and screaming.

As he fell to his knees, I swung my head forward, then threw it back as hard as I could. It smashed into the face of the thug holding me from behind. I smacked him with the back of my head a second time. He yowled, and his grasp loosened enough that I could swing around and break loose of his grip. Facing him, I smacked his face with the top of my head. The back of his head shattered the car window. His arm dropped to his side, and I threw a hard, straight jab into his face, ruining what was left of his nose. Then I saw the empty sleeve of his other arm tucked in his coat jacket.

He had held me with the only arm he had. He made a funny little sound and fell straight down as I turned to the other attacker, who was gasping for breath and trying to scramble to his feet in the mud. I stepped in close and threw a haymaker down to the side of his jaw just below the ear. Both his hands splashed into the mud, and I hit him again with a roundhouse right that knocked him up and over on his back. He lay there, arms flung out at his sides, his mouth open and gobbling rain.

I turned back to the first guy, who was on his hand and knees, and finished him off with another right, straight down to his temple. He fell face forward and splashed into a mud puddle without another sound.

The whole melee took less than two minutes.

When I rolled my first attacker over, to keep him from drowning in mud, his coat flopped open and I saw the badge pinned to his vest and the .32 under his arm.

I had been doing battle with my old pals Laurel and Hardy. I took a closer look at One Arm's partner and stared at an empty eye socket. I looked around in the rain for a minute but didn't see his glass eye.

"Well I'll be damned," I muttered to myself.

I was doubled over from the blows to my stomach but not too unsteady to reach down and rip the badge off the big guy's vest. Then I relieved him of his pistol, picked up my hat and paper sack with the dog bone, got in the car and drove off, leaving them both staring up at the rain.

I drove around the corner and past the park. Rain and wind had pretty much washed away all evidence of the noontime picnic, and the red words on the sandwich boards advertising FIREWORKS TONIGHT 9 P.M. ran down the length of the boards like streams of blood. I stopped in front of the municipal building, took the bone out of the paper sack, and put the gun and badge in it.

My ribs were throbbing and I had trouble standing up straight, but I made it up the steps and entered the police department. Rosalind had been replaced by a tall, slender rail of man in a blue uniform. He was smoking a cigar and reading *Life* magazine. He looked up through bored eyes as I put the bag on the counter.

"This is a gift for Captain Culhane," I said. "Please see that he gets it."

"Who shall I say it's from?"

"He'll know," I said, and got out of there. I aimed the car for L.A. and got the hell out of Dodge.

When I got to 101 I turned on my flasher and pushed the gas pedal close to the floor. Rain bubbled through the shattered car window and sprayed on my neck. My ribs felt like they were broken. Just the touch of my hand when I reached down to check brought tears to my eyes.

I turned off the flashing light and slowed down going through Santa Barbara, then flicked it back on and leaned on the gas again. I drove straight through to Sunset and headed east. The streets in L.A. were bone-dry. I was home by 10:30.

I pulled into the drive and sat for a minute. My gut was still throbbing. I got out of the car carefully, swinging my legs out the door first and then pulling myself to my feet with my hands on the doorsill. The pain didn't get any worse; it couldn't have. Stooped over, I made the door, unlocked it, and got inside. I went in the bedroom, pulled off jacket and tie, and opened my shirt and checked my torso in the bathroom mirror. Two dark red bruises the size of dollar pancakes formed a sideways figure eight at the bottom of my rib cage. The one-eyed man could hit.

I got the Ben-Gay out of the cabinet and went back in the bedroom. Rosie was scratching the back door, so I put the bottle on the night table and groaned my way to the back door. He was so happy to see me he jumped up on me and gave my a sloppy kiss. His paws hit me right at ground zero and added new pain to my aching gut.

"Jesus," I yelled. He jumped back, looking like I had whacked him on the rear.

"It's okay," I said, and got down on my knees and held my hand out to him. He came over and leaned against me, and the heat of his body felt good against the bruises.

"The old man took a bit of a beating," I said.

I fed him, gave him a bone, left the back door open, and went back

to the bedroom. I lay down on the bed and eased my pants off. The
Ben-Gay burned as I carefully spread it over my abdomen, but then it
began to work its magic. I lay there looking at the ceiling until the pain
eased. I don't know how long I lay there, thirty minutes maybe, long
enough for Rosie to finish with the bone and come back in. He put his
front paws up on the bed and looked down at me, his nose twitching
from the pungent odor. I scratched him behind the ears and took deep
breaths and waited for the ache to subside.

When I could move I got up, locked the front door, got the Canadian Club and a water tumbler, dropped a cube of ice in the tumbler,
and went back to the bedroom. I sat on the edge of the bed, poured
myself a half-glass of whiskey, rolled a cigarette, and lit up. Just inhal-
ing hurt.

Rosie sat at my feet, looking concerned. I patted the bed.

"Come on up," I said. He jumped on the bed and sat down and
looked down at me with concern.

"I'm okay, pal, nothing broken," I told him. That seemed to satisfy
him and he went to his side of the bed, did his little circle thing, and lay
down.

My trip had earned me more than a sore stomach. I was sure now
that the Wilensky woman's death was no accident.

I swallowed half the drink, smoked awhile, finished off the drink,
and doused the cigarette. The whiskey soaked up a little more of the
pain. I lay down on my back, worked my way under the sheet, and
turned off the light.

It had been a very long day. I was asleep before Rosie started to
snore.

CHAPTER 17

It was 7:15 when the phone woke me up. I don't know how long it had been ringing. I rolled over to reach for it and I felt a hot wire slash across my stomach.

"Oww!" I yelped. Rosie jerked awake as I reached across him and picked up the receiver.

"Yeah," I moaned.

"That you, Zeke?" I heard Bones say on the other end of the line.

"Uh-huh."

"What's the matter, you sound all in. Have a rough night?"

"You'll never know just how rough," I groaned.

"Want to stop by the morgue on your way in? I got the post-mortem ready for you."

"Right. Thirty minutes."

"No hurry," he said gleefully. "None of my patients is going anywhere."

"Cute," I said, and hung up. I called Ski and told him I was running a little late, and to call the precinct and tell Ozzie, who handled the radio, that we had to stop off at the morgue on the way in.

"How'd it go up there?" he asked.

"I'll give you a report when I see you," I said, and hung up.

I struggled out of bed and went into the kitchen to let the dog out, then realized I had left the back door open all night. Rosie was in the yard, watering the trees and shrubs. I went into the bathroom and turned the hot water as high as I could take it and let it wash over me for about ten minutes. Then I shaved; dressed in my tweed jacket, dark gray flannels, a dark blue shirt, and black tie; set out Rosie's food and water for him; and left to pick up Ski.

"What happened to the window?" was the first thing he said when he got in the car. Then he took a closer look at me and added, "What happened to *you*? You're as pale as white bread."

"I met Captain Culhane," I said.

"What'd he do, hit you with a sledgehammer?"

"That's about right," I said, and gave him a quick report as we headed downtown.

"It's a bust," I finished. "We can forget Verna Wilensky. Nobody up there is going to help, and legally we haven't a case for a subpoena."

"You going to let him get away with rocking you like that?" he said angrily, the blood rising to his face.

"Oh, I did my share," I said, and told him how the fight had ended, and about putting the gun and badge in the bag.

"The old man's gonna want to do something about this," Ski said. "He'll be mighty pissed off that a cop did that to another cop, especially to one of his."

"I made my point," I answered. "I don't want to hear the name Culhane or San Pietro or anything like it for the rest of my life."

"We could go back up there and make life miserable for him," the big man said.

"Ah, we'd be outnumbered. Of course, it seems like he only hires the handicapped. On the other hand, the one-eyed guy didn't need both eyes to damn near break me in half."

"I'd like to have a piece of the son of a bitch," Ski said. "You shoulda taken me with you, partner."

"You probably would have killed one of them. The last thing we'd want to do is spend twenty years in that place."

You can add morgues to a high place on the list of things I hate. Perhaps it's the smell of formaldehyde, blood, and alcohol that permeates the sterile confines of what Bones calls "the coolest place in town."

The room was white-tiled, with a bright light hanging from the ceiling over each of the tables, and a butcher's scale hanging from the ceiling beside the lamp. Each table had a ridge running all the way around it, and a sink at the foot into which water, blood, and any other unwanted material was channeled. A spigot hissed aerated water into the sink. The mixed odors of alcohol, blood, disinfectant, and death permeated the cold air in the room. There were half a dozen stretchers, elevated at the head and sloping down to the foot. Beside the table, a stenographer wearing a face mask sat at a wheeled desk, equipped with a shorthand writer. In the corner, almost inaudibly, a record player was providing something by Bach.

A large woman's corpse lay on its back on one of the tables, her dark hair showering over the raised end of the table. The body was the color of spoiled meat, and was split open from chin to Venus mound. Bones, in a white butcher's apron and wearing yellow gloves, was leaning over the corpse, digging around in the cavity, and dictating to the stenographer. He looked over the top of his glasses when I stuck my head through the swinging doors of the examination room.

"Zeke, m'boy," he said cheerily. "Want to take a look? See what cyanide does to the innards?"

"I'll take your word for it."

He stopped what he was doing and told the steno, whose name was Judith, to take a break. She stood primly, straightened her skirt, and left the room through a door on the far side. Bones peeled off the gloves, turned off the light over the table, and pulled off his gown. He dropped gown and gloves in a large trash bin near the door.

"Feelin' any better? You look like hell," he said.

"I sprung a couple of ribs," I said.

"She must've been quite the athlete," he said wryly.

"Don't I wish."

"Where's it hurt?"

He stopped and reached out with both hands, feeling the bottom of my rib cage.

"Right there," I said.

His nimble fingers worked around my sides and back again.

"Nothing broken. You'll probably be sore for a couple of days. Let's see what Mrs. Wilensky gave up." He led me to his office, which was adjacent to the laboratory: a cubicle of a room large enough for a desk, a couple of file cabinets, three chairs, and a table that held a coffeemaker, a couple of mugs, a tall sugar shaker, and a bedpan full of ice, in which a bottle of milk rested. There was a calendar on the wall, displaying a drawing of the human form with all the vital parts identified on it. The motto on the bottom read TOPFER'S SURGICAL INSTRUMENTS in large letters, and under that STAINLESS STEEL PRECISION TOOLS FOR EVERY OCCASION.

Ski was sitting in one of the chairs, staring stoically at the calendar. Ski could look at body parts all day long, but the aroma of death in all its incarnations really got to him.

I sat down next to Ski and Bones sat at his desk, which was piled with papers, books, a phone, and a human skull, which had an ashtray wedged inside it, just behind the gaping mouth. He rooted around in a desk drawer, ultimately coming up with a file folder, and proceeded to read from his report.

"Could you just reduce that to simple English?" Ski said after a moment or two.

Bones smiled, retrieved his cigarette, and leaned back in his chair.

"I make her closer to forty than forty-seven. Bleached blonde. In simple English, both lungs were full of water and traces of lye and other ingredients consistent with soap."

"In other words, she drowned, as we suspected," I said.

"Yes and no," he said.

"Now what does that mean?"

"She drowned all right, but remember what I told you about electrocution?"

"Yeah, it's the big freeze," Ski said. "Everything stops on a dime."

"Very good. So . . .?"

"So what?" Ski said.

"So how'd all that water get in her lungs?" He grinned like a man holding four aces.

It took a minute to sink in.

Ski said, "Uh-oh."

I didn't say anything. I just stared at him.

"In simple terms, boys, the lady was dead before the radio fell in the tub with her. You got yourself a nice, sweet homicide here. And a murder one unless the killer just happened to be strolling past Wilensky's bathroom on his way home and decided to hold her under water for four or five minutes. She broke a toe thrashing around and there's some skin under a couple of her fingernails."

"Please don't say 'I told you so,' " Ski said to me.

What had been conjecture on my part was now a reality. The assurance that Verna Wilensky was murdered in cold blood didn't make me feel good. It streaked through me like a cold wind had sneaked through my pores. It chilled my heart. And with that came the realization that perhaps Culhane knew the truth and was simply toying with me, safe in the belief that somebody had beat murder.

"My guess is that whoever killed her knocked that radio in as an afterthought," Bones said. "As most killers would, he probably thought he'd committed the perfect crime."

We both sat there and stared at him.

"Homicide," he said gleefully, and snapped his fingers. "Did I make your day or what?"

CHAPTER 18

I put on the red flasher, tweaked the siren, and made it to Pacific Meadows in a little under twenty minutes.

I didn't say anything on the way. Instead, my mind was working overtime. I was thinking of Verna Wilensky's last minutes.

She draws a hot bath, lights a candle, folds her bathrobe neatly, and puts it on the toilet seat. She tests the water with her toe. Then lowers herself carefully in the tub, settles, takes a sip of her gin and tonic. Lights a cigarette.

Sinatra murmurs a love song on the radio.

She doesn't hear the window in the living room slide up, doesn't hear or see the figure slip through.

He walks across the room, peers around the corner of the bedroom doorway. He sees cigarette smoke swirling in the light from the candle. He slips into the bedroom.

He takes off his gloves and suit jacket. Lays them on the bed. Rolls up his sleeves. Flexes his fingers. He sidles up to the bathroom door, peers around the corner.

Verna lolls in the warm water. She takes another drag on the cigarette and snuffs it out, drains most of her drink. She is feeling light-headed. She closes her eyes, hums a little tune.

She doesn't see the shadow wriggling on the wall as the candle dances to the movement the killer makes walking into the room. He walks up to the tub. Stands over her, flexes his fingers again.

His knuckles crack.

She opens her eyes. Looks straight up and sees the shape of her killer hovering over her. Before she can scream, he grabs a handful of her hair and thrusts her head underwater.

She begins thrashing.

Her killer is a shimmering silhouette filtered through water.

He plunges his other hand in the water and shoves her body against the bottom of the tub. The water roils as she fights to free herself.

She reaches up, scratches the killer's hand. He pulls it away and her head breaks the surface of the bath for a moment. He plunges his hand down and shoves her head underwater again.

She is kicking and flailing her arms.

The last pain she feels is her toe, breaking against the side of the tub.

Bubbles burst from her nose and mouth.

She looks up through heavy eyes, sees her deliverer's arms, wriggling as the bathwater floods into her lungs.

Then blessed sleep.

The killer holds her under until the bubbles stop. Until the thrashing stops. He stands up, looks down at his work. The music ends and the disc jockey's funereal voice comes on. He begins to introduce a Glenn Miller tune.

The killer leans on the shelf, jogs it, feels the screws rip loose from the wall. He jumps back, holding his hands over his head.

The radio splashes into the tub, hits her on the jaw as sparks pop from it. The water sizzles for a second.

Then it is quiet.

The killer, satisfied, returns to the bedroom. He wipes his arms free of water but does not dry them with a towel. He rolls down his sleeves, puts his gloves and jacket back on, leaves by the window.

A dog barking.

Too late.

"Jesus, look out!"

Ski's voice snapped me out of it. I was in the opposing lane. I swerved back just as the city bus rumbled by, its horn bellowing angrily.

"My mind wandered for a minute," I said.

"Yeah, so did the car."

"I was just thinking about the case."

Bones had already dispatched Oachi Okimoto, his best man, to the Wilensky house with a forensics team, and I had called radio dispatch and asked for King and Garrett to be assigned to us for the day. I told them it was for a neighborhood canvass but left out all other details.

Oachi Okimoto was already on the job when we got there. Okimoto was a short, thin, Japanese fellow with close-trimmed black hair, yellow eyes behind horn-rimmed bifocals, and delicate, manicured hands. He had on a white shirt with a striped bow tie, dark pants, and loafers. Okie was a pleasant little guy and very good at the trade. He had a map of the entire area spread out on the dining room table when we got there.

"Hi, boys," he said in a soft, very precise voice. "Big surprise, huh?"

"Oh, yeah," said Ski.

I explained that I had two uniformed cops on the way and would round up two more teams as quickly as possible. His three assistants were busy dusting everything in the house but the ceiling.

"Don't forget the toilet," Ski said. "Maybe he had to take a leak. Nobody wears gloves when they take a leak and flush."

Okie told us that Bones had already pulled the dead woman's prints for comparisons.

"She lived alone and, from what I gather, didn't have many visitors except maybe the people next door. They were close."

"I'll get prints on them," Okie said. The front door opened and Officer King stuck his head in. "Hi, Sergeant," he said, "what's up?" I motioned him in. Garrett was sitting in the squad car. King came in and stood at attention. He did everything but click his heels.

"This stays under your hat for now," I told King. "Wilensky is now a murder one."

"Wow," he said. "How?"

"That's what we're here to find out," Ski said, with a touch of sarcasm. He didn't like King; Ski didn't like attitude.

"I want that angle soft-pedaled," I went on. "I'm trying to keep this out of the papers for now, although it gets less likely by the minute. The story is: there was a heist in the neighborhood, we're looking for strangers starting early Monday morning up until say ten Monday night. On foot, in a car, you know the drill on that. Kids'll be a good bet, there's a lot of them in the neighborhood, they're all over the place on bikes. Be careful with them, though; they tend to make up things to get in on the act. I have to go back to the precinct now. Ski will be in charge. Okie has a map of the whole neighborhood. Use it to plan the canvass."

I jerked a thumb at the house on the corner. "Start next door and work this block first."

"The folks on the right are out of town," King said.

"How do you know that?"

"I checked when we came on the scene the other night. According to the Clarks, they left for San Francisco on vacation early Saturday morning. Be gone two weeks."

Ski walked to the living room window and stared thoughtfully at the house. "Bunch of papers on the porch," he said. "Apparently they forgot to put a hold on it." Then he turned suddenly and walked to a low, flat, coffee table near the front door. He picked a key off the table.

"I noticed this key when we came in that night," he said. "I figured it was an extra key to the front door, but maybe the vacationers gave it to Verna in case she needed to get in the house while they were gone. Neighbors do that." He handed the key to King and told him to check the door but not to go in the house if it worked. I left for the office.

Louie was washing a radio car when I pulled into the garage. The cream puff looked like it belonged in a circus. It was rain- and mud-streaked, and the busted window gave it the appearance of something you'd find on the back row of a used-car lot. Louie looked at it, then at me, then back at the car. Then he saw the window and his eyes bulged out of his head.

"What's that?" he said, doing a little nervous jig and pointing at the window.

"I had a little problem."

"What problem! Look at that window!" he said, and tears began to form. "Just look at that damn window!"

"A bird flew into me," I lied, handing him the keys.

"A bird! What kind of bird did that, a friggin' ostrich? A flying elephant? Did Dumbo fly into the car?"

He was still raving when I headed upstairs to the squad room. Moriarity was on the phone scowling when I walked in. He wiggled a finger at me and hung up the phone as I entered his office. I sat down across from him.

"Maybe you oughtta be in the hot seat," he snapped, for openers. "Louie just called me. What's this about a bird the size of Beverly Hills busting the window in the car?"

"It's a long story."

"Just give me the *Reader's Digest* version. I only got six hours left on this watch."

I gave him a blow-by-blow, starting with the black Pontiac following me, including my chat with Howland and the tour of the Hill with Culhane, and ending with my run-in at the diner.

"A couple of his cops tried to beat you up?" he said, his face storming up.

"I'd say that was on their mind."

"I'll call that son of a bitch and . . ."

"Hold on a minute. There's more . . ."

"I don't want you going back up there," he said flatly. "And forget Verna Hicks or Wilensky or whatever her name is. Frankly, I don't give a damn if she gets buried or not. I don't care if they embalm her and hang her off the city hall flagpole. And if you got a thing for dead broads, go over to the morgue and pick out a different one."

He was standing when he finished, his brow furrowed like a freshly plowed field. Then he added, "I like the trick with the gun and badge. That was inspired, Bannon." He started pacing, a bad sign. "Christ, I told you not to waste time and money going up there," he said. "Didn't I tell you that?"

"As I was about to say, there's something else."

"What?"

"Wilensky's lungs were full of water."

He flat-mouthed me. "She drowned, fer crissakes. What'd you expect to be in there, hundred-proof Scotch?"

"I just left Bones's office. He completed the autopsy. Verna drowned alright—before the radio ever fell in the tub."

He stared at me, letting that sink in. While he was working on it, I explained how drowning and electrocution work.

"Jesus. Aw, Jesus-fucking-Keerist!"

"Bones has sent a team from forensics back to the house, and I dropped Ski off there. I got two uniforms casing the neighborhood but

we really need at least two other teams. We got a homicide now, Lieutenant. I say Ski and I go back up to San Pietro and get serious with
those people."

"Damn it. Damn it, damn it." He paced the room again, this time
for a full two minutes, running both hands through his meager hair.
"The captain's gonna have a baby right in his office over this." He
paced some more. "You know the politics involved here, don't you?"

I nodded. "It's a murder one. Politics doesn't have anything to do
with it anymore."

"Oh, yeah. Tell that to McCurdy. He's gonna be gettin' it from
Chief Holman, and he's gonna be gettin' it from the mayor, who got it
from the governor, who got it from God-knows-who. I know what's on
your mind, Zeke. You're gonna try and pin this on Culhane, who is
about to announce his race for governor, and *that*, pal, is gonna rever-
berate all the way to Alaska."

I didn't say anything.

"You think whoever killed her was the payoff guy, right? The five-
C's-a-month guy through all these years?"

"Or had her iced. Yeah. That's a pretty good supposition."

"And you got your eye on Culhane for this, don't you?"

"It's a pretty good supposition."

"Stop saying that. It's giving me a stomachache."

I closed up again and sat there.

He whirled, and jabbed a forefinger at me. "Okay, why now? Why
pay off for all these years and then suddenly pull the plug on her?"

"You just said it, Culhane's running for governor. The price of silence suddenly went up."

"I suppose you already got a candidate for the guy who shoved her
under, too?"

"I've got an idea."

"Well, ain't that a surprise. It's your idea got us into this mess in
the first place."

"You're getting steamed up over nothing," I said. "Maybe they all
hate Culhane. Maybe they'll promote you."

"Yeah, and maybe the swallows will pass up Capistrano this year
and fly into the garage downstairs and crap all over Louie's goddamn
cream-puff sedan."

"It's a murder one, Dan; what do you think they're going to do, shove it under the carpet?" I shifted in my seat and that hot wire lashed across my ribs again. I winced. "Damn it!"

"Christ, you're a wreck," he said. "You seen a doc?"

"Bones checked my ribs. I'll be okay in a day or two."

"In answer to your question, no, they're not gonna sweep it under the rug, they're gonna look for a fall guy—which is you—which leads to me. I'll end up mowing the grass at city hall until I retire; and you? You'll be collecting garbage down in Tijuana. You'll have to turn wet-back just to get back across the border to get a decent meal."

He went back behind his desk and sat down and lit one of his sugar-coated cigars. Silence tiptoed around the room.

"Did it occur to you that maybe, just maybe, this don't have any-thing to do with Culhane?" he said finally. "Maybe she was shacking up with some guy, and his wife came over and did her in. Maybe she was running dope across the border on weekends and her Chicano pals gave her the bath. See what I mean? There could be a lot of scenarios. You got some coincidences workin' here and it looks like a closed case to you. Think about it, Bannon; you got to find the killer and tie him to Culhane and tie it all back to something that happened over twenty years ago."

"It's all we got for the present," I said. "Bones is going to misplace the autopsy report long enough for me to go up there and lay the story on Culhane and see his reaction. That will tell me a lot. Then if the banks want to keep playing hide-and-seek, we'll run over to Santa Maria and get Judge Wainwright to give us a search warrant. The money trail leads up there."

"And if it peters out?"

"We lose nothing. We take it to McCurdy when the post is released and let him tell us how to deal with it."

"I really don't like it when you fast-talk me, Zeke."

"It's logical."

"So was Custer's Last Stand."

"So what do we do? Shall I call Bones and tell him to send over the post? I'll do a report and then take it to McCurdy before it goes on file for the press?"

His eyes brightened when I mentioned that idea. He puffed on his

cigar and stared across the desk at me. "You got five minutes to con-
vince me otherwise." He looked at his watch.

I said: "When Culhane became sheriff he promised to clean the
mobsters out of Eureka, which is what San Pietro was called then. That
meant getting rid of Arnie Riker and his number two, Tony Fontonio.
Riker was arrested and convicted of murdering a young girl named
Wilma Thompson. It was a solid case because, among other things,
they had an eyewitness named Lila Parrish. The case went to appeal,
and Riker's sentence was reduced from death to life-no-parole because
Lila Parrish vamoosed right after the trial and nobody could find her.
Then a year later, Eddie Woods knocked off Fontonio, Eureka turned
into San Pietro, Culhane had the Fontonio case dead-docketed, and
everybody lived happily ever after.

"Now get this: Woods was in charge of the Riker investigation *and*
Woods burned Fontonio."

"And you think you can get all that together in an airtight package?
That's what it's going to have to be, Zeke. No holes, and right now all I
see is Swiss cheese in that story. For one thing, you're assuming that
Lila Parrish was lying and the Riker case was a frame and Eddie
Woods set it all up. How the hell do you plan to put that together? Your
chief witness, if it is Lila Parrish, is probably the dame on the slab in
the morgue."

"All I need to do is find one person who can identify the person
who sent the checks to Verna Hicks."

"And prove it was a frame. And Hicks and Parrish are one and the
same. And Woods did the number on her. And Culhane sanctioned it."

I didn't answer that.

He shook his head. "So far you haven't broken a lot of ice on that
pond," he said.

"It wasn't a homicide until this morning. That's a pretty good
icebreaker."

More cigar smoke puffed out of his mouth. He spun his chair
around and looked through the plate glass walls of his office into the
squad room for a long minute, then swung back.

"You plan to take Ski this time?"

I nodded.

"I told you to take the National Guard the first time you went up
there."

"Ski's better."

He sighed joylessly.

"When do you want to go?"

"Is this Thursday?"

"It was when I got up this morning."

"I got a date tonight. How's tomorrow morning sound?"

CHAPTER 19

When I left Moriarity's office, the switchboard operator called me over.

"You got a call from a Millicent Harrington at the West L.A. National Bank," he said. "Here's the number. She says she has some info for you."

"Thanks."

I went back to my desk and dialed her number.

"Hi," she said, "remember me?"

"If I forgot you, I'd need a brain transplant."

"I'm flattered, I think," she said with a light laugh.

"What's up?"

"I may have a tip for you. I called a woman I know at the South View Bank and Trust. It's on the list. Her name is Patty North. She remembers selling the cashier's check for Verna Hicks two months ago."

"Does she have a name for us?"

"No, but she has a great description of the man who bought it."

I looked at my watch. It was 10:50.

"How about I pick you up in thirty minutes. Maybe we can grab a bite of lunch after we talk to her."

"I'll call everybody on the list if that's all it takes to get you to take me to lunch."

I went down to the garage and told Louie to bring the cream puff around.

"Not you again," he snarled. "I just put the window in."

"Good. I'll try not to drive into any flying elephants this time."

Without another word, he disappeared with a swagger into the depths of the garage. A minute or two later I heard the Chevy crank up and then he came back, got out, and handed me the keys.

Millicent was waiting just inside the doors of the bank when I pulled up. She was so gorgeous I got a little numb when I saw her. She was dressed in a light taupe business suit with a pink scarf at her throat and a lime-green Robin Hood hat cocked jauntily over one eye. She never took her eyes off me as she walked toward the car.

"You look like you own the bank," I cracked, holding the door for her.

"Not quite yet," she said with a smirk. She sat on the seat, swung silk-sheathed legs in sideways, and crossed them at the knee.

"It's the South View Bank and Trust on West Sixth and Fairfax," she said as I got in the car. I slipped cautiously under the wheel but still got enough of a kickback from my sprained ribs to grimace a little.

"Is something wrong?" she asked with concern.

"Nothing serious. A confused cop tried to use me as a punching bag."

I let it drop there, although I could see her look of anxiety and curiosity. She lit two of her gold-tipped butts and handed one to me. Then she kissed two fingers and laid them on my cheek.

"Thanks," I said, and took a quick look her way. She was staring at me with obvious affection, her mouth slightly open.

"You can get in a lot of trouble with a look like that," I said.

"I hope so," she answered.

I drove down Western, grabbed a right on Sixth, and headed west to Fairfax. The bank was in the center of an upper-middle-class neighborhood. It was a one-story, yellow brick building boxed in by a women's clothing store and a pet store. Patty North was a tiny, well-groomed strawberry blonde in her mid forties, with bright eyes and a perpetually cheery smile. She was head teller and had a little cubicle in the rear of the bank. After introductions, we sat facing her and she took out a file, placed it on her desk, and laid one hand on top of it.

"This isn't quite kosher," she said. "But Millicent assures me it's for a good cause."

I didn't mention murder at this point. I didn't have to. She started right in.

"The gentleman came in a little after noon on a Monday, which was the first," she began. "He was five-eight or five-nine; about forty, give or take a year or two; trim, with a little tummy. Very tan, dark brown hair with some gray in it, and one of those skinny mustaches like William Powell's. He wore a wedding ring on the usual finger and a Masonic ring on the fourth finger of his right hand. He had a kind of cocky smile and he dressed with flash. A cream jacket with a thin red check, tan slacks, two-tone brown and white shoes, a brown fedora, and he was wearing aviator sunglasses, which he did not remove. He didn't say much. He put five one-hundred-dollar bills on the desk and spread them out like you would spread out a pinochle hand, and he put a twenty-five-cent piece on top. That's what we charge for a bank check. He didn't look at me straightaway but kind of kept his head down. He said, 'I require,'—I remember because he said it that way, *require*—'a five-hundred-dollar cashier's check made out to this person.' He had the name Verna Hicks written on a sheet of paper, which he slid across the desk to me. I said to him, 'Who is the issuer?' And he said, 'Is that necessary?' And I said, 'No, but it's customary.' And he said, 'Nix it, just give me a receipt.' That's the way he said it, *Nix it.* So I typed out the check and signed it, and he put it in a brown, letter-sized manila envelope. It was already addressed and stamped. He said thank you and left. The entire transaction took about five minutes. I did notice he had a jaunty kind of step to his walk."

As she spoke, a face flashed in my memory; a face I had seen in Howland's basement on one of the framed front pages. A flashy dresser, thin mustache.

"You have an amazing memory for details," I said.

"Photography is my hobby, particularly portraiture," she said. "There was just something about him. The flashy clothes, the little mustache, the sunglasses, and his voice. There was a harsh quality to it, kind of tough. He was distant but not unfriendly, just seemed to want to get the transaction done and get out of here. It was one of those faces you'd love to capture on film, although I could tell from his attitude that was the last thing he would have been interested in."

I thought for a minute or so and then asked Patty if she had a copy of the phone book. She reached in a large, lower drawer and got it. I flicked through it to the yellow pages and found what I was looking for. A quarter-page ad listed under PRIVATE INVESTIGATIONS. The ad told me that Eddie Woods was an experienced private investigator with eigh-teen years know-how, was bonded, and had references. His office was on the mezzanine floor of the Olympic Tower, on West Olympic and Al-mont. I jotted the phone number down.

I knew the place, a prestigious office building with a marble lobby only slightly smaller than the lobby of the city hall. It was known sim-ply as the Olympic. Eddie Woods was in high cotton for a private eye. Jerry Geisert was a divorce lawyer for the stars, and probably one of Woods's clients, since he was located in the same building and on the same floor.

An idea was gnawing on my brain. There was a sprightly little restaurant across the street from the Olympic called Francine's, which specialized in excellent home cooking. I closed the book and sug-gested all three of us go there for lunch.

Millicent looked at me out of the side of her eye, obviously disap-pointed that I had asked a third party to join us.

"I have an idea," I said by way of explanation.

It took fifteen minutes to drive to Francine's. I parked on the side of the building, went in, and found a table in front, facing the Olympic Tower. The place was just beginning to fill up with the lunchtime trade. The decor was as simple as the bill of fare. White-and-red-checkered tablecloths, menus printed up that day, paper napkins.

"Millie, order for me, will you? I want the turkey pancakes, and corn fritters with lots of maple syrup, and an iced tea. I'm going across the street. I shouldn't be more than ten, fifteen minutes. Patty, watch for me to come out and pay special attention to the person who's with me, if there is anybody with me."

"Is this detective work?" she asked, bright-eyed.

"You betcha," I answered.

CHAPTER 20

The lobby was all marble, bronze, and teak. Twin circular staircases curved up from each side of the room to the mezzanine where, the directory told me, Woods was located in rooms 106 and 107. I took the stairs up.

There was a doctor's office in the corner suite. Attorney Jerry Geisert's suite of offices took up about half the floor and Woods was located in the two offices next to Geisert.

The lettering on the pebbled glass door said EDWARD WOODS, CONFIDENTIAL INQUIRIES and it was locked. The door to the adjoining office was open. I walked down to it and stood in the entrance. The lettering on this door said "Private."

The office was neither flashy nor drab, small nor large. When I looked in, I faced a mahogany desk of average proportions. Against the right wall was a red leather sofa, beginning to show its age, as were the two matching leather chairs that bracketed it. Somebody had told Woods leather impressed people. They forgot to tell him less is better than more. There was a dark wooden hat tree in the corner near the door, and on the desk, a large glass ashtray that could have qualified as a deadly weapon, a leather-wrapped Ronson table lighter, a familiar green package of Luckies, and two phones, one a conventional black job with a handset, the other an old-time stand-up, which Woods was whispering into.

I stood in the entranceway and lightly tapped the glass in the door. He held up a finger without looking at me. A moment later he hung up, waved me in, stood up, and offered me his hand. Twenty years had changed him very little. He still looked younger than his age, still

230

sported the pencil mustache, still had a full head of hair as well as a bronze beach tan and bit of a paunch. His jacket was hanging on the tree. He was wearing a white silk shirt with a thin, pale blue stripe, and an inoffensive tie, red suspenders, and no belt.

"Edward Woods," he said with a practiced smile. "My secretary's gone to lunch."

"My name's Bannon," I said.

"Have a seat."

I dropped my hat on his desk, and as I sat down he looked straight into my eyes. His memory was getting a nibble.

"I'm about to go to lunch, too," he said.

"Nice fish," I said, nodding toward a six-foot marlin mounted on the wall.

"Two hundred and sixty pounds and every ounce a fighter. Took me seven hours to land that baby. I quit going after game fish after that. Anything that will fight that hard to stay alive deserves to die of old age."

"That's an admirable philosophy."

"Thanks. What can I do for you?"

"Ever heard of a woman named Verna Hicks? Or Verna Wilensky, which was her married name?"

His eyebrows drew together and his eyes went from interested to suspicious. He took a drag on his cigarette and blew out a couple of smoke rings.

"This a missing persons thing?" he asked. "You might do better starting with the police."

"I know where she is. She's down in the city morgue waiting for the state to bury her."

A casual smile crossed his lips and his eyes became less intense. He nodded more or less to himself and chuckled.

"Sergeant Bannon, right? Central homicide."

I nodded. "If we've met, you've got a better memory than I do."

"You've been in the headlines a few times. This about the dame whose radio took a bath with her?"

"You heard about it?"

"It was in the *Times*. Just a couple of graphs. No name on her. Didn't sound like a job for homicide."

"You read every line in the paper?"

"Always looking for an angle," he shrugged. "You'd be surprised what a guy can pick up if he keeps his eyes open and reads every page. I read the gossips, too."

"There's an angle in this one. She died with a lot of money in a savings account. I'm trying to locate survivors."

"Well," he said, standing up and walking to the tree to retrieve his suit jacket, "she's no relative of mine."

He slipped on the jacket and went back behind his desk but didn't sit down. My eyes wandered to the photographs on the desk. One was a sepia tintype of Woods, Culhane, and Buck Tallman. The other was a tinted studio shot of Woods standing with his arms around the waist of a pretty, black-haired woman who looked to be in her late thirties.

"Very pretty woman," I said, nodding at the picture.

"Thanks," he said. "I'll tell her you said so. That's my wife, Hazel. We're celebrating our tenth anniversary today. We check into a little hotel, have room service, put out the Do Not Disturb sign . . . a little tradition we have." He looked at his watch and then back at me, and raised his eyebrows.

I stood up, too.

"The Hicks woman died with almost a hundred grand in the bank."

It didn't shake him one way or the other.

"Most of it came in the form of five-hundred-dollar cashier's checks that showed up once a month over the last seventeen years. Most of them were sent from up San Pietro way."

"Is that a fact?" He came around the desk, took my arm by the elbow, and led me toward the door. "Come on, I'll go down with you."

He was a very smooth character. If I was annoying him, he didn't show it. He set the latch on the office door, pulled it shut, and tried it to make sure it locked. We walked down the marble stairs together.

"You see some connection between the checks and her radio jumping in the tub with her?" he asked on the way down.

"No. It just keeps gnawing at me. A woman with that much money in the bank, no will, and suddenly dead."

"Happens all the time. Nobody thinks they're gonna die. They put things off."

"I suppose."

As we walked out the front door, I turned around in front of him so he was facing the restaurant and stuck out my hand.

"Well, thanks for your time," I said. "I was hoping since you left San Pietro about the same time the checks started, the name might ring a bell."

"Sorry," he said with a pleasant smile. "I don't hear a thing."

As he started to turn, I said, "How about Lila Parrish? Didn't she disappear about that time?"

He stopped, and turned around. His eyes narrowed.

"What's that got to do with anything?"

"She's never turned up, has she?"

People scurried around us on the sidewalk. The street was full of cars going places during the lunch hour. A horn or two beeped. He walked over very close to me and said, "There's a lot of funny ideas in that question."

"I don't get you," I said.

"Sure you do. You tell me this Hicks dame was on somebody's pad for five bills a month. Then you tell me the checks came from San Pietro. Then you ask about the other broad, Parrish, who was a witness in one of my cases. I could hop about two feet and make something out of all that. Parrish skipped out, pal. Nobody knows where. I, for one, haven't seen her since the trial. Nobody else I know has either."

"Fair enough," I said.

"You know what I think, Bannon?"

"Nope."

"I think you're more interested in finding out who was sending money to that lady than finding her family."

"I'd like to see her get a decent send-off, that's all."

"Then pass the hat around the station house, you ought to be able to pick up twenty bucks. Here . . ." He reached in his pocket and took out a small roll of cash, peeled a five off it, and slapped it in the breast pocket of my jacket. "That'll get it started."

He turned and disappeared in the river of pedestrians.

I jaywalked back across the street to the restaurant. When I got to the table, Patty North was so excited she was bouncing in her chair.

"It's him," she said. "He's the one. How did you know that?"

"I'm a detective, remember?" I said, sitting down at the table. "That's what I'm supposed to do."

I reached in my pocket, took out the crumpled five-spot and dropped it on the table.

"What's that?" Millicent asked.

"He just started a fund to bury Verna."

"What a wonderful idea!" Her eyes brightened and she said excitedly, "We can go back to the bank after lunch and open an account. I'll put in fifty."

I laughed. "Millie, with fifty bucks we can lay her away in a solid silver coffin, with the Philadelphia Symphony playing 'Goodnight, Irene.' "

The waiter brought our meals and we dug in.

"Now, Patty," I said, "you are sure that's the guy who bought the check for Verna Hicks, aren't you?"

"Oh, absolutely," she said, nodding her head emphatically. "There's no question about it."

"You did a great job," I said. "Thanks."

We finished lunch and I dropped Patty North off at her bank with more thanks.

On the way back to the West L.A. bank, Millicent said, "He's the one you've been looking for, isn't he?"

"Yes and no," I said.

"I don't understand."

"His name is Eddie Woods. He was a cop up in San Pietro, got in some trouble, and left about the time Verna Hicks showed up down here. Now we know for sure he bought at least one of the checks. The next question is, who gave him the money to buy it."

"He didn't buy it himself?"

I shook my head.

"I don't think so," I said. "He wouldn't have had that kind of dough back in the late twenties and early thirties. Whoever made that deal with Verna was wealthy. He knew he could pay off for as long as it took. Woods wouldn't have driven all the way back to San Pietro to buy the other checks, everybody there knew him. I think his was probably a one-shot deal. I goofed."

"How?" Millicent asked.

"By looking for a single buyer. Obviously the checks were bought by different people through the years. Whoever was paying off Verna probably brokered the buy through a middleman. And that's going to make it even harder to trace them back to the number one."

"I'm sorry," a crestfallen Millicent said.

I smiled at her. "Don't be. It was a great break. She's a regular Charlie Chan. One thing I am sure of, thanks to her. Eddie Woods knows who the number one is."

"How do you know that?"

"He was too far up in the hierarchy not to. Maybe he *is* the middleman. I have to go back up to San Pietro tomorrow. I think I can get some answers now."

"If we have the money to bury Verna, can't you just forget it?"

"Not anymore."

"I don't understand."

I got very serious. "You've got to keep what I'm going to tell you under that cute little hat of yours for the next day or two. You can't even confide in your father."

"Alright, what is it?"

"Verna Wilensky was murdered. She was drowned, and whoever did the trick dropped the radio in the tub with her to make it look like an accident."

"Oh my God!" She covered her mouth with her hand. Tears suddenly gathered in her eyes.

"Now it's a homicide, and I've got to find out who killed her."

"Can't you ask Woods?"

I tried to smother a laugh. "I don't think that would work with Mr. Woods. He's not going to give up that information, not after all these years of covering it up. I may be able to hammer information out of him but I'll save him for later. First I want to see Culhane's face when I tell him this is now a homicide case and they'll have to stop playing coy."

I pulled up in front of her bank and struggled out of the car.

"Please don't get out," she said.

"They kicked in my ribs; they didn't kick my manners out of me."

I walked around the car and helped her out. As she stepped by me, she brushed my cheek with her lips.

"We still on for tonight?" I asked.

"We better be."

"I thought we might drop by the C-Note after the show."

She tossed me one of her million-dollar smiles. "I'd love that," she said. "Wherever it is."

I stood there and watched her disappear into the bank. And I thought to myself, *So* that's *what they mean by the luck of the Irish.*

CHAPTER 21

I made a call to Ski at the Wilensky house and got one of the forensics men. After I identified myself, he confided Ski was out in the
neighborhood.

"Anything new?" I asked.

"Ski thinks whoever iced the lady laid up all day in the house next
door and then went after her when she got in the tub."

"When Ski gets back, tell him I've got a call to make and then I'll
be on over."

"Sure," he said, and we hung up.

I made one more call and then drove across town to a little bar
called Murphy's Eight Ball, which was a hangout for off-duty cops and
newsies. It was 3:30, too early for any action. The bartender was un-
loading bottles of beer in a cooler behind an empty bar. In the rear, a
tall, rangy guy chewing on a wooden match was practicing side-pocket
bank shots at one of the two pool tables. Up front, the dozen tables and
booths all were empty. Jimmy Dorsey's "Amapola" was muttering from
the jukebox, its volume turned down to a whisper. The bartender
looked up through bored eyes and gave me half a smile.

"Zee," he said with a nod. "Little early for you, isn't it?"

"I'm meeting Jimmy Pen," I said. "Draw me one, will you?"

He took a frosted mug from the refrigerator and tilted it under the
beer spigot and jimmied the glass full without putting too much head
on it. I picked up a rumpled copy of the early *Times* edition and retreated to a booth as far away from both men as possible. Under a wall
lamp that put out about as much wattage as a penlight, I read the banner head: *BISMARCK* ATTACKED. The lead graph told me all I needed to
know: the British Navy had hunted down the German juggernaut,

which had sunk the HMS *Hood* and all its hands three days earlier. A battle royal was going on somewhere in the North Atlantic. I leafed back to the obits but there was no follow-up on the Wilensky story.

The door opened and a shaft of sunlight cut through the dark interior as Jimmy Pennington strolled in, hat on the back of his head and a newspaper folded and stuffed in his jacket pocket. He was carrying a brown nine-by-twelve envelope. The door swung shut behind him and he peered around the room until he spotted me.

He pointed to my glass and said to the barkeep, "Hey, Jerry, gimme one of these, will you please?" as he sat down, dropped his hat on the seat beside him, and laid the envelope by his elbow. Then to me, "I don't believe it, you can actually read," as he pointed to the dog-eared early edition.

"I can count all the way to ten, too, if I take my shoes off," I said.

"You must want something awful bad to offer to buy me a drink."

"I'm going to do you a favor, pal," I said.

"*And* pay for my drink? You don't believe I believe that, do you?"

"Why are all you newsies such cynics?"

"If I am, I learned it from you. So what's the scam for today?"

"No scam. I'm offering you a trade."

"Uh-oh."

Jerry brought the reporter his beer and a dish of pretzel sticks. I told him to put it on my tab.

"The last time a cop bought me a drink, we still had Prohibition."

"That's worth an item right there."

"I assume all this has something to do with the stuff you asked for."

"A reasonable assumption."

"What the hell are you interested in Mendosa for? It's off your beat by about a hundred miles."

"I'll get to that. First, I'm going to offer you an exclusive story. Your end is, you can't break it until the five-star tomorrow afternoon."

"How big a story?"

"It'll put a smile on your face."

"Front page?"

"Hell, I'm not an editor, I . . ."

"Don't hand me that shit, Zee. After fifteen years you know a banner story when you see one. Above the fold or below it?"

"What do I know about folds? Do we have a deal?"

"It's a pig in a poke. What's your angle?"

"You'll understand when I finish. After we're through talking, I'll go back and write my report, which will back up everything I tell you. You can write the story ahead of time but you have to hold it until 4:00 tomorrow. I'll file the report then, and that'll give you a scoop."

He thought for a minute and said: "Make it 5:00. We hit the street at 5:30 and all the competition'll be off and drunk by then."

"I can work that."

"This some kind of undercover job you've been working on?"

"You want to listen or play twenty questions?"

He took a sip of beer, took out a little green pad and the stub of a Ticonderoga pencil, and stared at me.

I gave him a pretty straightforward rundown on how we found Verna Hicks Wilensky, Bones's initial reaction, then got into the stuff in the strongbox, and finished with the five-hundred-a-month and the cashier's checks. That got his attention. I continued with my trip to San Pietro, how the bankers were giving me the cold shoulder, left out the encounter with the two cops, and then dropped the second shoe: Bones's reanalysis of the situation. He stopped writing and took a long swig of his beer when he realized he was on top of a murder case.

I then recounted the Wilma Thompson murder case, the appeal, and the missing witness, Lila Parrish, Eddie Woods's probable assassination of Fontonio, his connection with both cases; and finally the fact that most of the checks came from San Pietro. I didn't tell him I knew Eddie Woods had sent at least one of the checks; I kept that for my hole card.

"Is that it?" he asked.

"For Christ sake, you want me to write it for you?"

"You're trying to tie this to Culhane's tail," he said, and it wasn't a question.

"I can't tell you that, it's privileged."

He chuckled. "The hell you say."

"You didn't get to be top-slot reporter on the *Times* by having somebody else do your thinking for you," I said.

He tapped his pencil on the table several times and stared at me, then said, "You want me to grease the tracks for you."

"What do you mean?"

"Don't act dumb. You're going up against Brodie Culhane and you want me to point the finger in his general direction."

"I didn't say that."

"No, I said it."

"You want the story or not, Jimmy?"

"I *got* the story. Question is, what am I gonna do with it? And how are you going to tie this to Culhane?"

"You're beginning to sound like Moriarity."

"I'm sounding like my editor. Can I quote you that you're looking for a connection up in the San Pietro area?"

I juggled that around for a minute. Before I could answer, he said, "And how do you plan to tie Woods into this? So he lives in Los Angeles, so do a million and a half other people. And what's the connection with Mendosa?"

"Let's talk about that for a minute. What've you got for me?"

He slid the envelope over, opened the clasp, and pulled out a sheaf of clippings. "Most of this stuff was written by Matt Sorenson, who covered state news," he said.

"Where is he now?"

"The big time lured him to New York. But he used to talk about Mendosa. He wanted to blow the roof off the town, but it's outside our circulation area and the publisher squeezes every nickel so hard the buffalo gets a hernia. Most of what Matt wrote was what he could get over the phone, mixed with AP and UPI reports."

"You need these back?" I asked, lifting a handful of clippings.

"Yeah, but there's no rush."

"Tell me what you know about Mendosa."

He finished his beer and ordered another.

"Since when did you start drinking on the job?" I said.

"I'm through for the day. I'm gonna take full advantage of your tab." He lit a cigarette and started: "When Culhane got rid of Riker and Fontonio, the number-three man in the mob was Guilfoyle. He took a powder. He moved down south to Mendosa. It's in Pacifico County. It wasn't much of a town, a lazy little place. Its main claim to fame is a sanitarium, mostly a spill for drunks, druggies, and senile old folks their kids want to dump. Guilfoyle didn't have much trouble taking over and turning it into another Eureka. It wasn't quite as wide open but the town turned dirty from head to toe."

Pennington rooted around in the clippings and found a photograph. "Take a gander at Guilfoyle. He's a real package." He slid it across the table to me. I held it under the anemic light and saw a tall, beefy mutt in a light suit, uglier than a cross-eyed moose. He had thick features over a bull neck and two hundred pounds of muscle and flab. A cigar was tucked in the corner of his mouth and he wore a derby low over weasel eyes. His lips were curled into a smile that was closer to a sneer.

"Straight out of central casting," I said.

"So what's your interest in Mendosa?"

"One of the checks came from a bank up there."

"If you think you had trouble with Culhane, I'd steer clear of Mendosa. Guilfoyle could get you two years for disturbing the peace if you sneezed in town."

"Let me try something else on you. Supposing when Lila Parrish vanished she went down the road and hid out in Mendosa for a while. Then migrated down to L.A. and changed her name."

"You think Verna Hicks was Lila Parrish?"

"Think about it. All these events happened within about eighteen months, starting with Riker's trial in late 1922 and ending with the Fontonio hit in 1924, the same year Verna showed up in L.A., telling people she was from everyplace in Texas."

"That's another stretch, Zeke. Supposing Lila Parrish is living with her husband and family in Dubuque? Does the word slander mean anything to you? Do you have anything other than a hunch leading you there?"

I decided to play my hole card. "Can we go off the record a minute?" I said.

He pondered that. Reporters hate to go off-record for anything.

"Is it important, or one of your Canadian Club dreams?"

"It's fact."

"Okay, but I get it first when you're ready to go public."

"It's your story all the way."

"What a sweetheart. Okay, let's hear it."

"One of the more recent checks sent to Hicks was bought and mailed from here in town. The buyer was Eddie Woods."

That perked him up a bit. "You can prove this?" he said.

I nodded. "The teller who sold him the check ID'd him to me over lunch."

"It's still a stretch."

"Look, I've given you all the background we have on Hicks. You can point out that she showed up down here after Lila Parrish vamoosed. The dates are more than coincidental."

"How about the checks. Can I get photos of them?"

I nodded. "I'll list the number of checks and how many came from the San Pietro–Mendosa area. I can't give you the stats of the original checks because there may be some question about how I got them without a search warrant. I don't want to get anybody in trouble over this."

"How about her checks?"

"Fair game, they were in her safety box at home. I can also make the deposit books available to you."

"Exclusively?"

"Until the story breaks. Then anything in the report is fair game."

He laughed. "You'll be all over the papers again."

"I won't be here."

"Where will you be?"

"Up north," I said.

"Anything you get, I get first. That's part of the deal."

"Must be nice," I said. "Having me do your work for you."

"Works both ways, pal," he said, and then with a leer added: "By the way, mind if I mention that pansy dog of yours in the story?"

"Where did you hear about the dog?"

"I can't tell you that," he said. "It's privileged."

I had a different feeling going to the house in Pacific Meadows this time. Murder changes everything. Just knowing it happened is sobering. But inside the house, Ski was jubilant, as was Bones.

"Progress," Bones said. "We've got enough fingerprints from this place and the empty house next door to keep the F.B.I. busy for a month."

"I don't have a month. I don't have a week. Every day, this case slips further away."

"We've made some progress," Ski said casually.

"All talk and theories. I need some hard evidence."

"Oh," Ski said sardonically. "Well, how about this. The killer is about your size, maybe a little shorter, ten pounds heavier. He was wearing dark pants, a dark shirt, and a bowler. He cased the neighborhood for an hour or so the day before he killed her. At about 6:00 A.M. the day of the killing, the killer parked his car in the empty lot at the end of that strip of stores up on Main. He walked down six blocks to the house next door, after ascertaining that nobody was home from the papers gathering on the porch and possibly calling once or twice. He sat at a table near the front door for the whole day. Actually, he ate a sandwich, which he probably brought with him, and took the refuse with him when he left."

I sat there entranced as Ski painted a verbal portrait of the killing. And he was almost as good at it as Bones.

"When Verna went inside, the killer went out the back door, went to the side of her house, and watched her until he heard her drawing a bath. He wouldn't have used the front door, too chancy, but none of the windows were locked either. He went in, took off his gloves, went straight into the bathroom, and about 9:18 P.M. he shoved her underwater. He held her under for about five minutes. Then he noticed the radio, pulled down the shelf, and let it drop in the tub with her. He went out the same way he came in, walked back up to his car, and at about 9:50 he drove away."

"How do you know all this?" I asked.

"An old man two blocks over had a stroke six months ago. He sits on the front porch swing all day, every day. He saw the guy drive by four or five times. Tan-and-black ragtop. He thinks a Ford. A kid left his baseball mitt up at the ball diamond. He went up there on his bike to get it when he got up about 6:15 A.M. He was riding slow because he had a flashlight in one hand to see where he was going. When he passed the house, he saw the guy we described jimmy open the door. The guy had a small penlight in his mouth and the kid got a good shot of his hands. He was wearing black gloves. Gloves in May?"

Bones picked up the story: "He sat there all day, waiting for it to get dark. He sat by the front door so nothing would surprise him, even brought a sandwich, and ate it there. We know Verna never locked her windows. We found some threads under the bottom sill; he probably tore his jacket coming in. He went in the bedroom, saw her in the tub, took off the gloves so he wouldn't have to carry them away wet, then he rushed her, shoved her head underwater, and you know the rest. He left the same way, walked back up to the stores, and drove off into the night. We know that because a druggist and his wife were doing inventory, and they saw a guy in a bowler come out of the Meadows about 9:50 and drive off in the brown-and-black ragtop that was parked at the end of the strip all day."

"No facial description?" I asked Ski.

"No."

"License number?"

"No."

"Have you put out an APB on the car?"

"Yeah, but they can't stop every black-and-brown Ford in the county."

Bones said, "We got a fresh print off the shelf the radio was on. Another one off the commode trigger, like Ski suggested. We also picked up several prints off the table next door. Nobody eats with gloves on. We'll isolate the prints in Wilensky's bathroom and compare them to the ones on the table. If they match, and we can find the guy, we got our case."

"How soon will you know whether they match?"

He pursed his lips and thought about the question for a minute. "Five days?"

"Five days!"

"It's gotta go to Washington and then go through the F.B.I. process."

"Three days."

"I'll push for four. And that's fast."

I nodded. Then Ski threw one in from the deep outfield.

"I think this bird's an ex-con," he said.

Bones looked at him with surprise. "How do you figure?" he asked.

"Who else would set up a job where he has to sit in one spot all day but a guy who's spent a couple of years sitting in an eight-by-ten cell day in and day out."

Bones smiled. "If he is, his prints could be on file here in the state."

"It's too easy," Ski said. "We ain't gonna get that lucky. This guy's a pro. Casing the job, figuring out how to do it, noticing the papers on the porch so he knew there was nobody home. He had it all figured out."

"Yep," Bones agreed. "But even pros make mistakes. If he had just thrown the radio in the tub without drowning her first, she would have been killed instantly, and we would never have known the dif. Ironic, isn't it? That blunder may just get him a noseful of gas."

Me? I was wondering what kind of car Eddie Woods was driving these days.

CHAPTER 22

I was high up on Beverly Drive when I found Boxwood. I could see why Millie asked me if I wanted directions. It wasn't much of a street—barely two lanes wide and unpaved. The sign was lost among shrubs and trees. I made the sharp turn and followed the bumpy road around several curves. There was an occasional mailbox but the area was so heavily forested you could hardly see the houses from the road. Then the woods to the south began to thin out and I could catch fleeting glimpses of Beverly Hills and to its right, in the early evening haze, the sprawling Twentieth Century–Fox lot. I could see the big arc lights occasionally streaking into the evening sky from the sets where Tyrone Power or Gene Tierney or Don Ameche, the reigning monarchs of the studio, were probably shooting a scene in New York or Singapore, courtesy of the designers and carpenters who created movie magic.

I came on the property suddenly. The forest closed in on me again, I went around a shallow curve, and there it was. A stone wall about three feet high enclosed several acres of woods. The mailbox was imbedded in the wall. I could see the house flickering past through the trees, about two hundred or three hundred feet back in the woods. I turned in an open gate and drove down the dirt road that wound lazily around trees and wild bushes to the house.

It was a surprise. In my mind I had pictured one of those big Beverly Hills mansions, but this house was rustic, a high-peaked, one-story built of stone and wood. Cedar shingles surrounded an enormous chimney that was in the center of the structure. I drove past the carport, its door raised and the Pierce-Arrow Phaeton parked inside, up to a massive teakwood front door.

I was wearing my best suit, the blue linen double-breasted, with a pale blue French-cuffed shirt, a yellow tie with little blue dingbats, my best cordovan wing tips, and the small gold cuff links that, with $784, were my inheritance from my father. I had sixty-five bucks in my wallet including another ten Moriarity had given me for expenses. I was dressed to the nines and why not. I was going to take a Coldwater Canyon princess to the deli for dinner and to a free movie.

Chimes rang softly somewhere inside. The door opened immediately and she was standing there, her grin as wide as Sunset Boulevard and her eyes sparkling as they caught the rays of sun filtering through the trees.

"Hi," she said. "Any trouble finding the place?"

"Came right to it."

"I know, you're a cop," she said. "You can find any street in town and you remember phone numbers."

She took my hand and led me into the house, stepping aside as she did. The dog sat behind her. A pure white German shepherd, larger than Rosie, his pointed ears straight up on alert, his eyes, coal black at the center ringed with flecks of yellow, looking straight at me.

"I keep running into dogs every time I go through a door," I said.

"This is Montana," she said. "He's very well trained and very friendly, as long as you don't do something stupid."

"Is that supposed to reassure me?"

"He's a dear. You'll grow to love him, just like Rosebud."

"I'm calling him Rosie, after a prizefighter."

"I know who Slapsie Maxie Rosenbloom is," she said with fake exasperation.

"How come you call him Montana?"

"Because that's where he came from. Dad has a little spread out there, uses it for hunting. His caretaker's dog had pups and I got the pick of the litter."

A little spread. For hunting. With a caretaker. In Montana. What am I doing here?

I walked past her into a wide hallway that went all the way through the house. There was a staircase on the right side that curved around to the second floor, where what looked like two rooms were tucked into the eaves of the otherwise A-frame structure.

"I'll be ready in five minutes," she said, trotting up the steps.

"Make yourself at home." She stopped about halfway up, leaned over the banister, and pointed out directions to me. "The bar's to your left at the end of the hall, sitting room to the right, terrace straight ahead. Montana will show you around."

And she disappeared.

Montana stood up and walked slowly toward the rear of the house as if he understood every word. I followed him.

There were archways on both sides of the hall. To my left was the kitchen and to the right, a library, which smelled of leather, its shelves jammed with books. One chair, enormous with an equally enormous ottoman, held down a corner of the room, with a coffee table on one side of it, an unruly stack of magazines on the other side, a floor lamp behind it. The record player and her records filled almost an entire bookshelf behind the chair.

The main room was at the end of the hall and ran the full width of the place. It was huge. The fireplace, an island of brick and brass, served as a room divider, separating the barroom on the left from the sitting room on the right. The ceiling soared above, forming the back side of the A-frame. Skylights made both rooms bright and inviting.

The sitting room was furnished with white goose down sofas and chairs. It was a room decorated for comfort. On a table at one side of the living room were a dozen or so photographs: pictures of Millicent as a child in riding clothes on a black horse; family groups; Millicent on graduation day with her father standing proudly beside her. And one photograph of a roguish-looking young man in an RAF uniform with the insignia of the Eagle Squadron—a group of Americans who, in 1940, had formed their own flying squad within the British Air Force. Scrawled across the bottom was: "To my dear heart, Mill the Pill. Keep the faith. Hugh. 11/14/40."

An enormous window faced the terrace, with French doors on either side.

And what a terrace.

I followed Montana onto a length of neatly mowed lawn, twenty feet I guessed, up to the swimming pool, which stretched the length of the terrace and looked at first like a reflecting pond. I walked around one end of it out to the edge of the terrace and watched a broad facade of water, almost as long as the pool itself, pouring like a solid sheet straight down on rocks a dozen feet below and, in turn, running into a small pond surrounded by wildflowers. Then there was a tennis court, and beyond it the forest sloped down to a natural stream that tumbled down the hillside. The stone wall ended five feet from the stream, with a gate at its center. On the other side of the creek, nothing but trees. A sudden breeze took the heat out of the air and brought with it a guarantee of rain.

I was in a place far, far away from the L.A. I knew.

"So this is where Adam bumped into Eve," I said to Montana.

"I assume from that remark you like it," Millicent said, behind me.

I turned and walked back to the doorway. She was dressed in a pastel blue, lightweight cashmere blazer, white blouse, a pleated yellow silk skirt, and a matching silk scarf around her long, aristocratic neck. She was so chic she embarrassed the word.

"If Eve looked as good as you, Adam wouldn't have been interested in apples," I said.

She blushed, her lips parted slightly, and she stared up at me for several seconds. Then she smiled and said, "Wasn't it Eve who was interested in apples?"

We stood a foot apart, staring at each other, until she broke the spell. "Come on, we'll be late," she said. And to Montana, "Alert, Monty." His attitude changed. He suddenly got serious. He pranced around one corner of the pool and off into the woods.

"He's beautifully trained," I said.

"Thank you," she said brightly. "When he's on alert, he gets very officious."

"I can tell. Shall I close this door?" I said as we went back into the house.

"No, leave it open for him, he likes to patrol the place when I'm not here. Or take a swim. Or chase a rabbit. I lock the front door but it's for show. No thief in his right mind would take him on."

She turned on a couple of lights and we headed for the door.

"I've always had shepherds," she said, leading me toward the door. "My first was Buck. I named him after the dog in *Call of the Wild*."

"Buck was a malamute," I said.

"Not in my head he wasn't," she said with an arrogant lift of her chin.

When we got outside, she turned toward the carport and tossed me her car keys.

"Let's take the Phaeton," she said. "You drive."

"Aww," I said, "and I've got the company's best car."

"How did you swing that?"

"I have to go up the coast early in the morning."

"Is this about Verna?"

"Yeah," I said, "I'll be back tomorrow night late." And dropped it at that.

We made small talk as I kept the car in third gear and wound our way down to Sunset Boulevard, where I turned left, heading up to Hollywood. A block or two from Grauman's I pulled down a side street and parked in front of Harry's Absolutely Genuine New York Delicatessen.

BRITISH SINK *BISMARCK*

And the subhead:

NAZI JUGGERNAUT BLOWN FROM SEA;
ENGLISH FLEET AVENGES *HOOD* LOSS

I threw a dime in the cigar box on top of the papers and took two.

Harry's was just what it claimed to be. Black and white tile floors, red leather booths, white linoleum tabletops, wooden chairs with heart-shaped backs. Lots of light. The smell of salami and pastrami mixed with the rich aroma of the bakery.

Harry, at the front counter slicing turkey, looked up and yowled, "Hey, Zee, where ya been? I thought you died."

"I've been busy, Harry."

"So, you don't eat when you're busy?" He shook his head in disapproval. "Better not let Mama hear."

"Where is she?"

"Home with the grandkids. It's Tuesday. Who goes to the deli on Tuesday? Sit anywhere, Zee. Menus on the tables tonight."

We sat across from each other in one of the front booths and I gave Millie one of the two newspapers I'd picked up by the entrance. Her mouth was agape as she scanned the headline about the *Bismarck*.

I started reading the story. British dive-bombers had jammed the rudder of Germany's proudest battleship and it had circled helplessly while the British closed in and blew it to bits. According to the account, the *Bismarck* lost 2,400 men in its final battle.

Harry came to the table and read the headline over my shoulder.

"Harry, this is my friend Millie," I said. He stepped back, looked her over, and put his hand over his heart.

"Beautiful, exquisite," he said, rolling his eyes. "My heart goes pitty-pat. What you think, Zee. You think we get into this war?"

"You want to live in a world with Hitler on one side of us and Tōjō on the other?" I asked.

A two column yarn in the lower left corner of the front page described a near riot caused by America Firsters, pacifists who were against America getting into the war, and a group of American Legionnaires. There was a photo of angry men in overseas caps yelling at a group of businessmen carrying signs that said LINDBERGH SAYS STAY OUT OF EUROPE, and an ugly cartoon of a leering Roosevelt with Death swinging a scythe behind him and a caption that read ROOSEVELT THE WARMONGER.

"Now there's an irony. A bunch of business types on a picket line calling Roosevelt a warmonger, and the British and Nazis are blowing each other up in the North Sea."

"Corned beef and cabbage is the special," Harry said, to loosen up the tension. "I musta had a premonition you were coming, Zee."

"Sounds good to me," Millie said, and handed him her menu.

"On two, with draft beer," I said.

"Splendid," Harry said, and rushed off to the kitchen to get our dinner.

Millie shuddered. "Every day it's something awful," she said, turning her attention back to a war which couldn't be too far away. "My heart stops every time I see that photograph of the Nazis marching past the Eiffel Tower." She paused, and added, "You think we'll get into it, don't you?"

"Just a question of time." I nodded.

"Will you have to go?" she asked me.

I shrugged, trying to brush it off.

"Do you remember the war?" she asked.

Did I remember it? Oh, yeah.

"I was nine years old when my father went off to France," I told her. "I had a poster in my room. Uncle Sam without his top hat and coat. An angry Uncle Sam pointing straight at me and saying 'I Want You.' It scared me to look at it. Every day was a dread, every time the telegraph kid came down the street on his bicycle, we prayed it wouldn't stop at our house. I'd lie in bed at night and cry. I cried every night because I didn't think it was possible for my father to survive."

"I'm so sorry," she said, reaching across the table and taking my hand. "Did he?"

"What was left of him," I said.

I didn't tell her about the day my dad came home. My dad was a big guy with a crazy Irish sense of humor. The man who got off the train was like a shadow of that man. He had been gassed and it had reduced him to a wraith with sunken eyes who had seen a thousand horrors. His hands shook and he coughed a lot. He couldn't hold a job. He wouldn't talk about the war. I know now my dad had been dying. It took him twelve years, but each day he died a little more, until his lungs finally gave out. My mother died along with him. She lasted three years longer, the last two in such misery I still try to block it out of my mind.

This war, when it came, would be worse.

So I just said, "Sometimes I think it would be worse to wait at home than be in the middle of it."

"I've already lost someone in Europe," she said, staring blankly at the newspaper.

"When?"

"Nineteen forty. My cousin Hugh. Crazy cousin Hugh."

"What happened to him?"

"He was always crazy about airplanes. Learned to fly when he was a kid. When they formed the Eagle Squadron he raced off to London and joined up. I got a card from him after his first flight. He had shot down a Messerschmitt his first time out and he was so proud. Two days later he went down over France."

"I'm sorry." It sounded pitifully inadequate. I decided to lighten things up.

"I saw his picture in the living room. 'Mill the Pill'?"

It got a laugh out of her.

"That's what he called me. Hugh was the hell-raiser in the family and I was Miss Proper. Growing up we fought like brother and sister,

but when I was a teenager going to school back East he took me in
hand."

"So you turned into a hell-raiser, too?"

"I'm still trying."

"And what's the most audacious thing you ever did?"

She thought about it for a full minute.

"I sneaked over the wall at Miss Brownington's School for Girls
and went to see *King Kong* at the Radio City Music Hall."

I faked surprise. "Wow!" I said.

"That was a major step for me, sir," she said haughtily. "I could
have been expelled."

Not likely, I thought. *Not when your father owns half of Montana.*

The marquee said "Special Preview Tonight" and there was a long line
at Grauman's Theater when we got there, plus the usual crowd of
tourists looking at the wide walkway leading to the ticket booth with all
the hand- and footprints of the stars immortalized in concrete. Frank
was standing in the entrance in his tuxedo, smiling as the paying customers streamed in. He waved us over and led us into an almost full
house. There were three rows toward the back roped off in velvet for
the special guests.

Most of those seated in the "velvet rows" were studio execs. Pro-
ducers, flacks, and their friends. The stars, if they showed up, would
come in when the house lights dimmed.

Hedy Lamarr came in as the lights lowered, tall, dressed in a white
hooded dress, her jet-black hair framing porcelain features. The ice
princess, aloof, unreachable, the epitome of a Hollywood glamour
queen. Frank unhooked the velvet rope and she took the aisle seat.
Her escort, whom nobody noticed, stepped past her and sat down.

Jackie Cooper came in next, accompanied by an older woman I assumed was his mother. I hadn't seen Cooper in a movie since he was a
kid. Now he looked to be about fifteen. Judy Garland came in last, and
sat with a small, strange-looking man with bug eyes. The studio people
nervously awaited the audience reaction to what was obviously one of
their major pictures of the year. James Stewart, Lana Turner, Lamarr,
and Garland were the stars. It was terrific. Three young singers and
dancers make it big in the Ziegfeld Follies. There was a spectacular

Busby Berkeley dance number, but Garland stole the show with a heartbreaking rendition of "I'm Always Chasing Rainbows." The picture got a big hand from the audience and the stars slipped out while the cast credits were still rolling.

We stopped to thank Frank and then ran through the first drops of rain to the Phaeton. Big drops began to fall, splattering against the windshield as we got in the car.

"How about a nightcap?" I asked.

She leaned over close to me and said, "That would be very nice."

Maury's C-Note was on Santa Monica near Moreland, on the edge of Beverly Hills. Maury Castellano had started the club with a one-hundred-dollar tip from Victor Mature, which he'd gotten when he was maître d' at Robie's Nightclub on Vine, a popular hangout for the movie set. He had used the C-Note to option a large garage and raised money from friends to remodel it. It was a comfortable supper club with pretty good food and a piano bar. The walls were lined with photos of Hollywood's greats and near-greats.

I let Millie out at the door, parked the car, and ran through the rain to join her.

Maury held down the corner of the main bar and got up to jiggle my elbow when we entered. He did not like to shake hands.

"Hey, Zee, long time no see." He grinned.

"I've been fighting crime," I said with as straight a face as I could muster, and introduced him to Millie.

He bowed low, made a pass at kissing her hand, and said to me, "The Bucket?" I nodded.

The attraction for aficionados was the back room, where a bass player named Chuck Graves held nightly jam sessions with musician friends. The room had become a spot for big-name musicians to stop by and sit in with Graves's trio. Chuck's daytime job was as a studio musician, playing in the orchestra at Columbia Pictures.

The room, located in the rear of the club behind closed doors, was small, a mecca for true jazz lovers who cared more about music than decor and comfort. It seated about fifty people, on bridge chairs. The tables were just big enough to hold a couple of drinks and an ashtray. The place didn't really get jumping until around midnight but things were lively enough when we entered.

A cloud of cigarette smoke clung to the ceiling like fog. It was hot. The mismatched furniture looked like it had been picked up off street corners, the walls were painted black, and the stage was a platform supported on concrete blocks. A fan high on one wall over the rear door was doing a failed job of sucking out the smoke and heat.

I didn't recognize anybody in the room, although some looked interesting: a big man with lazy eyes in a checked sports jacket, who Chuck said was an actor, making a name for himself in westerns, and who leaned forward in his chair with his elbows on his knees, chain-smoking, listening to every note; a bald man doing a crossword, tapping his foot to the music but never looking up; a woman in a leopard coat, sitting with a little man in a tuxedo who was sweating like a sumo wrestler.

The group consisted of Graves; a tall, ebony-black piano player with a grin almost as wide as the hall; a horn player named Turk Ziegler, who used a mute most of the time; Bravo Jones, a balding alto sax man in the baggiest suit I ever saw—no tie; a skinny drummer in a striped shirt and a bow tie; and a diminutive colored man with a thin mustache, dressed in a Sunday suit and tie, playing electric guitar. They were wrapping up a lively version of "Airmail Special" as we entered. We sat at one of the dime-sized tables near the bandstand and ordered drinks from a waiter who looked like he was wilting.

Graves, a tall, rangy, good-looking blond with a musician's pallor and sad brown eyes, walked over to the table with a kind of loose limbed slouch. His soft, mellow voice drove the girls crazy, especially when he sang sad ballads.

"Hi, copper," he said with a wry grin. But he didn't look at me, he was staring at Millie. He kissed her hand and added, "Chuck Graves, at your service, ma'am."

"I'm over here," I said.

"Oh, I know, son, but I doubt anybody cares."

She looked embarrassed until it dawned on her that we were joking around.

"We can't stay long," I said. "Millie's a working lady and I got to go up the coast at dawn."

"That's cool." And to Millie, "Next set's for you."

The band came back, Chuck said a few words to them, and they looked over at the table. The piano man and Chuck laid down a beat, and Chuck started to sing:

I've flown around the world in a plane,
Dined on caviar and champagne,
And the North Pole I have charted
Still I can't get started
With you.

Chuck sang from the heart, soft as marshmallows, and finally wrapped it up:

I've been consulted by Franklin D,
Greta Garbo has had me to tea,
I got a house, a showplace,
Still I can't get no place
With you.

We stayed an hour.

When they wrapped for a break, Millie blew a kiss to Graves and I waved to the rest of the crew. I dropped a fiver in the bucket. From the corner of my eye I saw Millie add a hundred-dollar bill.

Maury held an umbrella over Millie's head as we raced out to the car. He helped her in.

"Hey, Zee," he said, "don't get lost so much. We miss ya." And to Millie. "Make him bring ya back, okay?"

He ran back into the club.

"Do you know *every*body in town?" she asked.

"This was my beat when I started out," I said. "It's my old neighborhood."

I started to put the key in the switch but she laid a hand on mine and stopped me.

"Was Chuck playing that song for me or you?" she asked.

"Which one?"

" 'I Can't Get Started.' "

"Maybe he was telling me in his own way that . . ."

"Stop right there," she said softly. "You can go anyplace with me, Zee. I'd fly around the world in a plane just to come home to you."

She laid both hands on my cheeks. Her hands were as smooth as fine suede. She drew me to her and kissed me. Her lips were soft and full and giving, and she folded into my arms.

I shoved the gear stick into second to get it out of the way and slipped over to her side of the seat. She shifted, facing me, and her leg slid over mine. She reached over, her hand moved down my spine and pulled me to her. I could feel the heat of her as she crushed against me.

We never stopped kissing but I could hear her sigh deep in her throat and she began to tremble as my hands explored her.

I don't know how long we were there.

Long after the rain stopped.

CHAPTER 23

I picked up Ski a little after seven in the morning and took the same route I had taken going up to San Pietro the first time. Ski spent most of the trip dead asleep, sitting straight up with his arms folded. He didn't like long drives.

When we passed the fruit stand on 101, I looked up on the hill but the beautiful young girl on the pinto pony wasn't there. Maybe it had been a vision. Maybe there wasn't any girl on a pony dashing across the hilltop. Maybe it was subconscious. Maybe Millicent was the young girl and the pony was her baby-blue Phaeton. Maybe I was thinking too much.

At the turnoff I nudged my partner.

"Almost there," I said. "Any time now a black Pontiac will probably drop in behind us."

But it didn't. I stopped at the overlook and gave Ski a quick visual tour of San Pietro, the Hill, and Grand View House. I looked out on the bay but the Grebe yacht was gone. We drove down into town.

I parked in front of the city hall. The maroon Packard was parked haphazardly a few yards farther on.

"That's Culhane's prowler," I told Ski as we got out.

"Does very well for the sheriff of a county the size of a saltine," Ski said.

"The county owns it," I said. "I guess that makes it legal."

Ski just snorted derisively. I left him to stroll around the park.

There was no sign of Culhane or Rusty, but I couldn't imagine them being very far from his rolling office. I went in to the police station. Rosie was behind the counter. She recognized me when I walked through the door.

"Hi," I said. "Remember me?"

She graced me with what might have passed for a smile and said, "He's fishing. It's Friday."

"Ah. Wednesday everybody plays golf at noon, Friday morning they go fishing. When do they take their ballet lessons?"

"The captain wouldn't know one end of a golf club from the other." She looked at the Seth Thomas on the wall. "He should be in any time now."

"I'll just go down and wait by the pier."

"It's a free world," she said, looking for something else to do. As I was headed for the door she mumbled, "He said you'd be back."

I went back to the car, drove to the foot of the street, and parked next to a silver Duesenberg Murphy convertible, which was sitting in a diagonal parking strip between the park and the pier area. Ski wandered over munching on a snow cone.

"That's a cute little buggy," he said. "Must be fifty G's worth of car, at least. Are you sure you're allowed to park next to it?"

"That's Gorman's car," I said.

"He's the shy banker?"

"Shy or ill-mannered or maybe both. Take your pick."

Along the length of the pier were several booths, capped with bright umbrellas, offering everything from hot dogs, soft drinks, and sandwiches to booze. Between them and the pier were patio tables with the same patterned umbrellas providing shade. Beyond the pier, the ocean stretched off to the horizon under a cloudless azure sky.

We sat down at one of the tables and checked out the harbor. To the north, on the public beach, a couple of kids were building a sand castle while their mother was stretched out on a canvas beach chair, reading a book. Farther down, four bobby-soxers were horse-wrestling in the water, the girls teetering on their boyfriends' shoulders. I raised a pair of binoculars to look up the side of the cliff to the overlook and then on up to Grand View. Only its spires were visible above the trees. Then I pulled the glass down below the overlook to the ledge. From my angle I could just see the edge of the ledge and the tops of the pine trees, bent and flat-topped from the ocean winds. Something started gnawing at the back of my brain but I couldn't sort it out.

"See anything interesting?" Ski asked.

"Not from this angle. There's a ledge about halfway up that mean-ass road on the side of the cliff."

"With the flat-top trees?"

"Yeah. There's also what's left of a 1920 Chevy on that ledge."

"No kidding. What's it doing there?"

"Some kid lost control of his car and went over." I handed him the binoculars. "See the little spur up there with the stone wall around it?"

"Uh-huh."

"It's foggy up there every night. Apparently he missed the curve. They put the wall around it after that. The road's closed now."

"Ain't you the fountain of information," Ski said. "You ought to ap-ply for a job as a tour guide." Then he said, "There's somebody up there."

I looked up, but the overlook was too far away to tell anything with the naked eye.

"It's a woman," he said. "Rich; she's wearing a hat and gloves. Car-rying flowers."

I took the glasses. Ski was right, she was rich. You can always tell. Even when a rich woman dresses down, she's dressed up.

She walked to the edge of the wall, looked out over the ocean for a minute or two, then down at the ledge, and threw the bouquet over the side. I watched it tumble end over end, catch the updraft, and skewer out flat before it fell off the wind stream and dropped almost straight down. It caught for a minute on one of the trees then vanished, cut off by the angle of my view. When I swung the glasses back up to the over-look, the rich woman was gone.

I pulled down the glasses and stared up the side of the cliff without focusing on anything. The nibble in my brain became a big bite.

I looked back out at the bay but there was still no sign of a power boat.

"I just thought of something," I said. "Have a hot dog; I'll be back in fifteen minutes."

"Are you embarrassed to take me?" he asked, feigning hurt feelings.

"Uh-huh," I said.

I got in the car and drove down the main drag to February Street and grabbed a right, followed it down to Third Street. Nothing had changed at the Howland house. The collie was still sleeping in the front yard and he didn't open an eye as I walked past. Mrs. Howland answered after my first knock.

"Remember me?" I asked. "Sergeant Bannon, L.A. police."

"Oh yes. My goodness, and I'm just a mess."

"Is Barney here? I won't be but a minute, I need to ask him a question."

"Yes. Come in." She led me to the staircase and called down to him.

"Barney, that nice young fellow from Los Angeles is back. Should I send him down?"

"Mr. Bannon? Of course," he yelled back.

I went down the steps and he was pecking away at his Royal.

"I have a question, Barney," I said as we shook hands. I walked over to the framed front pages and found the one I was looking for. The story in the right-hand lower column with the picture of a ruined car, which I had breezed over the first time. The headline read:

ELI GORMAN JR. DIES AS

CAR PLUNGES OFF OVERLOOK

I remembered Culhane telling me his life had changed one night at the overlook.

"Who was Eli Gorman?" I asked.

"The kid's grandfather. The dead boy was Ben's son, named after Mr. Eli. Mr. Eli owned the whole valley. He won it in a poker game with his partner, Shamus O'Dell."

"Of the Grand View O'Dells?"

"Yeah."

I looked back at the framed front page.

"The car wreck. What happened?"

"Eli Junior was goin' down to see a silent movie. He was a young hell-raiser, all those young-uns up there were always doing crazy things. He should never have gone down Cliffside; it was so foggy you couldn't see the end of your nose. He missed the first curve and went right off the overlook. The car burned but of course nobody even noticed that. They didn't spot it until the next day."

"What do you mean, nobody noticed it?"

"That was the same night Buck Tallman was killed."

*   *   *

When I got back to the park, Ski was still scanning the bay with the binoculars. A big Chris Craft with a mile-high flying bridge was entering the mouth of the harbor.

"This is probably our boy now," he said. Then, "How'd the quickie go?"

"I just got another chapter in the history of San Pietro."

"Ahh. Enlighten me." He lowered the glasses.

"That car wreck up on the overlook?"

"Yeah."

"It was Ben Gorman's son. The wreck happened the same night as the Grand View shoot-out."

"You ought to write a book."

"A lot of action for one night in the life of a small town."

"They happen that way. In threes. Something else big probably happened that night. Somebody's cat got run over. Somebody's Mercedes got a flat tire."

I looked back up the cliff. "I'll bet that was his mother. Or sister," I said.

"Makes sense," Ski said. "So what?"

"I don't know. So something."

"So why don't you ask old man Gorman. That's probably his boat."

"I've got better things to ask him."

"We going to ambush him when they come up?"

"We'll ambush both of them."

"My favorite endeavor," he said with a smile.

We drank lemonades—"fresh squoze," Ski informed me—and watched the big boat cruise up beside one of the docks. The engine growled as it went into reverse and the sea boiled up behind it like water boiling in a pot. Then Rusty appeared from behind us somewhere and strolled down to meet it. He was dressed, as always, in a dark suit, white shirt, and tie. He didn't acknowledge me. A deckhand grabbed the tie line, wrapped it around a cleat, and drew the bow in tight against some rubber tires attached to the side of the dock.

Culhane stepped off the cruiser as Rusty reached behind an ear and came up with a cigarette. Culhane lit it, then Rusty jerked a thumb back toward us. Culhane stared at us through dark amber sunglasses.

He was wearing a Hawaiian shirt, baggy khaki pants, and white deck shoes. He turned back toward the boat, and the cigarette bobbed in his lips as he said something to somebody I couldn't see. Then he came toward us with that loping, casual step of his. We held our chairs down. Rusty disappeared around the car and got in on the driver's side, to roll another cigarette, I assumed.

He came up to the table and said with a crooked smile, "You're a real bad penny, Cowboy. I see you brought the whole riot squad with you this time."

"Captain," I said with a nod. "This is my partner, Ski Agassi."

Culhane pulled his sunglasses down an inch and stared over them at me. He nodded at Ski, who sat as he usually does, straight-backed, with his melon-sized hands on his knees. Culhane went to the booth and ordered a lemonade.

"It really wasn't necessary; you made your point the other night," he said as he came back to the table and sat down. "I owe you an apology about that. There was some . . . miscommunication between the boys and me. I assume you didn't get mussed up too much, considering the outcome."

"The one with the one eye kicks like a mule. Did he locate it, by the way?"

He nodded. "It was okay after he washed the mud off. That was some fancy footwork you showed Max and Lenny."

"The one with two arms should have grabbed me."

"That would be Max. Lenny hits harder."

"Lenny hits very hard. I've still got a couple of very sore ribs. Out of curiosity, are all your cops walking-wounded?"

He looked over at me and said, "Lenny lost his arm and Max lost his eye in the same battle. And the reason Rusty doesn't say much is he caught shrapnel in the throat at the same time. It missed his jugular but took out his voice box."

I didn't know how to respond to that so I kept my mouth shut.

"Three damn good cops nobody else will have," he said. "There's a couple more around. You'll probably meet them if you make this a habit."

"That the fight you won the Silver Star and Purple Heart in?"

"You been doing your homework."

"It was in the *Times*. That's the kind of juice they always salvage from canned résumés. Which reminds me, Max broke the car's window with his head. It cost the city eleven bucks to fix."

"Did you have to pay for it?"

"No, thank God. On my salary that's a significant sum of money."

"Two and a quarter a month plus another fifty after you put in your first ten years."

"You been doing a little homework yourself."

"Public record. I'm a taxpayer; they have to tell me."

"What else do you know about me?"

"You made detective after only five years on the force and got kicked up to sergeant three years later. That says a lot about your capabilities. Got a bit of a temper, which gets you in hot water on occasion. You drive a four-year-old Olds, which cost you a hundred bucks used, live in a one-bedroom house. No debts to speak about. You're unmarried, thirty-four years old, went to college for a coupla years, California State, then dropped out to become a cop. Why, I don't know."

"I ran out of money," I said. "And got tired of slinging hash in the White House hamburger joint on Sepulveda for fifteen cents an hour when everybody else was getting rich playing the stock market."

"They all went broke two years later."

"Yeah. And I had a guaranteed job with a pension and a health policy."

"Somehow I don't think the amenities had a lot to do with it."

"What gives you that idea?"

"I told you before, I been around cops all my life. The best and the worst. I can read 'em all. You're the most dangerous kind."

"Dangerous?" I laughed.

"Yeah. You're a bulldog. When you're on to something, you bite it in the ass and don't let go, even when it's the wrong something."

"Is there supposed to be a message somewhere in all that?"

"You'll figure it out."

I let that go and backed up a few sentences. "Those amenities you were talking about get more and more important as time goes by," I said.

"The way you play the game, I'd take the short-end odds you won't be around to collect that pension."

I gave him a long stare and said, "You keep saying things that sound like you mean something else."

He chuckled. "Nah, just a guess. You like to play just off the edge, don't you?"

"Like how?"

"Like coming up here, announcing your arrival, annoying a lot of leading citizens, then going right back at it after I tell you there's nothing to be learned. You take down two boys twice your size and give me the message in a paper bag."

"Is that why you had your boys work me over?"

He looked out over the bay and sipped his lemonade before answering.

"My friend Brett Merrill once told me I should never make a wish out loud, there are people around who might believe me and make it happen. I do that. Something happens, I get a little pissed, maybe I say something like, 'I wish a piano would fall off a tall building on that guy,' something like that. I don't mean it, I'm just bitching out loud. Next thing I know, a Steinway lands on somebody."

"Lenny hits like a Steinway."

"You do a pretty good job taking care of yourself. Playing the edge. That's why you're a sergeant when most guys your age are still wearing out their shoe soles on a beat out in the boondocks somewhere. I'm not criticizing, mind you. In my book it calls for a certain amount of admiration."

I changed the subject suddenly. "You didn't tell me the victim in that car wreck at the overlook was Ben Gorman's son," I said.

He gave me the hard eye and said, "You didn't ask."

"It wouldn't have occurred to me."

"Me either. It was a car wreck. A young man we all loved was killed. What's that got to do with anything?"

"It happened the night of the Grand View massacre."

"Well, we didn't find the car until the next morning. Somebody coming up Cliffside spotted it."

"That was some night."

"It was the saddest night in my life," he said. "I lost Buck Tallman and my godson, back-to-back."

"He was your godson?"

"Ben Gorman is my best friend."

"I'm sorry, I didn't mean to sound . . ."

"Suspicious?"

"No. Unfeeling."

"That's a decent thought. Thank you."

"Is that what you meant by your life changing forever on the stone bench up there?"

"Isabel and Ben never got over it. Neither did I."

"I think we saw her about a half hour ago."

"Isabel Gorman? Where?"

I looked up the cliffside. "Up there. Dressed to the teeth. She threw some flowers down the side."

He stared up at the overlook for several seconds and then nodded. "She does that once a week. Has for over twenty years," he said, and there was a deep sadness in his voice.

Ski didn't say a word. He sat there with his hands on his knees, watching through eyes that revealed neither boredom nor interest. But he wasn't missing a thing.

Nobody said anything now. I looked back out in the harbor. The big cruiser was tied down at the end of the pier. Gorman was nowhere to be seen. The Duesenberg was still sitting there.

"So old Ben's going to give me the dodge again," I said finally.

"I keep telling you, there's nothing to be learned about that dead woman up here."

"Yeah, you keep telling me. You aren't trying to oil me, are you, Captain?" I said, smiling.

"I'd know better than to try."

"Wouldn't do you much good this time," I said.

"Oh? How come?"

"Ski?" I said, and the big man took two folded documents from his inside pocket, then laid them on the table in front of Culhane. He spread them apart with the flat of his hand and eyed them for a minute.

"Search warrants," I said. "For all the banks. One gives us access to the bank records, the other to safe deposit boxes at our discretion. Moriarity got them from Judge Weidemeyer down in district court."

He stared at the two folded warrants without speaking. A lot of things kneaded through his tough face. He shook his head ever so slightly, then he suddenly stood up. "I'm going to take a shower," he announced.

"I'd like to take a gander at the public records," Ski finally said. "Will that be a problem?"

"Nope." Culhane didn't bother turning around. "Second floor, records department. Ask for Glenda, she runs the department. Tell her I sent you."

With that, he got in his car. It made a U-turn, drove past the city hall, and turned right, toward the Breakers Hotel. Ski went up to City Hall. Me? I sat there by myself and stared at the Duesenberg.

CHAPTER 24

I'd been nursing my lemonade for about ten minutes when Rusty pulled up in the Packard. He gave the horn a toot, got out, came around and opened the back door, and wiggled a finger at me. I went over and got in, then he drove me around the corner and up three blocks to the front of the Breakers Hotel.

I followed him into the lobby, which was as quiet as a cemetery and as elegant as a tiara. It was about a hundred feet across the lobby to the French doors that opened onto the gardens, swimming pool, and a small outside café. The grass was so even I imagined a Japanese gardener on his hands and knees clipping it with a pair of fingernail scissors. Beyond all that, the Pacific Ocean graced anyone who could afford to stay in the place.

The front desk and the concierge's desk were pure mahogany, as was all the exposed wood in the room. The desk clerk and the concierge were both dressed in navy blue jackets with coats of arms on the left breast. About ten square miles of Persian rug covered hardwood floors. The chairs and sofas were plentiful, conservative, and expensive. To my left was a step-down bar, with about two dozen tables and a French slate bar on the far side. On the opposite side of the room from it was a café, with perhaps a dozen tables. The bartender was polishing a pebbled Waterford old-fashioned glass. He held it up to the recessed light behind the bar to make sure he hadn't missed any smudges, then stacked it on a small shelf behind him. In the restaurant, a waitress in a dark green uniform was arranging the sterling silverware on the linen tablecloths.

Nobody spoke above a whisper, if they spoke at all.

Rusty led me down a long hall, which was to our left and at right

angles to the lobby. On the left side of the hallway, more French doors
leading to the tennis courts. On the right were the rooms. The hall
ended in a T, which was Culhane's suite. Rusty tapped on the door,
then opened it with a key, and ushered me in. I heard the door close
quietly behind me and I was alone.

A large room. New carpeting, expensive hotel furniture but hotel
furniture nonetheless, more French doors facing the ocean. A fireplace in one corner, with a copper screen, and over it a large piece of
what appeared to be a hunk of very faded, red driftwood mounted on
the bricks. Beveled paneling stained the color of sun-blanched wood.
Light-colored curtains and drapes. Against the right wall, an old rolltop
desk with three framed photos on its flat top. A deep-piled white sofa
about eight feet long, with matching chairs on both sides, facing the
ocean. Bedroom and bath to the right and back toward the lobby. On
the left, an alcove with a wet bar facing the living room, and behind it, a
small kitchenette. A floor-model RCA radio in the corner adjacent to
the desk with a record changer on top of it, which was playing Edith
Piaf's "L'Etranger."

It was a bright, cheerful suite of rooms with a spectacular view, and
a surprise to me. I was expecting dark wood and masculine furniture,
with a stuffed marlin over the fireplace and a gun rack in the corner. I
was expecting a dirty shirt thrown over the sofa, ashtrays running
over with cigarette butts. A glass ring or two on the wooden table.
Then I remembered it was a hotel, decorated by the hotel's interior de-
signer. The few personal touches and the photographs were as out of
place as a waiter's thumb in a bowl of soup.

I walked over to the desk and saw what was apparently part of a
leg cast. There was a small gold lieutenant's bar pinned to it. It was
the only visible souvenir of his remarkable war record anywhere in
the room.

I checked the piece of driftwood. It appeared to be off the stern of a
boat. The black lettering, which was cut off by the shattered wood,
said *Dool* . . . and under it *Prin* . . . Both were faded by sun and sea, and
were barely legible.

"That's what's left of my old man's fishing boat," Culhane's voice
said behind me.

I turned. He was standing in the doorway that led to his bedroom, wearing a dark blue terry-cloth robe and scrubbing his hair with

a white towel. He threw the towel over his shoulder and went behind the bar.

"Irish Mist suit you?"

"Doesn't get any better."

"Straight up, one cube of ice?"

"That's a good guess."

"It's my drink."

He filled two highball glasses with more than generous slugs and dropped one ice cube in each. It was a little early for me but I wasn't going to pass up a glass of Irish whiskey.

"Tommy was a fisherman," Culhane said, handing me my drink. "He and Kathleen Brodie came over from Doolin, County Clare. She was fifteen when they married."

"When was that?"

"Eighteen eighty-four. They raced the stork all the way across the Atlantic. They were determined I'd be born on American soil and they just made it. I was born on Ellis Island in the physical examination clinic."

"How'd they end up out here?" I asked.

"No fishing in New York City. So they bundled me up and headed across the country to this ocean. Fishing was all he knew. He hired out until he saved enough money to buy his first boat, called her *Doolin Princess* after my mom, and painted her bright red, Mom's favorite color."

"I mean how did they end up in San Pietro?" I asked.

"Back in those days this was a fisherman's community. The natural bay, great fishing waters ten miles out there." He waved vaguely toward the Pacific. "Hell, there used to be an icehouse just about where you're sitting, ice to keep the fish fresh until they got back on the Hill. So this is where they settled. We lived in a little shack up in the village, when it was called Eureka."

"And you use your mother's maiden name instead of your father's first name?"

"That was his idea. He said one Tommy in the family was enough."

He turned and held his glass up to the piece of wood.

"Here's to both of you," he said.

"They're both dead?" I asked, joining the toast.

"Yeah. Tommy went out one day with his three-man crew. A heavy blow came up and we never saw him again. Couple of months later a guy down in Milltown who knew me saw that on the rocks. That's all we found. No other wreckage, no bodies. The Pacific has an ironic name. It can be damn unforgiving."

"I'm sorry," I said.

"He was okay, Tommy Culhane was. Good husband, good father, and one hell of a fisherman. Nothing breathing scared him." He chuckled, and added, "Loved a good brawl as long as it wasn't over anything serious."

"How old where you?"

"Eleven. My mom died two years later. In the state hospital, of pneumonia."

I knew about institutions like that. My mother had spent two years in and out of such dismal places, ending up in a state hole jokingly called a hospital. No matter how you dolled them up, nothing changed. There were always the smells of Lysol mixed with feces lingering in the halls and rooms; always burly men in sterile white pants and shirts, who called themselves "attendants" and resolved "incidents" by bending fingers back or hitting places that did not bruise easily; who slaughtered the King's English but used long medical terms as casually as a preacher throws around cynical hypotheses like "God" and "Christ." My mother's fingers were permanently crippled and her dementia was so deep that lethargy was a generous way of explaining her state of mind. She lay comatose for a month before she died of what was wryly diagnosed as pneumonia. I knew she was not comatose, I could tell by the way her eyes flicked briefly toward me. There was a momentary hint of recognition in that glassy stare when I went to visit her. I think she found some semblance of comfort in retreating into her own troubled and chaotic psyche. The last time I saw her she was skeletal and her gnarled fingers lay limp and useless at her sides. Truth be known, she died of starvation, which I learned is not an unpleasant way to die. For a few years after her death, my dreams were often haunted by the sudden intrusion of her mummified look and by the way her hand felt when I held it, like a bunch of twigs. I would awaken squeezing my own hand. Eventually these troubling images became less and less frequent but they never fully vanished.

And I thought about Brodie Culhane; about a thirteen-year-old kid left alone in a rough-and-tumble waterfront town like Eureka, a town without laws or morals; a kid growing up with a strong sense of justice in spite of it all, a sense of justice possibly tempered by expediency.

"What'd you do?"

He took a hard sip of his drink, let it roll around in his mouth for a second or two before swallowing it, and smiled. It was a fond smile, a good-memory smile.

"I became a stableboy."

"You're kidding."

He shook his head. "But I was the Gormans' stableboy," he said rather proudly. "After the funeral, Ben took me up to meet old man Gorman. Mr. Eli took me by the shoulder and said, 'I've got a job for you,' and led me to the stable. I had a small apartment over the stalls. I'll tell you, the old man could be a real pisser but he looked after me like I was a gold nugget. I was treated like family, rode to school every day in the shay with Ben, ate dinner with them at night. I even had a yarmulke for meals and holidays, but he had the buggy take me down to the Catholic mission every Sunday for mass."

"How come he treated you so well?" I asked.

"My mom was their washerwoman. And I was Ben's best friend. Still am." He went back into the bedroom. "I'll be about five minutes," he said.

I walked over to the rolltop and looked at the photos. One was a tintype, obviously Culhane with his mother and father. Culhane looked to be about seven or eight, a tough-looking little boy in a hand-knit sweater and a cap pulled down above one eye. He was wearing knickers and one leg sagged down around his ankle. Even at that age there was defiance in his wary smile. His father was a big, hefty, dark-haired man with a robust smile, his arm resting on Culhane's shoulder, while his mother was a wisp of a woman no more than five feet tall, dressed in a long skirt and a sailor's pea jacket. In the background was the *Doolin Princess*.

The second photo showed Buck Tallman in the saddle of a big Appaloosa. Culhane was standing in front of the horse holding its bridle. A good-looking kid in his late teens or early twenties, whom I assumed was Ben Gorman, was sitting behind Tallman, his hands around the big lawman's waist.

The last picture was of Culhane standing with a young man who had one arm around Brodie and his other around the waist of a small woman. She looked to be in her early thirties, striking and beautifully groomed, with the dark hair and sharp features of a Jewess. Next to her was Ben Gorman. I assumed the woman was Ben's wife, Isabel, and the young man their son, Eli, who had died in the car wreck. From their dress, the picture appeared to have been taken in the early twenties. It was an intimate photograph; they were all hunched together and smiling warmly at the camera.

He returned to the room dressed in black pants and a lightweight plaid shirt with the sleeves rolled up halfway to his elbows.

"Nice photo," I said, nodding toward the picture.

"Isn't it though," he said, and led me toward the French doors.

"Give you a start, brother?" Ben said. The two men rushed together, hugging and laughing like children. They walked briskly back to the house, both chattering away, cutting each other off with one story after another. Ben didn't talk about the future. He didn't have to.

"Eli and Isabel will be home in the morning," Gorman said. "The kid's dying to meet you. You're his hero, Brodie."

Culhane dreaded the meeting.

He was edgy when he and Ben had breakfast but tried to conceal it. They joked about the past, about kids who had grown up and moved on, about Delilah O'Dell and her infamous club. Ben drove them out to end-o'-track, and Brodie strolled back and forth trying to appear casual. He tried to roll a cigarette but his left hand was still stiff from a shrapnel wound and the tobacco fell out and was whisked away by the wind. He balled up the paper and stuck it in his mouth.

"Here comes the train," Ben said gleefully. "Come on, come on."

He took Brodie by the arm and they walked up to the makeshift station as the train rounded a bend and appeared through a thicket of pine trees. As the big engine hissed and puffed to a stop, he saw the kid on the platform between cars, looking through the steam, seeing his father and waving, and then, behind him, the tiny, dainty figure of Isabel, one hand holding her hat to keep it from flying off. The kid helped her off the train as Ben and Brodie went to meet them.

Time had been more than generous to her.

Or perhaps his memory was tainted.

He remembered Isabel as a tiny voice in the dark, the words chiseled in his brain. "First love is forever."

He smiled at her, stepped close, kissed her on the cheek, and gave her a hug. He could feel her heart quicken the way it once had so long ago and for a moment he was swept back to the greenhouse with her beside him in the dark on a horse blanket.

He stepped away from her. "You haven't aged a minute in twenty years," he said in a voice that the years and the Marines had toughened.

"Irish blarney," she said with a smile and, turning to the youth, said proudly, "Brodie, this is Eli, your godson."

He was taller than Brodie and shorter than his father. A husky kid in good shape: dark hair, brown eyes with a touch of mischief in them, and a solid grip when Brodie shook his hand.

"I feel like I know you already," the kid said, and looked at the bars on the shoulders of his uniform. "We followed the war from the day it started, wondering where you were over there. They didn't tell me you were a captain." Brodie could tell the kid was impressed.

"Last-minute thing," he said. "They upped me just before I got discharged. The pension's fatter. You play baseball like your old man?"

"Football's my game," he said. "More action. Baseball's kind of boring."

"Boring, then!" Brodie answered, and looked at Ben. "What have you been teaching the kid?"

Ben shrugged. "He's a halfback at the University of Pennsylvania," he said.

"One more year to go," Eli announced. "I took this semester off. Got a busted knee in the Army game so I'm taking it easy."

"Then what?"

"Haven't decided yet. I may stay back East for a while. I've got some friends in Boston."

"Male or female?"

A cocky grin: "Both."

"Wanderlust, huh."

Eli stuck his hands in his coat pockets and looked down at the ground. "I don't think I'd make a good banker," he said.

"Nothing to be ashamed of," Brodie said. "Neither would I."

The kid laughed, and looked back and forth at his parents as if to say, "See, he understands."

"I got a friend from the service who works down in Hollywood making

moving pictures. Maybe you and me, we could take a day or two and go
down, see how they do it."

"That sounds great!" the kid said eagerly.

As they started toward the car, Ben ran ahead. "Wait there a
minute," he called over his shoulder. He reached in the car and got his
Brownie camera.

"Can you work one of these?" he asked the conductor.

"I can try," he answered. Ben handed him the camera. "Just look
through here, hold it real still, and press the button."

So they stood together: Brodie, with his godson's arm around his
shoulder and his arm around the boy's waist, and Isabel with an arm
around Eli and Ben. And a stranger took their picture and Culhane
knew in his heart he was back to stay.

He opened the French doors and I followed him out to a redwood deck
facing the bay. Culhane took my glass and went inside to freshen our
drinks.

"Your partner's still in the hall of records, which is what we laugh-
ingly call it," Culhane said. "He says he'll meet you after lunch. I ordered us steak sandwiches and baked potatoes. Sound okay?"

"Sure, thanks."

I rolled two cigarettes and handed him one and lit them both. We
leaned on the railing and watched a sailboat tacking its way to the
mouth of the bay. I was wondering what he was thinking and why we
were suddenly getting so chummy. Then he said, "How did you ever
get in so deep with Palomino that time?"

He said it so casually it almost went by me. Then it hit me. I had
thought we had finished elbowing each other and were ready to get
down to business. Now he was bringing up my old business, a thing
that had been put to bed a couple of years ago.

"Touché," I said with half a grin.

"Just curious," he said with a shrug.

"I made a mistake in a poker game," I told him, without taking my
eyes off the boat.

"How's that?"

"I was playing on borrowed money. If you don't have the price in
your kick, never get in the game."

"You were playing on Palomino's money, right?"

"That's right, and it was his game." I shook my head. "That was my second mistake. Incidentally, it was never proven. That I didn't settle up with him, I mean."

"Well, killing him did raise some eyebrows," he said, raising his own.

"He more than had it coming," I said, looking at him. "He was holding a fistful of hot diamonds and had left a string of bodies behind to get them, when it all went sour on him."

"And three of his hooligans backing him up. That one was right on the edge, taking them all on like that."

"I didn't have much choice," I said. "They didn't want to go to the gas chamber and I was the only thing between them and the exit. We got all the rocks back, you should know that, having brought it up. Two hundred grand in hot ice. There wasn't an inquiry about the thou some people said I owed Palomino. That's why I have to wonder where you heard it. Sounds like something Eddie Woods might tumble onto."

"Know Eddie, do you?"

"You know I met him yesterday," I said flatly. "Until then, I wouldn't have known him if he'd walked up and kicked me in the ankle."

"That thing with Fontonio was unfortunate."

After a moment or two, I said, "Is it my turn yet?"

He smiled back with his lips. His eyes got a little bluer, a little less mischievous, a little warier.

"You want a look in my closet now, is that it?"

"It crossed my mind. How come you're not up at the club playing golf with the rest of the elite?"

"I have a bar tab in the clubhouse, that's as far as it goes. Sometimes somebody picks it up. Anonymously. That way it's not a bribe. The apartment and the car come with the job."

"I've never been that lucky."

"It's not luck, it's appreciation." He looked at me and his eyes had softened again. "Everybody knows I'm underpaid, just like you are. All cops are underpaid and underappreciated. All we get is the dirty laundry."

"So ask for a raise."

"I don't need a raise. I do what I do because it's my job, just like you do. I don't want any more money. I'd just end up buying a lot of crap I don't need."

The doorbell chimed and Culhane opened the door to a callow young man whose blue jacket was a little too broad in the shoulders and waist. He wheeled in the table, busied himself setting out sterling silver knives and forks, and lace napkins, and a sterling silver pot of coffee, then brought up sandwiches, still hot under stainless covers. Culhane gave him a dollar. There was no check to sign.

We sat down to eat. The sandwich was an inch-thick boneless sirloin larger than the slice of white bread that provided the sandwich part of the meal. The potato had been cut open, stuffed with butter, and mashed in the skin.

"What the hell are you *really* after, Cowboy?"

"The five hundred a month," I said. "I think it was blackmail."

"Maybe it was. But maybe it was a gift. And maybe you're looking in the wrong place."

"Where would you look?"

"Hell, I don't know," he said with a shrug. "I keep telling you, I never heard of this lady until you came along, and you've been in my hair ever since. You think I've been paying her five bills a month for all those years? I make *six* bills a month. I started at one-twenty-five. My raises come every three years and once in a while the council gives me a little Christmas bonus. I never take it unless my boys get the same. They provide me with this suite of rooms and the Packard, which belongs to the county." He waved a hand toward the rooms. "And I don't have a printing press in the back room cranking out C-notes."

"What do you know about electricity?" I asked, changing the subject.

"I know they use it to kill people back East. A hangman's knot is a hell of a lot easier. Even gas is kinder."

"When you get electrocuted everything stops. You heart stops beating, your digestion stops, your brain fries, you stop breathing. Instantly." I snapped my fingers. "Just like that."

"Well, maybe I'm wrong, it just seems like an ugly way to dispose of even the most serious felon."

"Verna Hicks's lungs were full of water."

I said it casually, between bites. He looked at me as if to say, So what? Then I watched the sun rise behind his eyes, like dawn crawling over a mountaintop. He looked at his sandwich and then back at me. He put his fork down, got up, walked to the railing, and stared out at the ocean for a minute or so, then turned to face me.

"You sure know how to ruin a guy's meal," he said. A growl, almost a whisper.

"You suspect this? That why you been sniffing around up here?"

"It's my *business*," I said.

"It's my *county*," he roared. "If somebody up here killed that lady, *whoever* did it, they'll answer to me."

"It was done on my watch and my beat," I said firmly. "If somebody up here's responsible, I intend to send them across."

His frigid eyes stayed on me.

"I don't know who killed her," I went on. "She's been down five days. You know how that is, every day the trail gets colder. The only clues I've got are those checks and a vague description of a guy who was seen in the neighborhood about the time she was dusted."

It got dead silent.

"Jesus, how I hate murder," he said. Then after a long pause: "And you say this lady had a decent life?"

"She was happily married and doing great until her husband was ironed out by a hit-and-runner four years ago," I said, rolling him the cigarette. "She was just getting back on her feet."

Culhane got up, and walked back to the railing of the deck, and smoked another cigarette silently for a while. I finished my lunch.

"I'll tell you this," he said finally, looking me directly in the eyes. "Nobody I know personally is capable of such an act. Or having it done. Take that or leave it."

"I have a hunch who she is. Or was."

"Yeah? Who would that be?"

"Lila Parrish."

Culhane looked stunned. "Lila Parrish?"

"The missing witness from the Thompson case."

"I know who the hell Lila Parrish is. Where the hell did you come up with that notion?"

"She vanished before the appeal. Then Verna popped up a year later in L.A. with no pedigree. She had four grand in cash, used it to open a bank account. And then there was the five hundred a month.

She saved almost all of it, bought a house and occasionally a new car, some antiques. She lived a simple life."

He stared at me for a long minute, letting that sink in.

"So naturally you figure she was being paid off to drop out of sight."

"You got a better idea?"

"I don't think much of that one."

"Maybe she was having an affair with somebody up here and took a powder, or was paid to," I said. "Maybe there isn't any connection with the Thompson case. But I have to find out. The money leads here, and I'll be here until I arrest the man or woman who killed her or I'm convinced otherwise."

He smoked the butt almost to his fingers. He flicked the end off it, split the butt down the middle, and dumped the remaining tobacco into the wind. Then he balled the paper into a fly speck and popped it in his mouth.

"That's the way a Marine does it," he said, and sat back down and poured us each a cup of coffee.

"How long were you in?" I asked.

"Two months short of sixteen years." He stared into his cup for a long minute. "It was fine until we went over there. The Western Front was a stinking, bloody burial ground. I lost most of my company in two days. But we got across the river." Then his lip curled and he repeated the line to himself, low with controlled rage and almost under his breath. "We got across that fucking river."

In the time I knew Culhane, I rarely heard the sheriff use that word. When he did use it, it was when nothing else was appropriate.

The doorbell rang again and he left the table, returning a few seconds later with a tall, deeply tanned, angular man, over six feet, with close-cropped salt-and-pepper hair, a hawk nose, and the saddest eyes I had ever seen. He was wearing a pale gray silk sports jacket and dark gray flannels.

Culhane introduced us. "Sergeant Bannon, this is Ben Gorman."

Gorman nodded at me and we shook hands.

"Want a drink? Cup of coffee?" Culhane asked.

"No thanks," Gorman answered. "Isabel's waiting on the patio. We're having lunch." He sat down at the table and looked across at me.

"Sorry if I've been inhospitable, Sergeant," he said. He took a folded 8½-by-11 manila envelope from the inside pocket of his jacket, unfolded it, laid it on the table, and slid it in front of me.

I opened the envelope. There were three cashier's checks inside, made out to Verna Hicks, one dated March the first, 1941. The other two were dated a year or so ago. The signatures on the checks were all the same: Marsha Whittaker.

"Is Miss Whittaker still with the bank?" I asked.

Gorman nodded. "She'll be there until two."

"May I talk to her?"

Gorman nodded. "She's expecting you."

"Benny, the woman the checks are made out to, Verna Hicks?" Culhane said. "She wasn't killed in an accident. She was murdered."

Gorman was stunned. He looked at me and then at Culhane, and said, almost in a whisper, "My God, Brodie, you told me she drowned in her tub."

"She did, only it wasn't an accident," I said. "Somebody shoved her head underwater and held it there until she died."

A minute passed and nobody said anything. Then Gorman, sounding genuinely upset, said, "You think someone in San Pietro had something to do with this?"

"I don't know, Mr. Gorman," I said. "I have a homicide on my hands. Somebody has been giving Verna Hicks five hundred a month for almost twenty years. That money trail leads here. That seems like more than a coincidence, and coincidence makes me nervous."

"On the other hand, it could have nothing at all to do with her death," said Culhane.

"Sure," I agreed. "We have people working a lot of angles in L.A. But right now this is the angle I'm working on. If it's a dead end, I'll be the first to admit it."

"Well," Gorman said, "I don't want to keep my wife waiting. Come say hello, Brodie."

"Of course," Culhane said. "We're just wrapping things up."

I followed the two men down the hall and through the lobby to the patio. Isabel Gorman was indeed the woman in the photo on Gorman's rolltop. She was as dignified in life as in the photograph, except her black hair was streaked with gray, there were lines around her mouth, and she had the same sorrow reflecting in her brown eyes as in Gorman's. She smiled sweetly when she saw Brodie.

"Hello, my dear," Culhane said, with a softness in his voice I had not heard before. He kissed her hand. She ran it tenderly down his cheek. "Dear Brodie," is all she said.

Gorman introduced her to me.

"What brings you up here, Sergeant?" she asked innocently.

"It's a homicide investigation," Gorman said gently. "Sergeant Bannon thinks the woman may have lived here at one time."

"Oh?" she said. "What was her name?"

"Hicks," I said. "Verna Hicks."

The name made no impression at all. She looked off at the ocean for a minute with her brows bunched together and then she slowly shook her head. "I don't recall that name," she said.

"We have to be going," Culhane said. "Just wanted to say hello."

"Thank you," she said, and patted Culhane's hand, and to me, "Good luck, Sergeant."

Gorman offered me his hand. "It was a pleasure meeting you," he said.

"My pleasure, Mr. Gorman. Thanks for your help."

I followed Culhane to the hotel entrance. When we got outside, Rusty was waiting and he offered me a ride to the bunk.

"No thanks," I said. "The walk'll do me good."

"Then I'll walk with you," Culhane said. We strolled down toward town. The ocean breeze rattled the palm fronds and cut the summer heat. As we entered the park we walked, in silence, toward the beach.

As we neared the far end of the park there was a small marble headstone at the edge of the sidewalk. Someone had put a bunch of wildflowers beside it and a withered apple. The inscription etched into its smooth face said:

CYCLONE

1897–1936

SORELY MISSED BY THE PEOPLE OF SAN PIETRO

"Who was Cyclone?" I asked.

"A horse," he said.

"A horse?"

"Everybody in town knew him. He used to jump the fence at the stable and wander downtown looking for a handout. Apples mostly. He loved apples. When he died, the people in town chipped in and bought him the marker."

We went to the end of the park. Rusty was waiting with the Packard.

"You got a lot of options," Culhane said as we reached the car.

"Which one do you like?" I asked.

He shrugged. "Take your pick," he said. He thought for a minute and added, "Just remember this: no matter how it comes out in the end, I'll be able to look you in the eye and say, 'I told you so.' "

"Now what the hell does that mean?" I asked.

He stared at me for a long time. I think he wanted me to figure it out.

Rusty opened the car door for him.

"It's about choices, pal," he said as he got in. "Every time you make one, you close a door and narrow your odds."

CHAPTER 25

The Chevy was parked by the docks where we had left it. I drove around to the diner but Ski was nowhere to be seen, so I cruised down to the Pacific National.

Marsha Whittaker was a pleasant woman in her early thirties, her blond hair cut in a short bob that emphasized a round face and wide hazel eyes. She was dressed in a pale green sleeveless pinafore. I showed her my badge and mentioned that Mr. Gorman had probably told her about me.

"Oh yes," she said "You're the gentleman interested in the cashier's checks."

"Yes, the ones made out to Verna Hicks."

"Well," she said, "I really can't tell you much. My predecessor, Miss Hamilton, died two years ago. I only remember three of them. One was March of this year and the other two were last year."

"Do you remember who purchased them?"

"I remember two of them. They were both purchased by young women. Very nicely dressed for San Pietro, that's how come I remember them. The first one, that would have been March 1940, was very pretty. She was wearing a two-piece suit. Light-colored, I think. Maybe beige. She came in, handed me an envelope, and said 'Will you please take care of this.' There were five one-hundred-dollar bills and a note to make the check out to Verna Hicks. After I made it out, she put it in a business envelope that was already stamped and addressed, said 'Thanks,' and left."

"Anything else you can remember?"

She hesitated for a minute, fell into deep thought again, then said, "No, I'm sorry."

"That's very good," I said.

"Well, you know, she was . . . different."

"How about the other one?"

"I remember her a little better, that was only a couple of months ago. She was small like the other girl but very . . . uh . . ."

"Voluptuous?" I tried.

"Thank you," she said, blushing again. "I think she was probably staying at the Breakers."

"Why do you say that?"

"She just looked like a tourist, the way she dressed and all, had a very heavy tan so I figured she'd probably been down on the beach. She was very friendly, you know, she smiled the whole time, but she didn't say anything but 'Please' when she handed me the envelope and 'Thanks' when I was finished. Oh, and she was wearing sunglasses . . . and she did have a kind of accent, a foreign accent it sounded like. But she didn't say enough to really tell. And the sunglasses she was wearing had white frames with little red hearts where the earpieces connect to the glasses. And she was wearing mascara. She really didn't need mascara, she was quite striking. She did the same thing as the other girl. Gave me the envelope and after I made out the check she put it in an addressed envelope. She walked very straight, like a model."

"Did you ever see either of them again?"

She shook her head. "Sorry I can't be more helpful."

"You've been a great deal of help. Thank you very much, Miss Whittaker."

"Welcome," she said, and I got up and left.

A Mrs. Higarty at the little Scotsman's bank added a new dimension. She remembered that one of the checks had been purchased by an Oriental gentleman in workman's clothes, who had presented her with five hundred dollars and a note to make the check out to Verna Hicks. He had simply nodded when she gave it to him. He, too, had a self-addressed envelope into which he deposited the check as he left. Her office was near the front of the bank and he walked away toward the post office.

I decided it was time to head up the Hill.

*   *   *

I drove around North End Park and past the guard at the entrance to the Hill, hoping he would be on a break, but no such luck. I could see his silhouette through the guardhouse window. There was no way I was going to get by him so I drove to the end of the street, took a left down a tree-lined avenue, and did a double-back to see if I was being followed. The street was empty. I drove around the curvy road until I reached the bottom of Cliffside Road. I sat there for a full five minutes trying to erase that trip down the steep, crumbling road from my mind. Then I got out, moved the sawhorse out of the way, pulled into the road, and put the sawhorse back.

I stayed in first gear and crept up the narrow strip. Rocks and dirt spat from under my rear wheels. I didn't look sideways at the beautiful view or left to the sheer wall a foot away; my gaze was frozen on the piddling excuse for a road. As I swung slowly around a curve, I saw, maybe ten feet ahead of me, a washout. An eroded arc in the road the size of half a hubcap faced me. I stopped and stared at it, hoping for a miracle. Hoping it would go away. I decided to chance it. There was no way I was going to back down to the bottom of the cliff.

I was two feet from the bite out of the road when I stopped the second time. I set the hand brake and leaned out, judging that the road at that point was a foot narrower. If I hugged the cliff it gave me a one-foot clearance. I released the brake and crawled up to the hole. As I started past it, I felt the car tremble. As the back wheels passed the defective spot, the car began to lurch. My mouth went dry. My throat closed. I turned the wheel inward and stepped on the gas.

The Chevy jumped ahead. Another chunk of the road fell away and dropped down to the ocean. The car sideswiped the cliff with a grinding squeal. I fought it under control and slowed down until I was barely moving. Sweat streaked down my cheeks. I gentled the gas pedal and went on. The car kept spitting debris, occasionally fishtailing slightly. I got to the top without further incident.

I moved the sawhorse, drove through, and put it back. I needed a cigarette. I drove up the road until I could see the gate to Grand View, stopped, and rolled one. My heart was still doing triple time. I counted to twenty as slowly as I could and brought my pulse closer to normal. I finished one butt, rolled another, and as I finished it a grocery truck pulled up to the gate. The driver got out and swung one half of the gate open and drove through. He left it open, so I cranked up and followed him, drove down the long driveway, and pulled around into the parking lot south of the big house.

I checked the car. The side of Louie's cream puff was going to need some work and the car would need a new paint job.

The wind coming up from the sea rattled the high hedge that bordered the side facing the cliffs. I walked down to the house. On the south side was another hedge, which hid a side door.

Nobody took a shot at me so I went to the front door and rang the bell. Somewhere inside I heard chimes playing the opening bars of "Anything Goes." I waited and rang again. Nothing.

I stepped back from the door and checked the house. There were no sounds of life. The place was like a sleeping cat. Then the silence was broken by a girl giggling on the north side of the place. I followed the laughter around the corner. A row of rose bushes flanked the north side of the house, the grass was manicured, several palm trees provided pools of shade. On the back side of the house, at the bottom of a low terrace, was an Olympic-size pool with several cabanas on the far side. Tables with gaily colored umbrellas were scattered here and there, and striped canvas beach chairs were lined up facing the sun.

Two of them were occupied.

I strolled down toward them. Two women were sunning themselves on the beach chairs by the pool, whispering to each other and snickering like high-school girls. One was tallish, with a pouty mouth, deep-set eyes, and auburn hair that matched her tan. She was wearing a pair of dark blue cotton shorts. Nothing else. The other one, shorter, slimmer, with perfect breasts, a mischievous grin, and jet-black hair, was wearing a nice tan, period.

The naked girl, who looked to be around nineteen or twenty, spotted me first. She sat up, crossed her legs Indian-style, and flashed a genuine smile. The other one's grin seemed more mechanical. Neither of them bothered to cover up.

"Aren't you cute," Naked One said without losing the smile. "Are you my five o'clock? If you are, you're extremely early."

"Now, do I look like your five o'clock?" I said, grinning back.

"I don't know," she said coquettishly, working her eyes overtime. "He's new. I never know; maybe you're a movie actor in disguise." The whole time she was showing me all of her assets.

"Do the seagulls ever bother you?" I asked.

Naked One giggled.

"My name's Zeke Bannon," I said, offering her my hand.

"Zeke?" the other one said. "What kinda name is Zeke?"

"Where are your manners, Emerald?" Naked One said. Then added, "Emerald's new. She hasn't finished the course yet."

"Is this a school?"

Naked One lowered her chin a notch and looked up at me.

"Miss Delilah's finishing school," she said. She leaned back on her elbows and said, "If you're not my five o'clock, I've got at least two hours free. Maybe I could give you a lesson or two."

"I'll just bet you could."

A voice from high over my shoulder said sternly, "Jade, you two put something on. This isn't a cattle show."

Both girls scrambled for cover. I turned around and looked up. The woman on the second-floor balcony had to be Delilah O'Dell. She was dressed in a long yellow silk robe with a pale pink striped sash, and yellow slippers with large fluffy balls on the top. And a hat. A pink feathery thing, with one feather arching down behind her ear and over her shoulder. She had flaming red hair and a rather full face with suspicious eyes. She could have been anything from thirty-five to fifty. She had a monumental figure, not voluptuous, just right, with a waist a wasp would weep for. Not beautiful, she didn't need to be; she was a package and knew it.

"Just make yourself at home, why don't you," she snapped.

"I rang the bell several times."

"Maybe I was out."

"You weren't."

"Maybe I wanted you to think I was. Most people would have come back later."

"You're Delilah O'Dell," I said.

"Really? Do I owe you anything for that information?"

I took out my badge and held it up so it winked in the sunlight.

"I'm a cop."

It neither surprised nor flustered her; nothing short of an earthquake would.

"I don't give a damn if you're King George," she said. "This is a private club and I don't remember inviting you in."

"I took a chance I'd catch you home."

"Did you now? Let me try and guess. You're Bannon."

"Word travels fast in San Pietro."

"Out of all mouths and into my ears. What are you doing up here?"

"I made a wrong turn."

"You sure did. Come around to the door." She vanished into the house.

I walked back to the front door, and a middle-aged colored man with graying hair and a build like King Kong opened it. He took my hat and nodded toward the stairs. I followed his instructions. I don't know what he did with my hat.

There was a living room to the right of the door as I entered, a large sitting room to the left, a door at the far end of the sitting room, and another door under the stairs, which circled up to a small mezzanine. It was fashionably furnished and in good taste. I went up to the top of the stairs. A hallway led off to my left and a door was to the right. I turned around and surveyed the downstairs sitting room. A moment later Delilah O'Dell came out of the door.

"Enjoying more of the view?" she asked.

"So that's where the Grand View shoot-out occurred," I said, nodding to the large room. "And you and Culhane were the only two who walked away from it."

"It wasn't the Battle of Gettysburg," she answered tartly. "Keep it in perspective. Come in here."

"Your man took my hat," I said.

"You'll get your damn hat back. Occasionally we have a guest who forgets his manners and wears his hat inside. This way we don't embarrass anyone."

"I should think at five hundred smackers a pop you wouldn't care."

"This is a classy place, Bannon, it isn't Steubenville, Ohio," she said, assuming I knew that Steubenville was reputed to be the whorehouse capital of the world.

Her living room was done in yellow and pale green. Chaise, sofa, three chairs you could sink in and disappear, white coffee tables. The lamps were Tiffany and overhead was a magnificent crystal chandelier that filled in the shadows in the room. A well-stocked wet bar in one corner. Billie Holiday was singing "I Get Along Without You Very Well" on the console.

I looked at the feather draped across her shoulder.

"Do you wear that hat to bed?" I asked.

"I don't wear anything to bed," she said. "How about you?"

"Silk pajama bottoms."

"You aren't the type."

"I live alone. I don't have company that often so I dress for comfort."

"You must not be trying very hard," she said, walking to the bar.

"To do what?"

"Have company. John Jameson alright?"

"Beautiful. One cube of ice, please."

She chuckled as she fixed the drinks.

"What's funny?" I asked.

"Two of a kind," she said half-aloud, shaking her head. She opened an ebony humidor, took out two thin cigars, and squeezed them between thumb and forefinger. Satisfied they were fresh, she snipped the ends off with a small scissor. She lit one, twirling it in the flame like an expert, and brought the drink and cigar over to me.

"Cuban," she said, nodding to the cigar. "I have a friend that brings them to me once a month. Why don't you give your legs a rest."

I sank into one of the big chairs. It was like sitting on a cloud.

"This is a great cigar," I said. "Of course, most of the cigars I've smoked cost a nickel and had 'It's a boy' printed on the wrapper."

She lit her own cigar.

"You do that with real finesse," I said. "Did your tricks come with the house?"

"I learned my tricks—as you call them—from a very experienced lady in Paris. I was her apt pupil for three years, starting when I was eighteen."

She looked me over with an experienced eye. "You shouldn't have any trouble finding company. Great eyes, nice nose, good strong jawline. Nice straight teeth. Trim. You could use a few hours in the sun. And not too tall. That's good. Anything over six feet I find intimidating."

"Who're you kidding? Nothing intimidates you."

"How would you know?"

"It's a measured guess. Is this how you size up your young ladies?"

"I'm not too concerned about height where the ladies are concerned," she said, sitting down on the chaise. "Some men like amazons, some like midgets."

"No kidding. I've never met a lady midget."

"Would you like to?"

"I can't afford it. A drink in this place would bankrupt me."

"Maybe a free sample, then. But I get to watch."

"Is that your monkey? Watching?"

"More like an audition."

"I already have a job," I said with a laugh.

"Not like the job I have in mind."

"I'm sure."

"Are you any good at it?"

"My job?"

"Yes, your job."

"Not bad."

"Brodie says you're a pit bull. Are you a pit bull . . . What's your first name?"

"Sergeant."

"Cute," she said sarcastically. "Is this where you go into your official act? Where's the blackjack?"

"We stopped using them, they leave bruises," I laughed. "My name's Zeke. And I assume Brodie told you to go mum on me."

"Brodie doesn't tell me what to do; I figure things out for myself. I think you're chasing some half-baked idea and you think if you talk to enough people, somebody's bound to tell you a lie you can hang your hat on."

"I suppose you could look at it that way."

She shook her head slowly. "Well, at least you're honest about it, *Sergeant,*" she said with a little spit in her tone.

"Why don't you call me Zeke."

"I don't think we're going to get that chummy."

"Really? I heard you have a thing for cops."

"I have a thing for *men.*"

"Ow . . . got a thing for acid, too."

"You don't chip easily, do you?"

"You're pretty good, but not *that* good."

"I'm just warming up."

"I won't be around for the finale."

"Really?"

"This won't take that long. What do your young ladies do for kicks?" I asked, making it sound as casual as possible. "San Pietro isn't exactly the Lido."

"They're driven into Santa Barbara or Los Angeles when they want to have fun. Sometimes they sneak into town for a movie."

"Do they do well? I mean, do they make a nice living?"

"Is this going to be twenty questions?"

"Curiosity."

"Jade, the naked sun goddess, is studying biology at U.C.L.A. She only works summers and holidays. So far, she's put herself through three years of college, makes straight A's, and will have a nice little nest egg when she graduates. That answer your question?"

"I was wondering where they bank," I said, and tried to blow a smoke ring, which fell apart as it left my lips. She blew three perfect ones and stared hard at me as they rose toward the chandelier.

"Do you shill for a bank on the side?" she asked after a minute crept by.

"I'm sure you know about the five hundred a month the woman Verna Hicks Wilensky was getting. I just talked to the notary at one of the banks. She described two of the buyers as five-three or five-four, a hundred and ten pounds, sexy, very fancily dressed for San Pietro. Pleasant, friendly, self-assured. The description could fit either of the naked goddesses down by the pool. And probably all the rest of the gals in your sorority."

"Or any other good-looking girl five-three or five-four."

"The descriptions of the buyers all follow the same line. Pretty, far too well dressed for your average San Pietro girl, in their early twenties. Well spoken, good manners, friendly but not overly so . . ."

"What are you building?"

"As you told me, your girls sneak off to Eureka for an occasional movie but don't spend time down there."

"It's called San Pietro. Eureka is history."

"Not from where I'm standing. Some things don't wash off."

"And you're different? Your badge makes you any better?"

I thought about that for a moment or two.

"Maybe you're right, Delilah. Maybe it's the same gutter no matter how you dress it up."

"Maybe you better sashay out of here."

"I'm not through yet. We were talking about your dollhouse. The girls wouldn't be recognized down in the village. They don't give their names, they hand the notary an envelope with five Ben Franklins in it and the name of the payee, get the check, put it in an addressed, stamped envelope, and get lost. I'd like to talk to some of the girls."

"Sure. Just as soon as I fall over dead on the floor."

"I could get pushy."

"You could lose that pretty smile of yours."

"We could do this the hard way, Delilah."

"*My* first name is *Miss*," she said harshly. "And you're up here chasing your own tail. Trying to pin something on me or Culhane or somebody else up here. Let me show you something."

She led me across the room and pointed to a small photograph mounted on the wall. It was a shot of Brodie and his crew, somewhere in France. The remnants of a town formed the background and they were up to their ankles in mud. Below the photograph, mounted on black velvet, were a Purple Heart and a Silver Star. She stared at Culhane's figure as though transfixed.

"Why did you leave, Brodie?"

He shrugged. "To see the world."

"Uh-huh."

"You want to know the truth? I was running away from what I just came back to."

She smiled ruefully. "You were sweet on Isabel, Ben was sweet on Isabel, and Isabel was sweet on both of you. Me? I was sweet on you and I couldn't make it to first base."

"Hell, we were just kids, Del."

"Doesn't make it hurt any the less."

"We were all good friends. Still are, I should hope."

"Nothing could ever change that, Brodie."

She went to the record changer and put on an up-tempo jazz record, "Aunt Hagar's Children Blues," and started to dance. Brodie had seen girls in Paris dancing like that, loose, legs flying, swinging to the rhythm of the music.

"C'mon, I'll teach you to do the Charleston."

"Can I do it on one leg?" he asked with a smile.

She stopped and lifted the needle off the turntable.

"I'm sorry . . ."

"Hey, it's nothing. In another month I'll be good as new. Still a little gimpy, that's all."

She sat down near him.

"Here's to us," she said, holding up her glass. When they tapped them, the fine glassware pinged like tiny bells.

"To us," he echoed. "A month from now you can teach me to dance. Give me an excuse to come by."

"You'll never need an excuse, Brodie. Just show up. I'll give you the key."

Without looking at me, she said, "Do you know about these men?"

"I've met most of them," I said. "Look, I'm not up here to give anybody grief, particularly a bunch of war heroes. I'm here because I've got a job to do and it involves murder and . . ."

"Go back to L.A. You think anybody up here will give you a nickel's worth of news? There's not a man in that picture wouldn't lie, kill, or die for Culhane. And you can include me in the club."

"I didn't say anything specific about Culhane."

"I think you're dancing with the idea."

"I think some of your girls have information that can help me. You want to do it the hard way?"

"Oh? And how would that work?"

"The scenario would go something like this: I send the black wagon up here from L.A. I come in with a fistful of warrants, and we haul a dozen of your ladies down to the city and go in the little room with the bare bulb hanging from the ceiling and get real serious. All we want to know is where they got the bucks to buy some cashier's checks."

"You'd have to wade through a couple of lawyers who make more money while they're taking a leak than you do in a year."

"I've done rounds with the best. Lawyers don't rattle me, although being in the same room with them usually gives me a rash."

"You're an arrogant son of a bitch."

"I've been called a lot worse."

"I'm sure you have," she said, standing up. "Well, that's what you're going to have to do, so you may as well trot on home and get your warrants."

"I think you've told me enough already."

"Don't bang your head on the wall, Sergeant. A couple of dozen very well heeled, very well connected gentlemen come through here every week. Any one of them could have slipped one of the girls some Ben Franklins and asked her to do that little chore. The girls don't know any of them by name."

"Then why are you getting wrinkles in your corset?"

"It's bad for business."

"So's murder."

"I think you should finish your drink and toddle along. You can take the cigar with you."

She walked across the room and opened the door.

"Swell," I said. "And I was hoping we'd get along."

"Save up your money for about ten years and come back; you'll find out how pleasant I can be," she answered.

"So long, Delilah," I said. "Thanks for the drink and the cigar."

The big colored guy was waiting for me at the front door with my hat.

"Good day, sir," he said.

"It could have been better," I told him.

I walked back toward the parking lot. I was guessing that the discreet side door hidden behind the hedgerow probably led to a private room for the locals.

Or maybe it was where the milkman made his morning delivery.

CHAPTER 26

$\int$ ki was in the diner when I got back there a little after three. He had commandeered a large booth in one corner and was leafing through his little black notebook.

Brett Merrill was sitting across the room in seersucker, a white shirt, and a blue tie, talking to a well-dressed gentleman who didn't look like he belonged in a diner. Neither of them did.

"The big guy in seersucker talking to the older fellow is the D.A., Brett Merrill," I told Ski.

"Ex-D.A.," Ski corrected. "He retired. He's Culhane's campaign manager now."

"So, how'd you do?" I asked.

"Not bad."

That was encouraging. Ski, who had been in the bureaucracy six years longer than I had, was a master of the noncommittal, having learned the trick from Moriarity. His responses ranged from "not much" to "not bad." Nothing less, nothing more. "Not bad" held promise.

"How'd you do?" he asked.

"Well, I had a steak sandwich and traded pedigrees with Culhane, met the Gormans, scored some points at a couple of banks, and then went to a whorehouse."

He shook his head. "I got six years' seniority on you and I get to spend the last three hours in the records room with a sweet little old lady named Glenda, listening to gossip, and blowing dust off old files. You eat steak, meet the snotty set, and get a matinee."

"Privileges of rank."

"Find out anything while you were eating and slumming with the rich?"

We started a familiar routine. Exchanging ideas and building on the evidence in some kind of logical order, trying to make sense of all the information we were gathering.

"I think I know who brokered the checks," I said.

"I'll take a wild guess," he answered, flipping through his notebook. No one, not even a cryptologist, could decipher Ski's scrawl. He looked over at me. "Delilah O'Dell," he said.

"You been snooping around the banks, too."

He nodded. "At least one check was bought by a working stiff I assume could have been her Japanese gardener. The rest of them were bought by sexy young ladies nobody knew. I get the feeling nobody wants to admit that the local madam has a chauffeur of color driving her and her employees around in a Rolls-Royce."

The man Merrill was talking to got up. They shook hands and the man left without so much as a glance at us.

"You think O'Dell was banking Lila Parrish?" Ski asked.

"No. I think she's the front. Her girls go into L.A. on occasion as well as San Luis Obispo and other towns along the route. Easy for them to make a five-minute trip to a bank. What did the records department give up?"

"A few interesting items. Some may fit in, some are just local history. For instance, there's a death certificate on an Eli Gorman Junior. He was born in Massachusetts in 1900, died September 1920. That's from the record. Isabel Hoffman and Ben Gorman were his parents. They were married in Massachusetts. Gorman was going to Harvard and she went with him. She was seventeen at the time. That's from Glenda."

"The kid was killed the night of the Grand View massacre," I told him. "He drove his car off the overlook. That was his mother we saw with the flowers up on the cliff."

"Eli Gorman, Ben's father, owned this whole valley at one time. The deeds are all on file."

"He won it in a poker game with O'Dell."

"Not all of it. O'Dell snookered him. He sold the deeds to the property that was then the town of Eureka to Riker the day of the game."

"And started a war," I said.

Ski thought about that for a moment or two.

"It probably started long before that," he said. "The old-timer, Tallman? He put up with the town's sins. After the shoot-out in Delilah's place, Culhane turned up the heat on Riker."

I finished the analysis. "And when Riker went up the river, and Fontonio was shot, Culhane ran Guilfoyle and the rest of the bunch out of town."

"I think I got a surprise for you. I took a stroll through the cemetery and came across a tombstone that's interesting." He looked at his notes. "Jerome Parrish. Born 1869, died 1908. Loving husband and father."

"The daughter was Lila Parrish," I guessed.

He nodded. "She was born in the clinic here, in 1900. Which would make her forty-one, close enough to fit Verna. Her mother was divorced when the kid was four. She remarried and divorced again. Her name now is Ione Fisher. Here's the kicker. Ione Fisher was, and still is, a nurse at the Shuler Institute, the sanitarium down in Mendosa. Very private. I understand Mrs. Fisher is head nurse now. She's sixty-two."

"That's a lot of stuff to get out of old records."

"Mostly Glenda. She's fifty-six, has a big nose, and loves to talk."

I said, "So Lila blows town, heads down to Mendosa, hides out with her old lady in a private sanitarium for a while, and when Guilfoyle moves on Mendosa, Lila slips down to L.A., gets a new ID, hikes her age up a bit, and becomes Verna Hicks."

"I have to wonder two things," Ski said. "If she was being paid off, why would she hide out twenty-five miles from here in a town run by Riker's boy? Seems a little risky, wouldn't you say?"

"You're forgetting the time element," I said. "Guilfoyle didn't move into Mendosa until after Riker's appeal, which was almost a year after the trial."

"You'd think if she was a key witness against Arnie Riker, Culhane would have found her when Riker appealed the case," Ski said. "Hell, if big-nosed Glenda knew who her mother was, Culhane certainly did."

"Sometimes what seems obvious isn't necessarily fact," a voice drawled, and we turned to face Brett Merrill. "Mind if I join you?"

He looked larger when confined in a small place. He was probably six-two and a hundred ninety or two hundred pounds. He sat down before we had a chance to answer him.

"Some things are bothering us," I said to Merrill. "Maybe you can help us out."

"I can try," he drawled pleasantly.

"Lila Parrish was your key witness in the Thompson case. It seems to us that you would have kept a leash on her—knowing Riker was sure to appeal his conviction."

"Yeah," Ski said. "And since her mother lives in Mendosa, you'd think Culhane would look for her there."

"Lila Parrish didn't live with her mother at the time of the murder," Merrill said. "She lived with another girl in a shanty in Milltown. She left her mother when Ione married Fisher. They were on the outs. Our people interviewed Ione Fisher. I'm convinced she wasn't hiding Lila down there."

"She was your only eyeball witness. How hard did you really try to find her?" I said.

Merrill shrugged and said in his easy drawl, "Lila Parrish vanished the day after she testified. Her roommate worked at the mill. When she came home from work, Lila's things were gone. Nobody's seen her since."

"And you couldn't find her?"

"Look, boys, sometimes you have to play the hand you're dealt. We had Riker dead-to-rights. He and his boat were covered with her blood. The Parrish girl had testified she saw Riker shoot Wilma Thompson and throw her in his car. Thompson's blood was all over the car. Riker had spent ten days in jail for beating her up once and she ditched him. Plenty of motive for a guy with Riker's reputation. And he had no alibi. He said he went to his boat that night, got drunk, and passed out. When he was arrested on the boat he was still wearing bloody clothes and there wasn't a scratch on him. He was lucky they reduced the sentence to life without parole."

I smiled. "Said like a true prosecutor."

"It was a solid case. The legwork was first rate. Woods and Carney gave me a preponderance of evidence."

"Where's Carney?"

"Died of a heart attack five years ago."

"When Woods shot Fontonio, why did you dead-docket the case against him?" Ski asked, suddenly changing the subject.

"I thought you were investigating an L.A. homicide," Merrill said softly. The smile got a little cooler.

"Just curious," Ski said.

"Making a case against Eddie Woods would have been a waste of time. There were no eyewitnesses. We had started a grand jury investigation against what was left of the Riker outfit and Eddie Woods went to Fontonio's place to deliver a subpoena. He says Fontonio went for a gun and he shot him. There was a gun in Fontonio's hand we couldn't trace."

"His wife and bodyguard said he never packed heat," Ski said.

"C'mon, boys," Merrill said, slowly shaking his head. "Would you go before a grand jury with a wife and a hoodlum as your only witnesses? The attorney general sent a man down from Sacramento to look into it. He looked over the evidence, said, 'Thanks a lot for nothing,' and went back to Sacramento. Then Eddie resigned."

He finished his coffee and dabbed his lips with a napkin.

Ski asked, "You came here from someplace else, didn't you? Just curious. Accents interest me."

"Everybody in California came from someplace else," Merrill answered. "I came from southern Georgia."

"Why?" I asked.

"I had a little law firm and a partner named David Vigil, who had kept business alive while I was off fighting the war. There really wasn't enough business for the two of us, and my brother and sister-in-law were barely scratching out a living on the family farm. One day I got a call from California, probably the longest long-distance call in the town's history. It was Brodie. He said, 'How'd you like to be D.A. of Eureka, California? I need some help out here.' So I packed my valise, took the bus to Atlanta, and hopped the train west. We kept busy. A shooting every week or ten days. Once in a while somebody stupid would rob the bank. If Buck Tallman didn't drop them in their tracks coming out the door, Brodie would ride them down. There was a lot of law but not much order." He stopped and chuckled. "Probably a lot more than you wanted to know. Southerners tend to go on."

"We're still trying to get a handle on the five hundred a month Verna was getting," I said, cutting off his monologue. "Somebody was paying her off for *some*thing."

"I wouldn't know about that."

"Does Culhane know?"

"You'll have to ask him," he said, grabbing his hat.

He laid a quarter on the table.

"Pleasure meeting you, Ski," he said, and strolled out, leaving us staring at the door.

After a minute or so I said, "Know what I think? I think we've run out of gas here. Nobody's going to tell us a damn thing."

"I'll tell you what I think," Ski answered. "I think Lila Parrish lied at Riker's trial. Merrill didn't have Thompson's body because Riker fed her to the sharks. So *somebody* arranged for Parrish to testify she had witnessed the murder, then paid her to vanish."

"Interesting theory, Ski. But why, after nearly twenty years, does she turn up dead in her bathtub?"

"If we knew that, we'd know who killed her."

"Maybe Merrill was giving us the shoo-fly about Ione Fisher. Maybe she knows where her daughter went."

"Maybe."

"There's only one person who might give us a straight answer," I said.

"The mother." Ski nodded. "And she's right down the road."

"Worth a shot," I agreed, and we headed south.

CHAPTER 27

The neon sign spelled ALBACORE POINT in startling red letters that burned the name into the fog. Under it: VACANCIES. At this time of year it should have said Full. Charlie Lefton apparently was too far off the beaten track to attract much trade. Or maybe he didn't care. Maybe Charlie was happy to have his little place by the ocean. Maybe he was independently wealthy and reclusive and used the place as a tax dodge. All Moriarity had said was that Charlie would give us a good price if we wanted to stay the night. Lefton's was perfect since it was on the way south to Mendosa.

We got to Lefton's by driving down a hard dirt road that led from Route 7 west toward the ocean and then curved around at a two-story hospital and followed the shoreline south. About five miles past the hospital, a sign had pointed off to the east to Milltown and a half mile beyond that was the paper mill, a black silhouette against the darkening blue sky. It was an eerie, ugly giant, a noisy complex with stacks that spewed reeking smoke and ash into the air. Man-made clouds obliterated a fiery sun sinking toward the horizon.

As we passed the plant, an early fog had suddenly surged out of the gathering dusk, not on little cat feet as Sandburg would have it but like a broiling storm cloud that had been grounded. Driving into it was like driving into a swirling, gray tunnel. The headlights reflected off it and were swallowed up. I switched to low beam and it gave us maybe ten feet of grace on the road. I was driving fifteen miles an hour when I spotted the red sign and slowed down, looking for the driveway into Lefton's place. I found it under the neon sign and turned onto a shell drive, the tires crunching beneath us as I eased down it.

"I hope the ocean isn't anywhere near here," I said. "If we roam off the road, we could end up in the drink."

After a moment, Ski said, "I can't swim."

I laughed at him. "Hell, you couldn't sink if you tried."

A sign jumped out of the fog at us, an arrow cut from a two-by-four, painted white with black letters: OFFICE. I felt disoriented, isolated in the middle of nowhere, with visibility of about five feet. I stepped out of the car and yelled, "Anybody around?"

My words sounded lifeless, without resonance, as the mist swallowed them up. Then a voice came back just as flat, "Who wants to know?"

"Customers," I yelled back.

A spotlight blinked on, a blurred orb somewhere off to our left. A shimmering image came toward us, a rail-thin six-footer, his face leathered and tanned by sun and wind, his windblown black hair in need of a trim, and his face covered with four or five days' growth of graying beard. He was wearing denim work pants, a clean white sweatshirt with the sleeves cut off and what was left rolled up over his shoulders, and light blue canvas deck shoes. There was a tattoo on his left biceps, a knife piercing a waving banner on which were the words DEATH BEFORE DISHONOR.

"Charlie Lefton?" I asked.

"Yeah, I'm Lefton," he said in a voice so quiet it was almost a whisper.

"I'm Zeke Bannon, this is my partner Ski Agassi. We work for Dan Moriarity. He said you might have room for us."

"Homicide cops, huh?"

I nodded.

"Follow me up to the lodge. Can't see shit in this soup."

We followed him down a slight embankment and into the arena of light formed by the searchlight. I could hear water beating against something.

"We close to the ocean?" I asked.

"About a hundred yards to your right," he answered. A moment later a small wooden bridge appeared through the fog. It led to the lodge, as Lefton called it, a strip of eleven rooms. The office was in the middle, five rooms on each side. A narrow walk surrounded the primitive billet and below it, a grid of four-by-fours supported it about five feet off the ground. Nearby, just out of the light's perimeter, I could hear a boat groaning against its tie lines, and much farther away, almost out of earshot, the ocean smacking against rocks.

"Where the hell are we?" I asked as we walked down to the office.

He pulled open a squeaky screen door and flicked on the office light and pointed to a map on the wall. It was a sectional of the coastline. We were on the back side of a narrow cove, like a finger pointing inward from the Pacific. Lefton's lodge was built on stilts in the event of an extremely high tide.

"Been here since '02 and never got a drop of water under the place," Lefton said. "Always have been a little too cautious for my own good."

The office barely earned the name. There was a scarred-up old desk against one wall, three straight-back wooden chairs, and a gray metal three-drawer file cabinet facing the desk on the opposite wall. An upright telephone, a small desk lamp, and a hot plate with a percolator held down the desk, and a 1939 calendar from a tackle shop adorned the wall.

"You guys just spending the night?"

"Yeah," I said. "We'll by pulling out about seven."

"Well, I brew up coffee at 6:30 if you need a jump start to get moving. Got some sugar and cream in my room, which is next door."

"You live here?" Ski asked.

"Here and on my boat. She can hold eight. I like to sleep on her. She rocks me to sleep." He spoke in that low voice, almost without modulation. I had the feeling you could set off a load of TNT in the next room and he wouldn't blink.

"Why don't you take 1 and 2," he said. "They got an adjoining door. They're open. Keys are in the top dresser drawers. You can settle up when you leave. Two bucks apiece sound fair?"

"More than fair," I said.

"Hell, they'd go empty anyways. Just gotta show a little profit. There's an ice chest filled with Mexican beer on the back side. Twenty cents a bottle. Throw the money in the tin can on the side."

"Thanks," I said.

"Come down from Pietro?" he said, making conversation.

I nodded.

"Where you heading this evening?"

"Mendosa."

Lefton seemed genuinely surprised.

"Jesus, why?" he asked.

"We have to interview somebody."

"Hmm. Well, don't mention the captain down there. You know the story about the feud between him and Guilfoyle?"

I nodded.

"Worst case of bad blood I ever saw. I'd walk light down there; your badge ain't worth a damn. One thing Guilfoyle really hates is big-city cops. He's mean as a constipated skunk but he's not as dumb as some think and he's got a real short fuse."

"So we've heard."

"He wouldn't get homicidal with a couple of out-of-town cops, would he?" Ski said with a smile.

"You seen the fog we got here. You could disappear into the Pacific and nobody would ever find you. It's happened a lot more often than you might think."

"To cops?" I asked.

"To anybody he gets a hard-on for."

"Great," Ski said dismally.

"How come Culhane doesn't go down there and clean the whole bunch out?" I asked.

Lefton shrugged. "It's a Mexican standoff. The captain doesn't give a damn, long's Gil stays on his side of the county line, which is about ten feet from here."

"You know Guilfoyle pretty well?" I asked.

"He brings a fishing party down here once a month or so. Doesn't like his guests to spend too much time in the daylight in Mendosa, if you know what I mean."

"Not exactly."

"They're his guests. Hard cases, I'd say; sounds like they're usually from back East somewhere. They fill up the place for a week. Or a month. Pay good, tip big. I don't ask questions."

I remembered what Jimmy Pennington said about Mendosa being called 'Hole-in-the-Wall' after the Montana hangout of Butch Cassidy and the Sundance Kid.

"Well, we're not planning to spend a lot of time there. Grab a bite to eat, gas up the jalopy, do our work, and come back."

"Mendosa's straight down the road about fifteen miles, just past the icehouse. Probably take you half an hour in this fog."

"Thanks, Charlie."

"Glad to do it," he answered. "Anything I can do for Dan."

That's all he said, although I was sure there was more to that story than he cared to tell. He walked in front of the car with a flashlight and guided us through a turnaround and back up to the main road.

It took us just under thirty minutes to crawl into Mendosa. We passed Ferguson's Icehouse on the right and about two miles from Mendosa we drove out of the fog as suddenly as we had driven into it.

"We got an address on Shuler's place?" I asked Ski.

"Yeah. End of Bellamy Street on the north end of town. Take a left at the second light, which is Main Street, and then right when the street forks."

I pulled into the first filling station I saw. The sign out front told us it was WARTHOG MILLER'S FILL-UP. The attendant was a short, mean-looking guy with a gimpy leg, oily hair, bad teeth, and the breath to go with it. I told him to fill it up and got out as he was pumping the gas. There was a lot of background noise. People, music, horns blowing. Friday night noises.

"You Warthog Miller?" I asked pleasantly.

"I suppose so," he snarled.

His eyes wandered to our license plate, the whip aerial on the back bumper, and the spotlight mounted beside the door on the driver's side.

"Lookin' for anybody in particular?" he said, too casually.

"Nope. Just gonna grab a bite to eat."

He finished pumping and asked if we needed oil.

"No thanks," I said, paid him two bucks for the gas, and got back in the car.

"Sounds like they're having a riot," Ski said.

"Friday night in a crooked mill town," I ventured.

"Ain't we the lucky ones."

As we pulled out, I watched Warthog in the rearview mirror. He scurried into the office and dropped a nickel in a pay phone on the wall.

"I think we got made," I said.

"What a surprise."

When we got to Main Street I sat for a minute, waiting for the light to change, then took a right.

"I said left at the light," Ski mumbled.

To our left, Main Street was as dark as a mole hole.

"I gotta make a phone call."

Main Street wasn't as bad as I expected. A small town with a tree-lined main drag. We drove six or seven blocks and saw three bars, a nightclub that advertised "dancing ladies" in neon, another that had a sign telling us it featured genuine New Orleans jazz, a gaming parlor with its windows painted black, a billiard parlor, a pawnshop, and a restaurant that bragged "We never close." Otherwise, there was the usual collection of hardware stores, grocers, meat markets, an ice cream parlor, and a movie theater. But it was a noisy town, with music spilling from the joints and streets filled with people looking in the doors and milling about. A lot of activity for a little town, even for a Friday night.

I drove another block and came to a restaurant called Ma's Home Cooking.

I parked and we went in and grabbed a table.

A waitress with henna-colored hair piled on top of her head and lipstick the color of blood sashayed over to the table and popped her gum for us.

"Hi, boys, what'll it be," she said. "The meat loaf's the specialty. It's so good the cook keeps the recipe in a safe."

"Just two coffees," I said.

"What kind of pie do you have?" Ski asked.

"What kind would you like, Shorty?" she said with a half-assed grin.

Ski's laugh rattled the place.

"How about banana cream?"

"You got it," she said. And to me, "Pie for you, too?"

"No thanks," I said.

"Two javas, one B.C., coming up."

I went to the phone booth in the back of the place near the rest rooms and looked up the Shuler Institute in the phone book, dropped a nickel, and dialed the number. A man answered the phone and I asked for Mrs. Fisher. She was on the phone within seconds.

"This is Superintendent Fisher."

"Mrs. Fisher? My name is Tyler Marchand the Third, from Santa Maria. I'm sure you've heard of Marchand Estates."

"Uh . . . yes, of course," she said. Took the bait.

"You've been highly recommended by several people in my club—I won't mention names, I'm sure you respect their confidentiality—and I'm sure you'll understand when you hear my predicament."

"Which is, Mr. Marchand?"

"My brother has become a real problem. He's a drinker and we have tried everything. He's very tight right now and I wondered if I might bring him by there."

"You mean now?!"

"I really need your help. I've been told you are a truly concerned establishment. I've driven over forty miles."

"Mr. Marchand, we require a letter of sponsorship and a substantial deposit prior to an examination. This late at night . . ."

"This is an emergency, Mrs. Fisher. He's been drinking for days. What better time to evaluate him? I can be there in ten minutes. I'll be glad to give you whatever deposit is required."

She hesitated for a few seconds and finally she said, "Alright, Mr. Marchand, but I'll have to talk to you before we admit him. There are a lot of details . . ."

"I'll be there in ten minutes," I said, and hung up.

The waitress was back by the time I returned to the table, carrying coffee in each hand and the pie perched on one of the cups.

"There you go," she said. "Shorty, you look like a man who'd just love an order of that meat loaf."

"And so I would," Ski said. "But we're running a little late for an appointment."

"Well, ain't that a boot in the ass," she chirped, and retreated to the back.

Ski took a long swig of coffee and glanced casually over the lip of the cup through the front window as he was drinking. He set the cup down, smiled, and said casually, "We got company."

"What kind?"

"Two guys. Dark blue Buick, spotlight on the side, tall aerial on the back bumper. Trying hard not to look at us."

"Sounds like my first trip to San Pietro."

"Maybe you just naturally irritate people, Zeke."

"Yeah," I said. "It's giving me a complex."

The front window of the place was behind me so I couldn't see our company.

"Somebody just lit a cigarette," Ski said. "They're still trying hard not to look over here. Think we can ditch 'em?"

"We'll give it a try."

He gulped down his pie and we left. I drove to the next intersection.

"Hang on," I said.

I grabbed a left, slammed down the gas, turned at the first left, and pulled in an alley behind the row of buildings facing Main Street. I killed the lights and waited. A minute later the Buick roared by. I pulled out of the other end of the alley, turned back onto Main, and drove toward Bellamy.

We had no trouble finding the Institute. It commanded several acres at the end of the street, a few blocks off Main, and was surrounded by an eight-foot stone wall with broken glass on the top. I wondered whether it was to keep the patients in or keep unwanted people out.

The main building was an enormous white Victorian gingerbread structure with a porch that surrounded it. It looked quite elegant. Three stories high with four spired towers topping it off. There were several outbuildings on both sides. The manicured lawn boasted trees and a small fish pond. Wooden porch swings hung from the heavy limbs of the sturdier trees.

Inside, things would be less cheerful. Drunks screaming with the D.T.'s would be locked away in rooms with padded walls; the elderly would be treated like children; schizoids would be locked away in padded rooms or strapped to beds chained to the floor. I knew about institutions like Shuler's and about dementia.

"Make like you're drunk, but don't make a lot of noise," I said.

We walked up the steps to the main office. Old memories flashed back and my stomach cramped as I entered the place.

A smallish, trim woman in a gray gabardine suit came out of an office as I entered the foyer. She had a stern face and her blue-white hair was mannishly cut in a short bob. She wore round glasses, her suspicious eyes framed in gold. She was followed by a surly hunk of a man in his late twenties, his body apparently molded by barbells. He was wearing a white nurse's uniform.

"Mrs. Fisher? I'm Tyler Marchand. We just spoke on the phone."

Ski staggered past them into the office, dropped heavily in a chair, closed his eyes, and started humming to himself.

I looked at the hulk and back at her.

"Can we go in your office and talk?"

Randy stood stiffly, arms hanging loosely at his sides.

"It's alright, Randy, finish your rounds," she said officiously, without looking at him.

"You sure? The lush is a big one."

"He won't cause you any trouble," I said. "He's a pussycat."

"Go on," she said, and Randy left. I followed Ione Fisher into her office.

"So you're Mr. Marchand?" she said with a snap in her tone.

"Yes," I said. "You'll have to forgive Raymond, my brother; he forgets his manners when he's under the weather."

Ski let his arms fall loosely, his mouth fell open, and he was still as a pillow.

Her office was pleasant, considering where we were. There was a vase of flowers on her desk and polka-dot curtains dressed the windows. I strolled over to the window facing the rear of the compound and looked the place over. The road made a wide arc around the rear grounds. In the center of the arc was a large, three-story building. There were no windows on the first floor; small, slitted oblongs of light every four or five feet on the second. The third floor looked like it belonged to a hotel. Sliding glass doors opened onto small balconies on the three sides I could see. I watched an elevator climb up one corner of the structure.

A muffled, inhuman cry echoed from one of the lower floors; a moment later I heard the sharp crack of a leather strap and the cry became a barely audible moan. Then the quad fell silent again.

"Seems pleasant enough," I said, and turned back to Nurse Fisher.

She sat down behind her desk and folded her hands on its top.

"How long has he been drinking?" she asked.

"About twenty years."

"No, no, I mean this time," she said, her frown deepening.

"Oh, let's see, it was Mother's birthday . . . sixteen days." I changed the subject. "Your place is quite impressive," I said. "These towered rooms on the floors above, is one of them available? I want Raymond to be as comfortable as possible."

"The tower suites are reserved for special visitors."

"Is that right. How does one become a special visitor?"

"Get elected to the board of directors," she said. "Have a seat, Mr. Marchand. I'll have to take down some information before we even consider accepting your brother."

"Thank you."

Before she went any further, a phone rang in the outer office.

"Excuse me, my secretary left an hour ago," she said, and went into the office and closed the door. I got up and looked out the front window. No cars. So far, so good.

She was gone about two minutes. When she came back, her expression had changed from stern to angry.

"Guess what?" she said.

I raised my eyebrows.

"There aren't any Marchands in Santa Maria," she said smugly. "No Marchand Estates. Nobody up there ever heard of you. What's your game, whoever you are?"

"You're very good," I said. I took out my wallet and showed her my badge.

"My name's Bannon, Central Homicide, L.A. Police," I said. "Raymond here is Detective Agassi, my partner."

Ski opened his eyes and sat up in the chair with his hands on his knees and offered her a brief smile.

"What do you want?"

I put it to her bluntly. "When's the last time you heard from Lila?"

She looked like I had thrown cold water in her face. The question stunned her and she just stared at me.

"Let me hit it from another angle," I said. "Did your daughter come down here and hide out with you after the Riker trial?"

She got control of herself.

"You better get out of here before . . ." She hesitated.

"Before what? Your sadistic flunky Randy comes back?"

Her face was white. "I haven't seen or heard from Lila in over twenty years," she whispered. "She left me when I married Ollie Fisher. She hated him. Look, people here at the Institute don't know about Lila. Nobody at this hospital was even here when it happened. Now please leave."

Her face tightened and fear began to take the place of anger.

"Be straight with me," I said. "Have you been in touch with Lila at all since Arnie Riker's murder trial?"

She lit a cigarette with a shaking hand. "I told you, she walked out of my life when she was fourteen."

"Never written? No phone calls?"

She shook her head.

"In all these years, she's never been in touch with you? No Christmas cards, birthday cards . . .?"

Her eyes widened. "*NO!*" She looked toward the front window and back at me. Ski walked over to the window and stared down the road.

"Why are you here? Why are you doing this to me?"

"A woman was murdered down in Los Angeles a few days ago. We can't track her back beyond 1924. Somebody was paying her five hundred dollars a month for all these years, and we think the dead woman may have been Lila."

She stared at me and tears welled up in her eyes.

"Sergeant . . .?"

"Bannon."

"Sergeant Bannon, why would you think that?"

"The dead woman showed up in L.A. in 1924—with no past."

"For the last twenty years I have lived each day hoping I would hear her voice. Or get a card. *Anything* to let me know she's alive. She was my only child. Do you have any children?"

I shook my head.

"Can you understand what that was like?"

"Yes, I can, and I'm sorry I have to bring it up," I said. "Do you have any pictures of Lila, even from when she was a child?"

She slowly shook her head.

"I couldn't afford to keep them," she said. "I was going to quit here and leave when she testified at Riker's trial but nobody cared about me." She hesitated for a moment and then said, "This girl who was murdered, why do you think it may have been Lila?"

"It's the only lead we have right now that makes sense."

"What happened to her?"

"She was drowned in her bathtub."

"Oh my God." The tears started working down her cheeks.

"We could be wrong, Mrs. Fisher," Ski said sympathetically. "We could be wrong, but we need to make sure."

She swallowed hard and said, "I was afraid to go and afraid to stay. Do you have any idea what these people are like? Have you ever met Guilfoyle?"

I shook my head.

"Guilfoyle heads security here. Sometimes he goes into what they call the rage ward. He likes to beat on them himself when they start getting out of hand. He calls it 'playtime.' Randy says he even brings his out-of-town friends in and lets them do things. Once, one of them broke a young girl's fingers."

"And you stayed here knowing that?"

"I didn't know anyplace else to go," she said. "It was a good job."

"Car's coming," Ski said.

"Oh my God," she cried.

"It's Guilfoyle," Ski said. "Now what's the play?"

I turned to Mrs. Fisher.

"Let me handle this," I said. "I'll cover you, don't worry."

"There's three of them . . ." Ski started, and the office door burst open. The man who came in was about five-eight. He was a ghost. White hair, no pigment in his skin. He was carrying a snub-nosed .32. He looked the room over with red eyes.

"You," he said to Ski. "In the chair."

Ski didn't move.

Guilfoyle came in behind the albino, shoving him aside. He was as mean-looking as the reputation that preceded him. Tall, round-shouldered, a beer belly tightening the vest of his three-piece suit, drooping dead eyes, a mouth turned down at the corners. A hairline scar etched one side of his face and he had big hands with gnarled fingers, which he kept flexing into fists. He was wearing a brown fedora with the brim snapped down over one eye.

A third thug came in behind him. More of the same. A feral-looking blond hooligan pushing six feet, who walked on the balls of his feet.

"There's no need for rough stuff," I said.

"Shut the fuck up," Guilfoyle snarled.

"We're police officers," I said.

"No shit," he said with a twisted excuse for a smile. "You were made before you got to Main Street."

"I don't know what you're all riled up about," I said. "We got a man in homicide named Red Marcus, who's got a drinking problem. We were told this might be a place could help him."

Guilfoyle snickered. "That's the biggest lie I heard since Santa Claus." He said to the albino, "Frisk 'em."

Ski got a little taller when he said it. The albino reached out to get Ski's gun and Ski grabbed his wrist.

"Nobody takes my gun," he said.

The other thug pulled a .38 and went toward him.

"It's true," Ione Fisher said. "They were just . . ."

Guilfoyle reached around and slapped her hard with the back of his hand, knocking her to the floor. "You speak when I say so," Guilfoyle said.

As he said it, Ski twisted the albino's wrist backward, snatched his gun, and threw him away like a wet bath towel.

Guilfoyle was distracted long enough for me to pull my Luger. I backed up a foot and aimed it at Guilfoyle's head.

"Why don't we all just relax," I said harshly.

Guilfoyle's snake eyes were ablaze. His tongue swept his lips like the tongue of an asp.

The albino scrambled to his feet.

The hooligan, aiming a .38 special, stopped three feet from Ski, who was aiming the albino's peashooter back at him.

Ione Fisher got slowly to her feet, her hand against her jaw.

"You don't really want a lot of shooting in here, do you, Guilfoyle? Think about it. You'll wake up all the guests in the place. Have the whole L.A. police force, the highway patrol, and half the A.G.'s staff down here?"

Guilfoyle's eyes flicked around the room.

"You wanna check out my story? Call my commanding officer. I was about to give it to Mrs. Fisher when the little squirt came busting in here flashing iron. That any way to treat a visiting fireman?"

"We got a call there was trouble out here," Guilfoyle said.

"You were misinformed." I took out my card with my free hand, took a pen from a holder on the desk, scribbled a number on it, and handed it to Guilfoyle. "His name's Captain Moriarity."

Guilfoyle didn't do anything for a minute. Finally he took the card, looked at it, and threw it on the floor.

I sat on the corner of the desk.

"Like I said, you don't want a lot of shooting disturbing the residents, do you, Sheriff? Most of them are disturbed enough as it is." I holstered the Luger.

"What did he ask you?" he said to Fisher.

"He told me about their friend and was asking about the facilities."

"What about 'em?"

"The usual questions. How much, what the rooms were like, things like that."

"Your pal wouldn't like it here," Guilfoyle said to me.

"I already figured that out."

"You shoulda called me. Professional courtesy."

"Why bother you? Besides, it's kind of confidential—or was."

Guilfoyle turned to the hooligan. "Put it away," he said. The hooligan did as he was told, pocketing the gun he'd been pointing at Ski. Guilfoyle took out a cigar, bit the end off it, and lit it from a folder of matches.

"Just a misunderstanding," he said finally. "We get a lot of rough trade in town. Can't be too careful."

"Sure," I said. "Anybody can make a mistake."

I got up and motioned to Ski.

"Let's go, partner. I don't think Marcus'd fit in here." I turned to Ione Fisher. "Thank you for your help," I told her, and headed for the door. Ski followed me.

"No hard feelings, right?" Guilfoyle said as we went out the door.

"No hard feelings," I said.

We went out and got in the car. Ski didn't say anything as I pulled away but his anger filled the car.

"Well, that went pretty well," I joked, trying to lighten things up.

Ski wasn't in the mood for jesting. He didn't say a word until we were almost out of town.

Then:

"Guilfoyle doesn't know we were talking to Fisher about Lila Parrish."

Silence.

Then:

"Guilfoyle's worried about some of his on-the-lam gunsels paying big bucks to hide out in Mendosa."

More silence.

Then:

"My guess is they're staying at Shuler's place, that's what got Guilfoyle's shorts in a bundle."

More silence.

Then:

"You kind of slapped his face in front of his boys."

"It comes naturally."

"You're dreamin' if you think it stopped back there, Zeke."

CHAPTER 28

I stayed on the speed limit until we got to the city limits, then I laid on the gas, but a mile later we hit fog again. It wasn't as thick this time but I had to slow down to forty. Both of us kept an eye on the rearview mirror.

"I been thinking about it," Ski said. "He's not dumb enough to kill a couple of cops. Do you think he's that dumb, Zee?"

"I hope not."

"I mean, how dumb could he be?"

"You heard what Lefton said. If he is that dumb, they'll kill us, run the car into the ocean, take our bodies out to sea, and feed us to the fish."

"I don't think he's that dumb."

"Don't bet on it. You're the one who said it first. We're dreaming if we think it ended back there."

We had made two miles before the fog slowed us down to thirty. I was beginning to relax.

A mistake.

Ski fell silent for a minute and then said, "So much for dreams. We got company again."

I looked in the rearview. Two circles of light shimmering in the fog. Pinpoints. But getting larger. Closing faster than they should have in the fog.

"Jesus," Ski said, mostly under his breath.

He reached up under the dash and snapped the 12-gauge pump from its saddle. He cracked it an inch. It was fully loaded. He checked his .38, opened the pocket in the dash, took out an extra clip for his

S&W, one for my Luger, and a handful of shotgun shells, and we were as fully armed as was available. We had roughly forty rounds.

The lights grew larger.

I turned on the spotlight, aiming it as far ahead as the fog would let me, lowered the beam on the headlights, and stepped on it.

"Remember what Lefton said about going off the road."

"They know the road, Ski, they're gaining on us."

He twisted in his seat as much as he could and hefted the shotgun up to his shoulder.

"Let 'em get close enough for me to put one shot through their windshield," he said.

"We passed an icehouse on the way down," I said. "It should be close. We need cover."

"They're right on our ass."

We were speeding in and out of the fog, strands of it swept by us. Through the mist I saw the sign pointing to the icehouse. Half a mile ahead.

"Hang on," I said. As I said it, they opened fire. The first shot exploded the back window and shattered the rearview mirror.

"Son of a bitch," Ski yelled.

He cut loose with the shotgun through the blown-out window. It hit the right side of their car and blew out the headlight. He pumped in another shell and the gun roared again, and I heard their radiator begin to hiss. The chase car swerved and tried to take us on the left side, so I let it, then hit the brakes, let the four-door Buick growl past, its ruptured radiator spitting steam.

One of Guilfoyle's goons aimed a .45 at us. I swerved into the rear of the chase car as he fired, and the gunshot whined off the hood of our Chevy. The other car slued in front of us. I smacked the rear of it again and it spun out just as I lost control and veered off the road on the opposite side, shattered the entrance sign to Ferguson's Icehouse, and skidded to a stop at the front door. The Buick screeched off the road behind us and hit a tree.

Ski and I piled out and ran up a bunch of steps to the door of the hulking, windowless two-story building. I hit the door with my shoulder and bounced back like a tennis ball.

"Out of the way," Ski yelled, and blew a hole where the doorknob and lock used to be. We charged into freezing cold as gunshots exploded behind us. Then the night was ripped with the sound of a tommy gun. I whirled around as slugs smacked into the heavy insulated walls, saw one of Guilfoyle's gunmen with the stutter gun spitting at us. I pulled the Luger, dropped to my knees, and fired half a clip at him. A bullet ripped into his throat and slammed him back against their wasted car. Blood spurted from his neck. He gasped like a dying fish and jackknifed to the ground.

From my left I heard two other guns start talking. One was heavy, a .357 or a .45. The doorjamb an inch from my face split open and showered me with splinters. Another gunman, a big man huffing as he ran, headed back toward their car, going for the machine gun. I slammed the door shut just as more gunfire erupted.

Behind me I heard Ski growl angrily, and turned as he fell against a mountain of hundred-pound cakes of ice. He was clutching his side.

I ran over to him, saw blood seeping through his fingers.

"Damn it!" he snarled. But it didn't slow him down. He grabbed a pair of ice tongs, dragged one of the big slabs of ice off the pile, and slid it across the floor, ramming the front door shut.

"How bad is it?" I said.

"Hit my side. Lots of padding. Don't worry about it."

Outside, more gunfire. Bullets smacking the heavy walls. Then the machine gun barked again. A dozen holes burst through the door. We dropped to the floor as the bullets stitched across the towering ice chunks and shards of frozen water showered down on us.

I grabbed the shotgun and crawled near the door.

It got quiet. I looked around. The room was freezing cold. My breath swirled around my face. The place was fifteen or twenty feet high. There were two or three wired lamps in the ceiling providing paltry light. To the right of the door there was a desk and chair. No other furniture.

The tommy gun barked again and ripped more holes in the door. More shards spit out of the stacked ice.

"How many do you make," Ski yelled.

"Three left. I took one down."

Tommy boomed again. The door was being shot to pieces.

"The hell with this," I said, leveled the shotgun at the wall in front of me, and pumped one, two, three shots into it. Bits of insulation and sheeting burst out of the hole. I fired again and saw a bit of light coming through the wall from our headlights. I stuck the Luger in my belt and put three more shotgun blasts into the hole. It opened up a three-foot hole in the side of the icehouse and I fell forward, pulled out the Luger, and peered through the gaping hole.

The albino was ten feet away, aiming a .357 at the hole I had just blown. Then suddenly he stopped and the .357 exploded twice in his fist. Bullets ripped through the hole inches from my face.

I laid the Luger barrel on the bottom edge of the hole and shot him. He was knocked backward into a tree. He looked amazed. Blood spurted from a hole in his chest. He fell to his knees and got off two more shots. I shot him again, this time my bullet tearing into his forehead. His back arched and he fell facedown.

The tommy gun was wasting the door.

I couldn't see the shooter with the stutter gun but the blond guy from Shuler's dashed into my view. He fired a shot with his .38 as he jumped behind a tree.

Off to my right I heard the circular magazine of the tommy gun click and fall to the ground, and another snap into its place. It began again, its thunder followed by the sound of .45-caliber slugs thunking into the icehouse door.

"Shoot over here at the hole in the wall," the blond hoodlum yelled.

I rolled away from the hole as a blast shattered its edges. The blond thug took a chance and slid around the tree, his gun barking as he did. I crawled back to the hole and emptied the Luger into him, and he whirled away with a scream, fell on his face, and rolled over, hands outspread, legs crossed at the ankles.

Five feet away, the remaining gunman, who was almost as big as Ski, hit the door with his shoulder. It splintered and fell inward, sending the cake of ice spinning across the floor. He stormed through the door, saw me, and grinned. I dropped the empty Luger and dove for the shotgun but he had the tommy waist high, aimed down my throat.

Ski's .38 bellowed behind me and hit the big hoodlum in the chest. He grunted and whirled toward the sound of the gun. I swung the pump gun up and fired into his belly. It doubled him up and knocked him against the doorjamb. His mouth dropped open with surprise. I charged another round into the chamber and shot him again. His chest erupted. Behind me, Ski emptied his .38 into what was left of him. He took them all and then spun around and fell backward down the steps, his legs flipping over his head before he landed facedown in the dirt.

It got as quiet as Sunday morning.

Smoke and steam whisked around the open door. I ran over to Ski, who was sitting on the floor with his back against the stored ice, and helped him up as best I could.

"Let's go, partner. We gotta get you to the hospital."

"You sure it's over?"

"It's over."

"Christ, we sure made a mess of this place," he said.

I got him up, gathered up our weapons and the tommy gun, and helped him out the door.

"Can you make it to the car?" I asked.

"Yeah," he said, and he staggered toward Louie's ruined cream puff.

I checked all three of them. All dead. I took their ID's and stuck them in my suit pocket, and ran back to the man by the car, the first one I shot. He was leaning against the tire, trying to breathe. Air gurgled through blood. He looked up at me with frightened eyes and then his eyes lost focus. They turned to glass and death rattled in his throat. He fell over on his side. I reached down and closed his eyelids with my fingers, reached in his pocket and got his ID.

"What are you doing?" Ski asked.

"I wanna know who we just killed," I said. I cranked up, spun around, and pulled back on the main road.

"Are they all dead?" he groaned.

"Yeah. Hang in there, partner. I'll have you in the hospital in five minutes."

"I can't believe that son of a bitch would try to kill a couple of cops."

"Dead men tell no tales. He thinks we know more about something back there than we know. Now, stop talking. Save your strength."

He ignored my advice.

"This is the second time in four years we've had to use bullets to get out of trouble," he sighed. "How come I'm always the one ends up getting shot?"

"There's more of you to hit," I said.

CHAPTER 29

I got immediate attention when I roared up to the hospital with siren and horn blowing. I pulled up as close as I could to the emergency entrance, and the security guard and an attendant rushed out with a gurney and wheeled Ski up a ramp and into the hospital. I didn't know what to expect but there was about twenty miles of lonely road between me and Guilfoyle, and nobody around to back me up, so I pulled the car around to a darkened side of the hospital, and went inside carrying our riot gun, my Luger, and Guilfoyle's tommy gun with the extra magazine.

There was an office inside the emergency entrance, and I walked in and laid out all my firepower on the desk.

"Jesus, you expecting the Japs to attack?" the security guard asked nervously.

"My name's Bannon. Get the captain on the phone—I don't care where he is—and tell him Bannon was ambushed at Ferguson's Icehouse by four of Guilfoyle's mobsters. My partner is shot and we're here at the hospital. I need help."

He rushed off, and I stepped into the operating room and stood beside the door. They were cutting Ski's pants off and Ski was beefing.

"It's my best suit, can't you just *pull* my pants off?"

"They're covered with blood, sir," the doctor said. "It won't clean off anyway. What's your name?"

"Agassi . . . just call me Ski, it's a lot easier."

"Good, Ski. I'm Dr. Butler and these are my assistants, nurse Gina Solomon and our on-duty intern, Dr. Knowles."

"My pleasure," Ski said with effort. "How bad is it?"

"There's no exit wound, so the round's still in there somewhere," he said to the nurse, and to Ski, "I'm fairly certain it missed your kidney and liver. So if we can just dig that little devil out, you'll be fine."

I moved a little closer and the doctor noticed me. He stared at me over his face mask and said, "And you are . . .?"

"Bannon. He's my partner."

He went back to work. "May I ask what happened?"

"He got shot."

The doctor gave me a wry look.

"I think it was a .38. There was a lot of shooting going on at the time and we were running for cover."

"Should we be expecting anyone else?"

"No," I said, "the other four are down at Ferguson's Icehouse waiting for a hearse."

"Well, that's a relief," Dr. Butler said. "So far tonight, I've had two broken legs and an old geezer who tried to swallow a bottle of gin in one swig. I'm a little tired."

"T . . . red?" Ski said.

"Say good night now, Ski," Butler said, "you're going to sleep."

"Awwrrii . . ." and he was in lullaby land. I left the room.

A few minutes later, Culhane's Packard came screeching into the parking lot. I was boiling mad inside but keeping it under control. Rusty got out and opened the door for Culhane. He was followed by a guy I hadn't met yet. Six-four, all muscle, dark-skinned with long black hair tied in a ponytail. His .45 was holstered on his belt and he was wearing a badge on his brightly embroidered vest. Nobody but a man that size would have the guts to wear a pale red vest with lizards embroidered on it.

"This is Big Redd," Culhane said. "You haven't met him yet."

He nodded and damn near broke my hand with his.

"How bad is your man hurt?" Culhane asked.

"He's got a slug in his side. The doctor says he'll be okay. Can we go inside and talk?"

"Sure. Redd, you and Rusty keep an eye open until Max and Lenny get here."

The big man nodded.

Culhane and I walked into the office. Culhane looked at the pile of guns on the table. He was about to make a crack but I didn't give him a chance.

"You been shining me, all along," I said, my voice trembling with rage.

He didn't say anything, just gave me that blue stare.

"My partner's in there with a bullet in him, Guilfoyle sent four of his goons to burn us, and I don't have a goddamn clue why! We killed four men tonight and *I don't know why*!"

"I wasn't grifting you."

"The hell you weren't. The first day we took a ride together, when we were sitting up on the overlook? I showed you a picture of Verna Hicks and you brushed it off. You *knew* it was Lila Parrish."

"I couldn't have recognized my mother from that clipping."

"I talked to her mother. She says she hasn't seen or heard from Lila in twenty years and I'm beginning to believe her."

"So . . ."

"So who was paying her off and why?"

"It's your case, Cowboy, you tell me."

"I think you're covering up for a murderer. Or, at the very least, for somebody who hired the killer."

"Get this straight, I haven't laid eyes on Lila Parrish since she walked out of the courtroom after she testified. If she was the Wilensky woman, I didn't know it. I don't know why she was killed. And I don't know why Guilfoyle sent his thugs after you."

I started pulling the ID's out of my pocket, flipping them open, and throwing them on the desk in front of him.

"Look at this. Two of these guys are special deputies. Guilfoyle sent *cops* to kill us."

"What the hell were you doing down there, anyway?"

"Ione Fisher," I said. "Ring a bell?"

"Shit," he said, shaking his head slowly. "She hasn't seen or heard from Lila in twenty years."

He flipped through the wallets I had thrown his way.

"You're a real collector, ain't you, pal." He laid them out side by side. "The two deputies are a big blond guy named Pierre Follet and an albino kid. This one?" He held up one of the wallets. "On the run for murder in St. Louis, picture's in every post office in the country. The other one I don't recognize but I'll bet you a year's salary he's got a sheet longer than the California coastline." He picked up the Thompson and slipped it up against his shoulder. "You should never've gone down there," he said.

"Well, thank you," I told him. "A little late, but thanks a bunch. I've got a wounded partner, a busted-up car, and four dead guys, including two cops, on my hands. That ought to be enough to attract the attorney general down here and clean Guilfoyle's tank. And Moriarity will probably assign me to some hick town they haven't even named yet."

"It was a fool's play by a goddamn pit bull." He laid the gun down and stared at me with hard eyes. "Now we got to get you out of it."

"Get me out of what?"

"Look, Guilfoyle may be dumb as a brick but he's a mobster and he thinks like one. You handed him an alibi when you snatched the ID's."

I didn't get it at first.

"Alibi?"

"Guilfoyle sends two of his cops and two hooligans after you and Ski. You think that was an accident? If all goes well, they dump your car in the Pacific, take you two offshore, and throw you to the sharks. If you knock over a cop or two, he blames the hooligans. You knock off the hooligans, his deputies cop the blame. By now he knows all four of his people are down for keeps. He probably doesn't know Ski was shot yet. That's a wrinkle he wasn't expecting, so his story will probably be his cops and the bad guys killed each other, and leave you out of it."

"And he thinks we're going to let him get away with that?"

"Who's 'we'?" he said casually. "I had no part in this, Cowboy. And if you think I'm going down to Mendosa and start World War Two because you made a dumb play, you're crazy."

"I don't think you have the guts to take on Guilfoyle," I snapped. "He's sitting twenty miles down the road running a hideout for the scum of the earth, he shoots a cop, and you're sitting here on your goddamn thumb."

He kicked the office door shut. "I'm going to explain the facts of life to you," he growled. "So listen up. My guess is Guilfoyle figured you were there snooping around in your off-hours hoping to pick up a couple of rabbits hiding out down there. That's why they call it 'Hole-in-the-Wall.' "

"So he decides to hit us?"

"It's the way he operates. He learned from the master—Arnie Riker, 'the Fisherman.' That's what we called him. I had a stoolie named Slim. He tipped me that there were four out-of-town shooters at Riker's hotel. They were the four who were killed at Grand View. The next day, Slim went missing. A month later, what was left of him after the sharks got finished washed up in Salingo, north of here. There was a bullet hole in the skull. We ID'd Slim from his teeth. That was how Riker took care of stoolies, card cheats, threats, people he didn't like."

"Wilma Thompson?"

"Just one of many."

I pointed to the buzzers on the table. "So, if Guilfoyle's that bad— now's your chance to blow the whistle on him. I got the evidence right there."

"Evidence, hell. I don't have the authority to give Guilfoyle a parking ticket right now. Why do you think I'm running for governor? If the day comes, Brett Merrill will be attorney general and we'll clean out Mendosa and a half-dozen other crooked towns like it. We'll set a fire under the damn legislature and we'll run the Rolls-Royce assholes who think they run the state out of Sacramento. In the meantime, I'm not throwing my political future in the shit can because you had an attack of stupidity.

"Now. Let's talk about your future for a minute."

"Future? My partner's got a bullet in him, there'll be a hearing, and . . ."

"There's not going to be any damn hearing, Cowboy. Guilfoyle has to take the out I'm gonna give him. That or explain to the attorney general up in Sacramento why two of his half-assed dicks paired up with two wanted felons to ambush a couple of L.A. cops. You think he wants to deal with that?"

"I've got my chief to deal with. Jesus, we killed four men tonight."

"I'll explain things to your chief."

"He won't buy the story."

"He will the way I explain it."

"I can't tell a bald-faced lie to my boss."

"Listen to me, I'll tell you what'll happen if you play this straight. First off, the state patrol'll get involved. Then there'll be a hearing and it'll come out that you and Agassi dusted two cops and their pals, and there you were, a hundred miles off your turf, snooping around, playing some hunch without so much as a warrant. So now you're on administrative leave without pay, and the attorney general will stick his nose in it, and you've already got a rep for doing things your own way . . . Do I need to paint a picture for you? You lose winning, Cowboy."

I didn't have an answer for that.

"Guilfoyle's stupid, but he's smart enough to work things out. You two were on your way back from dinner in Mendosa. All of a sudden the two cars came outta the fog, you got caught in their cross fire. Guilfoyle's cops chasin' Guilfoyle's thugs. Your partner caught one and you broke for the hospital. Now let's take a look at your car," Brodie said.

He got a flashlight from security, and we went around the corner and checked out the Chevy. The left side was crumpled where we sideswiped the chase car, there was a bullet scar across the hood, the left front fender was stove in, one of the headlights was knocked out, the windshield was cracked, the rearview mirror was gone, and there was no back window.

"You can't drive home in this," was all he said.

We went back to the emergency office, and he grabbed the phone and dialed a number.

"Jiggs," he said, "I want you to call Wilbur at home and tell him I got a '41 Chevy cabriolet needs a windshield, a rear window, and a rearview mirror. And the left front headlight's dead. Tell him to forget about the body damage. I'll need it by 7:00 A.M. If he starts whining tell him he gets double time." He turned to me and opened his hand.

"Keys," he said. I tossed them to him and he handed them to security.

"Tell Wilbur the car's at the hospital. Bergen has the keys. A guy named Bannon, L.A.P.D., will pick it up in the morning. He's staying at the Breakers."

"I got a room at Charlie Lefton's," I said.

"I'll take care of that. You think you'd last until morning down there? You'd probably end up getting Charlie whacked."

He scratched a wooden match to life on his belt buckle and lit another cigarette.

"I'll get you a room at the Breakers. And don't worry about being bribed—it's a trade for the tommy gun."

When we got to the hotel, he went to the desk, talked to the clerk for a minute or two, and came back with a key.

"Nice room overlooking the ocean," he said. "You can call your dispatcher and leave your number so they won't think you deserted the force. Your car'll be drivable by seven."

"Why all the favors, Brodie?" I asked.

"You're beginning to grow on me. Besides, I'd like to see you nail the one who killed that lady. I don't like murder any more than you do."

"And you don't have any curiosity about who was paying her and for what?"

"I'm not convinced they're connected."

"Supposing I told you Eddie Woods bought one of those checks?"

He looked genuinely surprised.

"Where'd you hear that?"

"From the lady in the bank who sold it to him."

He stared into his drink and didn't say anything.

As Merrill leads his men toward the embattled Germans, he runs past Culhane's foxhole and drops down beside him.

"The trap's working like a charm," he says, and then he sees Culhane's leg.

"Sweet Jesus!" he cries out.

"Don't let 'em take my leg, Major," Culhane says, his voice so weak Merrill can hardly understand him.

Merrill looks through the charging company of Marines and sees a red cross. "You, Corpsman, get over here!" he orders.

Culhane grabs a handful of Merrill's shirt.

"I got you your ten minutes, Major." His voice gets stronger. "Don't. . . let. . .them. . .take. . .my. . .leg." He begins to shake. Shock is setting in. The corpsman drops beside them and puts a tourniquet on Culhane's upper thigh.

"Promise me, damn it!" Culhane yells above the din of battle.

Merrill grabs a leatherneck by the arm. "Listen to me," Merrill bellows, shouting above the sounds of the Hell Hounds screaming, the peal of bayonets clashing, the thunder of guns. "You stay with your sergeant, get it? You stay with him when you get to the field hospital. You stay with him when they operate, and you tell whoever takes care of Culhane that I said if he takes off that leg, I'll personally take off one of his."

"Yes, sir, Major Merrill."

"Th'nks," Culhane stammers, and Merrill races into battle. He doesn't hear Culhane's last whisper before he passes out. "Good luck."

The young Marine leans over and eases the sergeant into a sitting position.

"This is gonna hurt, Sarge, but it'll be easier on that leg than if we go piggyback."

Culhane groans as the trooper slogs back through the mud toward the field hospital.

"What's your name?" Culhane asks.

"Woods. Eddie Woods. I'm in what's left of A Company."

"Thanks, Eddie."

He passes out and when he comes to, the field surgeon is leaning over him. His scalpel gleams in the lamp held by a corpsman.

"I'm putting you under again, Sergeant, this could hurt a little."

The surgeon puts a rag soaked in ether over Culhane's nose, and the last thing he remembers is Eddie Woods standing very close behind the surgeon with his bayonet held at his side.

"Just remember what Major Merrill said," Woods says in his ear. " 'You take the sergeant's leg off, I'll take off one of yours.' "

And then Culhane goes to sleep.

"Eddie Woods didn't kill Verna Wilensky," Culhane said quietly, after staring into space for a minute or two. "He wouldn't do in a woman, particularly that way. If Eddie killed anybody, they had it coming."

"Like Fontonio?"

He finished his drink and said, "Perhaps."

He got up to leave.

"I've got some phone calls to make," he said. "Don't worry about your partner, he's covered. As soon as he's ready, an ambulance'll take him down to L.A."

"You're going to call Guilfoyle, aren't you?" I said.

"Yep," he said. "And your boss. Just so everybody's straight about what happened up here tonight."

And he was gone.

*   *   *

I called the dispatcher in L.A., gave him the number of the Breakers, took a shower hot enough to wash away the smell of death, and crawled into a bed with a billowing goose-down pad over the mattress. I lay there wondering if Millicent's bed was that soft and comfortable. I thought about being beside her in it, smelling her soft scent, feeling her touch me.

She answered on the first ring. Her voice had the texture of fine silk.

"I was hoping it was you," she said softly.

"I was afraid I'd wake you up."

"I couldn't sleep."

"I, uh, I was thinking . . . uh, I was thinking about you," I said awkwardly. Then, "I'm not real good at this . . ."

"No need to apologize," she said. "I love hearing your voice. I've been thinking about you all day. When will you be home?"

"Tomorrow."

"What is Mr. Culhane like?"

"An enigma. There's something about these people . . . I can't put my finger on it."

I could feel her presence, as if she were in the room with me. And I remembered some lines I used to read to my father because he liked them so. "Read it again," he would say.

"My father loved some lines from a book," I said, staring at the ceiling. "I used to read it aloud to him . . ." And I whispered the lines:

> Alas! They were so young, so beautiful,
> So lonely, loving, helpless . . .

I stopped, forgetting the rest of the verse.

"That's from Byron's *Don Juan*," she said with a sense of awe. "I didn't . . ." And she stopped.

"Didn't think a cop read poetry?" I said with a laugh.

"I'm sorry," she answered, embarrassed. "That sounded kind of . . ."

I interrupted her. "We still have a lot to learn about each other," I said. "I hope we'll always be friends as well as lovers and we never have need to apologize for anything."

"What a lovely thing to say, Zee. Can't you come back tonight?"

"No. I'll be leaving first thing in the morning."

"Oh," she said, and there was disappointment in her voice.

"There's something I have to tell you," I said. "It's bound to make the papers and I want you to hear it from me first."

"Are you alright?"

"I'm fine," I said. "But there was trouble up here. There was some shooting and . . ."

"Oh my God . . ."

I started babbling. "Four mobsters tried to ambush my partner and me. Have I told you about Ski? I don't think we've talked about him much. He's a great partner. Every cop should be as lucky as I am to have Ski as a partner. Anyway, he took a bullet but he's okay. He's a big guy, it takes more than one bullet to do any serious damage. They're taking him back to L.A. Hospital by ambulance but he'll be fine. The thing is, we killed them, Mil. And the story you're going to read isn't going to say that. I wanted to talk to somebody and explain it . . . ah, hell, I wanted you to understand. I'll explain it when I see you."

"You don't have to explain anything to me, Zee."

"I want to," I said. "I want you to know it was them or us. We killed four men tonight and, and . . . I want you to know that this kind of thing doesn't happen often but it does happen and . . . it's not something I do easily—"

"I wish you were here," she said, cutting me off. "I wish you were here beside me and I could hold on to you." Her voice was trembling.

"You're here. You're all around me."

"Oh," she said, and stopped for a moment, then, "I'll stay home tomorrow. Please come over as soon as you can. I'll be waiting."

"You're really something, Mil. You're very special." I paused, and added, "To me."

"I hope so."

"Don't ever doubt it for a minute. I'll see you tomorrow."

"I'll count the minutes."

"Good night."

"Good night, my dear."

*   *   *

I kept thinking about her. It was my last thought until the jarring bell of the phone roused me from an exhausted sleep.

"Sergeant Bannon?"

"Yeah."

"This is Clampton, the dispatcher down at Central."

"Morning," I said in a voice still filled with sleep. I looked at my watch. It was 6:30 A.M.

"You got an urgent call here about a minute ago. Know a guy named Riker?"

That woke me up. I raised up on one elbow.

"Arnold Riker?"

"Yes, sir. He's up at Wesco State, says he needs to talk to you toot sweet."

"I thought he was in Q or Folsom."

"Yeah, well, he's at Wesco now. He says he can stand by the pay phone for two or three minutes." He gave me the number.

Riker was the last person I wanted to talk to. I didn't want to hear his *I been framed* litany, particularly at that hour. I am not at my best when I'm still shaking sleep out of my brain. But it was a call I couldn't ignore. I got the switchboard and gave them the number. It rang once.

"This is Riker," a sharp, edgy voice said.

"This is Bannon. What do you want?"

"Kind of brusque, aren't you, Sergeant?"

"Get to the point."

"I called to do you a favor," he said. It was a cold voice and surprisingly cultured.

"I don't need any favors from you," I said.

"Where are you?" he asked.

"None of your damn business. What do you want?"

"We need to have a little talk," the voice rasped.

"I'm a busy man, Riker."

"You haven't heard what I have to say yet."

"I've heard it from every crook I ever met. You were framed. You're an angel under your gruff exterior. You're . . ."

"You want to know who killed Wilma Thompson? I'll tell you straight up."

That got me fully awake.

"Okay, let's hear it. Save me the trip."

"Sorry, Sergeant. Not a chance. You've got to come to me. The warden's name is Jasper Rouche. He'll take care of the formalities when you get here. I'll be around." He chuckled. "My calendar's empty all day."

And he hung up.

CHAPTER 30

I showered and walked down to the garage, picked up the car, and tried to tip Wilbur, but he held up a hand and shook his head.

"The captain'd kill me if I took that," he said with a lopsided grin.

I thanked him, then called the hospital and learned that Ski was on his way to L.A. Then I got out of town.

It was an hour's drive to Wesco State Prison, which was forty miles south of Bakersfield and halfway across the state. In Santa Maria, I stopped in a little restaurant and ate a big breakfast while I read Pennington's story. As usual, it was a thorough, nonspeculative piece and as unsensational as a sensational story should be. There were three pictures: the fuzzy shot of Verna Wilensky, cropped from the shot of her at work, a small picture of Culhane, and a mug shot of Riker. The story was two columns wide, with an eighteen-point headline above the fold on the front page:

BATHTUB ACCIDENT
CALLED HOMICIDE

And under it the subhead:

DETECTIVE LINKS DROWNING VICTIM
TO TWENTY-YEAR-OLD MURDER CASE

The lead quoted Bones's conclusion from the autopsy and revealed that Wilensky had received the five hundred a month since 1924 and possibly before that.

It went on in the second graph to trace the checks back to San

Pietro and several other banks, possible links to the twenty-year-old Thompson murder case, and made a reference to the fact that "Homicide Sergeant Zeke Bannon was interested in locating one of the witnesses in the Thompson case." Wisely, Pennington avoided naming Lila Parrish, probably at the insistence of his editor.

Pennington then did a rehash of the Thompson murder and Riker's trial. It was a good story and one that wouldn't get me in trouble. Not that I should worry about that. The icehouse shoot-out, Ski's wound, and Louie's crumpled cream puff would be enough to deal with when I got back to L.A. and Moriarity's hot seat.

I paid the check, bought a package of Chesterfields, and headed east toward Bakersfield and the little town of Marasipa where the prison was located. I got there about ten. Wesco was a medium-security prison and relatively new, a two-story sprawl of brick buildings behind a double barbed-wire fence about twelve feet high. A prison guard in a starched brown uniform checked my credentials at the gate, directed me to the VIP parking lot, and told me how to get to the reception room.

Five minutes later I was met at the reception desk by a short little man in wire-rim glasses and blue prison garb, who introduced himself as Zimmer, a trustee and the warden's secretary. He led me to the second floor.

Unlike San Quentin and Folsom, which were grim, dank old dungeons with the lingering and pervasive smell of Lysol disguising the odor of old felons and older times, Wesco was clean and the color scheme was pale yellow, which brightened the surroundings. But the sense of hopelessness and desperation was the same as it is in all prisons.

Jasper Rouche was standing in the doorway of his office wearing a politician's broad grin. I had never been to Wesco, but I knew that Rouche was the brother of Harley Rouche, who had been in the state senate since Moses parted the Red Sea and was one of the most powerful politicians in the legislature. The warden's credentials were okay, considering his was a political job: a low-grade guard at San Quentin for five years, three more as guard captain, and later, assistant warden at Folsom, and finally warden at Wesco when it was built six years ago. He was dressed in a gray, off-the-rack business suit, a starched white shirt, and a clip-on bow tie. He stood a little under six feet and probably weighed two hundred pounds, with a florid face just beginning to gather wrinkles, slicked-back brown hair, and the beginnings of a beer belly. He also had feet big enough to kick a moose silly. A wad of chewing tobacco was resting low in one cheek.

"Welcome to Wesco, Sergeant," he said around the grin. I shook a hand that had manicured fingernails and skin as tough as a rhino's hide. "What can we do for you?"

"I'd like to talk to Arnold Riker," I said. "Sorry to show up without any notice."

"We were expecting you," he said, leading me into his office. "We can monitor the phones in con recreation when someone calls in, since they go through the switchboard—we don't listen to outgoings unless we got a warrant, which is just about never. So we heard you when you called him back."

"He's a clever bastard," I said. "He said just enough to con me into coming over here."

"Doesn't surprise me. I read that story in the *Times*. Through the years, Riker's probably talked to every other detective in the state, whistling the same old tune."

"Yeah," I said. "One of the ten thousand innocent cons doing time in state prison."

He laughed as he leaned over, and spit a dollop of tobacco juice in a brass spittoon beside his desk.

"By last count, there were about eight felons in the whole system who agreed with the jury that sent them up. I'll call over to block C and have them bring him over." He made the call and leaned back in his chair. It would take ten minutes to get Riker over there, so we had coffee and doughnuts.

"Tell me a little about Riker, Warden. All I know is what I've read in the clippings."

"He did ten years hard time in Q and four in Folsom, before he was sent down here," Rouche said. "That was six years ago, right after we opened. He's what I call a firecracker—straining to blow but you gotta light his fuse. Clean record in the other two pens and a little angel here. He reads everything. Two, three books a week, newspapers, magazines, and has a memory like an elephant. In fact, he runs the library. He's the only lifer we have here and he has a kind of gentlemanly quality about him, so he gets a lot of respect from the other cons."

"And he's been clean for all these years?"

"He had some trouble in Q," Rouche said. "You know, he went in with a certain amount of notoriety, so some of the long-timers tried him out. Story goes, a con jumped him in the shower with a shiv. Riker broke the guy's arm, dropped the shiv down the drain, and called the guard, told him the other guy slipped in the shower. After that, they left him alone. At Folsom he built up a circle of pals who covered his back. He never got in any trouble. That's why we got him. But he's tough, make no mistake. You don't do all that time without becoming a hard case. His sheet, when he was back in Chicago, had a murder rap and a couple of A&B's. He never took the fall for any of them."

"How about visitors?"

"Not too many. We keep a record of that. I can have Harve draw you up a list for the last few months. He's captain of the guards."

"That'd be swell," I said. "He indicated he had called his lawyer, too."

Rouche pressed a button under his desk and a minute later a mountain of a man came in.

"Harvey Craddock, this is Sergeant Bannon, L.A.P.D."

Harvey was two inches taller than Rouche and all muscle. He stared at me with the bored eyes of a man who had been around so long nothing surprised him anymore.

"Harve, how many calls did Riker get this morning?" Rouche asked.

"Three out, two in." He nodded at me. "You were one of them, Sergeant. Schyler was the other one. I don't know who the third call was to, whoever it was didn't call back."

"Sidney Schyler is Riker's lawyer?" I said with surprise. His nickname in the press was "Spring 'Em Schyler."

"The same," Harve answered.

I answered with a low whistle. Schyler was the bane of every cop from Sacramento to San Diego. He had sprung more guilty cons than all the other lawyers in the state combined.

Harve then volunteered that Riker had gone berserk when he read the morning paper. "He usually gets the paper first thing. Next thing, he was demanding he get to the phone in recreation. It's Saturday, so we let him. The first call went to Schyler, the second to you. Again, I have no idea about the third one. You called back immediately.

Schyler's call was about five minutes later but their conversation was blocked. Lawyer-client privilege, y'know."

"And that was after he read the paper?"

"Yeah, he had it with him, was raving on the phone to Schyler, waving the front page around," Harve said.

"Does Schyler call often?"

"Not really," said Harve. "I'll get the book out and check. Schyler comes up every three or four months. Henry Dahlmus visited him once, a while back."

"Who's Dahlmus?"

"Ex-con. He and Riker were roommates for about six months," Harve said.

"Dahlmus was illiterate," said Rouche. "Riker taught him to read and write. He did four years of a two-to-five for manslaughter. Shot a clerk in a grocery store down in Ventura."

"Anybody else?"

"Guilfoyle used to come over here every so often but I ain't seen him in a while," Harve said. "He calls Riker every now and again."

I finished my coffee and doughnut, and said, "Okay, let me take a crack at him."

Rouche gave me a small tin ashtray. "Bring it back when you're finished," he said. "They can be made into a shiv in the machine shop in about two minutes flat."

I had a feeling of déjà vu when I entered the interrogation room. I had seen it in various versions a dozen times before. Two chairs facing each other across a large metal table that was bolted to the floor. A high, screened window at one end of the room. Walls painted slate gray, the same color as the table, giving the room a depressing monochromatic look. Over the table, two 150-watt bulbs staring down through chicken wire.

Riker was sitting with his back to me when Rouche ushered me into the room. His right hand was handcuffed to one of the table stanchions, leaving his left free to drum on the tabletop, his thick fingers looking like the legs of a tarantula doing the lindy hop.

"Just rap on the door when you're through," the guard said. The bolt clicked as he pulled the door shut.

"Good morning, Sergeant," Riker said without turning around. "Took you longer than I thought to get here. Must have stopped for breakfast along the way." He spoke in a low but harsh voice that had the quality of fingernails scratching down a blackboard.

I walked around the end of the table and faced Riker for the first time. He was wearing blue denim prison garb and was shorter than I had pictured, five-seven maybe, although it was hard to tell since he was seated and slouched back in his chair. He was lean, with bony shoulders that emphasized a thin neck topped by a pale, creased, leathery face, ridged by years of hard time. His brown hair was cut scalpclose and streaked with gray. A thick nose separated dark brown eyes that looked almost black and peered up at me from a permanent squint. His thin lips struggled to keep from sneering.

More déjà vu.

A face I had seen in various incarnations in every pen I had ever visited. Suspicious, wary, bored, angry, tough, desperate, wily. Assets for any lifer who wants to stay alive and relatively unscathed. But unlike most cons, his English was impeccable.

I moved the chair two or three feet back from the table before I sat down.

"What's the matter, Sergeant?" he said coldly. "Afraid I'm contagious?"

"I like to stretch out my legs," I said. I put the ashtray on the table, along with the pack of Chesterfields and my Zippo. He shook one loose and fired it with the lighter.

"The indefatigable Zippo," Riker said, fondling its stainless steel case. "Invented in Bradford, Pennsylvania, 1932, by George Blaisdell. The unique feature is the patented windscreen. To date, it has outsold all other cigarette lighters in the world combined."

"You own stock in the company?" I asked.

"Eighteen years in stir," he said softly. "Nothing else to do but read. The library at Q was contemptible, same with Folsom. This one isn't bad. I've scrutinized almost every book in here. Actually, I'm up to the F's in the *Encyclopedia Britannica*. I read four newspapers a day, line by line, *and* do the crossword puzzles."

"Okay," I said. "You're a regular whiz kid. What do you want from me?"

I kept my eyes on him, watching all his moves. He didn't have many. He speared a forefinger at me whenever he made a point he thought was worth emphasizing and his left eye blinked occasionally as if he had no control over it. When he stared back at me, the light from the overheads revealed the telltale milky-white opacity of a cataract forming over the eye's lens.

"It isn't what I want, Sergeant," he said with a cryptic smile. "It's what *you* want from me."

"I don't have a lot of time," I drawled. "Just get on with it."

"How much did you have to pay that Pennington reporter for writing that laudatory piece about you in the *Times* today?"

"I bought him a beer," I answered.

He chuckled. "He sells out cheap."

I let the crack go by.

"I told you, I have information that will make your day—although not for the better I would guess." Riker tapped the ash off his cigarette but never took his eyes off me.

"I assume this great revelation is going to cost me."

He leaned forward, put his elbows on the table, and said, "Not one red cent. I don't indulge in blackmail."

"Then that's about all you didn't indulge in."

"A smart mouth," he said with disdain. "You think it's so funny? A person facing life for something that person never did? That's your idea of justice, isn't it? I bet you and Culhane got along famously."

"One murder's as bad as another."

"What does that mean?"

"It means you've dusted a lot of people in your time, Riker. You deserve every minute you've served, even if you were framed for the one thing they got you for. The one you keep whining about."

He jumped up, forgetting he was cuffed to the table leg, and his arm snapped at the end of the cuff. I didn't move, I just stared at him. He stood for a moment, his face reddening. Then he composed himself, smiled, and sat back down.

"I don't know what else you've lost in stir," I said quietly. "One thing you damn sure haven't lost is your rotten temper."

"I don't *whine*," he hissed.

Still staring at him, I said, "Whine, cry, whatever you call it. You're in here to stay."

He realized I was getting to him and his mood suddenly changed. He relaxed and slouched back in his chair again.

"He who laughs last, laughs best," Riker said.

"It's 'laughs best, laughs last,' " I said. "You're just full of homilies, aren't you? I'll tell you what, why don't you sit there and have a big laugh. Me? I've got a long drive ahead of me."

I started to get up.

"Who do you think you're kidding?" he said.

I was perplexed by the question. "About what?" I asked.

"That stuff about that Parrish dame?" he said. "You're showboating, Sergeant Bannon. To be crude about it, you're pissing in the wind." He leaned forward again. "You aren't any closer to Verna Hicks than I am to the King's palace in London."

"And you are?" I said.

"What do you think you're doing here? When I saw the front page this morning I *knew* what was going on. As soon as I saw the paper today, I knew you'd been grabbing at straws." He made a little motion with his hand, grabbing an imaginary speck in the air. "Grabbing at straws." Then he chuckled. "Been working this case what, five, six days? A week, maybe? Still on square one?"

He was annoying me but I didn't want to show it.

"Why don't you just say what you have to say."

"Maybe Lila's picking up five C's a month just like old Verna was. Maybe she had a little work done on her face. Culhane's easy with the favors—all those rich friends lay it out for him."

"That's what you think? Everybody who leaves San Pietro has a meal ticket for life?"

"Verna's paycheck ran out, didn't it, Sergeant?"

"Why would anybody kill her?" I said.

He shook his head and chuckled.

"Your boy's running for governor, certainly you've heard? The word is, he's going to announce this week. Maybe that's why Verna's no longer with us."

"Make your point, Riker. Why would Verna pose a threat to Culhane?"

"Verna Hicks could have blown Culhane out of his big, comfortable saddle."

"With what? What did she have on him?"

He leaned as close as the cuff would let him, and whispered. "You're supposed to be so smart, Bannon," he said, shaking his head. "Oh, it was my red jacket Lila Parrish saw the man wearing that night, my gun that was fired, my car Wilma got thrown into. But I didn't shoot Wilma Thompson."

I didn't say anything. I sat there looking stupid, waiting for the punch line, and it was a showstopper.

"Don't you get it, Sergeant? Nobody shot her. Wilma Thompson was Verna Hicks."

CHAPTER 31

"I knew it as soon as I saw that picture on the front page," Riker hissed softly, his black eyes glittering. "She was about fifty pounds heavier and she let her hair go natural and she had her nose bobbed, but I knew Wilma better than anybody. I knew she peroxided her hair back then because she thought it made her look like a movie star. I knew she had big dreams that wouldn't happen, knew she had broken her ankle hiking up near Monterey, because I was with her that day. I piggybacked her down to the first-aid station. And here's the clincher. I know that lady in the morgue, the one you found in the tub, has bridgework." He stuck a finger in the corner of his mouth, rubbed it across three teeth. "These three, right side on the bottom."

Worms of anxiety began to gnaw at me. I hadn't read the whole autopsy report, I had been out the door as soon as Bones told us we had a homicide on our hands. Riker couldn't have gotten that detail from the newspaper. The story had only quoted the paragraph from the report that pertained specifically to the fact that she was murdered.

"Anybody could have read that report and phoned you," I said.

"I didn't even see the paper until I got up this morning. It doesn't even hit town here until 4:00 A.M. And there's nothing in it except the information about water in her lungs and the radio causing it to look like an accident."

"Your lawyer called you this morning. He could have gotten a copy of that report with a phone call, called you up, and read it to you."

"Wrong again; I called him first, when I read the *Times*. He called me back the same as you, in no time flat."

I thought about what he was telling me. It made a kind of terrible sense. Someone paid to have Wilma's nose fixed to make her harder to recognize. Then she laid low for a while. Then someone arranged to get her a job in the tax office. Someone with clout.

Someone like Culhane.

"I considered the possibility that she wasn't dead," Riker said. "I always figured it was Eddie Woods who set me up on Culhane's orders. But what could I do? I'm in the can for life. Then I saw the picture this morning and read the story and I knew it wasn't Lila. So there it was. Verna Hicks was Wilma. I figure the little twist wanted to up the ante on Culhane since he's running for governor. And if he got elected, she'd probably jack it up again. So Woods did the job for good this time."

"Pure guesswork," I said bitterly. "You think you can *con* everybody into thinking Wilma Thompson's been alive for the last twenty years, something nobody can prove."

His lips curled into a sneer.

"Just another lousy cop," he snarled. "You don't want to know what really happened. You have any idea what it's like to live in a cage? The worst part about it is you have no options. You get up at the same time every day, shower at the same time, eat three lousy meals at the same time, and go to bed at the same time. One day is just like the next. You know it will never change for the rest of your life. And worst of all, you know you're innocent. Well, now it *will* change. I can change it because now I can *prove* I was framed. The dentist who did Wilma's bridgework still lives in San Pietro. His name is Wayne Tyler. I'll bet he's still got all the charts and pictures he took when he was working on her. If you're such a good cop, you'll go get it. And the coroner can see if I'm telling the truth."

His smile was an evil leer.

"You know what I like best about all this?" Riker threw his head back, laughed, and smacked his hands together. "The thing I like *best* is that you, the hotshot L.A. detective who's been sucking up to Culhane, are going to get me sprung, prove that son of a bitch framed me, and end his run for governor. Who else but Culhane would be paying her five hundred a month to disappear?"

I made a fist and dug my fingernails into my palms to keep from doing something stupid.

"You know something, Riker?" I said, standing up. "The thought of scum like you having one day on the outside turns my stomach."

"You'd better get busy," he snapped. "My lawyer's already on the case. It won't look too good if he calls a press conference and tells all those newsies who Verna Wilensky was, especially if you knew all about it and didn't do a goddamn thing."

I took the ashtray but left the pack of cigarettes in front of him.

"You forgot your butts," he said.

"They're not my brand," I said, rapping on the door.

Behind me, I heard him chuckling. "Thanks a lot, Sergeant. If you're half as good as you think you are, I'll be outside the walls suing everybody in sight before I need another pack."

CHAPTER 32

I stopped at the first pay phone I saw when I left Wesco and dialed the general operator in San Pietro. When I asked for Dr. Tyler's number, she informed me that he did not work on weekends.

"May I have his home number then?" I asked.

Pause.

"Is this an emergency?" she asked haughtily.

"Oh yes," I said.

"What's the name?"

I hesitated for a moment before I said, "Wilma Thompson. She can't come to the phone right now."

"Why not, is she in some distress?" the operator asked.

"Distress? Yes, definitely."

"I'll see if he's available. What's your number?"

"Can I hold?" I said. "I'm at a pay phone."

"Well . . . alright."

There was a long pause and then a man answered.

"Who is this anyway?" he said. He sounded younger than I imagined. And very annoyed.

"Dr. Tyler?"

"Yes."

"I'm sorry to disturb you but the operator was being overly protective. My name is Bannon, sir, I'm with the Los Angeles police."

"What's this about Wilma Thompson?"

"You were her dentist, weren't you?"

Long pause again.

"Why do you ask?"

"I don't mean to be impertinent, but you don't sound old enough. Perhaps I'm looking for your father."

"My father doesn't practice here any longer."

"He may be able to help me in an investigation I'm working on," I said. "It's urgent that I talk to him. May I have his number?"

"How do I know you're with the police?" he asked.

"Look, Doctor, I'll make this easy. Will you have your father call central homicide in L.A.?" I gave him the number. "Tell him he can call and leave his number with the desk man and I'll get back to him as soon as possible. My name is Bannon." I spelled it for him.

I hung up before he could argue with me and invested another half dollar on a call to the desk. The day man was Pete Craig.

"Pete, this is Zeke Bannon."

"Yes, sir, Sergeant."

I told him I was expecting a call from a Dr. Tyler and he should confirm that I was a police detective, then get his number and address.

"Okay," he said. "That was a helluva story this morning, Sarge."

"Thanks," I said. "I should be in radio range in about forty-five minutes. I'll contact you then."

"Right, sir."

I hung up and headed down 101 toward the city. At 2:00 P.M. I was crossing the mountains into Santa Clarita and I raised Craig on the radio.

"Any luck?" I asked.

"Yes, sir. Dr. Tyler left the information. He lives in Santa Monica, off California on Seventh Street, just west of Lincoln Park." He gave me Tyler's phone number.

"Good work," I said. "I'm heading there now."

"Sergeant, Lieutenant Moriarity is looking for you big-time."

"Is he there now?"

"No, sir. I'll have him call you on the radio as soon as he gets back."

"Thanks. Ten-four."

By now, Moriarity probably had an APB out on me. I wanted to have as much evidence in hand as possible when he did reach me. I envisioned a hard time in his hot seat.

I headed straight for Dr. Tyler's house instead of calling first, figuring a little charm and my ID would be harder to turn down than an impersonal phone call. Another thirty minutes and I was looking at street numbers. The house was a modest two-story stucco with a coral tiled roof and a flawless front lawn. The Saturday paper was on the front steps. I picked it up and rang the doorbell. A pretty woman in her late fifties opened the door.

"Hi," I said cheerily, handing her the paper and showing her my best smile along with my credentials. "My name's Bannon, L.A.P.D. Is Dr. Tyler in?"

"So you're the mysterious Sergeant Bannon," she said with a smile.

"Mysterious?"

"My son called us," she said, stepping back and holding the door open for me. "He tends to be a little melodramatic, although I must say, invoking Wilma Thompson's name raised my eyebrows. I'm Mary Tyler. I was Doc's nurse when Wilma was his patient."

"Then he did do some work on her?"

"Oh yes," she said, leading me through the house. "A terrible man, Arnold Riker, had the gall to bring her into the office. He said she fell and hit her jaw on the car door. Wilma was terrified of him, but she finally admitted that Riker had beaten her up."

"Did he pay for the work Dr. Tyler did?"

She nodded, then led me out the back door into the yard, a sprawling rose garden. The entire yard was ablaze in color, and the aroma, carried on a soft breeze, was intoxicating. Tyler was on his hands and knees in front of a rose bush, with a roll of tape in one hand, a small knife in the other, and a twig with a single pale mauve rose on it clasped between his teeth. He was using the knife to make a slit in the stem of the bush.

"Doc?" she called.

"Uh-huh," he said without looking up from his work.

"That detective, Sergeant Bannon, is here."

"Tell him to come on out," he said without taking the twig from his mouth.

"Thanks," I said to Mrs. Tyler, and made my way through the array of roses to his side.

"Hold this a minute, will you?" he asked, handing me a roll of tape, still without looking up. I watched as he trimmed the end of the twig to a flat edge, like the end of a screwdriver.

"I'm making a hybrid," he said as he worked. "The main bush is the recipient. I'm grafting this cutting onto it, hopefully to produce a new strain of rose." He traded the knife for the tape, carefully wrapped the incision, then got up, and looked down at his operation. Satisfied, he took off his gloves and looked at me for the first time, offering his hand.

"How do you do, Sergeant Bannon," he said. "Thanks for the help."

"My pleasure, Doctor."

"Call me Doc, everybody does," he said. Tyler was a cheerful man in his sixties, his brown hair just beginning to show a little gray. He was wearing a pair of baggy chinos and a faded Hawaiian shirt that probably had blinded people when it was new.

"Now what's this about Wilma Thompson?" he said.

"I understand you did some dental work on her back in the early twenties."

"I did," he said, and nodded.

"Did it involve some bridgework?"

"Uh-huh."

"Could you tell me about it, please?"

"You're playing hell with my curiosity," he said.

"I'll get to the point in a minute."

"When I came back from the war, I opened an office in San Luis Obispo, with a small clinic down in San Pietro," he said. "I'd go down there once a week. One day a man named Riker brought Wilma in. He said she had fallen and hit the side of her face. I knew he was lying the minute I examined her. It was clear she had been beaten. The bruise on her jaw and the injuries to her mouth made that quite apparent. You could see the imprint of his knuckles in the bruise along her right jaw. Two of her lower teeth on that side were so badly damaged they had to be extracted. She also had a hairline fracture right along here," he traced a four- or five-inch line across the jaw from his mouth toward the bottom of his ear, "and a chipped upper tooth on the same side."

"When was this?"

"I'll have to check the file. Nineteen twenty, as I recall."

"You have a vivid memory of this event," I said.

"Yes, I do," he said. "Particularly after what followed. I felt really sorry for Wilma."

"She told you that Riker struck her?"

He nodded. "The work was extensive, it spread out over a couple of weeks. She was obviously scared to death of Riker. With good cause, needless to say. I finally got her to admit that he had hit her—and it hadn't been the first time. But she was afraid to leave him. She was just a kid, eighteen at the time. Dreamed of going to Hollywood and becoming a star. She was a sad young lady. Pretty in her way, but it was obvious to me that Hollywood was not going to rush to her door."

"What exactly did you do?"

"I extracted the first molar and second bicuspid on the bottom. Then I made what we call a three-quarter crown on each side of the gap and bridged them with gold."

"Gold?" I said with surprise.

"Gold is inert," he said. "It doesn't corrode—doesn't react to anything in the mouth—and has the same consistency as a tooth. It was relatively inexpensive in those days. That's the way it was done. I also filled the first molar on top with silver. And I used stainless wire to draw the hairline fracture shut."

"Did you make any charts or reports on the work?"

"Of course. It's part of the process. First you diagram and assess the damage, then you chart exactly what procedure you're going to use to correct the problem. The charts are standard."

"Do you still have the paperwork?"

He looked at me strangely for a long minute before nodding.

"I have all my records. The inactive ones are in the basement," he said. "Why?"

"I have reason to suspect that Wilma Thompson wasn't murdered. She came here in 1924 as Verna Hicks, moved into Pacific Meadows, married happily. Her husband was killed in an auto accident about four years ago, and she lived alone until last week, when she was murdered in her bathtub."

He was genuinely shocked.

"That would mean she helped frame Riker?"

"So it would appear."

"Then who killed her?"

"That's what I'm trying to find out."

"My God. Little Wilma." He shook his head. "Well, she got even with him, if it's true. Believe me, I have no sympathy for Riker. He deserved everything he got. Is he still alive?"

I nodded. "He's in Wesco. His sentence was commuted to life without parole. He saw that picture this morning and called me. He's the one who told me about the work on her mouth. Could that be Wilma, Doc?"

He looked back at the picture. "She was a blonde back then," he said. "And you can tell how much weight she put on. But . . ."

He stared some more. "I couldn't swear to it, Sergeant."

"But it's possible?" I suggested.

He nodded. His shoulders slumped and he sat down on the steps. "Almost twenty years," he said, shaking his head. "And all these years we thought she was dead." Then the same thought that was burning a hole in me began to fester inside the doctor.

"You say you met Riker?"

"This morning. A nasty human being."

"But this may end up freeing him?"

His comment hit a nerve. I thought again about Wilma, the same thoughts that had provoked my interest in her "accidental death" to begin with. A kid with dreams, abused by a psychotic mobster, who escaped and lived a normal, decent life until time caught up with her. Now it had come to me to free the ferret who had started the whole tragedy twenty years ago.

"I'm not a judge, Doc," I said. "I just go where the evidence leads me."

"Tough job," he said.

"Sometimes."

"What exactly can I do for you?"

"I'd like to borrow your files on Wilma. I'll be glad to give you a receipt."

"I could have a lapse of memory about all this," he said.

"You could. It was a long time ago."

"I could say I didn't keep the files after she was killed."

"That, too. But you don't strike me as a man who would lie under oath, regardless of the consequences."

"And you don't strike me as a man who would let me get away with it if I tried."

"It's a tough call," I said.

"Tougher for you," he answered, and led me into the house.

* * *

I decided to check in on Ski, who was sitting up in bed and, between
bites of Boston cream pie, was regaling two nurses with tales of daunt-
less adventure. There was an empty dish of chocolate ice cream on the
table beside the bed.

"Hi, pardner," I said. "Spare a word?"

His face turned red. "Excuse us, ladies," he said quickly, "we have
business to discuss."

The nurses were all giggles as they left the room.

"I heard you spent the night in that fancy hotel," he said, feigning
anger. "What'd you do? Sleep till noon and have breakfast in bed while
I was being carried down here in an ambulance?"

I grinned at him. "While you were playing Andy Hardy for the an-
gels of mercy, I was busy finding out who Verna Hicks Wilensky was in
her previous life," I said. "I was up at 6:30, stopped for a bite of breakfast over near Bakersfield. Read the paper. Actually I thought Jimmy
the Pen did a pretty good job of . . ."

"What were you doing in Bakersfield?"

"Actually I was in Marapisa, it's about thirty . . ."

"I *know* where Marapisa is."

"Do you know what's in Marapisa?"

He thought for a minute. "Wesco State jam."

"Very good. And do you know who's in Wesco?"

"A lot of felons," he blurted. "Will you get on with it!"

"Does Arnie Riker ring any bells in that lame brain of yours? He's
currently in residence there. And he recognized Verna Hicks when he
saw the paper."

"Damn it, stop playing twenty questions with me. Who is she?"

"Did you ever read Bones's full report?"

". . . no. Did you?"

"No, but I'm going to. Meantime . . ."

I gave him a quick rundown on my conversation with memory-
expert Arnie Riker, my trip to Santa Monica, and the details of the
X rays. I handed him the yellowed charts. "Look who the patient was."

When he saw Wilma Thompson's name his jaw almost hit the
floor.

"You think it's possible?" he asked.

"If Tyler and Bones agree, school's out—and so is Riker. Our problem is, who killed Wilma Verna Hicks Wilensky Thompson? And why?"

I started out the door.

"Hey," he said. "What're you gonna do about Moriarity? He's on the warpath and . . ."

"Handle it," I said. "I'm busy."

It was about seven when I got home. I was exhausted, but Rosie's enthusiastic greeting cheered me up. I decided to clean up before calling Millie. We did the dog food–bone routine, and while he was out back gnawing on it, I took a long, hot shower. I put on a pair of slacks and a shirt and tie, and was reaching for the phone to call Millie when the doorbell rang.

When I opened the door, all I saw was Millie's eyes and that smile.

She was holding a sterling silver champagne bucket with a bottle chilling in it. There was a large wicker picnic basket beside her. The Phaeton was parked out front.

"Hi," she said. "I happened to be in the neighborhood . . ."

CHAPTER 33

I took the basket and ice bucket, and she leaned into me and kissed me. Her kisses were never desperate or hungry, they were soft and giving and inviting. We stood there locked together while Rosie circled us and whined for a little attention. Finally, I carried the picnic into the living room while she fussed over the dog.

I went into the bedroom, hurriedly gathered up my dirty clothes and towels from the floor and threw them in the hamper, got a blanket and brought it back, spreading it on the living room floor. I put a couple of pillows from the sofa on the floor, too.

She appraised the place, studying the orange-crate bookcases and the barren simplicity of the furnishings, her expression concealing any hint of either amusement or disappointment. I'm inclined to think it was exactly what she expected.

"Welcome to the Taj Mahal," I said.

She came across the room to me, her long legs sheathed in gray slacks, a pink V-neck cashmere sweater hugging her body, her eyes never straying from mine. She sat as close as two pillows would allow and studied my face.

"You're gorgeous," she said. "But you're sad." She ran her fingertips down one of my cheeks. "I'm sorry you had such a bad time and your partner was hurt. I hope you don't mind; I sent some flowers."

"His wife'll probably kill him," I said, and we both laughed and I kissed her again. Then I opened the champagne and filled two handsome fluted wineglasses. We toasted each other.

"I'll never intrude on your work," she said. "But I'll always listen if you need to talk about it."

"I'm okay," I said. "I'm sure Ski's in his element, lying to all the nurses and playing the hero."

"Good."

"I've learned some things about Verna's murder. I'm not sure where they're leading yet, but I think Culhane and his friends may be in for bad times."

"You like this man," she said. It wasn't a question.

"Irish charm," I said with a smile. "I think he deals with the law in a very expedient manner. I've done that a few times myself but I think this time he went over the line. I haven't told him what I know but I feel I should."

"Then do it."

"It's gonna be difficult."

"Has that ever stopped you before?"

"Not really. Culhane dropped everything last night when Ski and I got in trouble. Left a campaign fund-raiser. And he invented a lie—not for himself, he wasn't involved. He invented it to protect me and Ski."

"Did you go along with it?"

"So far. But it also protects the mobster who sent four killers after us. His name is Guilfoyle. A bottom-feeder."

"Why did Culhane do it?"

I thought about that for a while and then said, "I think he sees a lot of himself in me. If that makes any sense."

"I can understand that. Perhaps he sees the same things in you that I do. One of the things that attracts me to you is your impulsiveness. And your integrity. I've never known anyone like you, Zee."

"Integrity? I was way over my head, Mil. Way out of my territory, going where I was warned not to go in what turned out to be a blind alley, and then going along with a lie to cover up some very serious consequences."

"It's not over yet," she said.

"No," I said. "But I don't know if that's a good thing or a bad thing."

"Was the trip up there worthwhile?"

I decided to give her a taste of what it would be like to have a relationship with a cop.

"Yes and no," I said.

"What does that mean?"

"It's leading me places I hoped not to go. And now this case is turning around on me. I know who Verna was before she showed up in L.A., Mil. Verna was Wilma Thompson."

Her eyes grew the size of serving platters. "The woman who was murdered years ago?" she gasped.

"Apparently not," I said.

"Why did somebody do it now?" she asked, her voice filled with sadness.

"That's the question. Who killed her and why. I don't have all the pieces put together yet. I keep thinking I missed something along the way. Ever try to think of someone's name, and it's right on the tip of your tongue but you can't remember it?"

She laughed. "All the time."

"It's kind of like that," I said. "Something I saw or read or heard. But it keeps eluding me."

"Then forget about it," she said. "Let's eat."

I don't know whether she prepared the spread or had it done but it was a meal a king would have died for. I'm sure the champagne was from some prize vintage. I'd never had fresh strawberries in champagne or squares cut from the sweetest part of fresh melons or pâté from France. She had spread a dozen candles around the house and the odor was intoxicating.

While we were eating, my phone rang. I ignored it.

When we finished, we gathered up the remains and carried them to the kitchen, and gave some of the leftovers to Rosie. The phone rang again, and again I ignored it. I went into the living room and stacked several Tommy Dorsey records on the player. Soft stuff, with vocals by Sinatra, Jo Stafford, and the Pied Pipers. The first song was "Let's Get Away from It All" and we started to dance. Rosie curled up on one of the sofa pillows and eyed us ruefully.

She moved back a step or two from me and started to untie my tie. She did it slowly, as if she were taking the silk ribbon off a gift. She let it slide out of her hand and it fluttered to the floor.

"I've only known you for five days," Millie said softly, and began unbuttoning my shirt.

"You make love like nobody I've ever known in my life. Then you kill four men."

Another button. And another.

"You quote poetry. Now you're going to destroy someone you admire."

"I don't have any choice."

"I know that, Zeke."

She pulled my shirt out and let it fall open, and slid her hands around my waist and up my back. It was like being stroked by a velvet glove.

"I live in a dump and you live on a dozen acres on top of a mountain. You're caviar and I'm corned beef and cabbage."

She pressed against me and I could feel her heart beating through her sweater. Her lips were an inch away from mine.

Her lips caressed and engulfed mine. Her tongue found mine. There was nothing more to say.

We were both out of breath. She lay on her back staring at the ceiling. There were two candles in the room and their reflections looked like moths darting around overhead. Me? I couldn't keep my eyes off her body, a work of art tanned by the sun and shaped by tennis.

We didn't talk much. I could see the pulse beating in her throat. I don't know what she was looking at.

She turned her head and looked at me for a moment, then closed her eyes and rolled over against me and put one leg over mine.

"You throw a great picnic," I said.

"Mmm."

"You have a lot of hidden talents."

"So do you, darling," she said, and nestled her head against my shoulder.

We lay there quietly for a while longer. The record player had long since run through the ten LP's I had stacked on it.

"Miss Harrington, let's put it on the table," I said. "I make about three hundred bucks a month. I drive a car that's falling apart and smells like a junkyard and I live in a one-bedroom . . ."

She put two fingers on my lips and shut me up.

"Does my money intimidate you?" she asked earnestly.

"Sure."

"Why?"

"You're accustomed to a way of life that's—"

"Stop that!"

"I might begin to feel like a mooch . . ."

"Sergeant, you couldn't be a mooch if you tried," she said sternly. "You're devoting your life to doing a job that's dirty and dangerous, and doing it for damn little in return. I respect that. I find it very honorable. I also love the way you look and the way you think. We both know I have more money than I can ever spend. So why not let me enjoy sharing it with you. If you want to take me for corned beef sandwiches and beer at the deli, that's fine by me. And if I want to take you to Chasen's for roast duck and champagne, that should be fine by you. Doesn't that make sense?"

I had to laugh at her. It was such a pleasure to be around a woman who could change chicken shit to chicken salad with the turn of a word.

"So let's keep giving it a try, shall we?" she said. "I didn't ask to be born rich. Why let money spoil a beautiful thing?"

She laid a hand lightly on my cheek and kissed me with those soft lips to put an end to the conversation.

The candles burned themselves out.

I awoke to the smell of coffee. Mil was not in sight. It was 11:00 A.M. I lay there staring into space, thinking about the highs and lows of the last thirty-six hours. Then Millie came in the room carrying a tray with steaming coffee, more melon squares, and sweet rolls.

"Good morning," she said brightly, putting the tray on the bed between us. She had a sheet pulled around her shoulders and when she sat on the bed, it dropped off and she ignored it. If she was feeling nervous about the growing relationship between us, it certainly didn't show.

And my reservations were quickly dwindling away.

"I just realized, it's my day off," I said.

"Wonderful!" she said.

She leaned across the tray and gave me a good-morning kiss.

And the phone rang.

"Damn it," I said.

"Do you have to answer it?"

"If it's business, they'll just keep calling until I do."

She took the phone and put it between us, where I could reach it.

"Yeah?" I snarled, and she put her hand over her mouth to keep from laughing out loud.

It was Moriarity. The old man seemed to be in a pretty good mood, considering everything that was happening.

"You forget how to use the phone?" he said.

"I was working, boss. A lot's happening."

"Got a minute we can talk about what really happened to you two up the coast? Ski's acting a little coy about it."

"You read the report," I said. "It was signed off by Culhane and Guilfoyle. Usually they don't agree on anything, including the weather."

"I also heard from Charlie Lefton, whose place is less than a mile away from that icehouse. He says there was so much gunfire he thought the Japs were landing in Mendosa. What really happened? Just between us."

I told him about our trip to Mendosa, the brief interview with Lila Parrish's mother, and the ambush by Guilfoyle's denizens.

"It doesn't make sense, Dan. The trail keeps leading back to Culhane. Logically, that should make Guilfoyle giddy with joy. Instead, he sends four of his storm troopers to knock us off."

He whistled low and said, "You going to be home later?"

"It's my day off."

"Mine, too. That doesn't answer the question."

"Yeah, I'll be around."

"I'm gonna have a chat with the D.A. and put him on alert," he said. "I'm not sure where the department fits into this. Seems to me it's out of our jurisdiction."

"We have an unsolved homicide that is definitely in our jurisdiction," I said. "Be sure to bring that up to the D.A."

"How's that coming along?" he asked.

"Forget you asked," I said.

"Talk to you later," he said, and hung up.

"Great." I slammed down the dead phone, looked over at Millie, and said, "It isn't always like this."

"I figured that out," she said with a smile. "Now, what do you say we take a shower."

"Together?"

"Of course."

Then the phone rang again.

"Damn that thing," she cried.

It rang again. I sat there watching it. At six rings, I snatched it up.

"Yeah," I growled.

"I'm sorry to bother you, Sergeant," the desk man said, "but you got a funny message just now."

"Funny ha-ha or funny weird?"

"You tell me. He said, 'Tell Bannon that Sidney called. Tell him I said since we're going to be partners, we should talk.' Does that make any sense?"

"Yeah. And it's definitely not funny. That son of a bitch. What's the number?"

He told me and I thanked him, disconnected, and dialed the number he had given me.

"Who was that?" Millie asked.

"The desk man. The biggest shyster in the state is smirking at me." Sidney answered. His soft, oily voice said, "Is that you, Zeke?"

"It's Sergeant Bannon to you, Schyler, and today's my day off."

"So sorry to bother you," he said with a leer in his voice. "I wanted to check in since we're working on Riker's release together, in a manner of speaking."

It's hard acting tough when Millicent Harrington is sitting two feet away, stark naked and smiling at you.

"In a manner of speaking, my ass," I said, trying to put a snarl in my voice. "I want you to listen real carefully, Sidney. I am not working *with* you on Riker's release. I'm not working *with* you on the March of Dimes or the USO or anything else. Not if the Panama Canal freezes over."

"I'm trying to be nice. I can call a press conference in an hour and lay the whole story out."

"No, you can't, Sidney. All you got is a jailbird doing time for murder one. He's been crying 'Foul!' for twenty years. Nobody believes him anymore. It'll be the joke of the week. You have Riker's daydream and that's *all* you have. You want to stick your neck out? Go ahead. Otherwise sit there and count your toes until I tell you otherwise."

"Always the tough guy," Schyler said with a chuckle. "You will let me know, won't you?"

"I'll let my boss know. You want a statement, get it from him. See you around the courthouse." And I hung up.

"You're in the middle of the maelstrom," she said, obviously enjoying the action.

"If that means I'm in over my head, you're probably right. Well, the hell with them all. Damn it, it's my day off."

She moved the tray over and crawled up over me, one leg on each side, and sat down. She reached over and took the phone off the hook and put the receiver under a pillow and looked down at me.

"We don't have to get dressed today, do we?" she purred.

"Not unless the joint catches fire," I answered.

CHAPTER 34

The attorney general's hearing was held in an assembly room on the third floor of the city courthouse usually reserved for public meetings of the council. There was a large table at one end of the room with six chairs behind it, the seats of the mighty. There were two smaller tables facing the inquisitors, one on each side of the center aisle, a railing behind the tables, and six rows of pews on each side of the aisle for the common people.

The room had fewer than twenty people in it.

The inquiry was closed to the public and the press since it was an advisory hearing, a rare tribunal called by the governor. A gag order concerning evidence was in effect. The attorney general and two men, nominated by the A.G. and appointed by the governor, presided over the hearing. They would listen to the evidence and vote on the issue. The attorney general would then report the findings and recommendations directly to the governor, who would make the final decision. Then the record of the hearing would be made public.

Moriarity, Art Cannon—the city D.A.—Bones, and Dr. Tyler were seated at the table to the right, inside the rail. I was sitting behind them in the first pew when, about ten minutes before ten on Wednesday morning, Sidney Schyler entered with Arnold Riker, who was handcuffed to Harvey Craddock, the Wesco guard captain. Riker was dressed in a dark blue suit, white shirt, and a silk tie, probably courtesy of Schyler. If the objective was to make Riker socially acceptable, it didn't work. There was a feral aura about the man that a new suit and white shirt couldn't camouflage. Once a killer, always a killer.

When he saw me, Riker's lip curled into a mean smile. Then he winked at me and mouthed the words "Hi, partner."

He was enjoying his hour.

It did not go unnoticed by Cannon, a short, trim man with black hair parted down the middle and a wire mustache. He was fifty-two. He motioned to me and I leaned over the railing. "Don't let him rile you, Bannon," he said. "Everybody knows what he is, no matter what happens here today,"

"If he refers to me as his 'partner' one more time," I said, "I'm going to throw the son of a bitch out the window." I leaned back in my seat.

Sidney Schyler was a dandy. His thin blond hair was carefully distributed over his scalp in an attempt to cover a growing bald spot. He wore pince-nez, a yellow linen suit with a wide red check, and a vest with a watch chain that arced from one side of a growing paunch to the other. He spoke in a soft, unctuous voice, with a smile that was more of a smirk. But from everything I knew about him, he was scrupulously honest and one tough lawyer. He had been true to his promise. First thing Monday morning, while Bones and Tyler were working on the case, Schyler had called a press conference and announced that he had undeniable proof that Arnold Riker did not murder Wilma Thompson. He had requested an immediate governor's hearing, at which he would demand that Riker be exonerated of the crime and released on the spot. He got his request for the hearing, and a gag order pertaining to all evidence in the case was issued by a state judge. Par for the course.

Pennington, of course, jumped all over me for not tipping him off.

Schyler and Riker sat at the table on the opposite side of the aisle from our side. Craddock took the cuffs off Riker and sat him down in the chair with a firm shove on the shoulder. He went behind the railing and sat directly behind Riker, with a .38 revolver in his lap, covered by his fedora. I liked Craddock. He was all business.

At exactly 10:00, the governor's representatives arrived. They entered the room single file. These were the power boys. First was Alan Templeton, a pretty-boy, six-two, steel gray hair, a three-hundred-dollar tailor-made suit, a jaw squarer than Dick Tracy's, and the morals of an alley-cat. The ladies loved him. Three times attorney general, he could run forever and never lose. Behind him was Mike Butcher, a lean man with leathery skin and small, hooded eyes—state director of correctional facilities, former San Francisco chief of police, and one-time warden of San Quentin, who had weathered two investigations into brutality and inhumane conditions in the state prison system. The last one in was State Supreme Court Judge Thomas Levy, a little man with puffy hands, thick lips, and a face blotched with liver spots. Levy had been one of California's most feared hanging judges until appointed to the high court when he was two years past retirement age.

They sat at the table facing the room, with Templeton in the middle.

"Gentlemen," Templeton began, rapping his gavel for order, "this is a hearing to determine whether the woman known as Verna Hicks Wilensky, recently deceased, and the late Wilma Thompson, are, in fact, one and the same person. We are not concerned with facts regarding Mr. Riker's trial. If there were crimes committed against Mr. Riker or violations of the law, they will be brought before a grand jury and handled in the prescribed manner.

"We are aware that Mr. Riker was convicted of the felony murder of Miss Wilma Thompson. We are not interested in Mr. Riker's background prior to his arrest. We are not interested in any facts involving that trial. We are not interested in how Mrs. Wilensky died. We are only interested in the writ presented to this body by attorney Sidney Schyler, to wit: "That Mr. Riker has been wrongfully confined in state prisons for the past nineteen years for the murder of Wilma Thompson; that Miss Thompson was not the victim of a homicide in 1922, but instead she changed her name to Verna Hicks, moved to L.A. in 1924, married Frank Wilensky, and has lived here ever since, until her death ten days ago; that you, Mr. Schyler, will present physical evidence proving that the late Mrs. Wilensky was, in fact, Miss Thompson; that therefore Mr. Riker should be released forthwith from confinement in Wesco State Prison; and that the findings of the court in 1922 be vacated. Are these conditions true and acceptable to you, Mr. Schyler?"

"Yes, sir, they are," Schyler said.

"And do you intend to make an opening argument on Mr. Riker's behalf?" Templeton asked.

"Yes, sir."

"Keep it brief, and don't stray from the limited scope of this tribunal or I will cut you off. Understood?"

"Yes, sir."

"Is there opposing counsel present?" Templeton asked.

Cannon stood up. "Sir, I'm Arthur Cannon, the city district attorney. I am simply here to represent the city's interest in this matter, since one of our detectives is involved in the case. Actually, most of these events happened outside the city's jurisdiction."

"Then you have no objection to the proceeding itself?"

"No, sir."

"Alright, Mr. Schyler, get on with it," Templeton said tersely.

Schyler stood up, took off his glasses, and walked slowly back and forth in front of the three men, tapping his spectacles in the palm of his hand as he spoke.

"We are prepared to produce witnesses and evidence that will prove beyond a shadow of a doubt that my client, Arnold Riker, was convicted and has been incarcerated for nineteen years for the murder of Miss Wilma Thompson, a murder which we contend never occurred. A non-murder. We are not interested at this time in pursuing what really happened in 1922. Obviously, my client was framed, but it is up to the attorney general and the governor to instigate an investigation into that matter. Our purpose here today is to clear my client's name and to secure his immediate release from prison. If you find the evidence concurs with that conclusion, then I am presenting a writ demanding that the governor order Mr. Riker's immediate and unconditional release from Wesco State Prison, where he is presently incarcerated. For Mr. Riker to spend one more day in prison would be an outrageous miscarriage of justice. Thank you."

"How many witnesses do you plan to introduce, Mr. Schyler?" Judge Levy asked.

"Three, your honor. Possibly four."

"Any other questions?" Templeton asked, looking at Butcher, who shook his head.

"Alright, Mr. Schyler, you may proceed."

Schyler was a crafty attorney. He first set up an easel in front of the tribunal. His agenda was simple. First, he called Dr. Tyler and, after the dentist was sworn in, established his credentials as a dentist and oral surgeon. Tyler then described in detail the oral surgery he had performed on Wilma Thompson in 1921. Tyler's charts and diagrams showing the extent of the injuries had been blown up and placed on the easel. As Tyler described in detail the procedures he had performed on Thompson, Schyler used a pointer to illustrate the work on the charts and diagrams. Tyler also had taken two photographs of Thompson, a full-face close-up and a shot of her right profile showing the bruises on her jaw.

"Now, Dr. Tyler," Schyler said, "did you also examine the corpse of the woman who called herself Verna Hicks Wilensky?"

"Yes, I did."

"And did you make this examination in concert with Dr. Jerome Wietz, the county coroner?"

"Yes, I did."

"And did you recognize the corpse?"

"It was difficult. Mrs. Wilensky was bloated as a result of being submerged in bathwater for about twenty-four hours prior to being discovered. She also had had some cosmetic surgery performed on her nose. Her hair was natural. It was bleached blond when I knew her. And she had put on thirty, forty pounds. But my conclusion is that Mrs. Wilensky and Miss Thompson are and were the same person."

"This was a visual determination?" Butcher asked.

"Yes and no. I studied the diagrams and charts that Dr. Wietz prepared, and we made an overlay of Dr. Wietz's work and mine. They were identical, allowing for some gum shrinkage, which is normal over that period of time. I also saw comparative photographs of Thompson and Wilensky, and the drawing of Mrs. Wilensky with her nose reshaped. Considering that I had not seen Thompson in roughly twenty years, and allowing for the cosmetic surgery to her nose, it is my opinion that Thompson and Wilensky are one and the same."

"Thank you, Doctor," Schyler said. "Does the tribunal have any questions?"

"I am curious about something," Judge Levy said. "Were you able to recognize the bridgework as your own work, when you examined Mrs. Wilensky?"

"Not in an aesthetic sense," Tyler said. "By that, I mean a dentist does not do anything in constructing bridgework that would identify it as his own work. The procedure is common, sir. However, I will say that the bridgework in both women was identical, allowing for some degree of wear."

Templeton asked, "Was it possible to ascertain the extent of the surgery on Wilensky's nose?"

"I'd prefer you direct that question to Dr. Wietz," Tyler answered.

"My expertise is limited to the field of dentistry. He did, however, make copies of my photos of Thompson to make a drawing showing her nose before and after the surgery, and it was a significant visual aid."

There were no other questions.

Schyler called Bones and he was sworn in. Schyler had the diagrams and charts that Bones had prepared and several grisly photographs of the corpse. There was also a tracing Bones had made using the full-face photograph Tyler had taken of Thompson. On the drawing, Wietz had reshaped the nose to show how it looked after the cosmetic surgery.

Bones described the autopsy in general terms, then zeroed in on the dental work and cosmetic surgery in detail.

Bones said, "I think it's significant that my description of the bridgework and filling was precisely the same as Dr. Tyler's description at the time he did the work."

"Well, sir," Schyler said, "since the bridgework is a common procedure, wouldn't that always hold true?"

"I am referring specifically to the cause of the injury. We both had concluded that the injuries Miss Thompson had suffered were the result of a blow to the right side of her jaw."

"Why is that significant?"

Bones walked over to the exhibits.

"The nature of the injuries indicated that there was a sharp blow here." He made a fist and placed it against his own jaw. "The blow was made by a fist, which shattered the first molar and second bicuspid on the lower jaw. They were literally jammed against the upper jaw, which resulted in the chipping of the first molar on top and also a hairline fracture to the jaw. The photos of Miss Thompson also indicate this is true."

He picked up the photo of Thompson's right profile. "Notice the bruise on the jawline. You can see impressions of two knuckles here and here."

Then he picked up the diagram drawn by Tyler in 1921 and placed a sheet of tracing paper with his own sketch of the injuries over it. The match was virtually identical.

"Making allowances for gum shrinkage due to aging, it is my opin-

ion that they are identical and were caused by a blow to the side of the
jaw. What that means is both women had the identical jaw profile. Both
women were the same size. Both injuries were caused by a blow with a
fist to the same spot. And the injuries in both cases were identical."

He picked up the full-face photo of Thompson shot by Tyler and
the overlay showing how Thompson's nose had been altered.

"Miss Thompson's nose was thick in the bridge between her eyes
and it was too long. The cosmetic surgery narrowed her nose and
shortened it."

"What is your conclusion?" Judge Levy asked.

Bones said, "It is my opinion, based on the evidence presented to
me and my investigation, that Wilma Thompson and Verna Hicks
Wilensky are and were one and the same person."

"And do you concur with that opinion, Dr. Tyler?" Levy said.

"Yes, I do, Your Honor," Tyler said, nodding vigorously.

Bones and Tyler were excused.

"I have one more witness to question," Schyler said.

"Call your witness," Templeton said.

"Sergeant Zeke Bannon, L.A.P.D."

It was a shock to me. Although my presence had been requested,
I had not been subpoenaed. I walked through the gate and was
sworn in.

"Good morning, Sergeant," Schyler said with a grin. "I have just a
few questions. You are the investigating officer in the death of Verna
Hicks Wilensky, are you not?"

"That's correct."

"How long have you been investigating Mrs. Wilensky's homicide?"

Templeton interrupted. "Mr. Schyler, I think I made it clear
that the details of Mrs. Wilensky's death were immaterial to this
procedure."

"Yes, you did, sir, and I assure you this line of questioning is apro-
pos to the matter at hand."

"Alright," Templeton said. "But I caution you, proceed with care."

"Of course."

He repeated the question.

"Ten days," I said.

"Now, Sergeant, in the course of your investigation, did it become necessary to check into Mrs. Wilensky's background. By that, I mean to determine such things as date and place of birth, et cetera?"

"Yes, sir."

"And please tell this tribunal what you learned about her personal history."

"We couldn't establish anything prior to 1924."

"No date of birth?"

"No, sir."

"Place of birth?"

"No, sir."

"Where she worked previously?"

"Sir, as far as we can determine, Mrs. Wilensky had no personal history prior to moving to L.A. in 1924."

"In short," Schyler said, "Mrs. Wilensky did not exist prior to 1924."

"That is correct."

"Is that a normal situation, Sergeant?"

"No."

"And what conclusions, if any, did you draw from that?"

"That she changed her name prior to moving here."

"And have you drawn any conclusions from these facts."

"Not yet," I said.

"So yours is a continuing investigation?"

"Yes, it is."

"Oh yes, one other question. When did Mrs. Wilensky die?"

"May 25, about 7:30 P.M."

"Thank you, Sergeant." He turned to the tribunal.

"Any questions, gentlemen?" Schyler asked the tribunal.

Schyler had played it smart. Now it was up to the tribunal to ask the key question. The three men huddled together for a moment, then Templeton asked me, "Just for the record, Sergeant, what were the circumstances surrounding Mrs. Wilensky's death?"

"She was murdered, sir, and it was made to appear as an accident."

"Thank you, Sergeant. You are excused."

I returned to my seat in the first pew.

"I call Harvey Craddock," Schyler said.

The big guard was a little befuddled at first. He held the hat over his gun and sneaked it back into its holster, then left his hat, and went to be sworn in.

"Mr. Craddock, where are you employed?"

"Wesco State Prison. I am captain of the guard."

"So you know my client, Mr. Riker."

"Oh yes, for the last six years."

"Has Mr. Riker ever discussed the Wilma Thompson murder case with you, Captain?"

"Only every other day or so."

"And what did he say?"

"He'd just go over the whole night, picking out things he said proved he was set up."

"Did you believe him?"

"Nobody believed him."

"Would you consider him a dangerous prisoner?"

"Well, he's what we call a firecracker. Got a short fuse. Light 'em and they blow up in your face."

"And how many times did he blow up, Captain?"

Craddock paused for a few seconds before he answered.

"None."

"Ever create a scene, argue with other prisoners?"

"No, sir."

"In fact, he was the librarian, correct?"

"That is correct. Read four newspapers a day and could quote some of the stories almost word for word. Has an amazing memory."

"Even taught some of the other inmates to read and write, did he not?"

"Yes, sir, about six of them as I recall."

Templeton cut in.

"Mr. Schyler, is this testimony pertinent to anything?"

"Well, sir, my client here has been accused of a vicious crime. I think it is pertinent that he never gave any of the wardens in the prisons where he served time—San Quentin, Folsom, and Wesco—any problem. In fact, he was a model prisoner, helped other cons, was an avid reader."

"You made your point, counselor."

"Yes, sir," Schyler said. He dismissed Craddock, went to his table, took a swig of water, and dabbed his lips with his handkerchief. Then he turned to the tribunal and said:

"Gentlemen, it is the opinion of Wilma Thompson's dentist and the coroner of this county that the woman known as Verna Hicks Wilensky was, in reality, Wilma Thompson. Think about that, gentlemen. You have heard from the investigating officer in the case of Mrs. Wilensky's murder that she appeared here in L.A. in 1924, more than a year after my client's conviction for murdering Wilma Thompson, and that he and his investigators cannot establish any trace of her prior to 1924. She had to come from somewhere, gentlemen. I would suggest that Wilma Thompson was not murdered in 1922, a non-crime for which my client, Arnold Riker, has served nineteen years' hard time in state prisons. I would also suggest, gentlemen, that the probability of Miss Thompson and Mrs. Wilensky *not* being the same person is infinitesimal. Think about it: two women of the same size with the same bridgework, the same scars, the same surgery to the nose; and, finally, the opinion of two expert witnesses that the two women are the same person. And possibly the most profound evidence of all—Miss Thompson's body never was recovered.

"Mr. Riker does not fit the usual profile of a cold-blooded killer. In nineteen years, he never created a disturbance. He taught fellow prisoners to read and write. Ran the library. His character, therefore, is not in contention. I therefore argue that Mr. Riker is absolutely and undeniably not guilty of murder, manslaughter, or anything else, and thus should be released immediately from incarceration. We appeal to you to determine that Mr. Riker may walk out of this courtroom today a free man. Thank you."

The tribunal excused itself and went into an anteroom.

"What happens now?" I asked Cannon.

"They'll make their decision, call the governor, and make a recommendation. If the gov agrees, they'll come back in and announce that decision. If he doesn't agree, then Riker will have to sue the state and go through a retrial."

I went outside for a smoke. The first person I saw was the last person I wanted to see. Jim Pennington.He came across the hallway.

"Thanks a lot, pal," he said. "I was supposed to have the inside on this story, or did you forget that?"

"I couldn't stop Schyler from handing out the story that there would be a hearing, but the judge issued a gag order relating to the evidence."

"He told everybody you were partners."

"That'll be the damn day."

"You could have tipped me. Maybe Schyler would've given me an exclusive."

"You know he doesn't work that way, Jimmy. He gives it to everybody at the same time. He doesn't want to offend anybody, not even the scandal sheets."

"So how do you think it's going to work out?"

"He's got a tough jury. Templeton, Levy, and Butcher."

"Evasive. What's the evidence? You know Spring 'Em. How many times has he bragged about evidence that fizzles in the home stretch? Have you guys really got something?"

"I'm not in bed with Schyler, damn it. I produced the evidence."

"Why share it with him?"

"His client gave me the tip."

"*Riker!* You believed something *Riker* said? Hell, he's been peddling bullshit for all those years."

"It's not bullshit, Jimmy. I hate to say it, but I think Riker's going to walk."

"What the hell has Schyler got?"

I hesitated. But any minute now the tribunal would come back and everybody would know anyway.

"Dental records," I said.

"Dental records?"

"Think about it. As soon as the hearing's over, I'll give you my side of the story exclusively. I'm sure Schyler will have copies of all the evidence for the press."

Moriarity stuck his head out of the room.

"They're coming back in, Zeke."

"Is this on the level?" Pennington said.

"Yep," I said, and returned to the council room.

The three wise men trooped into the room and took their seats. Templeton rapped the gavel.

"Gentlemen, it is the unanimous opinion of this panel that Mr.

Riker was falsely imprisoned. The governor has accepted this verdict and has signed an executive order that exonerates Mr. Riker and vacates the verdict of the jury in his trial. Mr. Riker, you are released from custody."

Bang! went the gavel.

And Riker walked out of the room a free man.

CHAPTER 35

I sat in the first row and watched Riker swagger into the hallway, where he was immediately surrounded by reporters, photographers, and radio newscasters, all shouting questions at him as flashbulbs popped in his face. Behind him, wearing a Cheshire-cat smile, Schyler stood with his hands folded in front of him, watching the chaos and occasionally fielding a legal question. Bones, too, joined the madness, to explain how and why the tribunal had reached its decision. The three political appointees responsible for the madness scurried out a door in the front of the room and vanished.

I decided to follow them. I had nothing to say to the press. Bones, Riker, and Schyler would say enough. And now I had an open homicide on my hands that I didn't want to talk with the press about. In less than an hour, Riker's nineteen years behind bars had come to an abrupt end, and the verdict of the original jury had been thrown out on the testimony of a dentist, a coroner, and a cop. What had started as the simple investigation of an accidental death had escalated into a sensational murder case with lies, a frame-up, and vengeance at its heart, and political undertones stretching to the halls of the state lawmakers and the governor's mansion. All because the victim had too much money in her savings account and no early personal history—and her killer didn't know squat about electricity.

So I had a lot on my mind, not the least of which was Brodie Culhane. I had grown to like him in spite of myself, and yet there was an aura of corruption about him. Perhaps it was his way of brushing off the murder of Wilma Thompson Hicks Wilensky as if it were none of his concern. Perhaps it was the almost casual way he regarded Eddie Woods's murder of Fontonio. Now, more than ever, all roads led back to Culhane, San Pietro, and the events that had begun so many years ago in Eureka and culminated in Wilma's death. There was one character in the scenario who stood out in my mind, and I went to the hospital to talk it out with my partner.

Ski was half asleep when I entered the room.

"Feel like having a visitor?" I said.

"Hey, partner. What happened?"

"Riker walked."

"Well, that's no big surprise."

"Something still bothers me about this," I said. "I can't put my finger on it. It's just out of reach."

"About Riker?"

"Maybe. Hell, Schyler made him sound like Einstein. Son of a bitch read four papers a day and memorized every line. Taught other cons how to read and write. A real Boy Scout."

"Don't let it get you down. You did what you had to. Was Culhane there?"

I shook my head. "I'm sure the boys in Sacramento are already busy trying to figure the best way to bring him down. They know they can handle either Osterfelt or Bellini if they get elected. They've got a string on both of them. But if Culhane wins, they got a maverick on their hands. He'll get rid of all the department heads, guys who've been there forever, break up the political machine . . . he'll drive them all nuts. Life isn't a cat, Ski, it never lands on its feet. Culhane is going down and Riker walks."

"And we still got a homicide on our hands," Ski said. "Probably what's bugging you has something to do with that. Right now, Culhane had the most to gain by her death."

"I got my eye on Eddie Woods. He's the logical hit man and he knew about Wilma Thompson. He knew who she was. Hell, he sent one of the checks."

"I wouldn't take him on alone."

"Well, you sure as hell aren't gonna crawl out of bed and help me. This is nothing but a hunch, Ski. I can't put the arm on him with a bunch of guesswork."

"Walk cautiously."

"I'll keep in touch."

"I'll be thinking. Hell, I got nothin' better to do."

* * *

I went by the Olympic but Woods's office was closed up tighter than a miser's fist. I called Central and had the man on duty get Woods's unlisted phone number and address.

The house was in the Hollywood hills, a few blocks off Sunset Boulevard. It sat back from the street, behind a clump of trees and shrubs, a nice, one-story brick-and-redwood ranch. I drove up the driveway, which branched off at one end of the house toward a two-story attached garage, the other leg circling in front of the place.

Next door, a woman in a cotton dress was using an old-fashioned watering can to treat a cluster of thirsty lilies and carnations.

"I think they're probably on their boat," she said as I got out of the car. "I haven't seen them since day before yesterday."

"Thanks," I said. "I'll just take a look around."

She didn't seem too satisfied with the answer and watched as I knocked on the front door and peered through a living room window. I looked through the garage window, too. Two cars.

Bristles started tickling the back of my neck.

I went around to the back and checked the door to a screened-in porch. It was open.

Then I saw the hole.

A nice, clean, round hole about the size of a .32 slug in the glass panel of the back door.

The circle was bordered by streaks of amber. The color blood makes when it dries.

I looked through the window. A hallway led to what appeared to be the living room. To my left was the kitchen, connecting to the garage. To my right, what looked like a studio room, with a pair of legs in checkered pants on the floor leading into it.

Then the sweet smell of death eked through the bullet hole.

My heart was beating in my ears as I took out a pair of lock needles and jimmied the door open. The smell almost knocked me down. I covered my nose and mouth with a handkerchief and walked cautiously into the house.

Eddie Woods was lying on his side, one arm thrown back, the other trapped under his body. His eyes were half open, staring at the wall. His face was the color of dried putty. His light blue shirt was

soaked in dried blood but the two bullet holes in his chest were obvious. He had bled out on an Oriental rug.

Across the room, his wife lay facedown on the floor, her cheek
against the other end of the rug. She was a tiny woman, five-one or
five-two, and dark-haired. She might have been pretty at one time. One
arm was reaching toward a telephone on an end table. Her brown eyes
were wide open and frozen in an expression of pure terror. A scream
had died in her gaping mouth.

Two bullets in the back.

"Aw, damn it," I said half aloud, and then let it all out. "GOD
DAMN IT!"

I waited while Bones did the ABCs. Dead thirty-six to forty-eight
hours. A .32 did the trick. All four hits were insurance shots. The killer
had cut a square out of a side window with a glass cutter, and opened
the window.

"My guess is, Woods and his wife came in through the garage door
and walked through the kitchen," Bones said. "The killer was waiting
in the hallway. He popped Woods first, then the wife, who was trying to
get to the phone."

"Came in and waited, like he did for Verna Wilensky."

"Yeah, a very patient killer. We'll dust the place for prints and I've
got people checking the neighborhood. Got any ideas?"

"My idea is lying on the floor," I said.

I left the investigation in the hands of Bones and two capable homicide dicks who were on duty, and headed away from the scene, my
mind in a knot. I was a block away when the radiophone squawked on
the dashboard. I snatched it up. It was Ski.

"I been trying to raise you," he said. There was excitement in his
voice.

"Eddie Woods and his wife are dead," I said, and quickly gave him
the necessary details.

"It fits," he said excitedly.

"What do you mean?"

"You got me thinking," he said. "All I got to do is lie up here, eat
my pudding, and think."

"And?"

"Something you said about Riker reading four newspapers a day and remembering every line."

"Yeah?"

"So if he's such a genius, how come he missed that picture of Verna the first time it ran—last April?"

It took only a few seconds for me to see where he was headed.

"Keep talking."

"Well, if he read it in April, how come he didn't get wacky about it until he saw it last Saturday?"

"Ski, you're a genius."

I thought back to what the captain of the guard, Craddock, had said about visitors.

"One of the last visitors Riker had was an ex-con he bunked with for six months," I said.

"What's his name?"

"Uh . . . Dahlmus. Henry Dahlmus. He did four years on a two-to-five for manslaughter."

" Is he on parole?'

"Yep. Six months ago."

"Don't forget, pard, we got a fingerprint. If this Dahlmus was tried in Los Angeles County, we might have his prints in our own files."

"I'm heading back to the records department," I said.

Pulling the card on Dahlmus took fifteen minutes. The picture showed a short, chunky man with thick lips and a brush cut. I was more interested in the prints. The technician in the print department slipped the print we lifted at Wilensky's house on one side of the comparative microscope, and one by one fed Dahlmus's prints in the other side. After six tries, the tech looked at me and smiled. "Want to see something pretty?"

I looked in the scope. He had a match. No doubt about it.

Dahlmus was our killer.

I called Ski and gave him the news, but told him to keep it quiet until it broke in the newspapers. I owed Jimmy Pen that much.

I had the photo department run off a dozen copies of Dahlmus's mug shot and quickly typed out a physical description. Then I called

Moriarity and ran the whole story by him. I had never heard Moriarity chortle before. It was nearly 4:00 P.M.

"We need Dahlmus alive," I said. "He's the only one can tie the can on Riker's ass. Riker paid Dahlmus to kill Wilma and Eddie Woods. Revenge for framing him. And he raises a scandal Culhane can't ditch and ruins his hopes for governor."

"Let's call the newsies and get this story in the late editions and on the radio," he said. "Do you want to do the honors?"

"I've got an obligation to Jimmy the Pen," I said. "I want to give it to him and sit on it until he has an exclusive. When he breaks it, everybody will run with it."

"How much do we give them?"

"That there's an APB out for Dahlmus. That we have a positive identification from a print found in Verna Wilensky's house. That we're also looking for Riker, who's wanted for questioning. Let's leave Mendosa out of it for the time being, although my guess is, Riker's headed for Mendosa, if he isn't there already."

"Okay, give it to Pennington," Moriarity said. "It's a helluva story, Zee. Riker walks away a free man at noon, and by four he's on the run for complicity in killing the same person he didn't kill the first time, plus two others."

We hung up and I called Pennington at the *Times*. I caught him as he was walking out the door.

"How'd you like an update on the Riker story?" I asked.

"Gonna to be hard to top the one I got already," he said.

"Everybody's got that story. This one's a banner above the fold."

"I'm all ears."

"How about this for a headline: Henry Dahlmus, Former Riker Cellmate, Sought for Murder of Wilma Thompson. Riker to Be Questioned. And a side story: Dahlmus Also a Suspect in the Murder of Private Detective Eddie Woods and Wife."

Pennington almost jumped through the phone.

"I'll come over and give you the details along with his mug shot," I said. "Can you make the final? I want to spread his picture all over town."

"I'll get the desk to hold the first pressrun. We can replate the front page with a banner head and run this story as a box."

"I'm on my way," I said.

Before I left, I called Millicent and gave her a quick version of what was happening.

"It's gonna be a busy night," I said.

"I'll wait up," she answered.

CHAPTER 36

The *Times* hit the street fifteen minutes later than usual. Thirty minutes after that, the radio stations were on the air with it. By 7:00 P.M., Riker and Dahlmus were wanted men. Before the news broke, Moriarity had roadblocks everywhere and the airport covered.

I had my own agenda. I called Culhane before the paper hit the streets and gave him the news.

I could hear a combination of relief and excitement in his tone.

Then I told him about Eddie Woods and his wife.

There was a long pause.

"I told you . . . Eddie would never kill a woman," he said with a catch in his voice. "Did *you* find them?"

"Yeah." And then I said, "I'm sorry, Brodie."

"You ever sleep, Cowboy?" he said.

"It was Ski who came up with the answer," I said. "But I still got some questions that need answering."

"Such as?"

"Who was paying Wilma Thompson for going into hiding all those years?"

"That's out of your bailiwick, isn't it? You put a cap on your homicide. I'm sure the A.G. is going to be all over me, now that Riker's frame is public knowledge."

"They all tie together."

"First things first," he said. "You've got to nail Dahlmus and Riker."

"We have roadblocks all over the place. On the highways, at the airport. We got pictures of Dahlmus spreading all over town. But the minute this is news, Riker's going to turn rabbit, if he hasn't already."

There was silence on the line for a moment.

"Go on," Culhane said.

"I'm betting Dahlmus is at Shuler's Sanitarium right now, and that's where Riker will head."

"And then have a seaplane drop down in the morning and he'll be on his way to Mexico," said Culhane.

"We alerted the Coast Guard before we went public with this," I said. "I don't think he can take a chance on getting out of L.A. except by boat and going north."

"So you think he's headed for Mendosa," he said flatly.

"It's his safest bet at this point. I can get a judge to issue me a search warrant for Shuler's. Want to back me up?"

"You better hurry."

"I'll be on my way as soon as I can get the paperwork."

"I'll take care of that," he said. "Just get your ass up here."

"How long would it take Riker to get up there by boat?"

"Three, four hours. I have friends in the Coast Guard from the old days. I'll see if I can get a cutter to bottle up Mendosa."

"We need Dahlmus alive, Brodie, to testify it was Riker who ordered Verna Wilensky's murder."

"I know that."

"I'm on my way," I said.

CHAPTER 37

*T*he Pretty Maid *rocks gently at the Santa Monica pier. The captain, a trim, deeply tanned, hard-looking man with graying hair, in a blue blazer, a T-shirt, and white pants, is sitting at the controls listening to the radio.*

There are three others on the boat. One, slender, dressed in a gray suit, with a fedora cocked over one eye, looks like a ferret: narrow eyes, a long nose, thin lips. His name is Earl and he is definitely not dressed for boating. He is sitting on a deck chair and is as calm as a cat taking a nap. The second is dressed like a tourist from Ohio. Red slacks, a loud Hawaiian sports shirt with bright green palm trees, its tail hanging loose. He has red hair and is wired, moving around the deck of the boat snapping his fingers, impatient, singing under his breath.

The third one is a chubby man with a crew cut. Bulging eyes are constantly on the move in his round face. His tongue constantly licks dry lips. A gaudy tie is pulled down from a white shirt, sweat-stained under his arms and opened at the collar. His sports jacket is folded over one arm. He is holding a derby, his hands fingering the brim.

"Can't you calm down?" he snaps at the red-haired clown.

"This is calm,*" Leo snaps back. "You don't wanna see me agitated. Henry, here, don't wanna see me agitated, does he, Earl?"*

"I wouldn't know," Earl shrugs. He fingers a cigarette but doesn't light it.

"You're making me nervous."

"I ain't what's making you nervous, Henry." He giggles and goes back to humming "Bye-Bye Blackbird."

The captain looks down at Henry and says, "Why don't you go below, Mr. Dahlmus. Get out of sight."

"I get seasick easy. It's too hot down there."

"Well, you're too visible up here. They're giving your description every five minutes on the radio."

"Popular, ain'tcha, Henry." Leo chuckles.

The pudgy man turns and edges his way down into the cabin. He wipes sweat from his brow with his shirtsleeve.

"Here he comes," the captain's harsh voice says, as a black limousine approaches the pier and stops. The man in the backseat gets out before the driver can come around and open the door. He walks up the gangplank, a man who swaggers when he walks, his shoulders bunched up.

"Let's get outta here," he says to the captain in a razor voice.

"Yes, sir." The captain nods, and salutes with a forefinger.

The man turns to Leo.

"What are you so happy about?" he says to Leo.

Leo is taken aback. He shrugs. "You know," he says with a tight smile.

"No, I don't know. Sit down and relax."

"Yes, sir." Leo sits.

The cabin cruiser eases out of the bay toward open water.

The man with the tight shoulders climbs up on the bridge beside the captain.

"How are you, Jack?" he says, shaking hands with the captain.

"Doing okay, sir. Been a while."

"Yeah, too long. You know what to do?"

"Yes, sir, just like the old days."

"We got a situation."

"I know. I been listening to the radio."

"Everybody in town is listening to the damn radio. Open this thing up as soon as you can and get us into deep water."

"Done. We have to keep an eye out for the Coast Guard, Mr. Riker."

"So I've been hearing."

Riker goes below. Henry Dahlmus is sitting on a couch. He jumps up when Riker comes down the stairs.

"Hi, Arnie."

"Don't 'Hi, Arnie' me."

"Jesus, Arnie, I . . ."

"You fucked up royally."

"Aw, c'mon, Arnie."

"Just shut up."

Dahlmus shrinks into himself like a tortoise pulling into its shell. Riker goes to the bar and pours himself a drink. He sits down opposite Dahlmus, sips the drink, and stares across the cabin at the chubby man. Sits, sips, and stares as the radio drones on:

"We interrupt the program in progress to bring you a special bulletin. The Los Angeles Police Department has an all-points alert for two men suspected in the triple murder of . . ."

"Why didn't you just hire an airplane with a banner on the back and fly around town," Riker says.

A full moon lights the sea, its shimmering reflection accenting every wave. The captain's neck swivels as he looks for the telltale lights of other boats. So far, so good.

Below, Dahlmus is beginning to get sick. He can't keep his eyes off a cabin light rocking rhythmically as the cruiser chops through the waves, its heavy engines roaring behind them.

"I think I'll get some air," Dahlmus says. "I ain't much of a sailor."

"You're not much of anything," Riker says. "Go ahead, go topside and take a couple of deep breaths."

"Yeah, that's what I'll do."

He weaves his way to the stairs and makes his way up to the deck, leaving his jacket and derby behind. Riker watches him go, his cold eyes watching every move.

On deck, Leo and Earl are sitting on the seat stretching the width of the stern. Earl has his hat in his hand, his hair snapping in the wind. Leo has his arms stretched out on the back of the seat, eyes closed, head back.

"Ain't this the life," he says. *Earl has nothing to say.*

Riker comes on deck. He is whirling Dahlmus's derby on a forefinger. Dahlmus is leaning on the railing of the boat, eyes closed, gasping for breath.

Riker climbs up to the bridge.

"How we doin'?" he asks the captain.

"I got a shortwave from Guilfoyle. The Coast Guard is cruising around Mendosa Sound."

"So what do we do?"

"My suggestion is we swing wide around the sound and go in at a fishing camp run by a guy named Lefton. We know him, do a lot of fishing trips with him."

"Whatever you think."

"We can dodge the C.G. and slip in there. It's ten miles from town."

"How long?"

"Another hour and a half."

Riker goes back on deck. He walks to the stern and stands with his back to Dahlmus and says to Leo, "Slip me your piece."

"I thought . . ."

"You're not paid to think." He holds out his hand and Leo hands him a .38. Riker drapes Dahlmus's derby over it. He walks back and stands behind Dahlmus.

"Henry?"

Dahlmus turns and stands with his back to the sea. He sees his hat. Riker lifts the hat up and scales it out over Dahlmus's shoulder.

"What the hell . . ." Dahlmus starts, and then he sees the gun.

"I should have known better than to trust a two-bit stick-up man to do these jobs."

"I . . ."

"I told you, wait until she's in the tub and drop the radio in with her, but you had to get fancy. You made it a murder case."

Dahlmus began to whine. "I wanted to make sure . . ."

"Left your prints all over the place, you stupid bastard. And now that bulldog cop has tied you to me. But you're the only one can tie me to you."

He raises his gun hand straight out, a foot from the chest of Dahlmus. The gun barks twice, the bullets tearing into Dahlmus's flesh, the sound whisked away in the wind.

Dahlmus cries out once, "Ohh . . . ," and flips backward into the ocean. Riker watches as the body is caught in the wake of the cruiser, bobbing like a fishing cork in the moonlight.

Riker turns to Earl and Leo. He hands the gun back to Leo.

"Did you see that? No sea legs. Old Henry just fell overboard."

I lost daylight just after I passed through Lompoc. I turned on the siren and bright lights and put the speedometer on seventy. There was hardly any traffic and what there was got out of my way in a hurry.

Back in L.A., the APB had uniform cops and detectives shaking up their informants and stopping every brown-and-black ragtop, which is the last car we could put Dahlmus in. The big problem was how to bring Riker and Dahlmus in without invading Mendosa.

Guilfoyle would be their point man.

I pulled into the courthouse, and Hernandez, the hard-boiled deputy I met when I first came to San Pietro, gave me a look that would have frozen the gates of Hell.

"Do you know where I could find the captain?" I asked as pleasantly as I could manage.

"He's waiting for you, although I don't know why he should," she snapped. "Second floor at The Breakers." And turned her attention back to the magazine she was reading.

I drove around to The Breakers. A kid in a valet's jacket rushed up to the car and opened the door.

"Leave the car here," I said, locking the door and taking the keys.

"But . . ."

I ignored him and went up the stairs to the lobby. The ballroom was on the second floor. As I passed the desk, the manager said, "Excuse me, sir, may I help you?"

"No," I said.

I could hear music and voices, and followed them up the stairs. The ballroom entrance was right at the top. There were about a hundred people in formal dress gathered in the room. A banner across the stage said "Culhane for Governor." Red, white, and blue balloons clung to the ceiling and a small band was playing a lively version of "Shorty George." The mood was jovial, which surprised me. Two or three younger couples were off to one side doing the lindy hop. Waiters were cruising the room with trays of champagne, and there were two large food tables located on both sides of the dance floor. If the celebrants were concerned by the events of the day, you couldn't tell it.

Brett Merrill was waiting near the entrance. As I walked toward him, someone grabbed my elbow. I turned to face a giant of a man, probably six-five or six-six, wearing a green jacket with a small badge that told me he was the hotel's security officer.

"Excuse me, sir," he said, "this is a private party."

"It's alright, Carl," Merrill said as he walked up.

"He left his car parked and locked in front of the main entrance," the security man said.

I leaned over close to Merrill and said, "There's a shotgun under the dash and a .45 in the pocket."

"It's alright, Carl," he said. "Mr. Bannon is a police officer and my guest."

"Yes, sir," Carl said, and vanished as quickly as he had appeared. Merrill nodded toward a small dining room adjoining the main ballroom.

"Wait in there, I'll get him."

I went into the room and rolled a cigarette. It was a pleasant little parlor, with dark green wallpaper, paintings of famous horses on the walls. Before I could light my cigarette, Merrill returned with Culhane and the omnipresent Rusty.

"Let's sit down," he said. "I been standing up for two hours."

He sat at a table near the door and I sat across from him. Brett Merrill stood behind a chair but didn't sit. Rusty stood by the door with his arms crossed and looked out a window.

"You sure got busy after you left here," Culhane said.

"Look, if it had been my choice they would have gassed Riker nineteen years ago," I said.

He looked surprised. "I thought you were a stickler for the law. You saying you think they should have gassed an innocent man?"

"The law's one thing, justice is another," I said.

Merrill, who was looking down at me, stared off in the corner, thought for a minute, raised his eyebrows, and nodded approvingly.

"I've got my whole force on alert," Culhane said. "So far the Coast Guard hasn't picked them up. They have Mendosa's port bottled up. With any luck, they'll nail Riker before we do."

"Right now, I'm more interested in Dahlmus," I answered. "If he's on the boat with Riker, he's dead already."

"And if he was in Mendosa, Guilfoyle's taken him fishing by now," Culhane answered.

"So what's the plan?"

"We have to get past Guilfoyle's bunch and shake down Shuler's place. If Riker's there, we'll bring him in and let the state court deal with him."

"Can we do that?"

Merrill made a temple with his fingers and said sagely, "I hope Dahlmus is still alive and we get him, then we make a deal with him to turn up Riker. Otherwise he's looking at the gas chamber."

"And if Dahlmus is dead?"

"Then my hope is Riker will put up a fight," Culhane said with ice in his tone. "We have to sucker Guilfoyle out of Mendosa. Get him out in the open, then end-run him, and exercise our search warrant."

"How do you plan to do that?"

A phone call answered that question.

There was a knock on the door and the security man stuck his head in the room.

"Excuse me, Captain, you have an urgent phone call. They're patching it in here."

A moment later the phone rang. Culhane pointed to an extension. I kept my hand over the mouthpiece when we picked up.

"Captain, it's Charlie Lefton." His quiet voice was laced with fear. "I got a boat docking in here and I think . . ." Then there was a sound like a chair falling over and the line went dead.

Culhane slammed down the phone. He turned to Merrill. "Brett, keep everybody here happy." And then to me, "Let's go, Cowboy."

There were four cars waiting in front of the county building by the time we arrived. Big Redd, Max, Lefty, and Rusty were there, with four other deputies who were strangers to me. Culhane made fast introductions: Bobby Aaron, a man in his early fifties about my size, with the crafty look of a fox; Hank Foster, a well-built youngster with brown hair and a cockeyed smile on his face; a hard case named Joe Brady, who could have been anything from forty to fifty, with the face of a leather-tanned wrangler, and who just nodded at me; and another younger man named Randy Oldfield, who looked like an ex–football lineman.

Culhane had spread a county map on the hood of the Packard. The road south to Mendosa followed the shoreline, bowed out and curved around Lefton's, then back to the shoreline again. It was thickly forested for a half mile or so on either side of the fishing camp.

"Okay, here's the play," Culhane began. "We think Riker has landed by boat at Lefton's place. It's foggy down there so move carefully. Bobby, you and Brady take one of the cars down past Lefton's and see if you see anybody down there. Then pull off the road and park here, on the dirt road past the fishing camp."

Bobby Aaron, I would learn later, was an Apache Indian who had once been on the reservation police and had tailed a maverick Indian

all the way from Arizona, catching him in a bar in Eureka, before it became San Pietro. Culhane was so impressed he hired him on the spot.
Joe Brady was what he looked like, an ex-cowpoke.

"Big Redd, take one of the walkie-talkies and go down through the
woods on the ocean side. Check the place out . . ."

"I'll go with him," I said. "I'm in on this, too."

Big Redd looked at Culhane and shook his head slightly. Culhane
thought for a moment, then said, "Okay. Stay behind Redd and do what
he tells you. Use hand signals so we don't tip off anybody who might
be down there. Take the walkie-talkie and keep in touch when you
can."

He turned to the rest of his crew.

"The rest of us lay back here," he pointed to a spot on the map
about a mile from the camp. "We wait until Redd and Bannon reconnoi-
ter the place. If it's clear, we move down across the county line and
I'll try to lure Guilfoyle down there. If he bites, Bobby will pull behind
his cars and box him in. I have a warrant for his arrest for harboring
a felon. I'll serve it on him, then we'll play it by ear from there. Any
questions?"

There weren't any.

"Okay, let's get on with it."

Aaron got in a Pontiac sedan and cranked it up.

Big Redd earned his nickname. He was at least six four and built
like a tank. Dark skin, dark hair, wary eyes. He was wearing a .38 in a
shoulder holster and in his belt a cased bowie knife big enough to
slaughter a bull.

We drove down the road in my car until we hit fog, then pulled off
into the trees and started our trek through the forest.

CHAPTER 38

Redd moved soundlessly through the woods. I literally tried to follow in his footsteps to keep from making a sound. He would stop occasionally, kneel down, and just listen. Then we'd be off again. It took about fifteen minutes to get to the clearing. The lodge was deadly quiet. There was one light on in the office. As we crouched in the undergrowth, Redd saw something. He crawled to the right, toward the sea, and stopped again. He lay there motionless and beckoned me on. I crawled up beside him.

Down below us, in the small inlet that washed up to the edge of the lodge, Charlie Lefton was floating facedown, his back blown apart by a shotgun blast.

My jaw tightened so hard it hurt.

The office door opened and a man came out. He stood in the shadows outside the periphery of light from the office door and lit a cigarette. Then a second man came out and stood beside the first. They spoke back and forth for a minute or two, but we couldn't hear them clearly.

The first one was dressed in a gray suit. The other one looked like a clown. The guy in the suit was short, slender, and ferret-faced, and was wearing a fedora. The other one was wearing slacks and a loud sports shirt, and had curly red hair. The lean one was calm as a lake. The clown was jumpy, wired. The lean one pointed toward the office and they went back inside.

Neither one of them was Henry Dahlmus.

I pointed to myself and then to the grid of supports under the lodge, and indicated I wanted to go under there, come up on the other side of the office, and kick in the door. Redd would wait at the bottom of the steps leading to the walkway around the lodge and charge the door when he heard me kick it open.

Redd shook his head. Those weren't his instructions.

I pointed down at Lefton and then toward the two men in the office. He got my meaning. I offered a compromise. As soon as I hit the door, Redd could call Culhane and tell him to come in like the cavalry.

I didn't give Redd a chance to argue. I rolled through the weeds and made a run for the underbelly of the lodge. When I got there, I crawled through the crisscross of four-by-fours. A rat ran soundlessly away from me along one of the supports. I brushed spiderwebs away from my face. To my right, out in the bay somewhere, a fish jumped. I hesitated, waiting for a reaction from the pair above me. I heard the wired one say, "Just a fuckin' fish." And a moment later, "I don't think anybody's comin' down here."

No answer. I waited a little longer, then climbed carefully up the supports to the deck of the lodge and looked over. The door on my side of the office was closed. I climbed over the railing and fell against the outside wall of the office, drew my Luger, and wondered where Redd was. Then I counted to three and jumped into Lefton's office.

The two thugs were startled as I burst into the room. The lean, rat-faced little man with receding black hair had the smallest eyes I've ever seen on a human being. The wired clown in the noisy shirt and baggy pants was as nervous as a jumping bean.

He had a .38 in his hand.

It was a Mexican standoff. Rat Face just stood like a spectator.

Nobody did anything.

"Where's Dahlmus?" I said to Rat Face, ignoring the clown who was holding his pistol in both hands and aiming it at me.

Still no comment.

The clown giggled some more. His pupils were as wide as dollar pancakes, his hands shaking with anticipation. His trigger finger started twitching. I ignored the quiet one and turned on the clown. He was sweating. He bounced to my right and aimed straight at my face just as Big Redd moved silently through the door behind him, bowie knife in hand. Before the redhead could get his shot off, Redd said, "Hey."

The gunman whirled and as he did, Redd's knife flashed in a downward arc. The astonished gangster saw his own hand, still holding the gun, fall to the floor. Before he could scream, Redd stepped up and jammed the knife in an upward arc under his ribs to the hilt. Air rushed out of the wired freak. Redd slammed his foot into the dying man's chest and shoved him across the room. He crashed over Lefton's desk and ended in a heap in the corner. It all happened in the space of four or five seconds.

I swung the gun back on the lean one, who was so startled by the swiftness of Redd's attack he was rooted on the spot. He stared at the severed hand on the floor, with his mouth half open.

"He was squeezing the trigger on you," Redd said, nodding toward the dead man. He walked over, cleaned the knife on the dead man's shirt, and sheathed it. He pointed a forefinger back and forth between his own eyes and then at the corpse in the corner.

"Wired," he said. "You can't hesitate."

"Thanks," I said. "Call the captain to come on down." And to Rat Face, "Get rid of your heater or the same thing'll happen to you."

He opened his suit jacket, reached under his arm with two fingers, jiggled a .45 loose from its shoulder holster, and dropped it on the floor.

"Turn around and grab that wall."

Redd's walkie-talkie crackled to life. "Clear," he said. "One dead, one under control. They killed Charlie Lefton."

"What's your name?" I asked Rat Face.

"Earl," he blurted, turning and leaning forward on both hands. He knew the drill. I frisked him, lifting his wallet and a push-button knife. I backed up about five feet and reached out with my foot and dragged a chair over, picked up his gun and threw it on the desk. I sat down backward on the chair and let my gun hand rest on the back of the chair while I rifled through his wallet with my left. His license said his name was Earl Hirshman, that he was from Boston, thirty-two years old, five-seven, and weighed a hundred and thirty-five pounds. An ID identified him as a deputy sheriff in Pacifico County. A business card identified him as an "associate" with the law firm of Brophy, Myers, and Ragsdale. An associate, I assumed, was a private eye with a licensed gun. He had two one-hundred-dollar bills and four ones in the money pocket of the wallet.

I replaced the items, dropped the wallet on the table by my elbow, and pressed the button on the knife. A six-inch blade shot out. Both sides of the blade were honed to a razor's edge and the point was as sharp as a needle's. I put the point on the table and pressed the blade back into the handle and laid it beside the wallet.

"Okay, Earl, turn around, sit down, and rest your hands on top of your head."

He did as he was told.

"Very good," I said. "We're going to play one question. I'd ask you two but I doubt you and your dead pal there know why you were sent to kill Charlie Lefton. So I'm just going to ask you the one question. Who's paying the bills for this?"

His answer was a blank stare.

"We'll pull down the shades and swing that overhead light in your face when the captain gets here," I said to Earl. "Then he'll do whatever he does to get the conversation going."

Nothing. He had about as much expression on his face as a tree trunk.

"I feel compelled to tell you that Culhane and Lefton served in the Marines together," I said. "They were both wounded, but Lefton managed to carry Culhane back to the medics. Think about that while we wait for him to get here."

The story was partly true. Lefton had carried my boss, Moriarity, to safety, not Culhane.

Nothing changed in his expression but his tongue sneaked out and dampened his lips.

Outside, the headlights of Culhane's car flooded the road as he roared up to the fishing camp. A second car pulled in behind him. Culhane jumped out of the car and ran toward us. Then he saw Charlie Lefton lying on the dock. Redd had stopped to pull him out. Culhane's lips began to twitch with anger. He turned around, said something to Rusty which I couldn't hear, and Rusty opened the trunk of the Packard and brought him back a blanket. Culhane spread it over Lefton's body, took one of Lefton's hands from under the blanket, held it, and said something to Charlie Lefton's corpse.

He looked up at the office as an insane expression crossed his face. He stood, came up on the motel walk, and slammed through the door. He looked at Hirshman, then at me. Then he saw the severed hand and the body in the corner.

"A little slow, huh?" he said to Redd, who answered him by holding up a thumb and forefinger about a quarter-inch apart.

"Dahlmus?" Culhane asked.

I shrugged. "He's not here."

Two other cops joined us. Culhane told one of them to go to one of the rooms and bring back a blanket. He covered the dead man after relieving him of his wallet.

"Name's Leo Groover," Culhane said. "Baltimore."

He threw the wallet on the table with the rest of the assorted weapons and IDs. Then he walked over, grabbed a handful of Hirshman's shirt, dragged him to his feet, and hit him with a right cross that hurt *my* jaw. Hirshman flew halfway across the room and ended up on his back. He spit blood and looked up at Culhane with fear in his eyes.

"Back-shooting son of a bitch," Culhane said, and grabbed him again, dragging him to his feet.

"Easy," I said. "He's the only witness we have left."

"I'm not gonna kill him," Culhane said. "But I am going to hurt him some more." He hit Hirshman again, this time an uppercut. Hirshman went down and rolled over on his stomach. Culhane grabbed the back of his suit coat, jerked him up, and slammed him against the wall.

Hirshman stared at him through dazed eyes. His jaw was askew and he was bleeding from the mouth.

"Easy, Brodie," I said. "He's got a lot of talking to do."

"I haven't heard a peep out of the dirty little coward yet."

He closed in on Hirshman, his face a foot from the killer's.

"We're going outside where there's more room," he hissed in Hirshman's face, spun him around, and shoved him out the door.

We followed Culhane and Hirshman down the walkway, where Culhane kicked him and sent him spinning down the steps.

Rusty, Max, and three or four other policemen watched from twenty feet away and said nothing. Hirshman scrambled to his hands and knees, started to crawl frantically away from Culhane. Culhane turned to me and held out his hand.

"Gimme your piece," he said.

I looked at him with surprise, and he reached inside my jacket and pulled out the Luger. "I said gimme your damn gun," he said.

He walked slowly behind Hirshman. The mobster crawled up the embankment. As he reached the top, Culhane fired a shot. I jumped. The ground erupted an inch or two in front of Hirshman, who whirled over on his back.

"Jesus, don't kill me," he pleaded.

"Well, how about that," Culhane said. "It talks."

Earl looked at me and all he got was a dead stare.

"I'm not going to kill you, you useless little shit," Culhane said in a low, cold tone. "I'm gonna take off your kneecaps. They'll have to push you to the gas chamber in a wheelchair."

Earl was breathing hard but still silent.

"Let me explain something to you," Culhane said. "I'm old. And the older I get, the more I appreciate time. Right now, you're wasting mine."

Culhane looked at me and put the Luger against Hirshman's knee. "Ask him some questions."

"How did you get here from Baltimore?" I asked.

"I had to get outta town in a hurry," Earl blurted. "There was heat on me. I heard about this resort in Mendosa and called Guilfoyle. He said come on out, fifty bucks a day and I'd have to do whatever he told me to do. I took the train out."

"When?"

"About a month ago."

"Then what?"

"Guilfoyle says, 'I got a job for you in a couple of weeks.' I says, 'Doin' what?' He says, 'You got some limits I don't know about?' I shake my head, 'No.' He says, 'Good. I'll let you know.' "

"Keep going."

"Yesterday he tells me to get Dahlmus and that crazy freak inside, take the cabin cruiser down to this marina in L.A., and pick up this guy named Riker. Once Riker came aboard, he'd give the orders."

"Who ran the boat?"

"I dunno. It was called *Pretty Maid*."

"When did Riker show up?"

"A little before six. He was in a black limo. I didn't see who was driving."

Culhane was irate. His jaw was tight as a fist. He walked back and forth in front of Earl. Finally he said, "Why did you kill my friend?"

"I didn't shoot him. Leo was walking behind him and when Lefton told us to fuck off, he just swung the shotgun up and shot him."

Culhane looked down at the gunman. I spoke quickly.

"Who's paying you for all the dirty work?" I asked.

Earl was sweating. He wiped his mouth with the back of his hand.

"Who's paying you?" I repeated

"You're not doing real well, Earl," Culhane cut in. "You're hesitating! One more hesitation and I'll forget about your kneecaps. I'll just take off your pecker."

The gun roared and a geyser of dirt exploded a quarter of an inch from Earl's crotch. He screamed and scrambled backward.

"Where's Dahlmus?" I said.

"He's dead," Earl stammered. "Riker shot him on the boat."

"Who else was there?"

"Me, the cuckoo-nut, Dahlmus, and the guy who drove the boat."

"Okay, go on."

"We hang around a marina in Santa Monica and this big Lincoln pulls up and out comes Riker. He climbs aboard and says, 'Haul ass.' That's all he said until we're out about two hours and then Riker asks Leo for his gun. He goes over and caps Dahlmus twice. Dahlmus goes over backward. Then he says to us something like 'How about that, he fell overboard.' "

"You saw him shoot Dahlmus?" I said.

"Hell, I was three feet away. Surprised the hell outta me. Surprised Dahlmus, too."

"You take my breath away, Earl," Culhane said. "Keep talkin'."

"Riker says to me, 'I want you to call this Bannon and tell him to meet you at Lefton's fishing camp.' Then Riker says, 'Tell him you'll meet him there and you got plenty of information for him, but you got to make a deal. Tell Bannon if he comes in with anybody, he'll never see you again.'

"So we pull into Lefton's. Leo and I scout the place, and we see Lefton goin' into the office, and Leo follows him in, and he's on the phone. So Leo goes nuts, slams down the phone, and shoves him outside, and I ask him can he run a couple of us into town, and he's walkin' away and says 'fuck off' and you know the rest."

"They stole Charlie's car, too?" Culhane said.

"Yeah. By now Riker's getting nervous. He takes the dead guy's keys, tells us to wait here and call if anybody comes snoopin' around."

I asked him, "Where were you staying in Mendosa?"

"At Shuler's. There's a building back of the main place there with an indoor swimming pool and a workout room. There's a big room on the second floor, which is where they keep all the crazies, and there's four small apartments on the top floor. It's where I was staying. Dahlmus, too. And Leo the clown."

"How about the other apartment?"

"Empty."

"Is that where Riker is now?"

"I dunno, I swear. I never seen Riker until we picked him up at the marina. We sail past Mendosa because there was a Coast Guard cutter snoopin' around and end up here."

"What did he pay you?" Culhane asked.

Hirshman hesitated a moment and Culhane aimed the gun at his crotch again.

"Two bills for everybody I hit," he babbled. "He told me if a cop named Bannon showed up, he'd give me five hundred to hit him."

"Jesus," Culhane said, then dragged Hirshman to his feet and called Rusty over.

"Rusty," Culhane said, "take him into Lefton's office."

We followed them. The clown was still lying on the floor, his feet sticking out from under the blanket.

Culhane shoved Earl into a chair near the desk. "Now listen carefully, Earl. You're going to call Guilfoyle. Tell him that I showed up with Bannon and several men. Tell him there was some shooting and we killed Groover and you're trapped in Lefton's office. And you need help *now*. Tell him you can't hold out any longer, then hang up. You think you can remember all that?"

Earl nodded.

Culhane got the operator and gave her the number.

"You really think you can get Guilfoyle to come to us?" I asked Culhane.

"Oh, he'll come alright," Culhane replied with a smile. "His balls are a lot bigger than his brain."

"What are you going to do when he gets here?"

"Arrest him for aiding and abetting, conspiracy to commit murder, harboring fugitives, and I'm sure I'll think of a few other things by then."

Culhane had his men pull both cars up side by side, blocking the narrow road. He dispersed four of his men into the woods, two on each side of the road leading from Mendosa. Rusty, one-eyed Max, and

Redd stood behind him back by the cars, Rusty and Redd with shotguns and Max with the tommy gun.

"Where do you want me?" I asked.

"Out of the line of fire," he said.

"This is my game, too," I said. I reached under the dash of my car
and retrieved the shotgun, got the .45 from the car pocket and stuck it
in my belt. The Luger was back under my arm.

Culhane sighed with exasperation. "Okay," he replied. "Open the
Packard door on the driver's side and stand behind it with the window
rolled down." And to his crew: "No shooting until it's necessary. This
is between me and Guilfoyle. If the rest of them insist on a fight, we've
got them in a cross fire."

Culhane took off his tuxedo jacket, laid it out neatly on the front
seat of the car, and rolled his right shirtsleeve up to the elbow. He took
the warrant for Riker out of the jacket's inside pocket and slipped it in
his back pocket. He took a wooden box from under the seat, opened it,
and took out the six-gun, a Peacemaker in a tanned leather holster. He
slid it out of the holster, spun the cylinder and checked the load, then
dropped it back in its holster. He hitched the Peacemaker to his hip
and tied the holster right against his leg.

"Kill the car lights," said Culhane, and they blinked off. The only
light came from the garish red sign next to the lodge.

Wisps of fog dampened everything.

Culhane stood in front of the Packard, with one foot on the bumper
and his forearm resting on his knee.

All eyes were on the road from Mendosa.

A deathly silence fell over the blockade, interrupted occasionally
by a cricket fiddling for its mate or night birds talking to each other.

We waited.

But not for long.

CHAPTER 39

Thin and wispy, the fog began to creep in. It swirled knee-deep, pressed against the earth by cool night air. Light from the camp's red neon sign turned the mist into a red glow that enveloped the cars.

Culhane stared down the road toward Mendosa and smoked quietly. I wondered what was going through his mind. Was his political career ruined by the implications of an old frame-up? Or would it be enhanced by revelations that Riker was a monster who ordered up death the way some people order a steak dinner? Now Riker's hands were also drenched with the blood of Henry Dahlmus. And we had an eyewitness to prove he had committed that crime himself.

Culhane's play was to get past Guilfoyle to get to Riker. My play was to bring down Riker for arranging Verna Wilensky's murder.

In the darkness above the circle of light around the cars, I saw a new slender ridge of light appear. Culhane saw it, too. He straightened slightly and watched it grow, forming silhouettes of the trees as it got closer.

"Heads up," Culhane said.

The ridge of light grew brighter and reshaped into a pair of haloed orbs. Headlights, which rose over a slight crest in the road.

Culhane said, "Lights!"

The headlights of our cars clashed with the oncoming headlights like knights galloping toward each other full tilt. The lead car coming toward us slammed on its brakes and screeched to a stop thirty feet in front of us. The car following stopped a few feet short of rear-ending it.

Nobody moved. Fog swirled around us and was carried off by the wind.

Culhane split the butt of his cigarette, poured out the residue, balled up the paper, and popped it in his mouth.

"Is Guilfoyle in there?" he barked. "Or doesn't he have the guts to do his dirty work himself."

A minute crawled by before the front door on the driver's side opened and a long leg stepped out, followed by the rest of Guilfoyle's enormous frame. He stared into the lights. He was wearing a yellow suit with a vest, and a flowered tie. A brown derby was cocked over one eye and a cigar lingered forgotten in the corner of his mouth. He slammed the door behind him and said in a loud voice, "Everybody stay put until I say otherwise."

He hooked two thumbs in his vest pockets, strolled to the front of the car, and leaned against the front fender of his black Cadillac.

Guilfoyle took the cigar out of his mouth and spit at Culhane's shoe.

"What are you and yer Boy Scouts doing out tonight?" he sneered. "Do you get a merit badge for learning how to take a leak in the dark?"

"No," Culhane said, "we get our merit badges for landing two-bit bottom-feeders like you."

Guilfoyle's face clouded up. He paced back and forth from one side of the Cadillac to the other and stopped with his right side toward the car and put his right foot on the bumper. An automatic glistened threateningly from under his jacket.

"Watch out, he's a southpaw," I mumbled to Culhane.

While Culhane kept the uncouth Irish thug talking, Bobby Aaron pulled up behind the two mobster cars, blocking them in.

Guilfoyle looked back at Aaron's car, then at Culhane. Worry furrowed his brow.

"What the hell's going on?" he demanded.

Culhane reached in his back pocket and took out the warrant on Guilfoyle for harboring.

"I got a warrant here for your arrest, signed by State Supreme Court Judge Gray," Culhane lied. "I'd show it to you but you can't read."

"For what?"

"Aiding and abetting in first-degree murder, harboring known felons, attempted murder of two Los Angeles police officers. Want me to go on?"

"On what authority?" Guilfoyle sneered.

"You're in my county," Culhane said. He looked over his shoulder and said, "Show him, Max."

The one-eyed deputy flicked on the spotlight on the side of the Packard, and swept its beam to the side of the road about forty feet behind Guilfoyle's car. A sign read COUNTY LINE.

Guilfoyle's jaw began to twitch.

"Hey, Rusty," Culhane said without taking his eyes off Guilfoyle, "show this muttonhead our guest of honor."

Rusty opened the office door in Lefton's lodge and pulled Earl out. He stared across the road at Guilfoyle.

"Earl here's all the witness we need," Culhane said. "We been playing twenty questions. You know how to play twenty questions, Guilfoyle? It's like I ask him, what's bigger than a grain of sand and smaller than a pea, and he says, Guilfoyle's brain."

Culhane took a pair of handcuffs out off his pocket and held them up, letting them dangle like a noose in the lights of the cars. "Reach around with your right hand, take out that peashooter of yours, and drop it on the ground," he ordered.

To my right, I heard two shotguns click as shells were charged into chambers.

There was movement inside Guilfoyle's car.

"Fuck you," Guilfoyle snarled, turning full face toward Culhane.

"Either you throw down your gun or I'll take it away from you," Culhane said calmly.

Guilfoyle stood fast. The fingers of his left hand began to twitch.

"You, boys!" Culhane yelled to Guilfoyle's crew. "Don't be stupid. You're in a cross fire. Give up your hardware and nobody gets hurt."

He took a step toward Guilfoyle, and the big mobster's left hand flashed toward his automatic.

Culhane bent his knees in a crouch as he swept the .44 from its holster. He fanned the hammer back as he brought his gun hand up and fired.

It sounded like a cannon.

The big man grunted as if he had been punched in the stomach. Culhane's bullet tore into Guilfoyle's abdomen, knocking him backward onto the grille of the Caddy. He looked shocked but the bullet didn't stop him. Growling like a wounded animal, he pushed himself off the grille and blindly fired a shot. It chipped the road under the Packard and whined off in the dark.

Culhane fanned off two more shots.

Both into Guilfoyle's chest.

He screamed as he was knocked backward again. His elbow smashed out a headlight. His breath wheezed out of him like air wheezing out of a balloon. The derby flew off his head and bounced at his feet. Deep red blood oozed from the wounds in his chest and stomach.

He swung his gun up as his chin fell against his chest and fired another shot. It nicked Culhane's shoulder, kicking a tuft of his silk shirt into the air.

Culhane said nothing. He held his arm at full length and fired again. The last shot knocked Guilfoyle's head straight back. His eyes rolled up. He slumped and his right arm draped over the headlight support as his legs turned to rubber. He fell straight down and dangled from the support.

The passenger door flew open and a gunman jumped out, swinging a tommy gun. Culhane whirled, fell to one knee, and fanned off his last two shots. One smacked into the gunman's cheek. His head snapped back, its side bursting into a plume of blood and bone. His hat floated off and rolled into the darkness. The shot spun him around. His finger tightened on the trigger and the stutter gun ripped a trench in the ground at his feet, blew out the front tire, and sent the hubcap spinning away. He fell facedown, his feet crossed at the ankles.

Inside Guilfoyle's car a shape moved, a shotgun swung up.

"Look out!" Max yelled, shoving Culhane out of the way as he leveled a sawed-off shotgun at the windshield and fired both barrels. The left side of the windshield splattered and crumbled in on itself. Behind it, the mobster took the full blast in his face. Blood and bone showered the backseat as he was smacked backward.

The last gunman started screaming.

"Don't shoot, don't shoot, I'm finished," he cried, and threw his .45 out the car window. It was followed by his wiggling empty hands. Max pulled the door open, grabbed a fistful of shirt and tie, dragged him from the car, and threw him on the ground. He lay there whimpering, his face and suit splattered with the blood of his dead partner.

In the rear car, pistols and shotguns came flying out of windows. Hands were wiggling to show they were empty. One by one, four more of Guilfoyle's shooters tumbled out with their hands straight up over their heads.

The smell of cordite was whisked away by the wind.

Culhane stood up and brushed himself off. He looked at his shoulder. "Ruined my best shirt," he said.

"You okay?" Max asked.

"Thanks to you," Culhane said, and smacked him on the shoulder.

I did a dead head count as Culhane walked over to Guilfoyle, still dangling from the headlight support. He wrenched the .45 from Guilfoyle's taut fist, held it behind him, and Max took it. Blood showered down the side of Guilfoyle's face and spurted from the holes in his suit.

"Nice shooting," I said.

"Buck Tallman used to say shooting's just like swimming," Culhane replied, holstering the Peacemaker. "You never forget how."

He watched as the four hooligans from the rear car were herded up to us by Bobby Aaron.

"You know the setup at Shuler's?" Culhane asked me.

I nodded.

"How much security?"

"Lightweights. Ski and I got in without any problem—until Guilfoyle showed up."

"They know you?"

"They wouldn't remember me, it was dark."

"Bring Earl up here," Culhane said. "You know where Riker's holed up?" he asked the gunman.

"I wasn't there when he came in, but I'm guessin' he's on the third floor of the rage ward. That's where the VIPs usually stay. There's a swimming pool on the first floor, and the second floor is for the loonies, the ones they chain to the floor."

"How do we get in?"

"Only one staircase up to three. Got a steel door, so it's hard to break in. The elevator's the only other entrance to three. It's at the end of a short hall from a private door. It could be a death trap."

Culhane walked back and forth in front of him for a minute or so.

"Okay," he said to his crew, "here's the plan. We go in with two cars. Morningdale's gonna drive one car, with Rusty beside him and

Redd and Max in the backseat. Aaron drives the other car, with me and two backups. Morningdale will get us through the gate. You do anything fancy, Morningdale, Redd'll cut your throat. You understand that?"

"I understand," he nodded. A tear of sweat wriggled down the side of his face.

"What we want is surprise."

I heard myself say, "No," again.

Culhane looked at me with surprise.

"No?" he said.

"You're trying to count me out again," I said. "Riker's mine. I started this case and I'm going to finish it. You sit this one out, you've done more than enough. And you might still have a political career to worry about. I'll ride shotgun with Morningdale. Redd and Lenny in the backseat. Aaron drives with Rusty, and Max in the other car. We'll assume he's holed up in one of those apartments at the sanitarium."

"That's where he's at, the sanitarium," one of Guilfoyle's men, Bloom, offered suddenly. "I drove him and Guilfoyle up to building B from the boat. There's four apartments on the third floor."

"How many entrances in and out?" I asked.

"It's a fire trap," he said. "There's only three doors in on the first floor and one of them goes straight to an elevator—express to the third floor so the big shots can go in and out without entering the main building. There's staircases on each end of the building, but only one of them goes to the third floor."

"That's the one with the steel door to three?"

"Right."

I drew a little sketch with my finger in the dirt beside the road and studied it.

"There's also a staircase to the roof right next to the elevator," he said. "It's the only access to the roof."

"So if we cover the elevator and the third-floor door to the staircase, we've got him boxed," I said.

"If you can get onto the third floor," they both agreed.

"That is, of course, if he's there," said Culhane.

"Let's go find out," I said.

CHAPTER 40

It was a little past midnight when we drove through the gate in the eight-foot stone wall and kept going as quietly as we could, past the pond down to the Victorian main building of the Shuler Institute. The guard at the gate saw Earl and waved us through. There was a light over the door and a dim night-light in the main office, but the place was deserted.

We cut off our car lights and followed the gravel drive around the main building, guided by the moon. We stopped under a group of trees and turned the car off. The second car followed. I got out, walked to the edge of the trees, and listened.

It was deathly quiet. A cricket chirped way down at the end of the property and an occasional breeze whisked the leaves. Otherwise there was not a sound.

The rage ward loomed behind the main office building like a haunted Victorian mansion etched by moonlight. Like the main building, the third floor had four large gables, one facing in each direction, their spires reaching up like daggers toward the full moon. The second floor had several high windows on each side. That would be the ward for "the loonies" as Morningdale had called them. The first floor, apparently the gym and swimming pool, was windowless.

There was a single light on. It cast an eerie yellow glow from the gabled window facing west, toward the Pacific. Otherwise, the building could have been deserted.

"Is that where Riker's holed up?" I whispered to Morningdale.

"Probably," Earl said. "I know Dahlmus had the south room, and me and that nut from Baltimore each had a room."

* * *

In the darkness of the south room, Riker had watched the two cars drift under the trees and stop. Was it Guilfoyle and his bunch coming back? They had left in a hurry, he assumed to pick up Earl and that loopy one in the gaudy shirt. Riker sat on the window seat, saw two of the men come to the edge of the grove of trees and stare up at the building. He began to get nervous. He took out a cigarette, cupped his hand when he lit the match.

Big Redd squatted in the safety of the trees and stared hard at the one darkened window he could see. Then he thought he saw a flare. He squinted his eyes. Not sure. He focused on the dark window. Then he saw a red pinpoint brighten for a second. He picked up a pebble and tossed it at Bannon.

I felt a stone hit my leg, turned around, and saw Redd, hunched down. He made a motion for me to move back and with the other hand pantomimed someone taking a drag on a cigarette. Then he pointed to the dark window on the south side of the third floor. I moved back and focused on it, saw a momentary glow. Someone was in there. Smoking. Watching us. Now we had a problem. If it was Riker, we couldn't move from the cover of the trees without being spotted.

The gravel road wound down past several utility buildings and swept around the rage ward, almost to the end of the large compound, before circling back to the main entrance. There wasn't a cloud in the sky and the moon was so bright there was no possibility of making a dash across fifty yards of lawn to the entrance of the secured building without being spotted. Riker could be sitting there with a high-powered rifle, ready to take down anyone who entered the building.

There was one possibility. At a certain point, the driveway came within ten yards of the southwestern corner of the building. From the third floor of the building, it would be impossible to tell how many people were in the car. Also, from any one of the gabled rooms, it was only possible to see any three sides of the building.

I decided to send our two fastest runners, Redd and Aaron, to zigzag fifty yards across the lawn to the cover of two bays of trees under the south window. At the same time, one-eyed Max would drive straight to the northeast corner of the building, and one-armed Lenny, Rusty, and I would pile out of the car and blow the lock on the door Riker could not see. Once inside, our objective would be to cross the swimming pool room, to the stairwell on the southern side of the building. I would go up the stairs followed by Rusty, and hopefully trap Riker on the top floor, while Lenny and Max would cover the entrance to the elevator. Redd and Aaron would make a dash for the building and back me up. Riker's only option then would be the roof.

There was still that *if*. What if Riker was someplace else? Maybe making a run for it on a boat. Maybe some pilot was flying in to pick him up and fly him down to Mexico. Riker was a devious, psychopathic, cold-blooded killer. No time to worry about what-ifs. I had to move.

Riker watched the copse of trees, wondering what their next move would be. He had to assume that Culhane and Bannon were down below with plenty of backup. And if that was the case, he also had to assume that Guilfoyle had been trapped or arrested at Lefton's place. Maybe even killed. Riker had to get off the third floor. To stay there was suicidal.

Below him, two dark figures darted from the trees, dodging like rabbits in the moonlight, and behind them, one of the cars roared from the shelter of the small orchard.

The car was heading for the north side of the building. His blind side.

He had only one option. Get off the third floor and go through the second-floor ward to the north side of the building.

And create a diversion.

As he ran from his apartment and down the hall, he was smiling. Culhane and Bannon commanded the top of his hate list.

What a diversion he had planned for them.

Rusty handcuffed Earl to the branch of a eucalyptus tree.

"One sound outta you and you're morgue meat," I said, then jumped in the car.

We screeched down the gravel drive, slued around the corner, the car's rear wheels spewing stretches of lawn behind them, and slammed to a stop. The four of us piled out. The door's interior lock was a bar lock, a long steel slat running the width of the door. It could only be unlocked from the inside by a key.

"Lose the door," I said to Rusty, who swung his pump shotgun up and blew the hinges off. We charged through and ran around the pool to the exit on the south side. That door was unlocked.

As Lenny and Max headed for the elevator, I followed Rusty up the stairs, two at a time, to the third floor. There was a short flight of steps, a landing, then another flight up to the second-floor landing and the door to the ward for the insane.

Riker was waiting for us when we reached the first landing. As we rounded the corner, his shotgun roared, echoing up and down the narrow stairs. It deafened me for a moment but the blast hit Rusty in the legs, just below the knee.

I squeezed off three shots as fast as I could but Riker had spun back around the corner.

Rusty rolled down the stairs to the landing, his legs shredded by buckshot. I jumped down and pulled him around the corner just as Riker got off another shot. It ripped a three-foot hole in the wall. And once again, Riker was gone.

Eerie screams came from the rage ward. At first one or two, then a chorus of terrified cries and shrieks. I peeked around the corner just as Riker fired a third load of buckshot into the lock of the mental ward. Riker dove through the doorway, my shot missing him by inches.

Rusty was groaning in pain. I got on the walkie-talkie. "This is Bannon. Rusty's down with leg wounds. I think it hit an artery. Riker's in the mental ward, going north. Get a doctor and get some backup to the north door. I'm in pursuit."

"On the way," Max answered.

I took off my jacket, wrapped a sleeve around Rusty's thigh, and used the shotgun barrel as a tourniquet to stop the arterial blood pumping from one leg.

He pointed up the stairs. "Go, go," his lips told me.

Like the hounds of hell, screaming, moaning, babbling howls led me up the stairs into bedlam.

The mental patients were raving mad, chained to beds, clutching at Riker, tearing at his clothes. They were scratching his face, some looking for a savior, some striking out in fear. He was slashing at them with his shotgun and punching them, dragging them and their beds as he raced toward the far door. Another group rushed me as I charged in. Under the dim rays of the overhead night-lights, they were faceless hands and arms clutching at me, restrained only by the chains that bound them either to the floor or their beds. I spun around, trying to break loose, when I heard Riker's shotgun roar again. On the other end of the ward I saw two or three inmates spin away from him, screaming in pain. He turned and fired a second blast into another group. Bodies lurched as the buckshot ripped into them.

Then Riker saw me. He shook loose the last of his attackers, dodged through the door, and raced down the stairs leading to the pool room.

I holstered my Luger and tried to break free of the terrified people surrounding me so I could follow him.

Riker reached the first floor and ducked into the pool room. Adrenaline-spiked, he looked as crazed as the victims he had left on the second floor. He went to the corner of the room, pulled open the door. A broom closet. He went to the next. A large boiler rumbled in one corner, fed by gas and feeding hot water into the heated pool. Riker backed across to the room to the door, aimed at the gas valve, fired his shotgun, and dove through the opening.

I was halfway across the ward when I heard the boom of the shotgun followed by the gas explosion. The floor erupted, showering the room with bodies, bedding, chairs, shards of tile. An instant later, a geyser of flame burst through the hole. The searing blast struck me, throwing me on my back. The whole room began to tremble. Flames ate the deck, the ceiling, the walls.

Inmates were tossed around like puppets without strings.

A young woman staggered toward me, her brown hair ablaze. I scurried across the floor, pulled her down, and beat out the flames with my hands.

A crack jagged across the floor under me. I started to get up. There was another explosion. More debris swept through the room.

The floor split open and collapsed beneath me.

I plunged, arms and legs flailing, straight down into the swimming pool below.

It knocked my breath out. I was in a surreal world. A world of debris, of gowned bodies chained to sleeping-cots, a world tainted by orange flames reflecting off the surface above.

I hit bottom, got my legs under me, pushed upward through the wreckage to the surface, and burst out gasping for breath. The building was ablaze around me. As I reached the side, a hand grabbed my wrist and pulled me out of the pool. It was Max. He shoved me along the edge of the pool, shielding me from the flames, to the north door.

We rushed outside. Cool night air filled my lungs. Then I remembered
Rusty.

"Rusty?" I asked.

"He's hurting but he's okay," Max said, as we rushed away from
the flaming pyre.

"Riker . . ."

"I didn't see him."

Inmates in their white gowns were staggering around the yard,
babbling inanely, some pointing at the blazing ward and giggling,
some flailing at their burning gowns.

"He can't be far," I said. He went one way, I went another, both of
us working our way through the stunned victims of the fire. Behind
me, another fireball erupted from the burning building.

In the flare of the explosion I saw Riker.

He was twenty yards ahead of me, wielding a switchblade, slashing
at the crazed tenants. He grabbed one of the inmates by the hair, threw
him to his knees, slashed his throat, and pulled off his gown, putting it
on himself.

"Riker!" I yelled.

He turned and looked at me. I pulled my Luger and walked
toward him.

He looked down at my gun and then back at me and laughed.

"That pistol's soaking wet. It isn't worth shit," he hissed. He held
the knife toward me.

"Come on," he said, and rushed at me. I held the Luger at arm's
length and squeezed the trigger.

It misfired.

He was so close I could feel the heat from his burning body when
he slashed my arm with the knife. As he did, another screaming human comet rushed to him, grabbed him, and knocked him down. Riker
tried to struggle free but the human torch was twice his size. Flames
licked at Riker's purloined robe, etched up it, set Riker's hair on fire.
As fire engulfed them both, he kicked and screamed, and finally rolled
over and broke free of his fiery captor. His terrified eyes locked on
mine for a moment. He charged up at me.

He was three feet away from me, engulfed in fire, his face literally
melting from the flames, when I heard the *whoosh* and saw a flash of
silver an instant before the thick knife blade pierced his throat. It cut

windpipe and jugular and went all the way through his neck, stopped only by the hilt of the bowie knife.

Riker's scream was cut off as air rushed from his lungs and blood spewed from his jugular, and the vile mixture of breath and blood burst from his throat. Riker's mouth gaped open. I stared into eyes of pure madness and watched life flicker out of them before he fell dead.

Big Redd walked up and looked at my arm. He pulled out his shirt, tore a strip off the tail, and tied it tight just above the knife wound.

"Thanks," I said. "That's two I owe you."

"One," he said. "Charlie and I fished together."

It was the second and last time I heard him speak a word.

CHAPTER 41

In the morning's light, the back side of the Shuler Institute looked like a battlefield. The security building had burned itself out and collapsed into the swimming pool. All that was left was a huge pile of charred lumber. Firemen were rolling up their hoses, the last ambulance and the last of the hearses had pulled out.

A tall, burly man in a state trooper's uniform, with one of those Boy Scout hats pulled down low on his forehead, found me drinking coffee in a clinic they had set up in one of the smaller buildings. A kindly old doctor had used twelve stitches to sew my arm back together.

The trooper offered me his wolf's paw of a hand and said, "I'm Major Stacks, from up at the San Luis Obispo Station. Are you up to a few questions?"

"Sure," I said. "I could use a drink about now but people would talk."

He smiled formally and took out a pad and pen.

"What was the final death toll here?" I asked.

"Seventeen dead, fourteen injured." He said it as casually as if he were talking about the score of a football game. "Could you just kind of run over the events of last night for me?"

I remembered Moriarity's advice: "Keep it simple." I started with the APB on Riker and Dahlmus, gave him the front-page version up to the shoot-out at the Shuler Corral, and ended with Riker stabbing the defenseless mental patient and Big Redd's bowie knife ending Riker's days among the living.

"Well, that's pretty much the way the big Indian says it ended," Walker said.

"And far be it from me to contradict anything a big Indian with a

412

bowie knife might tell you," I said. Then I held up my arm. "Riker sliced about six inches out of this before Mr. Redd came to my rescue."

He flipped his book shut and nodded his thanks. "You will be around if we have any other questions, won't you?"

"You can find me at Central Homicide in L.A. anytime."

"Little off your beat, weren't you?" he said.

"I had bad directions."

He shook his head and smiled.

"By the way, did you hear about Captain Culhane?" he said, stopping at the door.

"Did something happen to him?"

"Osterfelt and Bellini announced this morning that they were joining forces. Osterfelt is running for governor and Bellini will run for lieutenant governor. Culhane announced he was cancelling his plans to run and dropped out of the race about thirty minutes ago."

"Thanks for the news," I said, but he was already gone.

It was noon when I drove up to The Breakers. I parked in front of the place, locked the car as usual, and went in. As I headed for the ballroom, the desk clerk waved at me.

"Sir," he said with a little spit in his tone.

I ignored him. I wasn't in the mood.

Then he snapped his fingers at me. *Snapped his fingers!* I admit I looked like hell. But snapping fingers at human beings does not sit well with me. I went back to the desk. He looked me up and down, and raised his nose an inch or two.

"Excuse me, sir. Are you *visiting* someone?"

I held my arm at full length under his nose and snapped my fingers four or five times in his face, real fast.

"Do you like that, pal?" I said. "Do you like being treated like a dog?"

He didn't know what to do. He started to babble, but I walked away and went up the stairs to the ballroom.

Little had changed since the night before. The ballroom ceiling was still covered with red, white, and blue balloons, with red, white, and blue streamers sagging between them. The tablecloths were still the same patriotic colors, as were the paper cups and platters. There was a small bandstand at the end of the room and the music stands were the national colors. But a lot of the balloons had lost air and were flitting around the dance floor under the ceiling fans. There was no band. The large tables on either side of the dance floor were covered with cold cuts, various kinds of bread, potato salad, and baked beans in tureens, but there was no one to eat all the food.

Culhane was the only person in the room.

His tie was off and his shirt open and his tux jacket was hung over the back of his chair. He was having a drink.

I walked the length of the room, kicking balloons out of my way, and stopped at the food table to put together a roast beef on rye bread with plenty of mayo and commandeer a bottle of Budweiser from a large tub filled with ice.

"Just like a cop," Culhane growled. "Never pass up a free feed."

I sat down across from him and took a swig of beer.

"And a beer drinker to boot."

"Only when I'm eating," I said, and held the bottle up in a toast to him.

"What's that for? You toasting to my defeat?"

"Look at it this way: you scared the hell out of them for a few days and took a walk. The voters deserve Osterfoos and Beldini or whatever the hell their names are."

I took a bite of my sandwich and washed it down with a swig of beer.

"If it's any consolation," I said. "I would have voted for you. Hell, I probably could have lined up half the L.A. police force for you."

He smiled ruefully. "I should have known those two had something up their sleeves. I wonder how they decided which one was gonna get the big job."

I shrugged. "Whoever had the most dirt on the other one."

"I hear you guys put on quite a show down there in Mendosa," he said, changing the subject.

"You would have loved it," I said. "We burned down half the institute and used up more ammo than you guys did in the Big War. Hell, it was like the Fourth of July." I finished the sandwich, then added, "Riker's right where he should have been all along. Dead."

"You did a good job, Cowboy. I once said you were a bulldog. Grab ahold and never let go."

"Thanks. Just for the record, if Redd hadn't iced the son of a bitch, I would have."

He looked across the table at me and smiled one of those enigmatic smiles of his. He knew what I meant. With Riker out of the way, the state would deep-six the case against Culhane for framing Riker. There was nobody left to file a complaint and why bother? It was a twenty-year-old case and Riker had proved to be a murderous psycho. They probably wouldn't have proceeded with it anyway, since Riker had finally ended up having Wilma Thompson killed. But I also knew Brodie would carry the stain of the frame-up for the rest of his career

"You know Osterfelt might even offer you the attorney general's spot," I said.

"Suure." He chuckled. "When the sun rises in the west."

"Why didn't you stay in the race? Everybody in the state would've known them for the bottom-feeders they are."

"It costs a lot of money to run that kind of race. Most of it would've come from friends of mine."

"They can afford it."

"I couldn't do that, Cowboy, take their money knowing I couldn't win."

"Maybe next time," I said. "When the voters have a taste of what those two are really like. If it means anything to you, I think you would have been a helluva governor for a year, maybe two. Before the money boys and pols and kingmakers got their claws into you."

"You think that would have happened?"

"It always happens. The key to being a successful politician is compromise, Brodie. And once you compromise, you're hooked. After that, it's downhill all the way."

"You are a cynic."

"Nope, a realist. It happens in all walks. A cop takes an apple. The next thing it's a buck. Then ten bucks, and the next thing you know he's sitting in the backseat of a police car altering ballots on election night for fifty bucks a vote. If I learned one thing about you, you don't compromise easily."

"Look who's talkin'," he said. "How come you never got hooked?"

"Because they don't have anything to offer me. I don't *want* anything. I'm happy doing what I'm doing."

"Everybody wants *some*thing, Cowboy."

"You're probably right. But in my case, it wouldn't have a price tag on it. You and I are alike in that respect. You sure didn't want to be governor for the money, you wanted to be governor to clean out that nest of crooks in Sacramento. Or maybe I'm wrong, Brodie, maybe just driving them all crazy would have been enough for you."

"We'll never know, will we?" he said, still smiling.

I finished my sandwich and washed the remains down with the rest of my beer. I wiped my mouth with the back of my hand. Then I heard a click behind me and looked around. In a dark corner, a lighter flared into light and I saw Delilah O'Dell's face for a moment. It snapped out and smoke curled from the shadows.

"Why don't you join us," I said.

"I'd rather listen to the two of you telling each other how swell you are."

But she got up and came over to the table anyway. She was in full blossom, as always. She was wearing a tan shantung pantsuit, with a maroon scarf around her long neck.

"How's the arm?" she asked.

"Just another scar to add to the ones I have already."

"That rich dame likes scars, does she?" Delilah said, taking out the makings and rolling two cigarettes.

"What do you know about that rich dame?"

She peered up at me and smirked.

"Who do you think you're talking to?" she said. "Where do you think Brodie found out about that sissy dog of yours?"

"Mata Hari, huh?" I said.

"She was a piker."

She lit the two butts, and gave Culhane and me each one. I looked around at what was left of Culhane's run for governor.

"Where are all those swells with the money who were making you look like a winner last night?"

"After I made my bow-out speech, they all went up to the golf course."

"How about Brett Merrill and Ben?"

"They feel bad for me. But I don't have to tell you that."

"That was cute, the way you got off the subject about the lady banker," Delilah said.

"You probably know more about her than I do," I said.

"You ought to marry her," Delilah said. "Better than working for a living."

"I'm not sure she's cut out to be a cop's wife," I said.

"I'm not sure you're cut out to be a rich boy," Culhane said.

We got another laugh out of that.

"Better go home and change clothes before you go by her place," said Delilah. "Unless you want to scare her to death."

"I got one question to ask before I head out," I said.

"Christ, you never change," Culhane said.

"It's for Delilah."

"Oh?" she said, raising her eyebrows.

"Did the shooting at Grand View happen just the way they say?"

She looked at me for a long minute and said, "It happened exactly the way Brodie said it did."

I nodded and got up to leave. Then I said to her, "But if it had happened some other way, you'd still say it happened the way Brodie said it did, wouldn't you?"

"You bet your sweet ass I would," she said with a smile, and without hesitation. Then she added, "You just don't get it."

"No. Maybe someday I'll understand why Wilma Thompson and Lila Parrish went on the lam. And who paid them to do it." I shrugged. "Who cares anyway, right?"

Wrong. I did care. I felt sorry for Wilma. After looking for happiness all those years, she still ended up dead.

"I'm sorry about Eddie Woods's wife," I said.

His face got very sad. He looked out the window as if there were answers out there to questions we all have about life and death.

Delilah started to say something but Culhane cut her off.

"Innocents always get caught in the cross fire," he said.

"What's the dif," I said. "By tomorrow, it'll be old news."

I got up to leave and we shook hands.

"For what it's worth," I said, "I think you're an honorable guy. We just play by different rules."

"Don't bet on it."

"Thanks for the sandwich," I said, kicking my way through the balloons on the way to the door.

"Hey, Cowboy," Culhane called after me.

I stopped and looked back at him.

"You're a helluva snoop," he said. "But you had your nose up the wrong dog's ass on this one."

"I think you're half right," I said.

"Don't you ever admit you're wrong?"

"Why bother?"

"Well, just remember one thing."

"What's that?"

He gave me a farewell smile.

"I told you so," Thomas Brodie Culhane said.

CHAPTER 42

I drove back to the house, made a big fuss over Rosie, and gave him two cans of dog food and an extra bone. I kept my arm out of the shower so the bandage wouldn't get wet, then dressed in my best navy slacks and blue shirt. I stopped by the drugstore and picked up the most expensive bottle of champagne they had, and went next door to the toy store to get a tin bucket, the kind kids take to the beach. There was a little girl, no more than eight or nine, selling roses on the corner. Ten cents apiece. She had sixteen left. I bought them all and gave her five bucks. I thought she was going to cry.

It was getting dusk when I turned into Millie's drive.

She opened the door before I got to it.

"Hi," I said, "I happened to be in the neighbor . . ."

She didn't let me finish. She pulled me in the house and put the roses and the pail with the champagne on a table near the door and she kissed my cheeks and my lips, and then took the pail and led me up the stairs and into her bathroom. She turned on the faucets to the tub and poured in a bottle of bubble bath. She unbuttoned my shirt slowly, kissing my chest as she did. She unzipped my pants and pulled them down, and sat me down on the edge of the tub and took off my shoes and socks. Then she slowly unbuttoned her shirt and let it fall on the floor, and slipped off her tennis shorts and panties. She stuck a toe in the water, eased herself down into the bubbles, then took my hands and led me into the tub facing her.

Then she noticed the bandage.

"My God, what happened?" she said with alarm.

"Later," I said. "How about the champagne?"

"Later," she murmured.

I settled into the tub and she slipped her legs around my hips and took my arm and gently kissed the wound.

"How bad is it?" she asked softly.

"Well," I whispered, "I think it may have ruined my dreams of becoming a concert pianist."

She locked her legs around me and slid me to her.

"Thank God," she whispered in my ear. "I hate Chopin."

EPILOGUE

1946

B annon got a card from Brodie Culhane once while he was overseas. Christmas, 1944. He was in some little town in Normandy. He didn't remember its name. There wasn't enough left to remember.

"I know how it is at Christmas," Brodie had written. "I'll think of you and hoist a glass of Irish Mist. One cube, please. Take care of yourself, Cowboy." It was signed "Santa C."

It had reached Bannon on January third, but it was the thought that counted.

Not a word since, except the card he had received two days ago. And now he was driving down the hill into San Pietro as he had five years before. Nothing had changed except the trees were a little taller and there was a different movie playing at the theater and Max and Lenny weren't riding herd on him.

He had said very little on the drive up, and the night before he had sat out by the pool, soaking his leg and rereading the file he had kept through the years. It was in a footlocker he had left with her when he went off to the army. He hadn't paid any attention to the old locker until he got the card, when they got back from their honeymoon.

He read it, showed it to her, then went down in the storm cellar, opened the trunk, and dug it out.

A closed case to everyone but you, Zee, Millicent had thought.

She didn't ask him about it and they had talked little about the old file on the trip up, but she knew that there were questions in its yellowing pages that had gnawed at him since he had come back from San Pietro that last time. She had sat quietly with her hand on his leg, watching the foothills grow into mountains.

He was going to find the answers.

He took a left at the bottom of the hill, drove up to The Breakers, and parked in front of the entrance.

The valet was a sharp little noodle in a tailored uniform, hair slicked back and a solicitous smile on his face. The closer he got to the car, the more the smile changed from con man to awe. He stopped beside the car and ran the flat of his hand very lightly across the hood.

"Fine," he said. "Italian paint job."

He backed up about six feet, checked her out, and came back.

"Twelve cylinders. Speedometer top: one-sixty."

"Close. One-eighty," Bannon said.

"British leather and I'll bet she's got a Sternberg radio in the dash."

"Muellenberg."

He whistled low with great appreciation.

"You think you could find a place to park this baby so she don't get dinged up or get a door scratched?" Bannon said as he struggled out of the driver's seat. The kid walked over to help him and he handed the youngster his cane.

"I can handle it," Zeke said. "Hold on to this for me." He got out and took the cane, then the kid ran around to the other side of the car and opened the door for Millie. She was stunning as always, dressed in pastel colors: a pale blue skirt and a pink blouse, and she was wearing a yellow straw hat, its brim flopping down around her ears, with her silken hair sweeping over her shoulders. The kid was dazzled. He forgot the car for a minute as he helped her down to the running board and onto the walk. Then he bowed from the waist.

"Thank you," she said, and flashed him a million-dollar smile. Bannon handed him a five-dollar bill but the kid shook his head.

"No, sir," he said, looking at the two rows of ribbons on Bannon's khaki shirt. "I ought to be paying you for the privilege of driving it across the street."

Then he ran around the front of the car, climbed aboard, and ran his hands lovingly around the oak steering wheel.

They entered the lobby, where Brett Merrill was sitting across the way. He stood up, loped across the room, and shook Bannon's hand hard enough to loosen a tooth.

"Good to see you, Zeke," he said with a smile that lit up the soft light of the lobby. "How's the leg?"

"It's fine," Bannon said. "I carry the cane to keep my balance. Millicent, this is Brett Merrill."

"How do you do, Mrs. Bannon," he said with courtly grace, and brushed the back of her hand with his lips. "What a delight to meet you."

As always, a Southern gentleman to the core.

"Let's have a drink," Merrill said.

They sat down in the barroom, which was an elegant recessed alcove off the main lobby. Nothing seemed to have changed in the hotel since Bannon had last seen it.

Merrill said to the waiter, "I know what the gentleman will have, unless his taste has changed. Irish Mist, neat, with one cube of ice." And to Millicent, "What will you have, my dear?"

"Amaretto on the rocks," she answered, her voice a startling blend of softness and strength. She reached over and held Bannon's hand. It was a gentle move, one that subtly proclaimed her affection for him. Her eyes said the rest.

When the army had sent Bannon to the hospital in San Diego, Millicent had insisted on coming to see him. He had resisted at first. He wanted to get through rehab, get himself back to together, be whole again. Get rid of the demons that follow all men home from the battlefield: guilt because he had survived when others around him had died; fear that is so real it tastes like acid in the throat.

But she had come anyway, driving down to the hospital every weekend, nursing him back with love and caring, cheering him up when he got the blues, chasing away the nightmares. The war had added a few years to Bannon's handsome features, but he seemed fit and looked well.

"The place hasn't changed," he said, making conversation as he looked around the lobby.

"No," Merrill answered. "It's reached that traditional stage. I have a feeling it *will* change, though. Times have changed. The old place will have to catch up."

"That's too bad," Millicent said. "There's something to be said for tradition, don't you think?"

"I do indeed," Merrill answered.

"Sorry it took so long for us to get up here," Bannon said. "That last card from Brodie was in a stack of mail that was forwarded to me from the hospital. I guess it had been bouncing around APOs for a month or two. Hope he wasn't pissed that I didn't answer sooner."

"Brodie? Never," Merrill said.

"How's it going with him?"

"Still alive," Merrill said with a smile. "You know Brodie. He defies the odds." There was a catch in his voice when he said it.

"Hell, I didn't really know him at all," said Bannon.

"Yes, you did. In some ways, maybe more than any of us. You got in his skin, and you know a lot about a person when that happens. Otherwise you wouldn't be here."

He swallowed a couple of times and went on. "He had a heart attack last November. Actually, the day after Thanksgiving. We had breakfast together at Wendy's and we were walking up the courthouse steps. He was glad-handing everybody, as usual. All of a sudden he stopped and sat down on the steps and said, 'I think I'm having a heart attack. I feel like my chest is gonna explode.' He was right. Massive coronary. He almost didn't come back from that one. Doc Fleming gave him a week. Then two weeks, then two months. Two months later, he gave him six more weeks, and two months after that Brodie was holding court every day out in the garden. Smoking, having a couple of drinks, everything he wasn't supposed to do. But he was going downhill fast. You could see a change every day. Yesterday, when I asked how it was going, Fleming said, 'He's sicker than most dead people I know.'"

Neither of them said much for a minute or two.

"You're right about Brodie, Brett," Bannon said. "I knew him for what? Two weeks? But he stayed with me. I thought a lot about him through the years."

"That's the way it is with the Captain."

"It's that damned army mail system," Bannon said angrily. "The card should've been here weeks ago."

"He understands that. When he read Pennington's story about you getting the DSC and the Purple Heart, he did an Irish jig around the apartment. 'And shot in the leg, just like me, wouldn't you know it!' he said. He was very proud of you. It doesn't take two weeks to measure the strength of a man."

"How true," Millicent Bannon said, and looked at Bannon adoringly.

A lucky man, Merrill thought. And aloud, "Had a rough time of it, didn't you?"

"Not really," he answered. "Most of the time I was a glorified traffic cop, moving tanks, jeeps, half-tracks, quarter-tons through bottle-necks, getting them up to the front. We were near the German border and a German Tiger tank broke through the lines. We were caught in the middle of a firefight. I drove over a mine. Next thing I remember, I was under the damn jeep, with a fifty-caliber shooting at everything that moved. We slowed the bastard down just long enough for our artillery to get its range. It didn't help win the war. Just another hour in the life of World War Two."

"That isn't exactly the way I heard it," said Merrill.

"That's exactly the way it happened," Bannon said.

Merrill looked past him, smiled, and stood up.

"Here's Del," he said.

Delilah hadn't changed a bit. Not a wrinkle, not a smile line, not a gray hair. *Maybe Grand View was sitting on top of the fountain of youth,* thought Bannon.

"Hi, hero," she said, giving him a peck on the cheek and immediately turning her attention to his wife.

"You must be Millicent," she said, offering her hand. Bannon watched her quick appraisal, saw the glint in her eye. *All class, that's what she's thinking.*

"How are things at Grand View?" Bannon asked.

"Nothing's changed," her dusky voice answered. "Things seemed to freeze in time during the war. You're looking fit as a fiddle, Zeke." She looked back at Millicent with a smile. "Must be the company you keep. Congratulations."

"Thank you," Millicent answered. She was a bit ill at ease, like meeting in-laws for the first time, and Delilah sensed it. Then Millicent said, "I feel as if I know you all. Zee has told me a lot about you. Actually, I met him the day before he came to San Pietro for the first time."

"We saw the announcement in the *Times* that you two tied the knot."

"We sneaked up to Monterey and got married. Neither of us wanted a big wedding. It upset my family but they'll get over it."

"I didn't get the card until two days ago. It's the damned army mail system . . ." Bannon started to repeat the excuse.

"That's exactly what Brodie said."

There was a moment of awkward silence and then Delilah said, "He's out in the garden. Bring your drinks, we'll freshen them outside."

"I have to beg off," Merrill said. "Today's our anniversary. I'm taking Susan up to San Francisco for a week. We're going to hole up at the St. Francis, have room service, and make believe we're twenty again."

"Congratulations," said Millicent. "I'm sure you'll have a grand time."

They said their goodbyes and Merrill strode out of the hotel.

"Prepare yourself," Delilah said, leading them across the sprawling lobby and out the French doors. "He's taken a licking."

It was a dazzling day, cloudless with a hint of wind, and the garden nestled between two wings of the hotel was a spotless oasis of emerald green grass bordered with flowers. Beyond it, the Pacific was as serene as a fish pond.

Brodie Culhane was sitting under a striped umbrella at a secluded table surrounded by acacia trees. His frame was spare. His failing heart had stripped away most of his weight and hollowed his cheeks. His skin was stretched tight over thick bones and had an almost translucent quality. His thinning hair was white as a swan.

There was a blanket over his shoulders even though it was a warm day. But though his body had betrayed him, his indomitable spirit had refused to surrender. He sat in a wheelchair, straight as a billiard cue, and his blue eyes were as alert as ever. As they approached the table, the Captain's crooked, arrogant grin brightened his withered features.

"Well, it's about damned time," he said. His voice had lost some of its timbre but the rascally quality was still there. He turned his attention immediately to Millicent. He reached out, took her hand, and held it for a long time.

"Saw your picture in the society pages when you got married," he said gruffly. "Beautiful, but pictures don't do you justice. No wonder it took him so long to bring you up here. Probably afraid I'd steal your heart and we'd run off together."

"We might still," Mil said with mischief in her smile as well.

"She dragged my sorry carcass back to the living," Bannon said. "She wouldn't let me feel sorry for myself."

"You're a lucky man, Cowboy."

They sat down around the table, relaxed like old friends. Brodie's nature dispelled any sense of awkwardness. There was a small table beside him, with a bottle of Irish Mist and a sterling ice bucket sweating in the warm day. A half-dozen rolled cigarettes and a cheap lighter lay beside the bucket.

Brodie stared across the table at Zeke Bannon and saw a look he was familiar with, a look he still saw occasionally when he peered in the mirror.

"You heard them, didn't you," he said.

"Heard what?" Bannon asked.

"You know what I mean. You heard 'em flapping on your shoulder. Lying under the jeep, you figured he was there, come to get you. I know, pal, I heard 'em, too, lying in that ditch in France. Those wings. The Angel of Death, waiting to take you. Then he just flew away, like a robin you walk up on and scare off. That's how close you came. Scared you right to the bones, didn't it?"

Bannon didn't say anything but Millie reached out and took his hand.

"Ever tell Millie?" Culhane said.

"He did," she answered. "In his own way."

"Fear's a hard thing to admit," said Bannon. "I never got that close to anyone." He looked at Delilah and added, "My loss." He turned back to Bannon. "So? How's the leg?"

"Still a little gimpy. Another month I'll lose the cane."

"That was quite a piece your pal Pennington wrote about you. Still suckin' up to the press, I see."

"Yeah. You know me, Headline Harry."

"So what're your plans now that you're all married and settled down?"

"No idea," Bannon said. "I'm checking over my options."

"Still thinkin' about playing cops and robbers?"

"I don't think so, Brodie. But you never know."

"How do you feel about that?" he asked Millicent.

"Whatever he wants to do," she said.

He laughed and shook his head. "Got it all, Cowboy. Well, you deserve the best."

"Thanks."

A waiter brought a bottle of Amaretto and Delilah busied herself making a round of drinks. Brodie reached for a cigarette, and Millicent produced her Dunhill and lit it.

"Remember the last time we saw each other?" Culhane asked.

"Sure," Bannon said. "Up there in the ballroom. You had just retired from politics."

"I think it's time to talk about it," he said. "I couldn't tell you at the time because it would have hurt too many people, people I loved and who loved me."

Bannon sat forward in his chair. He had been waiting five years for answers to questions he thought he'd never get. Millicent looked at Bannon from the corner of her eye.

"You don't have to do this, Brodie," Bannon said.

"Isabel died in 1942. Heart attack. Ben lasted another two years but he was lost without her. I think if it's true that you can die of a broken heart, then that's what Ben died of."

"Maybe I should take a walk," Millicent said.

"Nah," Brodie said gruffly. "What the hell, he'll tell you the story anyway. May as well get it firsthand."

He stopped for a moment, as if gathering his thoughts together.

"Actually Del knows more about some of it than I do, but I'll tell it my way and she can jump in if she gets the urge."

Bannon didn't say anything. He waited. And Culhane began to speak.

I never did tell you properly, but you played the Verna Hicks murder like the pro you are. Your instincts were right on target. Trouble was, you were stuck on one idea: that the Riker frame was a giant conspiracy between me, Eddie, Brett—the whole bunch of us. That's only partly right. But it wasn't about a frame-up, it was about loyalty and friendship that turned into murder and revenge. I didn't level with you then. I couldn't. Too many people to hurt. Too many secrets to reveal.

You were dead right about one thing.

It blew up that night at Grand View.

But the roots went way back to the poker game in 1900—the night Eli Gorman beat Del's old man, who left the Hill forever. And deeded off the town of Eureka to Arnold Riker.

I was an outsider on the Hill. Eureka was hometown to me, much as I hated it. Had it not been for Eli Gorman, I probably would have ended up a hooligan for that son of a bitch Riker. When my mom died, Eli took me in and showed me a life beyond any dream I ever had. I was a scared, lonely kid. No family left. But Eli and Ben and Ma Gorman gave me that in spades.

Eli was a dreamer. A rich man with a vision. The joker in the deck was Riker but we'll get to that.

Four of us kids were friends in the truest sense of the word. There was Ben, Isabel Hoffman, Delilah, and me. We went to school together, played together, and lived the sweet life together on the Hill.

That's where I first learned what the word friendship meant.

I learned about loyalty in France, with men who gave up their lives fighting for five miles of mud. I think Brett said it best. Courage is being there, heroism is staying alive.

I learned about love from a friend whom I betrayed, and who knew it and never mentioned it. He's still my best friend, although he's long gone. And his wife, dear Isabel, taught me that first love is forever.

Eli had our lives planned out for us. Ben and Isabel would marry. Ben would take over the bank. I'd take Buck Tallman's place when the time came, and clean up Eureka. Trouble was, I was in love with Isabel and she was in love with me. But she was engaged to Ben and she truly adored him, too. So one night, I packed my duds and left. Joined the Marines, traveled the world, and ended up in France in 1918. I truly thought I would spend the rest of my life as a leatherneck but the war put an end to that. You know how that can be. Fate can change your life in the time it takes a howitzer shell to go off.

Eli once told me everybody has to have a home to come back to. I guess that's why I came back to Eureka when I got out of the hospital. It was the only home I had left. I had a godson and a family, and Delilah was here. And old Eli's plan was waiting. I became Buck Tallman's deputy. It was still a tough town because Riker still ran it. But that was about to change. Delilah ought to tell you about how that night started. Unfortunately, I was late for the party or history might have a different story to tell.

It's still hard to talk about, Delilah said. *It was the worst night, the worst memory of my life. I remember every detail.*

Bucky was upstairs in my apartment. He always came by about six, for a cup of coffee and to listen to some opera records I had. It was a ritual. His deputy, Andy Sloan, was downstairs keeping an eye on things when the four of them came in.

I heard some swearing downstairs, walked to the head of the stairs and one of them, an out-of-towner, they all were, told me to come down and talk. I knew what they were, I could tell by looking at them. At that point, Bucky walked up beside me. The lead man sneered at Bucky, said something about him being Buffalo Bill, and Bucky walked down the steps and up to him. They were nose-to-nose. Bucky said, "You oughta brush your teeth sometimes, your breath smells like a dead cat's."

And just like that, the bastard pulled his pistol and shot Bucky in the stomach. And all hell broke loose.

Bucky grunted and staggered backward, pulled that Peacemaker and fanned three shots into him. Bangbangbang, just like that, so fast you could hardly tell them apart.

Five men were still standing and they all started shooting at once. It was unbelievable. Bullets shattered lamps and windows, and ripped into walls. I remember bits and pieces after that, like a collage: a vase of flowers bursting apart; the mobster standing against the wall to Andy's right, turning toward him and taking Andy's bullet in the face, falling on his knees and then doubling up, and falling forward with his head resting on the carpet; Bucky's .44 making twice as much noise as all the other guns; the thug near the inside bedroom door spinning around with tufts of gabardine flying off his chest and back; the bastard near the door firing a single shot at Andy, blowing open the back of his head, and knocking him backward over a large, stuffed easy chair.

It all happened in less than a minute. One of the hoodlums decided to run for it and Bucky shot him as he went out the door. Then Bucky fell against the staircase banister, started reloading his pistol, and the one who had shot Andy started to get up. He was crawling around on his knees looking for his gun. Then I heard a shot outside.

Culhane: *When I came through the door, there was Bucky, gut shot, trying to reload his Peacemaker, his hands so bloody the bullets kept slipping through his fingers and falling on the floor. Andy Sloan was dead on the floor. Everybody was dead but Bucky, me, and the last of Riker's men. He and Buck were both shot all to hell. They were across the room from each other, probably twenty, thirty feet apart.*

Through the years, I've played what happened next over and over in my head like one of those slow-motion movies, and I wish I could stop it. I wish I could turn off the projector and stop time.

I was twenty feet to the left of Riker's man.

He's struggling to his feet. He's raising his gun.

Buck slaps the cylinder shut on his .44 and his arm is going up.

I go for a head shot, figuring I'm closest. But even shot up as he was, Bucky was faster than me. Probably by half a second. Bucky shoots and I shoot. His bullet hits the gunman first, a split second before mine. His head snaps backward, and my shot goes right past him and hits the door to the bedroom on the first floor.

Bucky looks up at Del and says, "Wouldn't you know it. Killed in a whorehouse."

And then a woman screamed. She was behind the door to the first-floor bedroom, which was more or less reserved for locals. I ran across the room and kicked open the door. There was a man lying on the Persian rug, shot in the throat. Blood was spouting out of the wound. The woman was covered with his blood and hysterical. Her bloody hands were crossed over her face. She was shaking all over. But I wasn't looking at her.

"Get her out of here," I yelled to Delilah, and they were gone, and I was looking down at the youngster lying at my feet. I saw his eyes go blank.

It was my godson, Eli Junior.

My bullet killed him.

They both stopped talking. They were long past tears but the depth of their sadness swept through the garden like a cold wind. Bannon took Millicent's hand with both of his, held it tightly, and kissed it. Tears trickled down her face.

All I could think of was to get Eli out of there. I moved as fast I could. Wrapped him up in the Persian rug, which was drenched in blood. There was hardly any blood in the room except on the bedspread. I ripped it off the bed and threw it in the closet. Then I picked Eli up and carried him outside through the side door by the hedgerow, down to his car, and put him in the trunk. When I came back, the coroner was just arriving. I said as casually as I could, "Nothing in the bedroom." I had left the door open so he wouldn't see the hole in the door.

Then I made the toughest phone call I ever made in my life. I called Ben and told him to meet me at the overlook. It was foggy as hell. You couldn't even see your belt buckle. He met me there and we mourned over

Eli. We prayed over him and we talked to him and we were dying inside. We decided his mother could never know what happened. Killed in a whorehouse, killed by a man she loved. It would have killed her. He was her magic child, the mortar in a great friendship. So we cranked up the Chevy and I got behind the wheel, drove it to the edge, and jumped out. It seemed to take forever before it hit the shelf. And then a minute or so later, it exploded.

I don't know how Ben kept his sanity when he went home to Isabel. He had to wait until the next morning, until a newsboy saw the wreck on his way up Cliffside Road, and I went over and told them both.

He stopped and held his glass up. Delilah filled it. Bannon looked across the table at the old warrior.

"And you kept that secret until Isabel died?"

Culhane nodded. "Me, Ben, Delilah, and old Eli knew."

"And one more," Bannon said. "The girl young Eli was with— Wilma Thompson."

Millicent looked shocked. Delilah surprised. Culhane just smiled.

"Figured it out, didn't you, Cowboy?"

"It's the only way it made sense. The out-of-towners weren't coming to barter for a piece of the action. Riker sent them because he figured Delilah was hiding Wilma at Grand View."

"He had just done ten lousy days in the local jail for beating her up," Delilah said. "It should have been ten years. When she dropped out of sight, he sent those animals up to my place to find her."

Delilah is in her apartment when Noah taps on the door.

"It's old Mist' Eli," Noah says. "He's downstairs in his car. Can't come in 'cause of the wheelchair."

Delilah and Eli are friends, have been for years. Not social friends. Eli had never been to Grand View, but they talked on the phone once a week or so, about Eureka, about Riker. Delilah grabs her mink, wraps herself in it, and goes down. Raymond, Eli's chauffeur, holds the door for her and she gets in the backseat. Raymond wanders off in the dark.

Eli looks frail; even in the darkness of the car she can see the toll the shooting has taken on him. Six months and he is still mourning. Will always mourn the loss of his grandson. But his eyes glitter in the gloom. The window is cracked slightly and smoke from his cigar wisps through it.

"Does the cigar bother you?" he asks. Always the gentleman.

"Don't be silly," she says and lights a cigarette.

"There's nobody I can trust as much as I trust you, Del," he says. There is something in his voice, a cruelness she has not heard before. Anger, yes, but not cruelty.

She says nothing.

"The young girl, Wilma? You are protecting her, aren't you?"

Delilah doesn't answer at first. Then she slowly nods.

"She's not one of my girls, Eli. She does some work around the place and I pay her a salary, but she stays under cover."

"She meant a lot to young Eli, didn't she?"

Delilah nods. "She's a decent young woman. Just got mixed up with Riker. Those things happen."

"I have a plan," the old man says.

"What kind of plan?"

"To get rid of Riker once and for all."

Delilah just nods, wondering where he is heading with this.

"They call the son of a bitch 'the Fisherman' because he kills people and drops them at sea for the fish to eat. He probably doesn't do the killing himself, his kind never do. They have scum who do it for them."

Delilah still doesn't say a word.

"Supposing it appeared that he killed Wilma?"

"Kill Wilma!"

"I said 'appears.' "

Delilah stares at him, at the tip of the cigar glowing in the dark.

"You want to frame Riker?" she say cautiously.

"He lives on his boat. I hear he drinks heavily. Drunk almost every night . . ."

"You want to frame him," she says, and it is not a question.

He quickly outlines his plan.

Delilah sits quietly for a minute.

"Brodie won't buy it, Eli. Brett Merrill won't either."

"I know that. We need somebody else to do it, somebody who'll pull it off without a hitch, so nobody ever knows. Wilma can disappear, go anywhere she wants. I'll arrange for her to get a new license, a new identity, and make life easy for her for the rest of her life."

Delilah is quiet again. A long minute passes.

"This is a very risky thing."

"I know that, my dear." His voice is the voice of the crafty old fox. The man who outfoxed her father. Age and illness had wasted his body but not his brain.

"You want me to set this up?"

"No. Just find the right man. I'll do the talking. Only the three of us will ever know. When I die, I want to know we are rid of Riker forever."

"Let me think about it," she says after a little thought.

Two nights later she comes to his house. They sit in his library.

"Do you know Eddie Woods?" she asks.

"I met him when he first came on the force. And his friend . . ."

"Dave Carney. Woods saved Brodie's life."

"I know all about that."

"Woods is from Boston. A tough street kid. After he got out of the Marines, he was headed for trouble. Carney was a Boston cop. He and Woods served in Merrill's regiment together. They became friends. Carney was married, had two kids. But he had heart problems and the Boston police retired him early. Not much of a pension for a man with three mouths to feed. When Brodie called Woods and asked him to come on the force, he brought Carney in, too. You know Brodie. Once a Marine, always a Marine."

The old man nods.

"When he first came here a year or so ago, Eddie used to come by the place every once in a while. Then he started seeing some young girl from down in Milltown. On the sly."

"Is that important?"

"Woods may need a witness. Without a body, it will be hard to convict Riker."

"I see."

"And he may need Carney's help."

"That's a lot of people . . ."

"You, me, Eddie, Dave, Wilma, and the girl. Six people."

"I'll make it profitable for them all."

"You'll have to ask him, Eli. Woods is in awe of you. If the idea is presented by you, and he thinks it will help Brodie clean up the town . . ."

She lets the sentence die.

"Will you set up the meeting with Eddie Woods?"

"Tomorrow night." Delilah nods. *"Just the three of us to start with . . ."*

*   *   *

"It worked like a charm," Delilah said. "Woods worked out the details. He and Dave spent two months stealing blood from the hospital, a little bit at a time. They grilled Lila Parrish until she had her story down pat. Carney watched Riker like a hawk, knew every move he made. Carney's payoff was a trust fund for his wife and kids. He knew his ticker wouldn't last long. Eddie didn't ask for a dime. But after it was over and Fontonio took over for Riker, Eddie knew he had to take him out, too. Eli set him up in business and gave him twenty thousand dollars to get started."

"And Lila Parrish?"

"She went to college down in San Diego, on Eli's tab."

"And then Eddie married her," Bannon said.

Brodie is getting tired, Bannon thought. *The flash is drifting out of his eyes and his shoulders are beginning to droop. Or maybe just thinking about that night again sapped everything out of him.*

"You figured that out, too, huh," Culhane said.

"And you didn't know?" Bannon said to Culhane.

Brodie didn't answer.

"You handled the payoffs," Bannon said to Delilah.

She smiled. "You had that one right from the start," she said.

"You were on the right track," Brodie said. "But I kept telling you, you were after the wrong dog. I figured it was Guilfoyle who killed Wilma. You were the one who nailed Riker."

"Actually it was Ski who figured it out, lying up there in the hospital."

And Bannon thought: *It was Ski, too, who had wired for young Eli's birth certificate and figured out that Eli Junior was Brodie Culhane's son. "That's why Isabel and Ben Gorman went to Boston and married so soon after Brodie left Eureka," he had told Bannon while lying in a hospital bed. "I'll bet old Eli probably fixed the birth certificate, too. Showing Ben as the father." That was what Brodie meant when he said he had "betrayed a friend," what he meant by "the mortar in a great friendship."*

Brodie Culhane had accidentally murdered his own son.

There were some things in your past you could run from. But not that. No wonder Brodie seemed to have no fear. There was nothing left that could scare him. The greatest punishment he could have was to go on living every day knowing what he had done.

"How's that partner of yours doin'?" Culhane asked.

"He made lieutenant," I said.

"Good for him."

Bannon had one more question, but Brodie leaned over, reached under the table and brought up a gift-wrapped package. He slid it across the table to Bannon.

"Here," he said. "Call it a wedding present."

Bannon and Millicent looked at the package, then Bannon slid it over in front of her.

"You open it," he said.

She unwrapped it the way women do, pulling on the ribbon until the knot unties, then stripping the ribbon off and laying it carefully to the side. She unwrapped the paper with the same care, without even wrinkling the paper.

It was a walnut box with a small plaque on the lid that said:

BUCK TALLMAN 1899–1920

CAPTAIN BRODIE CULHANE 1921–1946

SERGEANT ZEKE BANNON 1946–

It was the Peacemaker. Oiled and polished and shined to a fare-thee-well. There was a card inside that said "Don't shoot your damn foot off."

"I hope you never use it, Cowboy," Brodie said. "Hang it on the wall or buy a table and display it in the library. But try not to use it. That's my wedding gift to you, Millicent."

Millicent leaned over and kissed him on the cheek.

"I have to ask you one more question, Brodie. When did you figure it was a frame-up? Riker, Wilma, Eddie. The whole thing. When did you know?"

He looked at me and suddenly the fire came back in his tired eyes and he got that crooked smile on his lips and his voice got strong.

"What's the dif?" he said.